JED MERCURIO

Jed Mercurio trained at the University of Birmingham Medical School and practised as a junior doctor before becoming a full-time writer in 1994. As a writer, producer and director his TV credits include the highly successful shows *Cardiac Arrest*, *Bodies*, *Line of Duty* and *Bodyguard*, as well as adaptations of *Frankenstein* and *Lady Chatterley's Lover*. Mercurio has been described by the *Telegraph* as 'the most successful writer working in television today' and by the *Independent* as 'the master of British Drama'.

Mercurio is the author of three novels. His first, *Bodies*, was chosen as one of the five best debuts of 2002 by the *Guardian*. In 2007 Mercurio published his second novel, *Ascent*, the story of a fictional Soviet fighter pilot and cosmonaut set against the background of the Korean War and the Space Race. *Ascent* was included in the *Guardian*'s list of '1000 Novels Everyone Must Read' and a graphic novelisation, illustrated by Wesley Robins, was published in 2011. Mercurio's most recent novel, *American Adulterer*, a fictionalisation of President John F. Kennedy's infidelities, was published in 2009.

ALSO BY JED MERCURIO

Ascent
American Adulterer

JED MERCURIO

Bodies

VINTAGE

19 20 18

Vintage
20 Vauxhall Bridge Road
London SW1V 2SA

Vintage is part of the Penguin Random House group
of companies whose addresses can be found
at global.penguinrandomhouse.com

Penguin
Random House
UK

First published in Great Britain by Jonathan Cape in 2002
First published in Vintage in 2003
This edition reissued in Vintage in 2019

Grateful acknowledgement is made to the following for
permission to reprint previously published material:

The Oxford Handbook of Clinical Medicine by R. A. Hope, J. M.
Longmore, S. K. MsManus and C. A. Wood-Allum (4th edition,
1998). Reprinted by permission of Oxford University Press

While every effort has been made to obtain permission from the
owners of copyright material reproduced herein, the publishers
would like to apologise for any omissions and will be pleased to
incorporate missing acknowledgements in any future editions

penguin.co.uk/vintage

A CIP catalogue record for this book is available from
the British Library

ISBN 9780099422839

Printed and bound in Great Britain by Clays Ltd, Elcograf S.p.A.

Penguin Random House is committed to a sustainable future
for our business, our readers and our planet. This book is
made from Forest Stewardship Council® certified paper.

MIX
Paper from
responsible sources
FSC
www.fsc.org
FSC® C018179

Contents

Contents

PART ONE

The Killing Season

... like the stars, these ideals are hard to reach –
but they serve for navigation during the night.

'Ideals', *The Oxford Handbook*
of Clinical Medicine

1: The Interior

Leaving behind the outside world I turn off the perimeter road and on the First of August I pass under the metal arch of the hospital gates. Ahead towers of concrete and glass carve blocks out of cloudless blue sky under which I'm swallowed into a city within a city with its own speed limits and language and even its own weather.

As I enter the building my reflection slithers over panes of glass. Windows reframe the sky into blue squares while my heels click on hard flat floors and echo off corridor walls. The air turns dry and sterile and as I burrow deeper into the hospital it cools to a constant twenty-one Celsius. Sunshine fades to a trickle then in its place humming strip lights burn.

Bracketed to a high white wall a sign throws down directions for wards and departments. Each destination is coded a colour and a line of that colour is etched into the floor and it maps the route ahead.

Standing here under the sign looking lost I look like what I am. I slip into my white coat, the same one I wore in finals but with a new badge that puts 'Dr' in front of my name, and with the white coat stiff like armour I plunge farther into the hospital.

Some people ask me the way to Pharmacy. I think I might be able to remember from the sign but I can't and I blush and I have to shake my head.

I say, 'It's my first day.'

They laugh. It's a nervous laugh. If a doctor doesn't know the way round his own hospital then maybe there are other things he doesn't know.

Ahead of me a straight white corridor drops away to a set of doors and through the glass of the doors I see another straight white corridor stretching to another set of doors. In the glass of those second doors I make out a third straight white corridor and all together the corridors and the doors are an ever diminishing series of arrows pointing me deeper in and I feel like I'm falling.

I'm falling through layers of brick, concrete and glass. In the weatherless vaults of corridors and stairwells outsiders dwindle. Here come only the sick, those who love them and those who look after them. From the perimeter road I've travelled inwards three-quarters of a mile. This is the interior.

On my home ward I meet the SHO. Rich is mixed race with light brown skin and pale eyes, tall with wide shoulders and hair razored to stubble. He says, 'At ten, there's an induction seminar for new housemen,' and then he gives me a list of jobs.

Word spreads that the new houseman's arrived. The nurses stack in front of me a pile of drug charts that each contains a patchwork of boxes for me to fill in. It takes me ten minutes to work out how to write up a patient for paracetamol. Even then I have to check with Rich. Later a nurse tells me she can't find Rich and she needs someone to look at a heart monitor. I stand at the foot of a bed and in it lies an obese man whose body smells of sweat and skin creams. Mysterious shapes float across the monitor's black screen. As I struggle to make sense of them my heart rate outruns the patient's.

I turn to the nurse. I open my mouth about to confess I'm worried so we should bleep someone more senior when she says, 'Oh. It's fine. He's stopped doing it now.' She pats me on the arm. 'Thanks,' she says and then she goes. I glance at the monitor but to me it still looks the same. I smile a nervous smile and then I leave the smelly fat man to return to my list of jobs.

At ten to ten the time bomb strapped to my body goes off at last. I shudder. It could be anything, anything at all, they want me for. I read the four red numbers displayed on my bleep's LED then with my thumb press a button to cancel the beeping but it must be the wrong button because the sound continues. I try all the buttons but the beeping won't stop. In the end I give in and dial the four numbers on the phone at the nurses' station with my bleep cycling through chorus after chorus of beeps and people looking at me to switch it off and me acting like it's not me at all – no, the noise must be coming from somewhere else.

At the other end of the phone line a casualty nurse tells me they've got a patient for me to see. I find Rich and tell him the one true fact I know I know for sure. I tell him, 'But we're not on take today.'

Rich reaches inside my white coat and presses the right button and my bleep stops beeping. He says, 'If it's an old patient of ours, it's us rather than the firm on call who have to clerk them in.' With a shrug he adds, 'It's a hospital rule,' and in shrugging them his shoulders rise like mountains and then he turns to go.

'But I've got this induction seminar.'

'I've got Outpatients. Sorry.'

Wearing my stiff dry-cleaned white coat and my badge saying 'Dr' I tread out into a building full of patients and diseases not even knowing the way to Casualty and halfway there or not there realising I don't know the way back either. Lost and late I arrive at last. A nurse laughs at me because I've run. 'Sorry,' she says but then she continues to snigger behind her hand.

In slick black marker the board in A&E displays the firms on take and the name plus bleep number of the doctor on call for each specialty. The casualty officers are screening patients and referring those in need of admission. The doctor listed for them to call is that firm's most junior, usually only a houseman like me. No one seeing patients here has been a doctor longer than a couple of years.

Through gaps in curtains I peer into the cubicles and see only old people with faces like skulls. Warts and moles and tumours add to their bodies; limbs and teeth and eyes have been subtracted.

One cubicle lies empty with its curtains pegged open on both the A&E side and the waiting room side. For a moment as I glide past I glimpse what seems part of the outside world. Civilians are waiting on banks of seats and chatting and some mill near the vending machines. I count no uniforms or white coats.

My patient lies in the next cubicle. I leave a gap in the curtain on my side but reach back to shut out the waiting room. I'm drawing the line between us and the outside world. He's crossed into this one now.

The patient is young, only twenty-two. He complained to his mother of waking up with a crushing headache, now he's barely conscious with a fever. The Young Headache Man lies on his side on a trolley and a blanket hoods his head. For the first time I'm witnessing acute disease. As a student we were led in groups to patients sat up in bed who put aside their newspaper or cup of tea to indulge our pokes and fumbles.

'Does the light bother you?' I ask.

He groans. 'Yes,' comes his mother's answer.

'Has he been sick or lost consciousness?'

'He was sick once, only a little bit.'

The Young Headache Man groans again and shifts position. I slide my fingers round the base of his skull and try to bend his neck forward, angling his chin towards his chest. He resists and groans. I draw his legs up towards his chest then try to straighten his knees. Again he resists and groans.

The thought pricks me: *This is meningitis.* But it's not big enough, this experience of being in the presence of actual disease with its potential to cause real-life death. Because medical school didn't try it's fallen to television to train me but the iconography of emergency is missing. For a few seconds I hesitate in this incongruous environment lacking any barking of orders or crashing of trolleys. Then I scan in a slow pan over the cubicles. As my blinks paste together the images, I register bleeding and no rush to stem the flow, a pregnant woman hunched retching on a trolley and no hands clamouring to support her, a screaming old woman and no hurry to divine the cause. Here isn't television. Here isn't the outside world. Here is somewhere different.

Hiding in the equipment room I knit through the pages of *The Oxford Handbook of Clinical Medicine.* First I must take blood. From boxes on the shelves I scoop a needle, syringe, Steret and reach into my white coat pocket to ensure I've got a tourniquet. Instead my fingers collide with an envelope and I pluck it out and open it. Inside lies a good luck card with an inscription from Rebecca, my girlfriend. I read her message and to myself I smile.

The Young Headache Man may be still but I'm trembling as I apply the tourniquet to his upper arm and slap the veins till they engorge. How much longer it is before this intimacy arrives outside; how even with Rebecca it was crept upon as if to a body buried in the woods. This close I witness the mortality in his face, the dulling of his eyes and the whitening of his skin, before with the glinting metal needle I puncture his vein. But when I draw back the plunger the syringe doesn't fill. I reposition the needle, he winces, I say, 'Sorry,' but still no blood flows.

I recall four attempts at taking blood during medical school, all unsupervised, all dependent on my own trial and error. Now on my first day as a doctor after five years' training I'm making attempt number five.

When I try again his skin breaks and the needle pierces the vein. I pull back to create vacuum and blood swirls into the syringe and the blood is red in the sunlight from the window behind and black under the strip light above. I gaze at the red sea parting from its greater self and smile up at the Young Headache Man's mother. Then I withdraw the needle forgetting to release the tourniquet beforehand and blood dribbles down his arm. I mop it with the Steret as my face turns the same depth of red.

I carry away the syringe of blood and search for the tubes to put it in. I can't find them and I have to ask a nurse and then when I do find them I don't know which colour tubes correspond to the different samples so I have to run back to the nurse again and by the time I've got the right tubes I'm thinking the blood must've clotted.

Panicking that I might have to go back to the patient and take blood all over again I press on the plunger harder and harder until the plug of clot at the neck of the syringe ruptures. Blood sprays out but I only lose a little bit of it. I squirt aliquots into the different coloured tubes. I label them, I label forms and put them in a tray marked for collection.

Then I walk, not run, to the phone and bleep Rich. I replace the handset and stare at it till it rings and then I say, 'I think we've got a meningitis down here.'

'Oh,' he says. 'D'you know how to do an LP?'

'No.'

'I'm still doing Outpatients.'

He measures a silence. My mouth dries. A spasm chokes my throat. My fingers delve into my pocket. *The Oxford Handbook* contains a page of instructions on performing a lumbar puncture in the manner of tuning a new VCR or assembling a shelf unit. But Rich sighs and says, 'Fuck. Hit him with ben pen and start an IVI. I'll be there when I'm there.'

I loom over the Young Headache Man and prepare to stab a Venflon into one of his veins. Taut elastic skin covers a body that isn't crumbling like the ones in all the other cubicles. His flesh lives like mine.

Yet again I fail in my first effort to puncture a vein. As it ruptures a blue-black bubble swells under his skin. 'Sorry,' I say. The mother presses her son's hand.

I try again with a different vein. Again it ruptures.

I move the tourniquet even farther down his arm. I'm running out of veins. This is a basic procedure I'm expected to learn on the job as part of my apprenticeship but I'm here on my own after five years of medical school in which I inserted a Venflon once and only then because the doctor who instructed me let me try because the case wasn't urgent and it didn't matter if I blundered.

I find a vein in the back of the Young Headache Man's hand. I slap it for nearly thirty seconds with the pulp of my fingertips till the skin flushes pink and the vein bulges like blue cable. Trembling I pierce it then withdraw the needle still trembling. This time as the needle retracts I spot blood backflowing up the cannula. I push the plastic tube and it slides up the vein and in.

Though in the department around me no one turns to acknowledge my triumph it glints in the vials of blood in the collection tray and on the green plastic cap of the Venflon piercing the Young Headache Man's arm.

I inject 2.4 grams of benzyl penicillin. The drug gushes through the Young Headache Man's blood to the diseased linings of his brain. But my heart leaps in my chest. This drug doesn't know I've passed all my exams.

Over the phone Rich organises an urgent CT scan to exclude

11

other conditions besides meningitis. In a white room where the air is cool and still I help a radiographer slide the Young Headache Man up to the metal drum. We retire to the control room and from behind plate glass we watch his head creep inch by inch through an invisible guillotine of X-rays.

While I wait for the film to be developed the Young Headache Man groans from time to time. At every sound I hope something catastrophic isn't happening to him – please, not here in the scanner where the radiographer will look to me, the doctor, to save his life. I worry about the groans but soon I'm worrying a lot more about the silences in between.

Rich arrives flushed and breathless with his tie loosened off his collar. 'How is he?' he says. I shake my head then offer an awkward grin. I need a new vocabulary.

The gallery of images appears on a transparency. The scan has sectioned the Young Headache Man's brain into planes like a butcher slicing ham. Rich throws the transparency up onto a light box and glances at it for no more than a few seconds before he nods and says, 'Right, then.'

Next we're up on the ward. The Young Headache Man is laid on his left side and his knees drawn up towards his chest. He moans and tries to straighten out. The foetal position stretches his spinal cord and in turn tugs on the lining of his brain that's inflamed like bees have stung it in swarms.

I've secured the assistance of a nurse. Her uniform is plain white instead of the pale blue of a staff nurse's. She's a student nurse, maybe the reason she smiled and seemed eager and agreed to help. Her badge reads 'Student Nurse III' then the initial 'D.' then her surname.

Rich nods towards her badge asking, 'So what's the D. stand for?'

'Oh,' she says glancing down – 'Donna.'

'What are his bloods?' he says to me.

'They've not come back yet.'

'Did you mark 'em "URGENT"?'

'I, er . . .'

'Mark them "URGENT",' he says. 'And chase them up if they don't call you with the results. ABC. Always Be Chasing.'

The Young Headache Man rolls on to his back. D. for Donna and I clasp his hands and roll him on to his side. His are hot and pink. Hers are cool and white and an engagement ring encircles her left fourth finger. With her I pull the Young Headache Man's knees back up and hook his left arm behind his calves and his right arm across his shoulder blades to hold him in position. He moans again. Though bigger than me and heavier he's too weak to overcome the leg-and-shoulder lock.

Rich takes over. He says, 'You do the LP.' He's sharp with me but the understanding is simple: I learn now how to perform a lumbar puncture so next time I won't have to call him.

'I'll get gloves in my size,' I say. I find a hiding place and in it once again I read line by line the instructions on performing an LP. I tell myself it's like installing a video or assembling an Ikea bookcase.

When I return Rich and the student nurse are waiting. She has long brown hair tied back and wears squarish black-rimmed glasses. Under their gaze I palpate the bony crests of the Young Headache Man's hip bones and draw an imaginary belt between them. I mark the spot and sterilise the surrounding area with brown sweeps of Betadine. With the tip of a needle I dig in then as I press out the dose of lignocaine I raise a quarter-inch dome under his skin. All the time Rich nods, gives hints, keeps me on track.

The spinal needle is long, narrow and very sharp and I push it into the Young Headache Man's back till as he moans, too ill to shriek, I encounter resistance. 'Push through it,' Rich says. 'Just

13

push.' I push harder. Something gives and the needle drives deeper.

Rich asks D. for Donna to uncap a specimen pot and hold it under the needle. I withdraw the black-capped metal stylet and expose the bore of the needle to air. We await CSF. D. for Donna holds the clear plastic pot between her thumb and forefinger and it oscillates with a nervous tremor. She's stooping forward and next to me I smell her scent and glimpse the pale skin of her cheek running down her neck and into the collar of her uniform. After a few seconds a bead of milky fluid forms and when it reaches critical mass it drips into the specimen pot with a faint plop.

'Well done,' says Rich and D. for Donna grants me a small smile.

We count three drops into each of two more pots and a glucose tube. We withdraw the needle and ease the Young Headache Man into a comfortable position.

Rich says, 'Now you've done an LP, you can show the other housemen. See one, do one, teach one.'

As I'm labelling the pots on the Young Headache Man's legs we count four purple stigmata that haven't been there before. Rich presses them but they don't blanch.

'Shit,' he says.

Later on one of the nurses finds me cowering in the storeroom.

'What're you doing?' she says.

'Nothing,' I say.

I slide back into my pocket *The Oxford Handbook* I've been attempting to digest page by page.

She mentions the Young Headache Man. 'Rich wants him to have a catheter,' she says.

'You mean *I* have to do it?'

She says, 'I'm not covered to do male catheters.'

I sense my hand creeping back down into my white coat pocket in search of *The Oxford Handbook*.

She peers at me with a look of irritation. Fighting a sudden impulse to flee I say, 'OK.' I wipe the dread from my face and like pulling down a blind I smile the new houseman smile that's the eager-to-please rictus of a dumb animal. I've witnessed catheterisation once in theatre on an anaesthetised patient.

Behind curtains the Young Headache Man lies semi-conscious clutching a pillow over his head and a rash of purple spots mottles his legs. I stretch on the gloves and wipe the Young Headache Man's glans penis with detergent-soaked cotton wool, removing enough smegma to top a pack of crackers. The stench of stale urine begins to bite into my nostrils. I open the catheter pack and begin by tearing a hole out of a sheet of sterile paper that I then lay over his groin with his penis sticking out through the hole like a dormant finger-puppet. I squirt local anaesthetic gel up the Young Headache Man's urethra then push up the tip of the catheter. I advance it trying to keep my hands off the latex and on the cellophane packaging but make little progress. In the end I pinch the latex between thumb and forefinger and feed it up. Accompanied by a semi-conscious groan from the Young Headache Man urine flows sooner and faster than expected, spilling off the polystyrene bowl the nurse holds. Splashes hit the floor and I stare down at my shoes where urine glistens like yellow beads. The nurse attaches the tube to a collection bag and I inject a few millilitres of water into the bladder balloon, clamping it in place.

'All done,' the nurse says and pats the Young Headache Man's abdomen.

Before I set about my next job her uniform transmits its pale blue, mixing to the burgundy of a blood bag another nurse is hooking up in a bay yellow with sunlight. Blood glints as it drips from the high bag into a giving set, by chance keeping time

15

with the beeps of a neighbouring patient's heart monitor. Phones ring. A bleep chimes in the distance. The cool still air, that of a secret vault, smells of healing.

On impulse I call Rebecca.

'Well?' she says.

'Well what?'

'*How's it going?*'

I say, 'Well, I haven't killed anyone yet.'

'No disasters?'

'No. Well, nearly. I had to put in a catheter.'

'A catheter?'

'You know – a tube up into the bladder, for urine.'

'Rather you than me.'

'It's the first penis I've touched, apart from my own. Not for the first time in my medical career, I've suffered a disadvantage from not going to public school.'

She laughs. I love her laugh.

'Thing is,' I say, 'now I've put one in, it's made me look like more of a doctor to the nurses. From now on a lot of my patients are going to get catheters whether they need one or not.'

Microbiology call to say the lumbar puncture confirms meningococcal meningitis and the Young Headache Man's blood is oozing from the two sites of my failed Venflon insertions. Rich rods a central line under the patient's collarbone into his subclavian vein, saying, 'Sometimes I think we only really impress anyone by how well we can drive sharp objects into body cavities.'

I decide to call Haematology.

'Always Be Chasing,' I say.

'Always Be Chasing,' he says.

Over the phone comes the news the Young Headache Man's

FDPs are up, his platelets are down and his clotting times prolonged.

'Is it DIC?' Rich calls from the bedside.

I've heard of DIC but I can't remember what it is. In an exam they'd move on to the next question but this is what the Young Headache Man's got and there's no moving on. Like an idiot I begin to fumble through the index of *The Oxford Handbook*.

Rich shouts, 'Is it DIC or isn't it?'

I whisper into the phone to the haematology technician at the other end. 'Is it DIC?' I say.

'I'm not allowed to make diagnoses,' he says. 'You're the doctor.'

With both his hands Rich is still grappling to insert a central line in the Young Headache Man's chest. Blood is gushing out of the puncture site under his collarbone and spreading in a sheet down his front. Rich is saying, 'Fuck, fuck,' and then to me he cries, 'I *really* need to know!'

My lips are trembling when I mumble to the lab tech, 'Please.'

'Yes,' he says. 'It's DIC.'

I call to Rich, 'Yes!'

'He needs two units of FFP!' he calls back.

'Can we have two units of SSP?' I ask the lab tech.

'*FFP!*' Rich shouts so loud his voice cracks – '*fresh frozen plasma!*'

'I mean FFP,' I say into the phone, turning crimson.

'And tell him we might be needing four bottles of the house red!'

Not understanding what the words mean I repeat them to the lab tech like I'm fumbling through a foreign language. He laughs when I say, 'Four bottles of the house red,' and says, 'OK.'

Rich and a nurse secure the central line. A pressure dressing

17

straps the puncture site and not long after the units of FFP flood his circulation. I observe it all from the periphery. No one even looks at me.

At the end of my first day as a doctor, my first First of August, I descend the stairs from my home ward and find myself in a long white corridor that looks the same as every other one in the hospital. I don't ask anyone the way. I'm a white coat now. I'm expected to know these things. But it takes me ten minutes to find the exit signs.

The signs channel me out through fencing layers of brick, concrete and glass where strip lights illuminate my path. In the next corridor light builds back to day. From windows that section the sky into blue squares, bars of sunbeams divide the next corridor after that into a grill of hot and cool. Slicing through them I feel each temperature change on my skin. In the atrium the air begins to diverge from twenty-one Celsius and my body passes out of the hospital's single constant season back into summer.

Here I peel off my white coat and hook it over my shoulder.

Outside the sun hurts my eyes but a breeze carrying the scents of grass and leaves and hot tarmac refreshes my skin. I climb into my car and follow the roadway round hospital buildings to the gates and when I drive through them I'm returning to the world.

2: The Way

The minute we get to work the following morning we check on the Young Headache Man. He isn't bleeding but instead his blood vessels are clotting off. His extremities are cold and pulseless. A purple dusk spreads into his fingers, toes and penis. His breathing shallows. His condition by the Glasgow Coma Scale is deteriorating.

Rich arranges for him to be transferred to ITU. He says, 'It used to be called the Intensive *Care* Unit, till they realised no one did.'

Before they come for the Young Headache Man I write up his notes at the nurses' station. Ward phones ring and as I take in lukewarm sips of tea visitors confer in whispers because they feel like visitors to the temple. Shoes slap the floor beside me and I look up. 'How is he, Doctor?' asks the Young Headache Man's mother.

'I'm afraid the infection is very serious. He's developed blood poisoning and a severe complication called disseminated intra-vascular coagulation. Some parts of his body are prone to bleeding, others to clotting, and it all creates a risk of organ damage and gangrene.'

'He's going to be all right, though, isn't he?' Her voice trembles and she looks down. The Young Headache Man's mother might be any kind of capable person in the outside world but so deep over the dividing line into this one she's meek and fragile and overwhelmed.

I say, 'I hope so.'

She murmurs, 'Please make him get better, Doctor.' Tears well in her eyes as behind her a nurse flags for me to attend my next assignment. The Young Headache Man's mother says, 'Don't let him not get better. He's all I've got.'

Till this moment I've been desperate to convince everyone including myself that inside this white coat of armour I'm a real doctor now. But the Young Headache Man's mother's emotions strike open a channel between us and in it I'm as meek and fragile and overwhelmed as she is. I've arced like current to the other side. For a moment I participate in the situation from her standpoint. She believes I, a doctor, exert more control over circumstances than my patients or their families. This I might once have believed but not now in this instant. A wave of melancholy gushes over me with such force it makes me fear I'll break down and sob.

Then the polarity resets and I'm launched back. Now I'm the doctor again and I'm angry. I'm angry with the Young Headache Man's mother for making a connection. She's luring me into promising her son's recovery because that's what counts, not the accuracy of the diagnosis or the spectrum of the antibiotics. No wonder I'm angry with her because I'm at a loss. I can't bleep my SHO and ask what to feel.

With a flick of my head I acknowledge the nurse still standing behind the Young Headache Man's mother and say to her, 'I'll be there in a minute.' The nurse goes and I turn back.

I've never told anyone they'll die. I've never told anyone and by that of course I mean not even myself. Sat here in the interior of the hospital with a protecting line drawn between me and the outside world I'm disputing the proposal that the Young Headache Man's mortality proves my own.

'Please tell me he'll get better,' his mother says.

'He will,' I say.

By morning we hear from ITU that the Young Headache Man's stopped being able to breathe for himself and he's been put on a ventilator.

I cross the hospital interior to the base of its highest tower where in the lift I ascend five floors. Outside ITU I remove my white coat as the notices instruct and I pass through frosted double doors beyond which machines maintain ten and only ever ten patients. Through a hose into his mouth a ventilator inflates the Young Headache Man's lungs and as his chest rises and falls in perfect regularity the sound of breathing isn't his but the machine's. On brackets overhead monitors beep and they sketch his body functions in waves of different shapes and colours. Lines fill him with blood and platelets and drugs while a tube empties his urine into a bag.

When his blood pressure plummets Rich sighs and says, 'Time to bung him on dopamine.' As he writes it on the drug chart he mutters, 'No-hope-amine.'

The next day the Young Headache Man's purple parts have turned black like the slick black of wet tarmac roads. His hands, feet and genitals have become gangrenous. 'It's the dopamine,' Rich says and he shrugs.

His mother hunches at his bedside as she's done for days. She combs his hair and recombs it and wipes the drool from his chin then a minute later rewipes it. She's preening him like a chimp and understanding about as much. She isn't the only one. What reason would He have for ruining this young body?

In the hall outside ITU a payphone hangs off the wall. I pump coins into the slot and count the rings picturing a building on the other side of the city and in the building an office and in the office a desk and behind the desk Rebecca. I picture her laying down her pen and marking her place with it and turning to reach for the handset and as she reaches the shoulder of her jacket rises into the black curls of her hair. She answers and I tell her about my day, about the Young Headache Man's operation. When I'm finished she says, 'What's gangrene?'

I try explaining again but there are more terms I have to elucidate. Then my bleep sounds. I cut her off. I tell her how much I miss her, that I'm looking forward to seeing her tonight, and she senses some change in my voice. It's just that I don't want to waste this last precious minute trying to explain what a fucking ventilator does.

Along the long main corridor sunlight beams through the spaced windows and as I tread to my next case I'm slicing through bars of molten gold. In between the air is still and cool. My skin registers the oscillating warm, cool, warm, cool. I trudge half a mile through the hospital's dry seasonless vaults while the Young Headache Man's brain grows so swollen it's going to get crushed inside his skull.

Then I spy Rich in a corridor. He's talking to a woman. She's tall like him and dark and she's holding a pile of hospital folders and wearing civvies. He acknowledges me with his eyes but their conversation appears intense so I pass them by.

We finish work at around six that night and Rich bleeps me to suggest the pub across the road. We click off our bleeps, fold our white coats like funeral flags and depart the hospital grounds.

Cold pints in our hands we sit outside where warm bright sunlight comforts me. Hospital buildings hew the sky into blue splinters and their shadows stretch long enough to reach our feet. I can flick out my leg and still be in their sway.

Rich slides out a cigarette and offers it me.

'No, thanks,' I say.

'You ever smoked?' he says lighting it.

'Tried one or two.'

'And never got hooked?'

'No,' I say.

He smokes and I drink. He drinks and later of the Young Headache Man he says, 'Poor bugger probably went to the pub like us. May even have pulled a condom over his head or photocopied his arse. Now he's fubarbundy.' He gulps his drink again. 'Don't be shy to paint it black. If the patient pegs it, the rels were expecting it and won't kick up a stink. If the patient survives, they think you're Dr fucking Kildare. Just being practical. That's the job.' He takes another mouth of beer, and adds, 'Can't play God. And why'd you want to? Worse hours and no prospect of promotion.'

I say, 'Who was that woman in the corridor?'

'Which one?' he says.

'The tall one with dark hair.'

'Her? She's one of the medical secretaries.'

'Not your girlfriend, then?'

'No,' he says.

Rich draws on the cigarette and exhales a puff of smoke. He says, 'You think the job's going to be like TV. You think you'll be saving lives with the tail of your white coat flapping round your arse like it's Batman's fucking cape.'

He drinks then his gaze drifts past me. Two nurses have come in, one who's young and spotty with a student's white uniform under a grey cardigan, while the other who's a few years older is good-looking with a pale blue staff nurse's uniform under a denim jacket. Rich tracks them with hunter's eyes as they cross to the bar. When his cigarette is spent he lights another.

'But it's not like that,' he says. 'It changes you. You think it won't, but it will.'

Standing he asks, 'Same again?' His glass is empty while mine's still more than half full. He strolls towards the bar and

23

offers to buy the nurses a drink and though he addresses them both his eyes are running over the staff nurse, the good-looking one. I glance at them for a moment and notice that the staff nurse is prettier but the student has the better body.

Then the Young Headache Man ruffles my thoughts. I know God's created a blemished existence so good must act to prevent suffering. I close my eyes and tilt my face to the sun. I feel warmth on my cheeks and rose light flares through my eyelids. The breeze tickles my skin and I know that amid the constancy of nature I too shall be a constant thing.

The next day the Young Headache Man's eyelids flutter at the sound of his mother's voice. I clench my fist and run my knuckles hard up and down his sternum and he shifts under me. I pinch the flesh on his forearm as hard as I can and eventually he jerks it away. When I look down I observe under his skin where I pinched the blackening bruise of ruptured capillaries.

His mother says, 'It's good news, isn't it? He's going to get better, isn't he?'

She's stroking his head and not looking up at me as with gentle loving strokes her fingers fall through his hair. Her face shines with hope.

I say, 'It's early days. We have to see if this improvement continues.'

She says, 'But you did say he'd get better, didn't you? He will, won't he?'

'I think I spoke too soon. I shouldn't have. I'm very sorry. We have to wait and see.'

She says, 'What are you saying now?'

'He's very poorly. It's still possible the illness will be too much.'

She bends low and kisses him on the forehead. I'm an intruder. I leave the bedside. I glance back and see her sob and

24

then she hides her sobbing as she carries on stroking his matted hair over and over like Greyfriars' Bobby at his master's grave losing something precious and unable to comprehend why.

In the storeroom I lock myself away for a minute. I lean on the sink and peer out of the window at the paths and shrubs backing far below on to the buildings of the hospital interior. I pick over my exchange with the Young Headache Man's mother and I can't remember if I made it clear to her it's still possible he'll suffer greater injury, even possible he'll still die. Maybe I thought I painted it black but maybe I only drew her a shade of grey. But I can't face going back to her now and saying it straight.

My bleep goes off and I recover and respond to it.

Round the wards Rich is wearing a hangover. I left the pub after the second drink but I overhear gossip flicking between the nurses that matches him with the student nurse rather than the staff nurse. He and I wander from ward to ward checking on our patients ahead of our consultant's round.

In the corridor we encounter the tall dark-haired medical secretary he was talking to yesterday. She sees us and tightens her grip on the pile of files she's carrying and drops her eyes. As she passes us her gaze drags along the floor and her head doesn't lift till we've crossed.

I say, 'D'you think she heard about the student nurse?'

'No,' he says. 'I think she heard about the wife.'

After two more days in which antibiotics exterminate infection and transfusions replenish his blood the Young Headache Man blinks his eyelids to commands and he starts trying to breathe for himself again.

'We're going to take the breathing tube out,' Rich says. 'Blink twice if you're ready.'

The Young Headache Man blinks twice. His mother reaches for a black hand but stops herself and instead grips his elbow.

An ITU nurse unties the tape holding the endotracheal tube in place and then with small upward slips of her hands it begins to emerge streaked with spit, phlegm and blood. The Young Headache Man blinks over and over, signalling 'No, no, no', and the beeps of his heart monitor start stacking together like machine-gun fire. His mother grips his elbow all the harder but the nurse says, 'It'll be all right,' and brings out the rest of the tube. His mouth gapes in panic then he takes a first choking breath.

'That's it,' says Rich. 'You're breathing.'

He tries to shape words but only animal sounds emerge.

'You won't be able to speak just yet,' Rich says. 'Your vocal cords will take time to recover.'

He can barely move but with his eyes he glances round at us. I stand at the foot of the bed while Rich mans the ventilator. Our eyes glance back at the bruised invaded mutilated young body with its dead hands and dead feet and hidden beneath a sheet there are dead genitalia.

Rich says, 'You'll feel very strange to begin with. You may not remember anything. You had meningitis, mate.'

The Young Headache Man blinks twice. 'Yes,' he's saying.

'You fell into a coma and you got blood poisoning.'

He blinks twice again.

'Because of the blood poisoning you developed another problem. You got gangrene in your hands and in your feet and in your genitals.'

Rich leaves a pause but the Young Headache Man doesn't blink. His eyes are animal eyes staring up at us all. 'You got gangrene, mate. Did you hear? Did you understand?' Now he blinks twice. His eyes glisten with tears and his mother hangs her head and begins to weep too.

'There's nothing we can do,' says Rich. 'I'm sorry,' he says.

The Young Headache Man fights to say words but he can't and all he can do to express himself is weep. Rich flicks his head for us all to leave. He's first, followed by the nurse.

His mother clings on to the Young Headache Man's mutilated body. She cries and mumbles to him, 'It's all right. You're all right.' She lays her face against his and her tears flow into his. I turn to go whispering, 'I'm sorry.'

'You said he'd get better,' she says.

Without thinking I say, 'He did.' The words have come out and there's nothing I can do to retract them but I cross to her side of the bed and never having done it to a stranger and not knowing how I fumble a hand on to her shoulder. She rises and pours her pain into my eyes and as I glance away she slaps me across the face. But through the air her hand slows to no more than a pathetic pointless gesture by the time it strikes my cheek.

'I'm sorry,' I say with it sounding like I'm returning the pathetic pointless gesture. Then in the end, not knowing the thoughts of God and struggling to understand my own, I go.

In the lift I fall five floors to the long sloping pastel corridor, the spine of the hospital that steers me out from its interior of wards and departments. I turn corners and mount steps and pass through doors. In minutes I reach the atrium. I peel off my white coat and cross into daylight. I do it all without thinking because now I know the way.

3: The Night

Rising from deep in the interior I mount the staircase of a high tower till I reach windows from which I can watch the evening sun sink behind city buildings. The August sky is shedding its violet skin to bare dark meat beneath. I've been on call since nine o'clock this morning when one of the other housemen handed over the red crash bleep. He was stubbly and dead-eyed and grateful to unburden himself of it. So far Rich and I have clerked in sixteen patients. Soon he'll exercise the SHO's privilege and go to his bed leaving me alone to enter night.

On the wards drug trolleys rattle from bay to bay. Their axles squeak. Sleeping pills dot small plastic pots before the patients swallow them with sips of water. The strip lights wink out and a nurse clicks on the night lamps while in her other hand she cradles the night shift's first mug of tea. Sounds fall away to silence though the silence is not silence but the background hum of machines like ripples on the surface of a lake no longer being disrupted by traffic and at last allowed to radiate to the banks.

While the interior slows into midnight the front of house bustles. Around me casualty officers combat the first volley of post-pub pathologies by branding them PFOs, PGTs, PDEs, but they do so in whispers for fear of a drunk realising he or she's having their piss taken. Here where the two worlds collide the power shifts at night from the doctors and nurses to the louder and more aggressive patients and visitors. The staff no longer stride from cubicle to cubicle. They don't look people in the eye. They find places to make themselves small and go about their work.

Over the next couple of hours I don't move from Casualty. I clerk in patients seventeen, eighteen and nineteen.

Later when I trudge back into the interior along the long pale corridor I see no one and I hear no one. People cram these halls by day but no one comes through at night bar the skeleton staff on call. Passageways plunge away to the gloom of deaf telephones, sleeping scanners, locked clinics. Long empty corridors and tall empty stairwells are silent. Long flat walls echo only to the clicks of my heels. The air tides to my breath. I feel alone.

I call Rebecca. When she answers sleepiness strangles her voice and I realise I've woken her.

'Sorry,' I say. 'I didn't realise how late it was.'

'No, it's OK,' she croaks. 'I'd gone to bed early. I miss you.'

'I miss you too,' I say.

From the stairs I peer out over the hospital campus towards the city and the sky. An airliner's navigation beacons blink in and out of cloud. There's no moon and city glow blanks the stars. A few lights glimmer in the windows of office buildings signalling the last souls in the outside world still at their professions yet brightness still dapples the whole hospital campus. Hours beyond midnight it remains a city of light and industry.

My bleep summons me and I return to Casualty where I admit a congestive heart failure and a stroke, patients twenty and twenty-one.

I shuffle to my on-call room and I lay my personal bleep and red crash bleep on top of the dusty bedside table before slipping off my shoes. I lie on top of the bedcovers but I can't sleep. Though summer heat swelters I daren't remove my shirt in case I'm called to a cardiac arrest. I slide up the window and flakes of paint break off and a spider's web ruptures. Into the room flood the roars and rumbles of generators and ventilators, of ambulances and taxis and drunks. I close it again. Now I lie hot in my tight clothes beside a clock ticking towards daylight with the crash bleep blinking like a detonator and pipes trickling and the sound of footsteps on the floor above and an Islamic prayer seeping in from the next room.

My bleep guillotines the turmoil. My heart rate leaps. Is it real? Have I been bleeped, or dreamed it? Flicking on the bedside lamp I read the green glowing digits of the LED and dial. Seven rings sound before I hear, 'We've got an eighty-three-year-old lady who's off legs and her pulse has gone up to a hundred and fifty – blood pressure's one hundred over seventy-five.'

I hear the words but in my semi-conscious condition I don't know what they all mean. After a few moments I say, 'OK,' and I hear the click of the line being cut and then I'm alone in the room trying to figure out where I am and who'd be calling me. It's nearly five minutes before I realise the telephone receiver's still in my palm and with a lumpen hand I replace it. I glimpse my bare feet and unhitched trousers and unbuttoned shirt. I search the hot gloomy room with its flaking paint and ugly furniture and in doing so I orientate myself. I step into my shoes, stand to fasten my trousers, hook my bleeps into the belt, scoop up my white coat and leave, buttoning my shirt as I shamble to another ward, another set of nurses.

They glance at me with my ruffled hair and creased shirt and bloodshot eyes then return to their talk and their tea. The staff nurse leads me to the patient, this eighty-three-year-old woman, while I study the notes. She was found on the floor of her room by the staff of her warden-controlled accommodation and because she was unable to get to her feet again she was admitted for investigation. The notes conclude, *Turf to Geriatrics mane.*

I feel the patient's pulse for myself and find it soaring towards one hundred and eighty. I ask the staff nurse if we can put her on a monitor and while she leaves to find one I examine Off Legs. She has one of those geriatric bodies with bits missing and bits added on. Her left hand is short of a little finger and surgery of her parotid gland craters the angle of her jaw. Added on are white rings round her corneas, a hairy wart on her cheek, a cyst on the back of her neck and red striations branching from beneath pendulous breasts.

We paste three electrodes to her chest, switch on the monitor and soon I study sawtooth peaks and dips that tight together are surging from left to right. The staff nurse glances from the screen to the side of my head. Eventually I mumble, 'It's a tachycardia of some sort.' She tuts. I ask, 'You wouldn't know what it was, would you?'

She combines a shake of her head with a shrug. 'What are we going to do about it?'

I say, 'A twelve-lead ECG.'

'You'll have to do it. I'm not happy to. Oh, and I don't know where the machine is.'

On foot I search the neighbouring wards then trundle back with an ECG machine. It's so out of date there are suction cups for electrodes. The new ones with decent electrodes and a computer print-out languish behind locks in the ECG Department kept for use by cardiographers during routine hours only. The suction cups won't stick for long to Off Legs' body and there are twelve of them so keeping them attached during the ECG is like performing the trick of the spinning plates. I've never done an ECG before. I proceed by trial and error and working off the fading instructions on the machine's top panel. It takes me half an hour though the print-out is faint, wavy and to my eyes inconclusive.

The rest of the ward is trouble free so the nurses sit at the nurses' station and distribute another round of tea. They don't offer me one. While they chatter among themselves I consider Off Legs' notes. She was admitted through Casualty this afternoon (yesterday afternoon) through a different firm because she was an old patient of their consultant. The notes describe an admission ECG as *NAD*. Looking to compare it with the new one I search the folder and eventually find it already crumpled and tucked into a sleeve at the back. It shows what I think is an MI.

I call Rich and tell him about the tachycardia, the inconclusive ECG and the old one I think shows a missed MI. He's on Coronary Care dealing with patient number twenty-two after the nurses there called him direct because they thought the case was too complicated for the houseman.

'Are there P waves?' he wants to know.

'No. I don't think so. I'm not sure.'

'Go and look at the monitor. Tell me if there's P waves and if the complexes are narrow or wide. I'll hold.'

'How wide is wide?' I ask.

'Wider than narrow,' he answers.

I scrutinise the screen again till the lines and blips burn tracks on my retinas. When I return to the phone the nurses have opened a packet of biscuits.

'No P waves,' I say. 'I don't think the complexes are very wide.'

'This is bound to be an SVT. Give her adenosine, 3 milligrams, IV bolus. Just whack it in. I'll be there in five or ten minutes. Oh, oxygen too.'

I convey Rich's advice to the staff nurse. She gazes at me over

32

a chocolate Hobnob that's half in her mouth and half snapping off between her thumb and forefinger. 'How much oxygen?' she says munching.

Not knowing for sure I guess, 'Thirty per cent?'

'You can't have thirty per cent. It's twenty-four, twenty-eight or thirty-five. Besides, on this ward we do it in litres per minute.'

'How many's the usual?'

'Two to four.'

'OK.'

Like talking to a moron she says, '*Which*? *Two* or *four*?'

'Four,' I say, still guessing. 'No. Two.'

The adenosine works and Off Legs' heart rate drops to a hundred within seconds. An oxygen mask veils her face but her eyes stand out with their white rings round the corneas and in them flashes a sudden look of surprise and fear. She clutches her chest and lets out a long moan. The staff nurse becomes alarmed and sets herself to scurry to the phone and hurl out an arrest call. I'm paralysed of course.

But then the heart rate levels out at eighty and in a second or two Off Legs stops moaning.

'How d'you feel?' I ask her.

'All right,' she says.

When Rich arrives he laughs off the moaning and chest-clutching. 'Oh, yeah,' he says, 'sometimes they do that with adenosine. Should've mentioned it, I suppose.'

He's wearing theatre blues comprising a V-necked vest stamped with the name of the health authority and baggy trousers tied by an elasticated waistband. I show him the two ECGs. The new one he scans but soon loses patience. 'This is shit. It's like a spider with diarrhoea crawled all over the paper. How's anyone expected to read this?'

'Sorry,' I mutter.

'It's not your fault. It's those fucking machines. If you want a decent ECG out of hours, you have to sweet-talk the girls on CCU. Not that that's any easier.' Now he studies the admission ECG. He sighs and says, 'Yep. Anterolateral MI. No wonder she's off those big sexy legs.'

'That's why she's had a run of SVT.'

'Yep.'

'They missed it, didn't they?'

'The Caz officer probably glanced at it. Maybe he thought it was high take-off or something. Left it for the medics to figure out. Then the houseman looks at it, isn't sure, so reads that the caz officer, who's an SHO and therefore should know more about it, thought it was OK. Then the medical SHO, who'd definitely have picked it up, gets the abridged version – "Off legs, investigations NAD, looking to turf to Gerries."'

Rich writes in the notes. I peer over his shoulder. His body leaks an odour of sweat and sleeplessness. 'So they missed an MI,' I say.

'Sure, it's a fuck-up.'

The staff nurse leans on the trolley that Rich is balancing the notes on. 'Well?' she says.

'She's had an MI,' he says. 'Go and give her an aspirin.'

Rich writes: Δ: *SVT secondary to MI. Admission ECG: NAD. Suggest now follow cardiac protocol – aspirin stat. + o.d., GTN infusion, Tinziparin b.d., monitor, serial ECGs, serial CEs*, then folds up the original ECG and stuffs it in his pocket.

I want to know, 'What're you doing?'

'I'll have a quiet word with them all in the morning. It's up to them what they do with the ECG.' Rich steals a chocolate hobnob and rises. 'Bleep me if there's anything else you need help with.'

I'm lumbering back to bed when my bleep goes off. It's

Casualty with another stroke to see. I drop by the doctors' mess and make myself a cup of tea, spending ten minutes waiting for the low-power kettle to boil. Health authority regulations ban appliances of normal wattage in doctors' residences. I picture a bureaucrat fretting over the risk of the hospital's electricity generators diverting current from some premature baby's incubator into a houseman's sandwich toaster. There's no milk left so I cool it with tap water and drink it black. I never drink tea black. It's gulped down.

The stroke is eighty-nine with nicotine-stained fingers, a mouth missing half its teeth, dense pink elbow patches of psoriasis and a lipoma added onto his shoulder. I clerk him in, patient number twenty-three, concluding my notes with *? turf to Geriatrics mane.*

But I know I'm not going to bed yet. Before I even finish examining the stroke I glimpse patient number twenty-four, a blue breathless heart failure, being wheeled into a cubicle and a nurse posting the notice MEDICS TO SEE.

Now I'm seeing the heart failure who's a blue bloater with blue tongue, lips and fingertips and fluid swelling his body into a shiny tight balloon. I press hard on his skin and my thumb crater remains like lunar footprints. Meanwhile another trolley rolls in and patient number twenty-five is marked for me, this time an upper GI bleed.

And now I'm seeing the bleeder. He's frightened, confused and possibly senile. I roll this old man on his side and a nurse hauls his knees up towards his chest while I draw on surgical gloves and lubricate my right middle finger. I tell him what I'm about to do then with my left hand flat on his buttock that's so wasted I can feel the hunk of his ischial tuberosity I inch my finger into the old man's anus. The ring of muscle constricts and he moans and he starts mumbling to himself, 'No, no, no, no, no.'

'It'll all be over in a second,' I say. 'It's part of making you well again.'

The sphincter muscle hardens in protest. I push and his voice rises.

'No, no, no, no, no!' he shrieks.

But I ream the ring until at last I feel slackening and the muscle surrenders. I slide up through lubricant and he begins to sob. I roll my wrist feeling with one digit for anything out of place. Then it's withdrawn and I glance down at my gloved finger smeared with blackened bloody shit.

'All done now,' the nurse says.

'All done now,' I say but he just lies there weeping.

'I'm sorry,' I say then I go because I want my bed.

The first shafts of sunlight slice into my on-call room. When I get up the dusty washbasin splurges urine-coloured water and I have to run the tap till it's as clear as it's going to get before I can splash my face. In the mirror I glimpse my face. My hair is flattened on one side and sticks out on the other. I peel off a weave of fluff that's somehow snagged in my stubble. So now my body from its time in hospital has bits added on. A whitehead bulges at the edge of one nostril. I pincer it with my fingernails and out ruptures pus then I wash my face again, this time sensing the sweat and grease sedimented over the last twenty hours.

My bleep clangs.

The patient is a chest pain. I see him on CCU where they run off a crisp clean ECG and from it I diagnose a heart attack. Treatment commences and he's soon comfortable, Mister Patient Number Twenty-Six.

I get more bleeps. It's 6.30 a.m. and I'm resiting a drip. It takes three or four attempts while around me the auxiliaries serve the patients breakfast. The scent of food makes my stomach churn. I'm running on empty.

At the nurses' station I'm answering another bleep. While on the phone I rub my face and feel dirt and stubble and grease in my hair.

A cup of tea clinks by my arm. It's Donna, D. for Donna. She must've just come on duty. She lifts the cup from the auxiliaries' trolley. 'You look like you need it,' she says.

I sugar the tea. The sugar is my breakfast.

Donna's skin is clear and she smells fresh with the scent of having just bathed. I slip my hands round the cup. Its warmth comforts me. Daylight blasts through windows and my body begins to charge again like a leaf unfolding to the sun.

The night shift of nurses are dribbling out of the hospital and home to bed. The early shift are on duty now and they're waking the patients, encountering problems and bleeping me, the houseman, till nine o'clock when stubbly and dead-eyed and grateful to unburden myself of it I pass the crash bleep to the next houseman. Then with no time to shave or shower or change clothes I join Rich and the rest of the firm for the post-take ward round.

4: The Sacrifice

So we tour the hospital ward by ward reviewing our twenty-six new admissions. Doctor H. heads the firm. He's the consultant. He appoints us all and we answer more to his needs than to the patients'. Our SPR is Anita. She's Asian, plump, always seems short of time. When she speaks words tumble out like paratroopers.

As we trundle round the wards I push the trolley and Rich scribbles in the notes and Doctor H. signals his disapproval if the nurses ask us about our old patients instead of the new ones. Rich and I have to promise them we'll come back later.

Short-cutting through a surgical ward we skim past a row of patients and among them I glimpse an old one of ours. He's a man in his early twenties. Orthopaedic harnesses elevate his arms and legs. Big white bandages wrap amputated hands and feet so it appears that for limbs he owns four giant Q-Tips. A sheet covers his groin and under it where his penis should be instead lies a bloodied white pressure dressing. Though his hair's long after weeks in hospital I recognise that this is the Young Headache Man as he is now. After the meningitis he became the Young Gangrene Man so we gave him to the surgeons. When his hands and feet and genitals didn't fall off of their own accord they took him to theatre and cut them off anyway. Now he's the Man with Q-Tips for Limbs and a Scabbing Crater for Genitals.

Before his eyes swing up to mine I turn and hurry to catch up with the ward round.

Come one o'clock we still aren't finished. We attend the lunchtime medical meeting in the Postgraduate Centre where failure to show is anathema. As we march out of the hospital building across the hot sticky tarmac of the car park Doctor H. says, 'You're here to learn.' Sandwiches languish outside the lecture hall. We're the last to arrive and get the scraps. I crave a hot meal. Doctor H. seats himself on the front row with the other consultants. Rich, Anita and I stand at the back. Rich confers with one of the other medical SHOs in hushed tones talking serious talk. They're discussing the missed MI. She and her houseman glance in my direction. I glance away.

In the meeting the A&E consultant, Mister M., gives a case presentation. Meanwhile my feet swell. Weariness aches in my shoulders and back. The stench of my own body odour ascends from my shirt. Sleep tugs on my eyelids. I feel warm and dry and this shitty lecture is droning in my ears. Rich nudges me awake as I'm about to topple. As I grunt and focus I see Mister M. fix me with a cold glare.

I slip out to the bathroom where I douse my face with cold clear water. I drink and spit, drink and spit, then swallow. Cold clear water soothes my throat. I shut myself in a cubicle, lower the toilet lid and sit. Aches slither from my shoes and under the cubicle door and out into the world.

My bleep startles me with a message from Rich. It's ten past two. The meeting's over and I must've fallen asleep in the Postgraduate Centre toilets.

We review the last of the twenty-six new patients at quarter past three. Doctor H. mentions a couple of things that he feels weren't good enough and departs. Anita follows a minute or two after. Rich and I work back round the hospital, completing jobs assigned us on the post-take round and dealing with the backlog of issues relating to our old cohort of patients.

When I'm on her ward I sneak a look at Off Legs' notes. Her team thank us for our intervention and log that the ECGs suggest an evolving MI. They're careful to use the word 'evolving' to remain consistent with that 'normal' admission ECG. As for the patient herself she's sitting up in bed and her heart's beating out a rhythm like a metronome.

We finish at six and trudge out of the hospital with our overnight bags slung over our shoulders, heading home at last into low sun blinding our red eyes.

'You talked to them,' I say, meaning the female SHO and her houseman I saw him whispering to, 'about the missed MI? You talked to them after the meeting?'

'It's August,' he says. 'New housemen, new SHOs, new caz officers. Mistakes are more likely. No wonder they call it the Killing Season.' Then he sighs and adds, 'She had a run of SVT and now she's fine.'

'What if she'd had an arrest and died? It might happen, next time.'

'And what I'm doing is the best way of preventing a next time. *The – best – way.* Those guys looked at the ECG and all went, "Fuck – an MI – how could we have missed it?" They'll learn from their mistake and try hard not to make it again.'

'You know what that sounds like, Rich? "Close ranks. Bury your mistakes."'

'If you screwed up, what'd *you* want? You'd want your colleagues to cover your arse, wouldn't you? You'd want to be given a quiet nudge, and a chance to learn from it – wouldn't you?'

I reach my car that's the same heap I had as a student and figures as a contributor to my overdraft that still masses over two thousand pounds. I chuck my bag on to the passenger seat and say, 'No, mate – that's *you*. It's not me.'

The click of the front door's enough to wake me. Rebecca finds me on the sofa, dozing on a pile of cushions. She's been working late and she sighs because it's my turn to cook. 'I'll nip out for a takeaway,' I offer but signalling zero intent of rising.

She measures a pause, irked by my body language. We have a miniature olive tree on the coffee table. Rebecca picks a fallen leaf out of the pot, flicks it into the bin and says, 'No. I'll do tonight. You do tomorrow.'

Then she lays her newspaper and briefcase on the floor and slips out of her jacket. I get a sudden impulse of wanting her to continue. I want her undressing, I want her naked, I want her body against mine. She passes the window towards the kitchen threshold. I picture her stripped with the window behind her and framed in it streetlights glowing out of evening gloom and she's offering me her soft warm body.

'Come and sit down,' I say.

My hand spiders along her shoulder to the back of her neck, up into her curls of black hair, round, then pulling her head to mine. Her breath brushes my skin before noses slide over each other, lips into lips, flesh into flesh that's warm, wet, young, living. I hook her waist and squeeze her into an embrace. My hand delves between her thighs.

'No,' she says.

The heel of my hand massages her crotch. Her hand I take and clasp it on to the erection rising inside my trousers.

'Not now,' she says.

We met a year ago. Like me she'd got a faith and she'd saved herself. Then we shared the long summer between my passing finals and starting house jobs and we found a flat together. Now I want the sex we've had only three times and on each occasion sex followed by her tears and guilt then reaffirmation of the agreement to wait till we're married.

I smother her mouth with mine. Now I want more than mutual masturbation, that compromise we've struck. I want it despite her having surrendered her virginity to me, that sacrifice she made.

'No,' she says.

'Why?' I ask, though I know the answer is that I've promised never to pressurise her again out of consideration for *that sacrifice*.

'You know why,' she says and she pulls away leaving me alone in the room while she scurries into the bedroom.

But Rebecca hasn't witnessed the decay lurking to ambush our bodies or met the Young Headache Man whose body was once as complete as ours but now is being measured for plastic hands and feet since he woke up with no dick.

'Don't take this the wrong way,' she says on her return in jeans and a T-shirt, 'but you could do with a shower.'

I nod and say nothing for a time and then I want to tell her about the missed MI but by now she's in the kitchen expressing herself in the clash of pots and pans.

So I shower. Sweat and stench are leaking from my body. Water cascades off my scalp and shoulders. Warm as it is it reminds me of the tea Donna gave me, the tea that was warm in my hands. I recall peering down at its milky surface and it was swirling like water down the plughole at my feet, like circles pulling me down into a warm wet place. An erection pulses again. This time I urge it in quickening beats of my hand while hot water thrills my skin and I'm shocked by how fast, in spite of my tiredness, how fast I come.

5: The Language

As well as Monday to Friday nine to five I work one of every four nights in the hospital and one in every four weekends. Dread consumes the evening before the day on call as I sense impending confinement, discomfort and sleeplessness and I consign myself to an early night. Torpor swallows the evening after the night on call. As August fades to September I learn to cherish the one night in four I can accompany Rebecca to the cinema and not fall asleep. On one night in four I know I'm not going to be shaken awake by her with the restaurant bill paid and the waiter returning my jacket. These things we learned the hard way.

This evening is one of the one-in-four but I've travelled straight from hospital because we finished late. I'm still in work clothes – plain shirt and tie, comfortable trousers, brogues, no jacket. I don't wear a jacket because that's where the white coat lives. Splashes of blood crust the cuff of my shirt so I roll up my sleeves. I remember my bleep and unclip it from my belt then decide to carry on wearing it albeit switched off as an emblem at least as strong as the suits and mobile phones around me.

No one here in the restaurant is from the hospital. They're normal with normal jobs. Their shop talk revolves around the size of offices and the size of expense accounts, holidays booked, openings elsewhere. I'm on a different plane and I discuss work with other doctors in jargon no civilian can comprehend or is meant to comprehend. Already I'm starting to feel I don't belong with civilians or they with me.

'Great, you're here,' she says when she arrives and we kiss. Her skin's soft and warm. She's wearing her usual scent. Her hair's still damp from the shower.

'Working late,' I say. 'Curing ills, saving lives.'

I buy her a drink and she spots her friends. I'm introduced to them, a man and a woman. Rebecca and her friends lead us into the restaurant then a waiter guides us towards tables. I suggest, 'How about sitting outside?'

We're seated with a view of other bars and restaurants, boutiques, some steps leading down to the canal and on the far bank the red-brick plaza of the sports arena and conference centre. City buildings crowd the sky but the hospital hunches out of sight.

I stretch my hands behind my head and breathe in fresh air. Knots slacken in my back muscles. Pressure bleeds from my feet. A cool breeze prickles my skin with a warning summer's soon to end but not yet.

'Alfresco,' says the man, Rebecca's friend's husband.

Indicating the departing waiter I say, 'D'you know him then?' but Rebecca's friend's husband only frowns.

Menus jostle for space among plates, cutlery and elbows. The woman's a solicitor in the firm where Rebecca's doing her articles, her husband an estate agent. We embark on a bottle of wine.

'So do you specialise?' Estate Agent asks me after Rebecca's mentioned I'm a doctor.

'Not yet,' I say. 'Next year I'll decide whether I'm carrying on in hospital or heading out into general practice. I'm still a houseman.'

'You're, what, doing all that hundred-hours-a-week non-sense?'

'*Everybody* does stupid hours these days,' says Solicitor.

'It's more the pattern of work,' I say. 'If someone in business does a thirteen- or fourteen-hour day plus some time at the weekends, that's a seventy-two hour week, the same as I do. But they don't go without sleep two or more nights a week.'

They respond by glancing down at their menus. Rebecca says, 'So, anyone else having a starter?'

My rant continues, 'We're assumed to work half the hours we're on call, even though we work nearly all of them, so sixteen hours we're up through the night only count as eight, and forty-eight over a weekend become twenty-four, which means that a week where I'm on call over the weekend plus one other night, which is actually a hundred and fourteen hours – overtime, unpaid and unaccounted for, normally takes that up to a hundred and twenty – that week is officially considered to be seventy-two hours, which, magically, is also the legal maximum number of hours designated in law.'

But of course I'm saying none of this. Instead like them I'm studying the menu of modern international cuisine. The food looks good and after we've ordered my doctorly thoughts start drowning in burgundy. High-rises gulp the sun's embers and with the air cooling around us day ends. I try to put out of my mind that the next sun I see will presage three days and nights of captivity.

Over the terrain of starters and main courses the conversation visits legal cases, house prices, prices in general, a new car, a new film and so on. It continues like a procession with another lawsuit and someone being gazumped and a Christmas holiday being planned. And so on. The things people talk about, the things *I* once talked about, now seem meaningless against beats of life and death within the hospital.

I say, 'Anyone for another bottle of wine?' Their glasses remain half full while mine is empty and Rebecca's on mineral water because she's driving. Estate Agent shrugs and makes a neutral noise so I flag the waiter.

Then as I'm pouring and drinking Estate Agent mentions a case in the news of a surgeon facing an allegation of malpractice.

'What's the allegation?' I say.

'I think he misdiagnosed a number of patients who all turned out to have cancer of one sort or another.'

'The problem is no one knows who these bad doctors are till they make a mistake,' says Solicitor, 'by which time it's too late.'

'But surely that's the definition of a bad doctor,' her husband argues – 'one who's made a mistake.'

I say, 'There's a difference between negligence and error. *Negligence* is what's committed by incompetent doctors.'

Rebecca says, 'And who decides what's negligence and what's error, who's bad and who's to be excused?'

'I think it's hard for people outside the job to know. You don't even think of your colleagues as being "good" doctors or "bad" doctors. Some are more adept at the academic side, some the practical, some are better organised, some have a slicker bedside manner. They're all essential qualities but, in this case in the news, we're only talking about one: diagnostic ability. Let's say a doctor misses a heart attack. That sounds like negligence. And it is, if it was a barn-door inferior MI with towering ST elevation in II, III and aVF on the ECG. But suppose the doctor isn't in cardiology or a related specialty and it's a more obscure infarct . . .'

I trail off. They're looking at each other and they're half laughing, half frowning at the chunks of jargon I've flung their way. But they're civilians discussing medicine as if they understand it and I rejoice in proving they can't. How could they? Fuckers.

Gulping the dregs of my glass I pour more out of the wine

bottle. Rebecca narrows her eyes at me but in my condition I don't care.

'I think what you're saying,' says Solicitor, 'is it's technical,' and everybody grins.

A couple of tables away some designer-suited wanker's watch chimes and I leap up, sweeping away the tails of my absent white coat and fumbling for my silent bleep.

They're staring at me. I'd wanted to be under the sky but now as night chills the air I'm shivering. I roll down my shirt sleeves and though I'm showing blood on the cuff I don't care. 'I'm cold,' I say even though it's my fault we're out here but by the time the waiter's fired the heater they've called for the bill.

Travelling home I watch late-night streets glide past the car window. Rebecca's breathing sounds heavy in the silence between us. I glance across at her and her eyes are locked through the windscreen at the road ahead. Buildings shrink from offices to homes, pavements darken and I say, 'We had a patient who'd had an MI and no one picked it up till she started having an arrhythmia.'

She says nothing.

'I'm sorry,' I say.

'You shouldn't drink so much. It's not like you.'

'I'm sorry,' I say again.

She sighs and though she never takes her eyes from the road I sense her soften. 'An MI's a heart attack, isn't it?' she says.

'Yeah.'

'What's an arrhythmia?'

'An abnormal heartbeat.'

'What happened?'

'Nothing. She got better and went home.'

'You're not in trouble, are you?'

'No. It wasn't me who missed it. It was another doctor.'

'Has she made a complaint?'

'She never knew it'd been missed.'

'No one told her?'

'No. I suppose, you know, no harm done et cetera.'

'And who made that decision?'

'All the doctors involved, I suppose.'

'Your consultant?'

'No.'

'Rich?'

'He said, "Every doctor makes mistakes."'

She says, 'But you didn't do anything about it.'

'No,' I say.

Neither of us speaks again till we're trudging through the front door of our building. As we mount the communal stairs I'm already craving sleep.

She says, 'But what if something serious had gone wrong? What if she'd died?'

'You know what I'd do.'

'What would you do?'

'I'd speak out. Of course I would.'

We enter our flat. I strip off my tie and fling it through the open bedroom door but it falls short of the bed. At the desk by the front door Rebecca as is her routine glances for a message signed in the flashing red light of the answering machine. I assume the discussion's over but there are no messages so she looks up and says, 'You'd tell the authorities?'

'I don't know *how* I'd do it. I'd find someone I could report it to, I suppose. My consultant. A manager. An official of some kind.'

'So there isn't a specific person you're supposed to report this kind of thing to?'

'I don't know,' I say. I shrug. 'No.'

Slipping off her shoes she asks, 'I can't believe you don't even have someone who deals with this kind of thing.'

'Look, I was just trying to let you in on something about my life. I was trying to give you some insight into what my job's actually like, not what everyone imagines it's like. If I'd known all I was going to get back was . . .' I trail off.

She goes to the kitchen. I hear a cupboard open and the tap run. Rebecca returns taking sips from a glass of water and asks, 'Are you not enjoying your job?'

After a while all I say is, 'It's not always what I expected.'

'What d'you mean?' she says.

I've no stamina for the explanation. With civilians I need to find a language in which to describe the job and it's a language I've wearied of sifting for.

'Nothing,' I say and slip into the bedroom.

Rebecca peers through the open door for a moment and though I can sense her eyes on me I don't look up from unlacing my shoes. I hear her sigh with a short sharp aggressive burst of air. I register her shape receding from my peripheral vision then I hear her stamp into the bathroom and slam the door behind her.

I'm sitting by myself on the edge of the bed. Knots harden in my back, pressure pulses back into my feet but I know it's not her fault. When she comes back I'll tell her I'm sorry.

But when she comes to bed I can tell by her movements she'll remain pissed off with me even if I do say I'm sorry, so fuck her, I'm not saying anything.

Tomorrow at work I'll do a ring-around, hospital to hospital, and bleep my former housemates. I'm going to start making it a regular thing that on my precious one night in four I socialise with other doctors.

Though still in my clothes I'm already drifting into sleep. In the hospital I go to bed in them all the time, to speed the possibility of sleep and to be prepared for the ready-set-go when I'm woken. Of course she says, 'You're not going to sleep like that,' but that's exactly what I do.

6: The Weekend

And in the next moment my body jerks awake. A noise concusses my ears and as noises and smells and feelings acquire form I identify it as the clang of the crash bleep. Now I realise I'm not at home but in the hospital, in bed in an on-call room, and Rebecca's four miles away and three nights in the past. Next I remember it's Saturday night. No, it's *Sunday* night. It must be morning but it's dark and I don't even look at my watch as I tumble off the bed in my clothes. As I swing upright the pressure in my head changes and it arcs a stiffening charge down my spine and I feel my brain slop inside my aching skull. I smell my own sweat filling the hot stifling room and it coats my skin and mats my hair. My throat stings and when I swallow it hurts and dry crusts congest my nose. Now I remember I've got a cold because I had a sore throat on Friday and by yesterday I was streaking handkerchiefs with custard snot. My bleep's phosphor glow lights the path to my shoes. Then I'm running.

Feeling sick with fear, fever and fatigue I gallop down the stairs from the landing of on-call rooms and out of the doctors' mess. Every bound pounds my skull and even the ruffling of my hair jerks every follicle. Gloom flares into the harsh humming burn of strip lights. Long empty corridors drop away from me in every direction and while the sweat chills on my skin and I shiver with fever I hesitate for a moment at the centre of the hospital interior as if I've forgotten the purpose of my being here. Then like from a dream I discover among the sights and sounds and smells of the last few seconds the sound of the crash-bleep message that shattered me awake and from it decipher the words: *Cardiac arrest, Ward S19. Cardiac arrest, Ward S19.*

I pick the corridor and then I'm sprinting towards the surgical wards. I hear the clatter of my shoes reverberating along empty halls and the smashing open of doors jars my wrists and the repeat chime of the bleep echoes around me. For a few seconds I believe or maybe I only imagine other footsteps in another corridor converging with mine. It's quiet and empty this deep in the hospital at this time of night but I wonder if it can be so still that the sound of a doctor running would seep through layers of concrete.

My nose begins to run and I wipe away the drips with the back of my hand. My throat feels swollen and rough as sandpaper. I'm still blinking sleep out of my eyes when I reach the surgical ward. No one else undergoes this transition. Policemen have time to wrap their bags of chips into a ball and fling them out of the squad-car window on to the pavement. Firemen finish their snooker shot before sliding down that stupid pole of theirs that reminds me of something you'd see in a fucking Village People video. No one suffers this but us anywhere apart from the battlefield.

A marble body lies splayed on a bed with a bloody Redivac hanging from its side. Rich and the anaesthetist are already at work supported by two ward nurses and a surgical houseman. Under their flicking hands pink tracks of old operations scar the body's belly that bulges like a tight fluid-filled mound. On the monitor a jumbled white line strings from left to right. The nurses stick two slick square orange defib pads over the chest and after Rich turns the dial to two hundred joules he hits the CHARGE button and the machine hums with power. The defib tones and Rich calls, 'Clear,' and he presses the paddles on to the orange pads and when he clicks the triggers with his thumbs electricity fires into the patient. The body twitches and the monitor fuzzes to peaks and troughs before condensing into a flat white line. 'Oh, shit,' says Rich.

I've been a doctor for over a month and this is the first true cardiac arrest. Once I might've imagined I'd be facing three or four a day and responding to them with barked-out orders and the tails of my white coat flapping like in a scene from television. We run three cycles of CPR and adrenaline then add atropine then three more cycles then lignocaine then another three cycles and then Rich calls it off.

Afterwards in the doctors' mess I reread the protocols at the back of *The Oxford Handbook* while holding the book up with one hand while with the other making two cups of tea that are black because there's no milk again. Inside a plastic bag two slices of bread sweat and turn stale. The vending machine in the hall gulps my coins without spitting out a chocolate bar so I return to the kitchen and tear out the mouldy patches of bread and though what remains looks like Swiss cheese gone bad I eat it anyway.

My head throbs with fever and my muscles ache but if I go off sick I'll be leaving Rich to cover the weekend alone. So you don't take sick leave. Sick leave means you're dumping on your colleagues. The one thing you never do is dump on your colleagues. As for patients being exposed to my germs I think as regards nosocomial illness a cold ought to be the least of their worries.

In the empty junior doctors' common room I hand Rich his tea but before I drink mine I sneeze and have to fill my handkerchief with snot. He grimaces. In a few minutes the clock will creep to midnight and technically it'll be Monday morning, thirty-nine hours exactly since we came on duty. Rich and I down our tea and agree to split up and sweep the wards, him starting on CCU, me on Geriatrics, and work the three-quarters of a mile towards each other.

On the wards I rewrite drug charts, I append fluids to IV rotas, I replace troublesome Venflons, I strengthen painkillers, I tail off antibiotics. I cancel out the minor duties that'll disrupt my night. I defer major problems to the teams coming back on at nine o'clock.

I leave Geriatrics but then I'm called back. Someone has fallen out of bed.

'A patient?' I say.

'What's that supposed to mean?' says the nurse.

Hospital rules compel me to perform an examination and fill out an accident form. The patient has senile dementia. Either that or she fell from a very high bed.

A notice warns me not to venture outside but ignoring it I plod through a fire exit into the night air. I wander along a narrow concrete path that snakes through shrubs and along the way encounter a yellow board reporting A MEMBER OF STAFF WAS ASSAULTED HERE that gives a time and date and requests witnesses. I press on and before I can re-enter the hospital I have to negotiate a building site of skips and tarpaulin-covered brick piles.

Here cold refreshing rain sprinkles my face. My last shower was nearly three days ago. This evening (yesterday evening) I shaved for the only time this weekend and had to do it in two stages, first the left-hand side of my face then an hour later the right-hand side and under the chin, as in between I was called to a patient who'd dropped her blood pressure. I'm using Rebecca's present of an electric razor to save time but from chin to collar my skin's broken out in itchy purple blotches.

In the gloom I don't see a stray building site brick and I stub my toe on it and trip into the mud. Now my big toe throbs, I've grazed my palm and silt splatters my white coat and trouser leg. I limp all the way to the on-call room, clean out the graze on my palm and change back into the clothes I discarded this morning. They're screwed in a ball at the bottom of my overnight bag still reeking of the first twenty-four hours' patients, sweat and fever. I don't have a replacement white coat and the hospital laundry shuts at the weekend so I rinse it at the sink as well as I can.

Then hobbling up the long corridor I'm bleeped and answer it at the next phone.

'I'm sorry,' says a nurse from yet another ward, 'but one of our gentlemen has a headache and I want to give him a paracetamol.'

'Sure.'

'So you wouldn't mind coming here and writing him up for it, please?'

'Just give it and I'll sign next time I'm there.'

'I'm sorry. I'm not happy to give it unless it's signed for. We had someone suspended last week.'

'For giving paracetamol?'

'For giving an unprescribed IV.'

'That's a lot different.'

'Still, I'm not happy to give the paracetamol unless it's signed for.'

I'm damp and smelly, my shaving rash has bubbled into whiteheads and the pain in my big toe is beginning to bite but I still go there and do what she wants.

Next I'm on one of the medical wards and the night sister mentions a patient who's complaining of breathlessness. She tells me, 'She was complaining of being very short of puff earlier this evening, but I think she was putting on a bit of a show for her visitors.'

'Yeah?'

'Her doctors think she's a Munchausen.'

'So she's OK then?' I say.

'I think so,' she says.

'Do you want me to see her?'

'You should, I suppose.'

The Breathless Lady is old the way everyone else here is old. Bits are added on to her body and bits taken away. Moles mottle her leathery skin and the fat has left her chest uncovering ribs like shutter slats. On her fleshless arms joints bulge and veins stand out like blue cables. She sits propped up on pillows where she's half asleep but breathing fast. 'Hello,' I say.

'It's my breathing,' she says at once.

In the Breathless Lady's pulse my fingertip feels splashes of blood like they're little scared taps coming from inside a locked cupboard. I say, 'You've got yourself worked up into a state, I think.'

'No,' she says. 'It's my breathing. If only I could get my breath.'

'Try and get some sleep.'

I want to get some sleep too. Instead Casualty bleeps me to see another admission.

I snap my bleep out of its belt and kick it across the floor of the ward with my good foot and staff at the nurses' station turn to gape at me. I wish I could hum like the corridor strip lights that burn twenty-four hours a day. But I'm tired and limping and I've got a cold and when I stoop to retrieve the bleep – it's intact – knots tug in my back muscles. All I can think to say to the night sister is, 'Shit, sorry.'

I abandon the Breathless Lady and plod to Casualty and clerk in the next patient.

Back in my on-call room I loosen my shoe and roll off my sock. Blood inks my toenail and a crack splinters it in two. Red blood stains the gutters of my toes. I swing my leg on to the bed and the pressure drains but it's too painful to lay a blanket over so I try to sleep with my leg outside the covers.

I don't know if I've slept or not. It could be I blinked and the dank on-call room blacked out and the plash of rain lulled but as I open my eyes again I'm awake to the sound of my bleep and the glow of its LED. Cold embraces my leg. Rain beats on the window. Wind shivers its frame. I'm a cold empty body in a cold empty bed. I limp out of the doctors' mess. Each step shatters stiff joints. While I'm still en route the bleep's upgraded to urgent. By the time I get there it's being put out as a cardiac arrest. I think it can't be an arrest. There can't be none for a month then two in the same night. How does that make any sense?

The patient is the Breathless Lady.

Her body like leather splayed over knobs of bone lies flat and still. The bed's drawn out from the wall and its head is folded down. At the head end one nurse squeezes an Ambu bag while over the body another, the night sister, pounds out chest compressions. A third untangles monitor leads by twisting and separating coloured wires. Shit stains the bed between the Breathless Lady's legs in streaks of ejecta referring to a brown explosion at the moment of death.

'I'll take over chest compressions,' I tell the night sister, 'you help connect the monitor.' We swap places. 'What happened?'

'We don't know. She just went off.'

The monitor sparks and the picture that forms is a flat white line. 'Asystole,' I say. Then, 'Fuck.' Then, 'One milligram of adrenaline.'

The adrenaline comes in a Minijet. I bite off the cap and plunge the contents into the Breathless Lady's Venflon then it's back to chest compressions.

Rich and the anaesthetist arrive at virtually the same time. She takes over the bagging while Rich demands to know what we've given so far.

The anaesthetist pivots back the Breathless Lady's head and

opens her mouth. She snaps the laryngoscope blade out to a right angle and into the back of her throat. She requests a pause in the chest compressions so she can feed in an endotracheal tube. The anaesthetist wiggles the tube down towards the opening of the vocal cords. She's plump and pear-shaped and bent forward wearing theatre blues with a deep V-neck her big pale breasts jiggle in rhythm to the tube. I notice her bra cuts crescents out of her areolae. The anaesthetist levers on the laryngoscope and one of the Breathless Lady's front teeth snaps out of her mouth on to the floor by my feet before the tube slides down through the cords into the bronchus and the anaesthetist says, 'I'm in, thanks.'

I resume chest compressions. Rich orders another milligram of adrenaline. An oxygen line hisses from the wall to the Ambu bag. The anaesthetist squeezes once for every five of my compressions. I glimpse a crop of three or four coarse black hairs between her big white breasts. The stench of the Breathless Lady's agonal shit rises to my nose. The monitor line splinters into peaks and troughs in time to my compressions. Each time I react with hope. Each time the flat line reforms before I press again. Rich injects the adrenaline. The Breathless Lady's tooth lies broken at my feet.

A wave of nausea pumps a gush of saliva into my mouth. I'm going to be sick because of the stink of her shit and the broken tooth and the dead body but I fight it because I'm a doctor and these things shouldn't get to me. Spasms twist my stomach and with an embarrassed mutter of, 'I'll be right back,' I break out of the curtain and fling my head into the nearest sink. When I retch I throw up spit and snot and brown tea. I run the tap and with scoops of cold water I wipe my chin and rinse the acid taste from my mouth before turning and scurrying back behind the curtains.

'Sorry,' I say and take over from the nurse who's performed

chest compressions while I was away and one thing tonight I'm grateful for is that no one says anything.

Half a minute later Rich calls a pause and feels her carotid pulse. I stare at the constant white line on the square black screen on the other side of the bed. Rich reaffirms, 'No pulse, asystole,' and calls for more adrenaline and for atropine. The syringes cross between hands and from Rich's the drugs drain into the Breathless Lady's stagnant circulation. I continue chest compressions and the anaesthetist continues ventilating and on account of these twin efforts we hope to move drugs and oxygen round to her dying organs. We have to kick her heart into a rhythm, any kind of rhythm, something at least we can treat, but what we can't treat is a flat line because that means it's a dead flaccid heart that won't answer to drugs or electricity. Why didn't I perform a better examination? Why didn't I check her gases? Why didn't I do something when she said she couldn't breathe?

A snap like the sound of a stick of celery breaking judders my hands. 'Easy, tiger,' says Rich. Now I feel the crunch of her broken ribs every time I press on the Breathless Lady's chest.

We give more CPR and more adrenaline and I carry on peering at the flat line, the broken tooth, the shit and the anaesthetist's tits with the strange crop of hair growing in the valley. Now Rich gives lignocaine and we follow the injection with another three minutes' CPR, another dose of adrenaline, I break another one of her fucking ribs, that shit keeps stinking though I don't think I'm going to puke again and the tooth jerks on my peripheral vision like a speck on a car windscreen.

'Bicarb?' Rich suggests to the anaesthetist.

'Has anyone done gases?' she wants to know.

She means now as part of our resuscitation but I think of earlier in the night when I first saw her and I should've done gases then to make sure she wasn't faking and when I tune back into the debate between Rich and the anaesthetist over the Breathless Lady's now dead body I hear the anaesthetist conceding, 'Could give it a whirl, I suppose.'

The drugs in labelled boxes all slot into a polythene sleeve hanging from a metal stand. One of the nurses slides out the bicarb and breaks open the box. It's on the lowest rung of the sleeve.

Now Rich injects the drug. I kick the tooth out of sight. It's part of her, part of her body whether alive or dead and maybe we should keep it to bury with her but I still kick it anyway and I do it with my bad foot just to feel pain jolt me like lightning.

'Why don't we try some shocks?' I say.

The anaesthetist says, 'They won't do anything to asystole.'

'She's dead,' I say. 'It's hardly as if we can make things any fucking worse.'

Rich nods and flips the paddles out of the defibrillator. While a nurse lays two square orange pads on the Breathless Lady's chest Rich clicks the knob round to two hundred joules, punches the CHARGE button, reports, 'Charging,' and presses the humming paddles to her chest. The hum crescendoes to a couple of blip tones, Rich calls, 'Clear,' and the second we all step back he pulls the triggers. Current straightens the tan leather body and like a rag doll's her head shudders atop her limp neck.

The scrawl of current collects back into a flat line as Rich thumbs the carotid pulse. 'Asystole. No pulse. Two hundred, charging.' Rich charges, clears and shocks again. 'Asystole. No pulse. Three-sixty, charging.' He dials the knob to three hundred and sixty joules, clears and shocks again. The Breathless Lady's scrawny body quivers. The flat line reforms and we topple forward into another three minutes' CPR, another shot of adrenaline and three more three-sixty shocks but nothing changes on the screen or on the dead body or in the shit, the

60

tooth, the anaesthetist's tits or in my guilt. When at last Rich says it I'm grateful. He says, 'Thanks, everyone, but I'm calling this one off.'

7: The Munchausen

'At weekends, the patients are like ships adrift on the ocean. On Friday afternoon, we all plot them a course for the following two and a half days, hoping that on Monday morning the buggers haven't slid off the radar. Most of 'em just end up becalmed. It's a big hospital, after all. Unfortunately, this old Doris crashed on to the rocks. If you think weekends are bad, you wait till Christmas.'

Rich is flicking through the Breathless Lady's notes in the ward sister's office with the door closed while I pace back and forth in front of him. Guilt smothers me like a foam jacket, killing every sensation bar the pain in my ruptured big toe.

'It's all in the notes,' he says waving them at me.

I say, 'She died because I made a mistake. She had a PE, didn't she? She had a PE and I didn't diagnose it.'

'You made a mistake. True. But so did every other fucker.' He points out entries in the notes. 'It's all here. The reg thought she was a hysteric. The consultant wondered if she was throwing off microemboli. The houseman was supposed to book a spiral CT –' he plucks a form out of the back of the notes and waves it at me – 'only she forgot to. No one chased it up. ABC. Always Be Chasing. In the meantime, no one thought to anticoagulate her or even give her a pair of TED stockings.'

'I should've read all that. Then I'd've done gases. She'd had a small PE. It was a warning of what was going to happen. I could've treated her.'

'Probably she'd've died anyway.'

I stop pacing and perch on the edge of the sister's desk. My shoulders curl inwards, my hands fall limp on to my lap and I mumble, 'Who knows what would've happened?'

Rich drops his voice to say, 'You said the night sister said she was a Munchausen.'

'I was the one who examined her. She was tachycardic and tachypnoeic. How can I have been so fucking stupid?' I thump my knuckles on the desk. The shock wave jars the splinter in my big toenail. I wince. I wince at the pain across my hand, the pain ripping into my toe and wince at my own fucking fucking stupidity and snarl, *'How can I have been so fucking stupid?'*

'The night sister still could've – still *should've* – checked on her after you'd seen her. Would've picked up she was still breathless and tachycardic. Would've bleeped you. You would've done all the stuff you're talking about, but it would still've been too late.'

'Why is this everyone's fault but mine? It isn't!' He waves me to lower my voice. I gaze at the floor. 'I had the chance to save her, and I fucked it up, and I don't know why. I don't know why I was so stupid. I just don't fucking know.'

'Listen,' he says, 'mistakes are never one person's fault. Every one of the people who were supposed to treat this old woman let her down. You were one of them – yes. In your view, the most important – hmm, maybe. But the sole cause of her demise? – no way. No amount of guilt is going to bring her back.'

I glance away. Guilt like quicksand encloses me. 'Why didn't I even do gases? If I'd done gases, I'd've diagnosed the PE. Why didn't I do gases?'

Rich lets my word hang then says in a low voice, 'I don't

know why you didn't do gases. But I understand how it happened that you didn't. How many times have you left home without your keys? How many times have you dialled a wrong number?'

'It's nowhere near the fucking same.'

'No. You're wrong. It *is* the fucking same. We all make mistakes. Because we happen to be doctors, our mistakes have larger repercussions, but the process is the same. The human mind is prone to error. Forgetting your keys. Dialling the wrong number. Having a cold and a knackered toe and being dead on your feet then not thinking that woman might've had a PE. They're all the fucking same.'

I glare holes in the carpet. My eyes start feeling wet and I blink back tears. The carpet blurs. As long as tears don't swell over my lids and break on to my cheeks then that means I'm in control. As long as they don't break over my lids then I'm fine.

Rich says, 'You made a mistake. You'll learn from it. I did.'

I daren't look his way to acknowledge his confession in case those tears shake loose.

'I was a houseman,' he says. 'The first few weeks. The Killing Season. We had some guy come in, no proper history, couldn't make a diagnosis, did a whole load of bloods. Never heard anything from the lab, so assumed everything was OK. That was the line I took, anyway. I should've chased it up, but, for some reason, I never did. Still can't explain why. Can you?'

I don't say anything. I remain hunched on the desk cratering the floor with my stare while Rich's words radiate into the walls and furniture.

'You see,' he continues, 'one of the blood samples, the important one, was lying in a tray somewhere, because I'd forgotten to call a porter or mark it urgent. That's three mistakes. Not bleeping the porter, not marking it urgent and not chasing it up. If I'd chased it up, I'd've got the diagnosis and treated it. The next morning, I'm on the ward and I hear the whole fucking thing happening. Nurses shouting, the crash team arriving. He's arrested and died. The lab run the blood routinely that morning, and call me to say one of my patients has a raging DKA. Him – the one who's just died. Everyone knew I'd fucked up. Everyone knew if I'd picked up even the glucose when I was supposed to, we'd've been able to bring his numbers down and he wouldn't't've arrested. I was gutted. I didn't sleep for weeks. I felt like shit for what I'd done. But no one said a thing, because it happens. It'd happened to all of them to one degree or another. I learned from my mistake. ABC. Always Be Chasing. After tonight, I guarantee you'll never dismiss a patient's symptoms again. You'll never miss a PE, either, no matter how remote the possibility. From making this one mistake, you'll be twice the doctor you were before.'

He stands and says, 'In the morning, I'll make sure I'm the one who talks to the family. You do an ERCP.'

Before I can ask what the hell he means he's gone.

My bleep chimes but I don't even look at the LED.

My eyes track round the room poking at the furniture our words have radiated into: the desk, the chair, the filing cabinet, the Breathless Lady's notes, a styrofoam cup holding a pool of cold coffee, sweet wrappers, the telephone, the window, the ward outside veiled by a blind, the walls, the staff rota on one, the calendar donated by a pharmaceutical firm on another.

My guilt forms the screen onto which as flickering frames the micro-events of earlier can project. I see myself wandering towards the Breathless Lady, counting her breaths, feeling her pulse. The reel rewinds and in it the night sister's saying, 'She's a Munchausen.' *Then* I'm seeing the Breathless Lady. She's propped up on pillows and she's breathing fast. 'It's my breathing,' she's saying. I don't remember counting her breaths. I didn't count them. I'm feeling her pulse. I remember it being more than a hundred. 'You've got yourself in a state,' I'm telling her. 'It's my breathing,' she's telling me. 'Try to relax and get some sleep,' I'm telling her. Then I'm bleeped and kicking my bleep and leaving for Casualty. I don't recheck her pulse to see if it's settled. I don't listen to her chest though probably I won't have heard anything abnormal. Why don't I consult the notes? Why don't I do gases?

The flickering frames loop back to the beginning. The sister's saying, 'She's a Munchausen,' and the Breathless Lady's taking breaths I don't count, her pulse is batting along and she's saying, 'It's my breathing,' and I'm back to the sister, saying, 'It's nothing,' and I haven't looked in the notes and I haven't listened to her chest (though probably I wouldn't have heard anything abnormal) and I haven't done gases.

My bleep goes off again. I still don't look.

The reel loops over and over again. I search for the one fragment of memory that'll provide exculpation but I can't recover it because it's not there. The images spin till they dissolve. They dissolve into three frames. The three frames flash in my face: the Breathless Lady gasping, 'It's my breathing'; me not examining her properly; me abandoning her.

For the third time my bleep sounds. I glance down at the LED, lumber to the phone and dial the number.

'You've a patient here to see,' a casualty nurse says, 'a CVA.'

'OK,' I say and I limp away to see the patient.

In Caz I'm nervous while I confront elements of the outside world but then I withdraw deep into the interior where no one's watching me tread the long empty halls. Shivers of fever make me wrap my white coat around me like a blanket. I'm pale and sweaty and breathless but I see the next patient and the one after that.

Later I make it back to my on-call room and I want to phone Rebecca but it's the middle of the night. I hunch on the edge of the bed with my back ridging into tense struts of pain and there's no one I can talk to. There's no one else in the world who isn't fast asleep.

Me, I don't sleep. Instead my eyes inspect the grey shapes of the room. Then when it goes off I'm grateful for the bleep that swings me to my feet and out of the door into the hard constant light of the corridors. There's someone vomiting blood on a medical ward and to see him I have to ascend three flights of stairs every step of which hurts. From the top I peer out of the windows at the city outside and among the nameless glimmers of light I sense no one feels what I feel or does what I do. I'm all alone with what's happened as I turn away from the plates of glass and to the man who's vomiting blood.

When I need to discuss this new case with Rich our sentences are clipped and our terms direct but walking behind them like a shadow is the death of the Breathless Lady. I feel the whole hospital's blurring into fog. Patients, staff, beds, trolleys, drugs, monitors, masks and diseases are all congealing. Above in clouds temples of glass and concrete are frosting over. A single blow will bring them shattering in a million fragments on those of us below.

Later, much later, the Breathless Lady's notes hang from Rich's hand and I gaze at them across a mug of black tea I'm not drinking. We slouch in the doctors' mess with 6-a.m. light beginning to spread from the windows and he says, 'What I mean by "ERCP" is *emergency retrospective clerking of patient.*'

I don't take the notes. He waves them at me. 'I haven't written up the arrest yet,' he says. 'There's space for you to buff the notes.'

'I don't want to cover my arse. I killed that woman.'

'You slit her throat? You put a bullet through her head?'

'You know what I mean, arsehole.'

'Yes. That's the whole point. I *do* know what you mean.'

Rich leaps up and hurls his tea splashing into the sink. 'I'm sick of this shit. *You're* the arsehole. That woman cried wolf once too often. Christ, she was a fucking Munchausen.'

'She wasn't a Munchausen,' I murmur but Rich continues,

'And, if you think telling the world is going to absolve you, forget it. They won't even understand what you feel. The outside world won't even figure out that a doctor would feel guilty about his mistake. A postman puts your letter through someone else's door and it's just a mistake. A cashier gives you the wrong change or a chemist gives you someone else's holiday snaps or a plumber mends a tap but it still leaks. They're just mistakes, human errors, but, when doctors get it wrong, the reaction is different. But if you think they'll understand *what you mean*, then go ahead – *tell them*!'

He flings the Breathless Lady's notes on to the chair beside me. 'In medicine,' he says, 'this is the worst that happens – but all it is is some stranger dying.'

Forty-eight hours after I came on call nine o'clock arrives and with it Monday morning begins for the rest of the hospital. Doctors who've had the weekend off are bounding into work. I hand over the crash bleep. Under stubble my shaving rash is calming down. I dump the muddy white coat at the laundry and claim a fresh one to lay over my dirty smelly clothes. Now I enter the working day with its minimum eight more hours.

'Have you hurt yourself?' asks Anita, our registrar.

'I'm OK,' I croak.

'You've got a cold. You don't need to go off sick today, do you?'

'Can't really. Too much to do.'

'Hmm,' she says. Then she says, 'I heard about the Munchausen,' and develops an earnest expression.

'She wasn't a Munchausen,' I mutter.

68

But words like paratroopers are tumbling over each other to leap from Anita's mouth. 'You know as a houseman you have to keep your wits about you. Once I was asked to give a diamorph injection and the dose was supposed to be 2.5 milligrams but when I'd given the 2.5 milligrams I just forgot and kept on squeezing the syringe and I'd drawn up five milligrams so the patient got a double dose and that could've been very, very serious.'

'What happened?'

'Nothing. He was fine.'

I'm disappointed. Somehow I'd feel better if every other doctor had killed someone by mistake. I grunt, 'That's not very serious then.'

'No but it could've been and that's the point I'm making about keeping your wits about you when you're a houseman. OK, the post-take round's going to start at ten o'clock and we're starting on CCU so see you there and there's a lot to get round today.'

Anita departs and I stare at the Kardex lying on top of the notes trolley. I peel open the pages as if I'm committing a crime. I search through backward-sloping script and circles instead of dots over *i*s and *j*s till I encounter remarks concerning the Breathless Lady. The night sister has made two entries. The first is: *12.35 am. C/O SOB. S/B HO. No action taken.* The other is: *3.10 am. Found not breathing, no pulse. Called 222. Resuscitation involving RMO, HO, anaesthetist on call – not successful.*

I read them again and my gaze locks to those three words *No action taken* that record a doctor doing nothing in the face of a warning of what was to come. While my eyes remain down a group gathers round the nurses' station. Their glances twitch from patients in states of semi-dress to curtains drawn across secret practices to doctors and nurses gliding about their business and before I even look up those twitches alone betray them as civilians.

An old man and woman stand in their best clothes that must be ten years old and from their side a middle-aged man in a boiler suit approaches me. He introduces himself and I realise he's the Breathless Lady's stepson. He's called in before going to work. The old man and woman are her brother and sister-in-law. 'The ward sister telephoned us,' he says. 'She said there was a doctor who'd speak to us here,' and then he glances down at a piece of paper and makes a hash of pronouncing Rich's surname.

I'm still staring at the Kardex etched with those three words *No action taken*. I close it and slide it under a shelf and say, 'Yes, I can bleep him for you.'

The stepson in the boiler suit nods and thanks me and he's about to turn away to wait with the others.

Then I say, 'Wait.' He stops and turns and I say, 'I know this other doctor won't be able to see you for quite a while. But I was there when she passed away. I'll speak to you.'

I stand and shake his hand. I say to him, 'Would you all like to take a seat in the office?'

'Thank you, Doctor,' says the old woman, the sister-in-law, and the three of them file in.

I shut the door behind me and when I take a seat I'm forcing my feverish aching back to hold up straight. I say, 'Let me start by saying how sorry I am for your loss.'

They gaze into me and my stubbly face and crumpled clothes. The stepson has unzipped his boiler suit and knotted the arms at his waist. Oil stains the T-shirt covering his chest. 'How'd it happen?' he asks.

'The honest answer is I don't know. We know she'd complained of breathing difficulties on and off for some time. Without wanting to sound unsympathetic, the doctors looking after her felt that some – and I emphasise "some" – of her problems were due to panic attacks. Panic attacks are understandable in an elderly lady who's concerned she may have breathing problems. It must've been very upsetting for her.'

'That's right, Doctor,' says the brother. 'She was very upset.'

'I'm aware that her own doctors were looking into the possibility that blood clots were lodging in her lungs. That was never proved. We can't know the cause of death, if one can be determined, without a post-mortem.'

They exchange glances. None of them wants that.

'Think about it,' I say. If a PE that I missed killed the Breathless Lady the only way of knowing for sure is a PM. I'm pushing for the truth to come out and I'm not even sure why. 'It's the only way to know. You don't have to make up your mind today.'

The brother asks, 'Could it have been that, though, Doctor – a blood clot?'

'A large blood clot can cause sudden death. I think it is the most likely explanation in this case.'

I imagine the Breathless Lady when the fatal pulmonary embolism clogged her lungs experienced a sudden awful sense of collapse. She was terrified and in the moment she grasped her doom she shat herself. I say, 'I know it can be some consolation at a time like this to know whether a person suffered, and I can assure you death was sudden. She didn't suffer. She wouldn't even have known it was happening.'

They take it all in with upset eyes. Then the brother murmurs, 'I'm glad she didn't suffer.'

Now I peer at them wanting the truth to emerge. I want my guilt to be known and to be punished. I'm willing them to ask the question. I'm willing them to ask the question that will let out the torrent of guilt inside me that makes me want to proclaim the truth that is that I killed the Breathless Lady, and the stepson asks it. He asks, 'Was there anything that could've been done to save her?'

I picture temples of glass and concrete crowning a city within a city then within this place a long corridor strut by bars of sunlight and from this spine articulate wards and laboratories and theatres and departments.

Monitors beat to the drips of healing fluids. Pink repaints anaemic bodies. Yellow drains from jaundiced eyes like a bath being emptied. Warmth returns to cold clammy hands. Ulcers shallow, wounds close, hearts pump, lungs clear, livers and kidneys cleanse, spleens shrink.

Nights pass without sleep. Lives end but the saving of others brings fulfilment and hope is recycled by the triumph of medicine. Morning rises and my body recharges like a green leaf unfolding to the sun.

Facing up to what I'll lose I'm shaking. Rich committed a fatal error but it drove him to preach the 'Always Be Chasing' ABC that's saved who knows how many since. I can be the same.

'Was there anything that could've been done to save her?' they say.

'I doubt it,' I say.

My voice quivers. My hand's trembling. I press it on my lap. I cough, I fix the Breathless Lady's brother, sister-in-law and stepson with a look of conviction and I repeat,

'I doubt it.'

Then I continue with, 'She'd had a panic attack around midnight. Even if that was due to one of these blood clots lodging on her lungs, it could only have been a small one, nothing like the one that caused her death. If we'd diagnosed a blood clot at midnight, and given her treatment to thin her blood, I doubt there'd've been time for it to prevent the big one, the killer. I think everyone did the best they could and nothing could've prevented this tragedy. I'm very, very sorry.'

They exchange looks through sad eyes then one of them speaks for them all when he says, 'Thank you, Doctor.'

I take the medical notes to the neighbouring ward and find space at the nurses' station. There I buff them. I describe being called to see the Breathless Lady, a patient suspected of Munchausen's syndrome, who is manifesting anxiety. Her pulse is a hundred, her respiratory rate twenty-four. I reassure her and she calms down. Pulse seventy, resps twelve. I diagnose a panic attack and plan to review her. I write that, should she suffer further breathlessness in the night, I will take arterial blood gases. If gases suggest a PE, I will anticoagulate her.

Rich comes by and he asks, 'Everything OK?'

'Everything OK,' I say and chuck the notes on the pile with the other discharged or dead patients.

Then I scurry to the staff toilet in the aisle leading off the ward but it's occupied and I decide I'll head all the way to the one in the doctors' mess. Each step that isn't a run convinces me I remain in control. When I get there I lock the door behind me and take deep breaths. The wave of nausea ebbs. Then the gush of saliva in my mouth fires a warning and a moment later spasms convulse my stomach and oesophagus. I heave once, twice, three times before yellow watery puke spurts into the shit-specked white porcelain of the toilet bowl.

I promise. I'll be twice the doctor I was before and never again miss a PE or distrust a patient's symptoms and I know before I wanted to confess but now I'm going to fight for what I have. I have the chance to carry on being a doctor. I have the chance to help people and save lives and all these things I promise in return for a second chance.

After wobbling to my feet I splash water from the basin over my face, wipe the puke from my chin, gulp mouthfuls from the tap to rinse out the taste and then at five to ten I muster for the post-take round.

As I wander through the interior I register how it's filled with staff and visitors. Voices and a herd of shoes clicking on hard floors have conquered the silence of the night gone by. The sun beams through the spaced windows of the long main corridor and I limp through gold bars of light while in between them the air is cold but to my feverish skin the temperature seems not to vary.

Doctor H. saunters across my path carrying a pile of notes tucked under his arm and he's still wearing his reading glasses. I think about veering off but it's too late. He sees me and says, 'Morning.'

'Morning,' I say back.

We walk together but I keep the space between us wide to spare him my stench and ugliness. 'How was the take?' he asks.

'Not too bad,' I say. 'Forty-one patients.'

'Weekends are the worst,' he says.

'They do nothing for my chances of winning the hospital beauty contest. Maybe I should do surgery – perhaps I'll do better in life if I'm wearing a mask.'

He laughs and meaning nothing in particular he asks, 'So how's it all going?'

I measure a pause but then I say, 'Fine. No problems.'

'Good,' he says. 'Very good. It's a real baptism of fire. I've been through it. If ever there's anything you want to talk about, I'll make a real effort to look like I could actually give a toss.'

I laugh.

We walk to the top of the corridor without adding any more. I feel an urge to break into a run. It swells inside me with shocking suddenness and I lie to him that I need to chase up a result ahead of the round.

'See you in a minute,' he says as he recedes through doors.

Corridors tunnel up to the rim of the main hospital buildings then I plunge into a small square of shrubs between the entrance and the front of CCU. Outside the air thrills my face and I suck in lungfuls till my lips and fingers tingle. I'm overcome by a compulsion to charge and run away or I'll be sick but there's nowhere to go and when I retch there's nothing left to bring up.

8: The Burial

Rebecca's body lies turned to me or away from me but in either case always on her side and her slow breaths slide into the gutter between our pillows like oil seeping into pavement cracks. She sleeps while the Breathless Lady lives on in my thoughts.

My eyes are always open to meet the dawn. That it comes later each morning only serves to prolong my vigil till first light dribbles under the curtains. The bedroom forms in grey around me. I study the shape of the shade that hangs over the ceiling bulb. I trace the lines of the wardrobe and the chest of drawers. Another hour fortifies the light. Bright rods dagger from curtain borders slicing the room into sections. Now as if undergoing the effect of a prism the grey divides into the pale blue of the walls and the rich wooden brown of the furniture.

Later I bury my head to rediscover darkness under the covers and there torment myself with the same questions over and over again. *Why didn't I do gases? Why did I believe the night sister? Why didn't I look in the notes? Why didn't I consider a PE?*

This morning almost a minute passes before the first sign Rebecca's climbing out of unconsciousness and this morning that first sign is a sound. A noise issues from her throat that's part breath and part groan. Then she rolls away from me on to her back and continues over on to her other side. Curls of black hair now cascade on to the pillow in the opposite direction. Her arm twitches before swinging towards her face. Moments later her shoulders twist and rise.

'Hiya,' she says.

'Hiya,' I say back.

The crack in my toenail has healed so I suffer no pain pacing barefoot to the bathroom where I shave and shower. I might not get chance tomorrow morning because I'll be on call. In the mirror I notice flashes of eczema over my eyebrows. I haven't had it since finals and not this bad since A-levels. I claw my fringe down. It's nearly long enough to cover the redness.

Over breakfast Rebecca scans some faxes before folding them into her briefcase. I place a mug of tea beside her and tell her, 'I'm on call tonight.'

'Yeah,' she says, 'I've got it in my diary. I'm meeting Emma for a drink.' Emma is a friend of hers from university. I think she might have two friends called Emma.

'Have a good time,' I say.

I pick up my overnight bag and a coat. I need one now.

'See you tomorrow,' I say.

'See you,' she says.

I shuffle out of the flat without telling her something I've known for two days. This morning they're conducting the Breathless Lady's post-mortem.

Rich remains up on the ward holding my bleep while I'm in the basement of the hospital explaining to one of the pathology technicians that I was involved in the care of the deceased and I'm curious to discover the cause of death.

'I'll ask the pathologist if it's OK for you to go in,' she says.

A trolley rattles across the floor above my head.

'She says it's OK,' says the technician, 'but she says you'd better wear wellies.'

There's a spare pair in the department. Leaning against a wall

77

I swap them for my shoes, hook up my white coat then follow the technician into the examination room. Body fluids trickle off tables on to the floor that remains wet from its most recent mopping. In the chill air I shiver and I smell meat and preservatives and the smell of preservatives is so acrid it at once sours the back of my nose and the back of my throat.

'We don't often get one of the clinicians down here,' the pathologist says.

'Why ever not? Corpses, body fluids, pickled organs – you've got the lot.'

The technicians have already prepared the Breathless Lady. They've sawn open her thorax, sliced open her abdomen and removed vital organs. An incision circles the head at the level of the tops of her ears. The technician has peeled the scalp forward, crumpling the face into a mound of flesh, then uncapped the skull and excised the brain before replacing the coverings. I recognise her because her face is still on.

A workbench runs along three edges of the room. There on a set of scales the pathologist weighs the Breathless Lady's lungs. She slices through the red holy tissue and almost straight away finds strings of thick black clot plugging the blood vessels.

My spirits plunge but I try not to show my feelings to the pathologist. Maybe she'll find something else.

The brain waits for us at another station on the workbench. The pathologist weighs it and examines it. I gaze upon the ritual with hope vanishing. The pathologist reports the brain as normal. The other organs are weighed and they too are all found to be normal.

I know now as a fact that I killed the Breathless Lady.

When I glance up shivering against the cold air that seeps through my shirt I see the pathologist returning to the Breathless Lady's body and stripping out leg veins. 'Funny,' she says, 'I can't find any clots in her legs.'

I snap, 'They're all in her fucking lungs, that's why.'

Now the PM's been performed the Breathless Lady's firm can write her death certificate. I'm not there when the family come in to collect it but by all accounts they're grateful for the care their loved one received. The following week the Breathless Lady is buried and with her my mistake.

Tonight I'm home before Rebecca. I've worked days and nights and the next days and not a minute's crept by without my thinking of the Breathless Lady. I sit in silence with no CD playing and no television on as outside day fades and street lamps flare. I don't get up to turn on the house lights. I sit and stare into space and gloom congeals round me.

On the coffee table next to our miniature olive tree a paper bag from the chemist's contains a tube of hydrocortisone cream. The packet lies unopened while the red flashes over my eyebrows have over the course of today become confluent with a blotch in the middle of my forehead.

I'm like a bottle of fizzy drink shaken hard then laid out for someone to find.

The front door clicks and seconds later electric light bursts over me.

'You're home,' Rebecca says in surprise.

'Must've fallen asleep,' I lie.

She sheds her briefcase and lays her newspaper on the table next to the olive plant. 'You wouldn't fancy nipping out?' she says. 'Just grab a bite and a glass or two of wine? Not a late one, promise.'

I don't stir. My body's the weight of lead.

She sighs and says, 'OK, then,' ripping off her coat then flinging it over the back of a chair.

I want to tell her the truth. I want to confide that more than a week ago I was crouched over a shit-specked toilet puking and at the same time begging for my future in medicine and ever since through sleepless nights I've plummeted into despair. So many times I've been close to shaking her awake and confessing my crime but I've always held it in where it twists my insides and now it seems to be rotting my skin. Now at last I say to her, 'I think I might've made a mistake at work.'

'What kind of mistake?' she asks standing in the middle of the room.

'A mistake,' I say.

She stands still in front of me. I wish she'd sit down. Then she says,

'But I thought you were a good doctor.'

She's reacting like a civilian, one of them, who can't understand, who won't understand. I know now I shouldn't have confessed to her and moreover how right I was in not confessing to the Breathless Lady's family.

'Everyone makes mistakes,' I say. 'Good doctors do, good lawyers, good drivers – *everyone*.'

'We talked about this. I thought we said good doctors don't make mistakes.'

There's a note in her voice that deadens me. The note is shame.

She goes on, 'What have the hospital said?'

'They don't know about it.'

'I thought you said, if something like this ever happened, you'd come clean about it?'

She stands for a long time, not looking at me, just standing there. I know she's not going to sit down and it hurts me. She mumbles, 'I thought you said bad doctors should be punished.'

I say, 'I am being punished.'

'How?' she says.

'Like this,' I say.

Then I look away.

In the morning I return to the work of the firm where Rich and Anita never mention the Breathless Lady and as far as I know Doctor H. isn't even aware of my mistake. I've set about keeping my promise. I take careful histories and perform thorough examinations. Before instituting treatment I refer to *The Oxford Handbook*. I never fail to chase up results and while the walls of the interior protect me from those who might accuse I withdraw into the community of my own kind.

On the ward Donna, the student nurse, mans the nurses' station alone. She's holding the telephone receiver away from her ear and punching digits on the keypad. She transmits her bleep message then replaces the handset.

I sit beside her to write an entry in a patient's notes. My eczema's bubbling into blotches but I flick my fringe down over it and try not to scratch my face. My bleep chimes and I reach for the phone in front of me.

Donna's telephone rings. A diamond squatting on top of a silver band glints as her left ring finger travels with the rest of her hand. She picks up and says, 'Yes,' to whoever's on the other end, 'I'm bleeping you about the gentleman with pneumonia you saw earlier. He's complaining of pleuritic pain. Could you write him up for something, please?' She listens then says, 'OK. I'll give him a dose now and you can sign for it later.'

She ends the call and we down phones at the same time. Her engagement ring swings over as her wrist rolls. She writes an entry in the prn section at the back of the drug chart, attaches a note reading *Dr to sign* and scoots to the treatment room, emerges carrying a pill in a small plastic tub, crosses into a bay, gives the pill to a patient in his seventies and leaves the ward.

I finish my paperwork. As I move away to attend my next task, the one I've been bleeped about, I glance down at the chart and notes Donna was dealing with. Although he's not my patient I know something about his history and I spot the clash with the painkiller she's just given him. So I cross out her entry on the drug chart and replace it with the appropriate one. I bleep the houseman and tell her, 'Listen, you gave a verbal order for a non-steroidal, but he's got a long history of GU.'

'Shit,' she says.

'Don't worry. I've put him on something else, if that's OK.'

'Of course it is. Thanks. Is he all right?'

'He's fine.'

'I wasn't thinking . . . What the fuck was I thinking of?'

'It happens,' I say. 'Don't worry about it.'

Now I visit the GU Man and advise him to let the nurses know if he gets any stomach pains. As usual I come to the ward on and off throughout the morning. Every time I glance over at the GU Man he appears comfortable. By afternoon I've stopped looking because I know he's going to be OK.

Later I'm trudging down a corridor. I'm in the heart of the interior where I feel secure. Ahead of me Donna is strolling back to the ward. A black scrunchy cuffs her brown hair back off the pale clear skin of her face away from her squarish black-framed glasses and narrow neck. She wears the student nurse's plain white and I notice her small breasts bulging under the thin cotton of her uniform. The collar opens over her sternum from which clavicles spread like wings and they make ridges in thin tight skin.

'Still here?' I say as we cross.

She says, 'Home now, thank God.'

I pause and call her back. 'Have you got a minute? I need to tell you about something.'

'What is it?'

'That verbal order you took this morning. The patient's fine, so don't worry, but he's got a stomach ulcer and you gave him a non-steroidal.'

She looks shocked. 'He's all right, though?'

'Trust me, it's the least of his problems. I changed the prescription and OK'd it with his houseman. You were off the ward before I realised. I hope you don't mind.'

'God, no.' She peers down at her feet. 'What if something had happened?'

'It didn't.'

'You're positive he'll be OK?'

'Positive.'

She nods and glances down and away, not to her feet, to the side.

'These things happen,' I say.

Her face lifts and she peers at me through her black-rimmed glasses and I worry her gaze will harden but, no, her eyes stay soft. Her hand flicks past her breasts and clavicles and neck to loosen and recuff her hair and my eyes catch the diamond ring and in that moment I think, *Engagements can be broken.*

'These things happen,' she says back.

9: The Secret

A slab of eczema scalds my forehead. Notes, charts, results strips and X-rays lie strewn before me. The phone rings but I ignore it. I sit at the nurses' station inspecting every one of my cases. I chase results that aren't back yet, even routine ones. The on-call biochemist becomes sharp with me but I manufacture an argument for their importance. I write out forms for the next day so they're not forgotten in the scramble of rounds. It's 8 p.m. and I should've finished two hours ago. In truth I *did* finish two hours ago but here I stay nailing every blood count.

By the time I'm home Rebecca's reading in bed. 'You never said you were on call tonight,' she says.

'I wasn't.'

'We had plans.'

'I forgot. I should've phoned. I'm sorry.'

The next night is worse. I'm driving home and rain fogs my windscreen with one wiper failed while the other waves surrender to the downpour. Uncertainty clinches me and I loop back towards the hospital. I park among the waggling beams of visitors' headlights and dart into the hospital to check a blood result. It's there, noted in my hand, already acted upon.

I remain at the nurses' station wearing no white coat but a jumper over my shirt and tie with my wet hair dripping on to the notes and I can't move. I don't know what to do next, whether to stay and find more work or to go home. I'm as vulnerable and powerless as the patients around me. I recognise it in the faces of these old people with their bodies added to and subtracted by disease who don't know what's going to become of them.

The following night is an on-call night and two paramedics burst a trolley through the fogged plastic doors of Casualty. A rush of wind dissipates into the department and the doors swing back with a slap like leather and in that time voices have begun colliding in the air around the trolley patient.

'Into resus!'

'Where's the reg?'

'It's an arrest!' which leads on to a cry directed at Rich and me of, 'Get in here!'

We start towards the resus room but the staff nurse is panicking and she shouts, 'Do I have to put out a 222? *Get in here!*'

The staff nurse and paramedics heave the patient from the trolley on to the couch in the middle of the resus room. While one of the paramedics continues chest compressions the other one, who's bagging, says, 'No pulse or spontaneous resps for five minutes –' but he's speaking to the SHO who's Spanish and she's gaping between the patient and the paramedic and isn't doing anything.

I say, 'If the reg isn't available, maybe we should call the A&E consultant.' No one responds. It's like they haven't heard me. 'I said, "If the reg isn't av–"'

'We'll take over chest compressions,' says Rich with a nod to me. The paramedic steps back and I step forward. A bag of fluid lies across the patient's chest running into a green Venflon in the back of his hand. Rich transfers it to a stand, snatches a couple of brown Venflons and promises, 'I'll get better access.'

The Spanish SHO twitches and moves towards the patient but doesn't start doing anything. While with slick fingers Rich passes his first Venflon the staff nurse runs round the patient's head, transfers the oxygen supply from the paramedics' portable cylinder to the wall socket and opens the valve to fifteen litres per minute. The tiny ball inside the glass leaps to the top of the gauge. Now she takes over bagging and over the gush of oxygen Rich asks the paramedic, 'What's happened?'

'Gunshot wounds –'

Excitement pricks us all. We're in a rare televisual moment and we gasp with enthusiasm.

'Gunshot wounds – one to the abdomen, one to the head. Someone at the scene said he'd been trying to nick a car.'

'Picked the wrong car.'

'Looks like it,' the paramedic laughs.

'Cheers,' says Rich.

'Cheers, Doc,' he says back.

The paramedics saunter out of the resus room. A couple of seconds later we hear the slap of the plastic doors and another second after that receive the rush of wind. The staff nurse reaches and pulls a heart monitor to the bedside. The Spanish SHO not having a role unravels the leads and then dials the tuning knobs till a flat line appears.

Something appears and disappears in my peripheral vision. It happens again and a third time and it looks like a small greyish balloon being blown up and let down, blown up and let down, blown up and let down. Now I glance round and at the moment I recognise what I'm seeing I also realise the inflations tally with my chest compression.

'Rich . . . '

'What?'

'I'm stopping chest compressions.'

'Why?'

'Because they're making his brain come out of his head.'

Rich glances up. The bullet's blasted an opening in the

86

patient's skull above his ear and splintered bone into his hair. Yet the anatomy of his head and face is intact enough for a first glance to miss the injury.

'Do a compression,' he says.

'No,' says the nurse grimacing.

I press Hole in the Head's chest and a white-grey mush bulges out of the hole and leaks down the side of his head. The Spanish SHO screws up her face.

'You know,' I say then, 'this abdominal wound isn't doing much in the way of bleeding.'

Rich and I peer in. A bullet's punched a slit to the side of his navel. Layers of skin, fat and muscle pucker with uniform pallor. Though blackened the loop of bowel inside leaks no red.

Now a man I recognise as Mister M., the A&E consultant, steps into the room. The Spanish SHO without a word to anyone scampers out.

'Where's the bloody registrar?' Mister M. wants to know.

No one knows.

'What've you got here?' he asks.

We tell him and he rubs his hands together. He throws his jacket over a trolley, rolls up his sleeves and starts pulling little used equipment off the shelves. While I continue chest compressions he makes a nurse help him into theatre greens. I stand back and he begins by making a scalpel incision between Hole in the Head's ribs and slides a clamp into the opening.

'Carry on chest compressions,' he says to me.

'I'm not scrubbed,' I say.

He tuts and says, 'Oh, just put some bloody gloves on.'

Rich shakes his head in disbelief but I put on the gloves and resume chest compressions.

Mister M. turns the handle and the clamp widens, retracting the ribs from the wound. Not a drop of blood drips out. Mister M. squeezes Hole in the Head's heart by hand until he gets cramp then he makes me do it. Flesh crowds round my hand and wrist. Thick cold muscle fills my palm and squeezing it is like squeezing a tennis ball made of rump steak.

Rich whispers to me, 'This is a complete fucking piss in the wind. His entire circulating blood volume's spilled on the pavement somewhere between this hospital and a drug baron's limousine.' He raises his voice to Mister M. 'Sorry, we've got medical patients to see.'

'This is an excellent teaching case.'

'Sorry,' says Rich, pulling me away by the elbow.

'Fuck off, then,' Mister M. mutters under his breath. Then he wields a big electric saw. 'You won't see this very often,' he says to the nurse who looks like she's going to throw up and as we pass out through the doors we hear it buzz to life.

Admissions occupy us till midnight. Rich clerks in three to every two of mine. Every question of the history I ask twice over because they'll change their answers. Every item of the examination I inspect or feel or listen to till I'm certain and if I'm not then I draw a ring round it and label it unknown. I'll look in their blood or their spit or their X-rays and keep looking till I've made it known. I must because they all have *her* capacity to catch me out.

We sweep the wards for problems. When Rich bleeps me I lie and tell him I've completed my share of the sweep and he can go to bed. I carry on chasing up results and assessing patients' progress for another hour, falling behind with an admission that awaits me in Casualty.

'You've already got two more to see,' the charge nurse tells me. 'What's taking so long?'

The admissions peter out by four but I don't finish handling them till six. This is my longest stint so far without even a minute's break, twenty-one hours, a quarter of them of my own making. Results not filed flash like warning lights in my mind but I think through them one by one and remember they're all in, all dealt with.

At 6 a.m. and entering autumn it's not light yet.

In my on-call room I smear hydrocortisone cream over my forehead. I'm exhausting a tube a fortnight. I can no longer apply soap to my face in case it induces a rash. Leaning into the mirror above the basin I inspect my skin's pinhead black speckles where grime's clogged the pores of my nose and cheeks.

I lie on the bed not even loosening my tie or my belt or removing my shoes. Thoughts dip and swerve round my head like kites but sleep still begins closing round my body.

The Breathless Lady lies in a grave somewhere on the outskirts of the city. Her body putrefies and inside it the blood clot I missed blackens like tar.

My bleep clangs.

I roll off the bed, sliding my knees on to the carpet, my cheek pressed on the mattress, and I weep. I'm weeping with tiredness. My shoulders quake as sobs dribble out from my chest and on to the blankets like blood spreading from a head wound.

When I look up from the next patient's notes I see someone as near death as any still living thing can be. Cancer has consumed his body, excavating fat from his eye sockets, his cheeks, his neck and his hands. His skin is the grey of rotting meat and rods of grey stubble dot his chin but have stopped growing. His eyes cannot focus. They're dead. His body is dying from the outside in, beginning with skin and muscle decaying to a grey shroud before the organs that support life wither and collapse.

'Your stomach cancer has spread very badly,' I tell him. 'Do you understand me?'

Breath rasps in his throat till they gather into a word that might be, 'Yes.'

'Your doctors will have explained that you are very, very ill. Do you understand me? We'll do everything we can to make you comfortable. Do you understand?'

He can't answer.

'Why've they brought him in?' I ask the charge nurse. 'Shouldn't he be in a hospice?'

The charge nurse shrugs, 'You'd've thought so, wouldn't you? Anyway, he's made it here now.'

'Yeah, and you could say the Hindenburg made it to New Jersey.'

I'm trying to install a subcut diamorph driver when the rasp in his throat thickens to something fluid and he's drowning and he gags and two or three litres of dark red blood gush from Grey Meat's mouth over his chest. Focus deserts his eyes and they darken into death. Ten seconds later I'm still standing poised to prick his grey skin with words of comfort forming on my lips, still as I was at that moment, his moment of death.

I look from dark dead eyes down into the blood and see lumps I think can be pieces of tumour or even parts of his stomach. I feel a sudden overpowering urge to giggle. I feel a compulsion to giggle like a child because I feel in this moment I've been let in on the great secret about life and death and the great secret is that there is no great secret. It's like having been in awe of a magic trick and then suddenly spotting the strings.

I back away and sit at the table in the body of the department. It's a few seconds before I draw my pen from the breast pocket of my white coat and compose an entry in the notes.

I remember lying on my bed as sleep enclosed me like the water of a deep warm bath. I wish the last half-hour had been spent in that sleep. It would have been if Grey Meat had died in the ambulance before he got to Casualty. I wish he'd died in the ambulance so I could have slept instead.

I begin to look around and in doing so my eyes track over the clock and I realise fifteen minutes have passed since Grey Meat died. Two white coats revolve around each other at the far end of the room. One goes into a cubicle and the other into X-ray. Nurses console a toddler who's crying whose parents use wide strokes of their arms to make a point. A middle-aged woman on a drip glides towards me in a wheelchair pushed by a porter.

I glance down at my hand and observe sentence after sentence inscribed in Grey Meat's notes. While my higher self sat paralysed the primitive motor inside me has carried on turning over because the next case is waiting. I'm like the most refined medical instrument. I pass through without friction, without being decelerated or deviated or dulled. Once I feared how much all this would affect me. Now I fear how little it does.

10: The Autumn

Rainclouds have snuffed out their glow and the blue skies of August have faded like a lost golden age. Damp darkens concrete towers to charcoal and their glass no longer glints. Trees that in dotting the hospital perimeter resemble fenceposts decay to skeletons. Their brown leaves crumble into soil and become fuel for other living things.

In the interior I reclerk a Vague Yellow Woman who's a hand-back from overnight. The whites of her eyes are dyed bright yellow as if they're boiled sweets. Her skin's yellow-brown. The beds of her fingernails are yellow. Grey flecks her black hair. Her nightie is cream with small pink flowers. She's too forgetful and vague to give me a history but her husband is helpful and concerned and tells me of a three-week deterioration characterised by sleepiness, irritability and confusion. I ask about alcohol and he nods and shows a pained look when he answers that she's drunk too much for too long.

'She's jaundiced,' I tell him. 'For some reason, usually related to the liver, bile pigments are accumulating in her blood stream. We need to do more tests to find out the cause.'

Doctor H.'s round started about twenty minutes ago but having not progressed beyond the ward they're down in the bottom bay by the windows overlooking the car park. I'm with them only a minute or two before Donna scurries down, apologises to Doctor H. for interrupting and whispers to me about the Vague Yellow Woman.

'There's something wrong with her,' she says.

Doctor H. and Rich eavesdrop for a moment before returning to the case in hand.

'What's wrong?' I whisper back.

'Something *dead* wrong.'

I say, 'She's just nodded off.'

'I might only be a student but I know a dead person when I see one and she's dead.'

The ward round moves to the next patient, crossing Donna and me. They glance up the ward to the top bay where nothing out of the ordinary appears to be happening.

'What's happening?' Rich noses.

'Nothing,' I say.

'All you had to do was clerk her in,' he laughs, 'not kill her.'

'Houseman gone and killed a patient?' Doctor H. says, swinging up the next one's X-rays. 'Hope it's one of mine. One less to see on the round.'

'I'm going to see what's going on,' I say. 'And you two – you two can just fuck right off.'

Rich and Doctor H. laugh. I stride back up the ward with Donna. She's scowling. 'This isn't a joke, you know,' she says.

'I know. I'm sorry.'

The curtains are drawn round the bed and the husband stands outside. His body rocks to and fro as if to plunge through the curtains then withdrawing for fear of what he might discover. 'She's taken a turn,' he says. I assure him I'll deal with it and slip through the curtains.

The Vague Yellow Woman lies on her back, her arms limp at her side, her lips parted, her chest still. The yellow eyes stare at the ceiling, the yellow-brown skin hangs loose. I go through the motions of examining pupil reactivity, carotid pulse, heart and breath sounds but like Donna I know a dead person when I see one. Already her body's cooling and she's received no CPR. Calling an arrest now will be more trouble than it's worth especially with the ward round in full swing. So I search for clues but find none. I pick over every point of the history, every particle of the examination, and I know I've not missed anything that was there to find. Why she's dead is a mystery. Maybe the bloods will tell.

Now I remember the husband. Her 'turn' has been a huge fuck-off detour. I take a big breath and step out. 'How is she?' he asks at once.

'Let's go into the office. We can talk in there.' He nods and follows. He doesn't ask me to hurry up and tell him what's wrong but I still think he suspects the worst. Relatives don't shout and scream and cry through a gamut of emotions. They're too numb and powerless. They save what they feel for later, for their friends and families, sometimes for the nurses, but not for us, the white coats.

'This is going to come as a hell of a shock,' I tell him, 'and there's no easy way to say it. I'm afraid your wife is dead.' He holds his look to me for a second or two before his head sinks. He pinches the bridge of his nose. Seconds pass and then in a tiny burst he lets out a sob.

Rebecca doesn't talk. Nor for that matter do I. I call her to say I'm going straight out from work and she says, 'OK,' and that's our only conversation in a couple of days, because I've been on call. I meet with friends from medical school who're housemen now like me. We go round the table swapping tales and after our second or third pints when it's my third or fourth turn I spin them the story of the Vague Yellow Woman. Drinks go down and we talk more shop till we've gone round the table and it's back to me again.

When I creep into our bed Rebecca's already asleep and for the first time that night I remember that somewhere not so many miles distant the Breathless Lady's flesh is sinking to carrion and out of the rot her bones are rising.

The Vague Yellow Woman's blood-test results have shown jaundice and liver damage but they're not severe enough to cause death so I've requested a post-mortem that takes place a few days later. The pathologist finds no fatal lesion. She comments, however, that the condition of the Vague Yellow Woman's body, most likely as a consequence of alcoholism, is that of a much older person.

That night Rebecca and I accept an invitation from a couple of friends, more hers than mine, and when I'm drunk I tell the one about the Vague Yellow Woman and her comic death. Rebecca interrupts a couple of times to say, 'Why are you swearing so much? You didn't used to.'

In my mind I compare her to a stylish pair of shoes but a pair that pinches my toes. All this time when I've looked at them I've tried to tell myself how well they suit me and ignore how ill they fit. To me she appears as the sum of her parts. I see features, a mouth that's like this and a nose that's like that, no longer an image beautified by love. I see a body.

We arrive home and of course I've had too much to drink. Rebecca is leaning over the phone to play messages. I slot behind her with my insteps shunting her heels and I sweep aside her hair and kiss the back of her neck and hook my hands under her top. I work them up from her tummy into her breasts.

'What're you doing?' she says.

My left hand cups her left breast while my right plunges down to her cunt and I pull up hard lifting her away from the phone that's playing her a message about a lunch meeting and turning her round towards me. I stumble back and we topple on to the carpet. My leg bumps the coffee table knocking the miniature olive tree on its side and ejecting soil from the pot and the impact makes Rebecca wince.

'What're you doing?' she repeats.

I'm winded but now I'm on top of her dividing her knees with mine and kneading her breasts, pressing my mouth on to hers.

'No!' she cries.

I stop. I bring myself up and off her. All the time she's staring up at me with a mix of anger and confusion. I try not to let her see my eyes but I can't and I look down, all apologies.

My next night on call evolves in slow motion. The clock in Casualty creeps round from one to two to three while my hand writes two pages of notes, four blood forms and an X-ray request for every patient I admit. This is a week night and a quiet night when the drunks sleep it off in rubbish skips and incoming patients are all old. On trolleys they sail into bare cubicles. At times I'm alone in the department examining one body after another ravaged by age, gazing at warts and tumours and surgical scars and legs so corrugated by varicose veins they look like a motorway map. My young body aches with weariness but I respond with the same serenity as the old give to their decay.

I have to phone Rich for advice and that's rare now. Ours is the first conversation I've had in six hours with someone whose name I know. While on the line his bleep alerts him to an outside call. I overhear him accepting a woman in her nineties with end-stage respiratory failure.

'I'll see her, if you want,' he offers.

'Thanks,' I say, 'but I'll be OK.'

I complete the previous patient's clerking and hand her notes to the porter who trolleys her out of the department and into the interior of the hospital. A middle-aged nurse tears the paper covering from the couch in the cubicle where I examined the patient and straightens the pillow to make it ready for the next one. She crosses to the office and begins reading a book. At the viewing box an Asian casualty officer studies a wrist X-ray. I spoke to him when he came on shift but he had nothing to say. The patient is a paramedic who was pushed backwards down some steps by a member of the public.

A cubicle curtain sweeps open and a middle-aged woman in a dirty coat locks eyes with me. 'Are you going to see me yet?'

'I'm not a casualty doctor,' I say. 'One of them will see you.'

'I know what I've got,' she says. 'Just give me the antibiotics.'

'We can't write a prescription without making a diagnosis.'

The woman strides towards me and I smell alcohol and urine and vaginal secretions before she hurls a slap across my cheek. She pushes me away saying, 'I know you're all pissheads anyway,' and strides out of the department.

My cheek stings. From the other end of the room the nurse and the paramedic and the SHO are gazing over at me. I rub my cheek and the gesture that seems appropriate is a shrug. The others shrug in return and resume their work.

The clock reminds me I'm in the time between three and five when my body slumps to its weariest. I attempt to mount energy enough to lumber through the hospital to my room but I know my sleep will only be measured in minutes.

Instead I recede into the interior and shamble through silent unpopulated vaults to the doctors' mess where I gulp a dark bitter flood of tea from a cracked mug. Late-night television blinks on mute from the corner of the room making fast cuts to nowhere interesting. Alone here I might as well be the sole doctor at large in the hospital.

Rich bleeps me. 'Good news,' he says. 'The old woman with

respiratory failure died in the ambulance. You can go to bed.' I do with gratitude that she's dead.

Deep in the night with the body's defences at their weakest more patients succumb than at any other time. Life's grip on life dwindles to its most fragile. Doctors are themselves diurnal creatures and they shrink too.

After the post-take round I'm on the ward stumbling with tiredness through a list of jobs ordered by Doctor H. and one of the nurses tells me there's a man who wants to speak to me.

'Me personally?' I ask, surprised because I'm just a houseman, I'm a nobody.

'Yes, you, personally, by name,' she says.

In the sister's office sits the Vague Yellow Woman's husband. He rises half to his feet to shake my hand and I slump opposite.

'I wanted to ask you about this,' he says.

He opens a supermarket carrier bag and draws out the dead woman's cream nightie with the pattern of small flowers. He unfolds it and holds out to me material marked by a bloodstain.

'I don't remember her having any blood on her when she died,' he says.

'No, neither do I,' I say.

'I wonder if you know how it might've happened.'

'No, I don't. It must've been there before she died. But, I'm like you – I don't remember it.'

'Where's it from?' he asks.

'I don't know. I'm sorry. Do you want me to try and find out?'

'Like an investigation, you mean?'

'No, just try and find out.'

He thinks. 'No,' he decides.

'I'm very sorry about this. It must've been awful for you when you saw the blood.'

He nods. I shift in my seat. Through the glass behind the dead woman's husband I see Rich throwing me a look. I furrow my eyebrows so he nods, dials a circle in the air with his finger and steps to the phone.

'I don't know if you'd want to look,' the husband says now, 'but I brought in some photos of her. You only saw her, you know, the way she was when she came in. This is what she was like before.'

He slides the photographs out of an envelope, half a dozen of them of different sizes in black-and-white and colour. I feel the pressure I felt from the Young Headache Man's mother to turn me to liquid and decant me into a vessel shaped like her pain.

My bleep goes off, from Rich just outside the door at the nurses' station, offering me a lifeline out of the room.

The Vague Yellow Woman's widower glances down at my bleep then up at me and his eyes pour his pain into me but I don't go just yet.

In the photographs her eyes are clear white and her skin is palest pink and her hair is black with no grey. I look at them and he cries. His sorrow opens to the air and I feel it crushing me into a mould made in its shape but I resist.

'I'm sorry,' he says.

'That's OK,' I say, feeling nothing, and now I go.

That night I'm telling Rebecca about my night on call. We sit at the table by the window with a CD playing. I look at her and she's a member of the public, a civilian, the kind who shoves a paramedic downstairs and slaps a doctor's face and believes ones who make mistakes should be vilified. I want to retaliate so I say, 'An old woman died in the ambulance before she even reached us.'

Rebecca sips her juice but doesn't look up from the dinner table.

'That's sad,' she says.

I eat. She eats.

'Maybe it's true what they say,' I say. 'A houseman would rather sell his own granny than have to get out of bed to admit her.'

'Sick medical humour,' she says. 'No one means it.'

'*I* mean it. I was grateful. When I heard the woman had died. I felt glad.'

'Why? What do you mean?'

'I didn't have to clerk her in, admit her. An hour's work turned into an hour's kip. It felt . . . like an answer to a prayer.'

'You prayed for her to die?'

'Of course not.'

Phrases churn in her mind while food churns in her mouth. She chooses, 'That's cruel. I know you can't mean it.'

Sudden rage rises and I want to shout at her that I had a feeling that seemed appropriate at the time and now like her I know it was sinful but it's an index of what the job's done to me, it's something that'll help her to understand, because the person she remembers me as, the person I was only three months ago, would've mourned that old lady not rejoiced in her death. I mourn her now but tomorrow I'll still be this instrument, this frictionless glinting scalpel, that slices through human misery without being decelerated by it, and I want to snap at Rebecca, 'It wasn't me who decided she should die,' meaning God did and He's the one who's cruel not me.

'There's something I have to tell you and there's no easy way to say it.'

I speak in the metre of breaking the news to the family. But it's not the relative of a dead loved one I've spoken to, it's Rebecca, and I go on, 'I don't want to live here with you any more.'

She clashes her fork on to her plate and her face closes like a shutter.

'I know you can't be shocked,' I say. 'One of us was going to say it sooner or later.'

She says, 'We're *engaged*.'

I pause because it's been so long since she's said the word. We had an understanding, when we moved in together that one day we'd be married. In the early days that's how she described us – 'engaged'. I never said it. I never referred to her as my fiancée, always girlfriend.

'That happened because you said we shouldn't live together unless we were going to get married. We were just going along with it. There was no ring. We never set a date.'

'You wanted to. You said you wanted to.'

'I did. Then. Maybe. I'm sorry. You can stay here. I'll move into hospital acc–'

'We've hardly talked. You can't give up on us like this.'

'I'm sorry,' I say and go to the bedroom just to be in a different place. When she comes through she's crying. She sits beside me on the bed and I hold her and she cries and cries with deep sobbing moans from the very centre of her.

And I feel nothing. That's my job, isn't it? To feel nothing.

In my hospital room a suitcase lies eviscerated on the bed surrounded by a chest of drawers, a basin, a wardrobe, a desk, a pot plant and pinned to the wall an on-call rota. I share a lounge, kitchen and bathroom with two neighbours.

I lay my hands on the radiator under the window and gaze out at the hospital campus. The flats in a horseshoe overlook the roadway down to Casualty and look up towards the car park and medical wards. Beyond sprawls the city and somewhere in it a grave where flesh is falling from bones. A snake of blood clot, the one I missed, hardens to stone.

The pot plant on the desk is the miniature olive tree from our flat. All its fruit, all its leaves, are moulting. Rebecca warned this would happen when she gave it me. The plant responds to a change of environment by shedding its embellishments, existing only as the stripped-down essence of a living thing.

In dusk the hospital buildings loom into low cloud and beyond them squats the city smudged by fog. I stroll from one side of the campus to the other, a mile, to the pub where I'm meeting Rich.

Through the windows I see doctors and nurses standing inside in clusters. Those of us who work in the interior constitute a society twice removed, once from the outside world and once again from the borderlands of the hospital. As I push open the door it releases conversation rich with the jargon that identifies our enclave and it makes me feel at home.

I step in and let the door swing shut behind me. Outside light fades and the bare trees like skeletons are interred by darkness.

PART TWO

All Things Red

Their senses in some scorching cautery of battle
Happy are men who yet before they are killed
Can let their veins run cold [. . .]

Having seen all things red,
Their eyes are rid
Of the hurt of the colour of blood for ever [. . .]

Their senses in some scorching cautery of battle
Now long since ironed,
Can laugh among the dying, unconcerned

From 'Insensibility', Wilfred Owen

11: The Bones

This morning I'm in Casualty where a twenty-year-old girl has taken a paracetamol overdose. She's fat with rosy cheeks like a cartoon face and she sits on the trolley with her hands behind her head wearing her own clothes rather than a hospital gown to signal she's not ready to cross from the outside world into this different one.

'How many did you take?' I ask.

'I'm not sure. A lot.'

'Ten, twenty, thirty?'

'Twenty or thirty.'

'Which? Twenty or thirty?'

'Nearer thirty, I suppose.'

'And when did you take them?'

'A couple of hours ago. Maybe four or five o'clock. I'm not sure.'

I press under her ribs into her liver. 'That hurt?'

'No, I really feel fine now. I didn't think I needed to come in. Rob - my boyfriend - he made me come in. I didn't mean it. I was drunk. I'd had a row with him.' She starts explaining why she took the OD but I just want to get on and when she sees I'm not listening she dries.

The nurse is named Carol. She's middle-aged and severe-looking and she says to me, 'None of the staff nurses who do gastric lavage are on at the moment, so you'll have to do it.'

So I read the page in *The Oxford Handbook*.

Minutes later Didn't Mean It is lying on her side and the nurse named Carol is holding her still. 'But I didn't mean it,' she whimpers before I push the tube into her mouth and ask her to swallow. She gags and tries to fling the tube away. 'Come on now,' I say and push the tube to the back of her throat, 'swallow . . .' This time she pukes but though it's not much more than a spit it splatters the floor by my feet causing me to skip clear.

I give her a sip of water and give her the tube again. 'Come on for me now,' I say, 'swallow . . . that's it . . .'

We continue in this fashion through a dozen attempts and one more spit of puke.

Self-doubt sets in. I need a second opinion.

'You've OD'd before, haven't you?' I ask her. They usually have.

'Yeah,' she says.

'I'm doing it right, aren't I?'

'Yeah,' she says and we start again. Five minutes later I feel the tube slide down her throat. She gags but can't expel the tube and tears stream from her eyes. I feed it down into the stomach until I feel it bump to a stop.

Then the lavage begins. We pour tepid water through a funnel into the tube, massage the side of her belly to slosh it around inside then using a big syringe siphon off gastric contents comprising an acrid-smelling mixture of stomach juices, alcohol, a kebab and half a dozen tablets. Repeated siphonings liberate more tablets and more of the kebab. When no more tablets appear in the wash-out we stop.

'Let me see,' says one of the caz officers, a German SHO, peering into the bucket of gastric contents. Then waving me towards him he whispers, 'Hey, you like to see mine?'

He leads me into another cubicle where a demented woman in her eighties sits on the trolley with the side rails racked up to stop her hurling herself to the floor. Her calves and ankles are elephantine from chronic oedema and the surface of the left shin has cratered into red-blue ulcers that ripple with maggots.

'Cool, yeah?' he says to me.

I sigh and return to Didn't Mean It. I overhear the German SHO saying to one of the student nurses, 'Hey, you like to see something cool?'

'What?' she asks.

'Come and look. Come.'

'OK,' she says and I suppose she pads after him to see the old lady with maggots in her leg ulcers.

Dawn arrives as I lumber to my bed. I doze and glance at the clock then doze again till I've let the time slide through eight thirty. I'm living in my own room that's no more than a box of blank plaster walls but I've surrounded myself with my own stuff like a rota on the wall with dates marked in yellow highlighter, a colour portable, CDs and a player, the stark skeletal olive plant and a New Testament in the bedside drawer.

With the first breaths of day I suck in the weight that crushes my chest and that weight is the Breathless Lady.

I button my shirt and tie my tie. I'm putting on the same clothes as yesterday and as they go on I notice a puke stain on my trousers. I recognise it's from Didn't Mean It when her spit splattered the floor and I thought I'd succeeded in jumping clear. From the black plastic bag in the corner I choose my cleanest pair of dirty trousers.

In the mirror I see my hair needs cutting. It needed cutting weeks ago. It's falling down into my eyes and over my collar at the back. I rub cream into the red band of eczema over my eyebrows. I'm using three times the recommended dose but I still can't prevent it breaking out on bad days. At least my hair hides the worst of it. A couple of spots rise among stubble. I scratch off their heads then press out yellow matter.

From my window I watch as the postman leans his bicycle against a wall and deposits letters in the entrance hall of the block of flats opposite mine. Drizzle divides the quad like layers of curtain. The postman crosses the quad towards this block. He disappears under the window frame and seconds later I hear letters slap the floor of the entrance hall as they fall from the slit in the front door.

My bleep sounds. 'We've got another overdose,' the Casualty nurse tells me.

'It's ten to nine,' I say. 'Can't she wait till the next houseman comes on?'

'She's here and she needs to be seen. If you want to pass her over at nine o'clock, that's up to you.'

I put the phone down and to myself mutter, 'Fuck.' You don't pass work on. You don't dump on your colleagues.

Clipping my bleep into the right-hand pocket of my trousers I put on my white coat and check its pockets for pens, pen torch, stethoscope, tourniquet, brown Venflon, notebook and *Oxford Handbook*. I descend the stairs into the entrance hall. One of the letters is for me bearing the sticker denoting its redirection from what was mine and Rebecca's address and is now Rebecca's alone.

When I leave Casualty I plod up to the ward to see Didn't Mean It. I've had to wait four hours since ingestion to measure the level of paracetamol in her circulation. She's sitting up in bed looking hungover with a thin clear fuse of fluid trickling into one arm from a bag of N-acetylcysteine. The other arm I slap to engorge a vein and then I take the blood sample.

All I can do now is wait for her numbers. It's all in the

numbers. I send the blood to the lab like a witch doctor rolling bones.

Donna conducts Didn't Mean It's nursing admission. The questions about mobility and special diets and medication skip between them in seconds.

'Do you require assistance in walking?' Donna asks.

'Only on a Friday night,' says Didn't Mean It and they laugh.

'Do you find it difficult to get in and out of the bath?' Donna asks and begins to giggle.

Didn't Mean It is shaking her head to them all, giggling too. Donna tells her they're questions for the old folk but she's got to ask them anyway. Didn't Mean It says something and Donna starts laughing, then Didn't Mean It follows, because the idea of ever becoming so old you can't put on your own shoes is ludicrous to them both.

At the nurses' station Rich says to me, 'I bet she's going to need a new liver. What do you think?'

'I think she might too.'

'How's that any kind of bet?'

I say, 'I never said I thought she'd get one *in time.*'

He says, 'Now *that's* a bet.'

Then I get the call. I prepare to check the level on a graph against the time elapsed since the pills were taken and this point on the graph will fall above or below a certain line and where it falls will foretell her future. I'm looking at her, at Didn't Mean It, as the biochemist gives over the figures and my eyes flick down to the graph then over to the infusion in her arm. I count one drop, two, three-four-five like pills falling from her hand into her mouth. Donna says something else and Didn't Mean It laughs again. They're both laughing as if they're already mates on a night out together. But these numbers I'm hearing are bad numbers. They're bad bones.

12: The Call

The alarm clock tones and I ascend from sleep. I inhale and from the air in the room I draw in that weight that leadens my body. At the sink I wash and it being a ward round with Doctor H. this morning I shave. Thoughts about patients to see, a result expected, an investigation to perform, all jumble in my mind but among them hulks the immovable lead jacket of the Breathless Lady's memory.

I shamble to the ward. In Didn't Mean It's eyes yellow rises like suns. Liver numbers climb. Clotting times stretch. We've gone to her first on our round. Among heart attacks and strokes and pneumonias she's the sickie, the one you worry about. We work her up for half an hour, me on the phone, chasing every last result out of the labs, Rich writing all the charts, Anita committing Doctor H.'s verdict to the notes. Didn't Mean It is in liver failure. Doctor H. confers with the Liver Unit and she gets booked for the journey across the city to the University Hospital.

Before she goes I'm bleeped to change her Venflon. A blood bubble inflates under her skin and it ruptures on to the bed sheet. I count a dozen or more bruises looking like black coins, the currency of passed drips. Her arms extend in spasm, straightening at the elbows and flicking up at the wrists with both arms in symmetry as in a ballet pose. She may know I'm here. She may not. Then the arms relax again and minutes will

112

pass before the next spasms in the choreography of a poisoned brain.

I don't look at her. I see blood and bruises and tubes going in but this is not to be considered a person. Though I'm beside her I'm not part of the moment or part of another life ending for no reason I can comprehend. I'm a passer-by captured in a photograph who's an out-of-focus streak of lines flashing through the frame and then gone. I'm a cold scalpel-sharp instrument slicing through scenes in other people's lives and not ever being slowed.

In the sluice room Donna is crying.

'When will we hear?' she asks me.

'I don't know. Maybe tonight. I can let you know, if you want.'

She nods and writes a phone number down for me.

When the ambulance crew comes for Didn't Mean It it's like giving her up to strangers. Perhaps this sense of demotion is what relatives feel as the curtains draw across their faces and I take charge.

The ward round continues till lunchtime and in the canteen I know today one person is going to die. This time the number is certain. That one person will be a healthy man or woman of a certain size and tissue type in a hospital under certain criteria with a certain intention stated before death or it will be the girl who Didn't Mean It.

For lunch I choose pizza.

In the afternoon I'm bleeped for an outside call.

'Hi,' Rebecca says.

'Hi,' I say. 'How are you?'

'I'm well. You?'

'Yeah, fine,' I say.

She says, 'The reason I'm calling is because, well, you've still got a load of stuff here.'

'I know. I'm sorry. I'd been hoping I could make space for it in my room, but I don't think I can.'

'It's, well, beginning to piss me off.'

'And, *well*, I'm sorry I'm only living in a shitty little hospital room while you've still got the flat.'

Silence springs between us like a rod. I'm expecting a click and a tone but she holds the line. I sigh and say, 'I'll sort something out. But I can't do it till the weekend after next – I'm on call for this one coming.'

'That's nearly another two weeks,' she says. She sighs. 'OK,' she says.

Doctor H. was conducting his outpatients' clinic when he got a call from the Liver Unit. Anita was in the next room and overheard. 'So did you ask him what they said?' I ask her. She tells me so in her gabbled speech I get the full story in one sentence without a pause for breath.

Alone on the ward I unfold the piece of paper in my pocket and transcribe Donna's number into the telephone keypad. I don't recognise the voice so I ask, 'Is Donna there, please?' but it's her, she just sounded different.

'It's bad news,' I say. 'They didn't get a donor in time. She was taken off the ventilator about an hour ago. I'm sorry.'

'Thanks for letting me know,' she says then nothing.

'Listen, maybe it's the last thing you feel like doing at the moment, but I'm not on tonight, if you fancied meeting for a drink.'

'I'm already doing something tonight,' she says.

'OK,' I say. I'm about to back off but I can't fight the compulsion to add, 'I'm nearly done now, actually. I don't know how you're fixed, but I could meet you in half an hour. A quick drink, and then you can go on to whatever you've got planned.'

'I don't know,' she says. 'It's ... I don't know.'

'That's OK. I understand. I'll see you around tomorrow. Have a good night,' I finish.

'See you,' she finishes.

I sit at the nurses' station. I don't get up. Sat here deep in the hospital interior with my skin pale and blemished under unblinking strip lights I picture the fixtures of my room. I picture the bare wooden furniture and the narrow bed and as my mind's eye scans the only animation it encounters resides in the screen of my portable television and the only voice in the CD player and the only life in that fucking stripped-down abbreviation of an olive plant.

I stare at the patients through the glass partition of the bay in front of me. The spotty young student nurse that's the one Rich slept with is taking temperatures and blood pressures. I watch the fall of her clean white uniform from her shoulders and hips. I register the bulge of her breasts and the curve of her buttocks. Belted, her waist narrows where arms would go to pull her close, where hands would press before gliding down to her vagina.

I hear my bleep clang to an outside call.

'It's me,' says the voice on the end of the line.

'Donna?'

'I could meet you at the pub near the traffic lights, the one just before the Chinese. If you still want to.'

'Yeah. I know the one.'

'Just a quick drink, though. I've got to be somewhere later.'

'Sure,' I say.

'Seven o'clock OK?' she says.

'Seven o'clock,' I say.

I calculate time enough to shower and shave, to apply deodorant and aftershave, to deaden the reek of my day.

But first I bleep Rich.

'You know our bet,' I say.

'What about it?'

'I won.'

'Shit,' he says. 'That's a curry I owe you.'

The pub's only half a mile from the hospital. I find Donna seated at a table by a big stone fireplace though the fire itself is unlit. Her brown hair hangs loose to her shoulders and across her forehead into the black frame of her glasses. She's wearing a pale jumper and dark jeans. It's the first time I've seen her out of uniform.

She looks up as I step towards the table. 'You found it then,' she says and smiles.

'I needed a compass and Boy Scout troop to get me here, but I made it. What can I get you?'

'I've just got mine. Sit down, I'll get you one.'

'You sure?'

'I've bought drinks before. If I get mixed up, I'll squeak for help.'

My eyes track her to the bar. She could pass for a civilian, a schoolteacher or an accountant, as could I. She turns and catches me staring and though self-conscious she smiles back.

When she returns to the table she sets down the drinks and sits and slides a pack of cigarettes out of her bag. Flipping open the lid she offers me one but I say, 'No, thanks.'

She ignites her cigarette and takes a drag and when she exhales the smoke gives her evanescent tusks.

I say, 'I didn't know you smoked.'

'No?'

'No.'

'D'you mind?' she says.

'No,' I say.

116

'You ever?'

'Smoked? No.'

'Never got addicted to the weed?' she says.

'Never got addicted,' I say.

We drink and talk. I give her more details about the girl who Didn't Mean It because she wants to hear them. At the end she asks, 'What happened to her, in the end, I mean?'

'Pretty much everything packed up. But thanks to all the paracetamol, her period pains were never better.'

She laughs and I find myself giggling. We find we're both giggling.

She says, 'We had a bloke who'd got asbestosis and after he died it took two weeks to cremate him.'

She erupts with laughter and so do I. Tears are streaming down our faces. People are turning round to look at us.

We recover our composure. She drinks and says, 'She said it was silly. Her boyfriend had been in touch with his ex about something. She said it made her feel like he didn't respect her, didn't respect her feelings. Maybe there was something to it. Maybe there wasn't. Whatever it was, it wasn't worth dying over.'

'No,' I say, 'it wasn't.'

'Nothing is,' she says.

'I think you're probably right.'

'Why?'

'Why do I think that?' I say.

'Yes,' she says.

'Because it's commonplace. It's nothing special. Everybody dies. Who doesn't die and want it at least to mean something? But a person's death usually has no meaning, because there's too many of them, because it's just a piss in the ocean.'

She drinks and after a bit says, 'I think that's the truth. I think that's the fucking truth.' She raises her glass to me and looks away, tears glistening in her eyes.

I lean across the table and prod her arm. 'Hey, we have a right old time when we go out, don't we?'

She laughs and wipes her nose.

I buy the next round and when I return I say, 'So, who're you engaged to?'

'My fiancé,' she says and I laugh.

I say, 'So where're you off to tonight?'

'I'm meeting up with some people from my group.' She glances at her watch. 'Actually . . .' She trails off seeming hesitant. She looks at her watch again and gives me a rueful smile.

I take a gulp of my drink. I look at her face and the strands of brown hair mingling with her eyelashes, her thin tight skin, and I say it. I say, 'Don't go.'

She casts her look off the side of the table into the wooden floorboards by her feet. She glances into the fireplace and across to the bar but not to me.

I lean closer. 'Don't go.'

She sips her drink and still without looking at me reaches into her bag for her mobile phone.

We drink more and have Chinese. As we leave the restaurant we hesitate then I turn towards the hospital and she follows. We reach the part of the road from which a path winds up to the hospital flats. I pause and turn towards her. 'You can come in for coffee, if you like,' I say. 'Or I can call you a cab. It's up to you.'

She hesitates though in doing so she finds a smile as she glances down and away. When her face lifts again I meet her lips with mine. They sting with cold before the thrill of the warm wet mass of her tongue and the heat of her breath. Her spit tastes of drink and spices and cigarettes and I know mine can't be any better. But my arms loop down into the small of her back and I draw her closer to me while her hands press on my shoulder blades to pull me closer to her, then after a minute my head tips and my nose slides over hers and her head makes the reciprocal change and we continue without interruption.

Then after another minute or so she withdraws her mouth. 'I can't do this,' she says.

I lean towards her again and again she accepts me. We kiss in the cold still night with traffic Doppler-shifting by while through our mouths we pour heat into each other's bodies.

'I'm sorry,' she says breaking for the second time. 'I can't do this.'

I say, 'Come up with me. I really want you to.'

She looks down. I lift her chin to kiss her again but this time she rears her head free. 'No,' she says. 'I'm confused. I need to be somewhere, to think.'

'Come up with me,' I say. 'We can talk. Just talk, that's all.'

'No. I have to go home now.'

'At least let me call you a cab.'

'It's OK. I'll go up to Caz. There's always minicabs outside.'

'You're sure?' I say.

'I'm sure,' she says.

'OK. I'm sorry if . . . It was great seeing you. You'll be on the ward tomorrow?'

She thrusts her hands into her coat pockets and taps her feet on the pavement. 'No,' she says. 'I've finished. Today was my last day. My group's moving to Orthopaedics. That's why we were all meeting up tonight.'

Stiffening I snap, 'It's getting late. I'm going in. You've got my bleep number.'

Her eyes widen at the sharpness in my voice. Then she nods and turns and trudges a short distance along the pavement, cutting up into the hospital campus heading towards the main buildings.

I watch her go and an ache claws at my chest and throat. I want to go to bed with Donna. I want to go to bed with her. I don't want to go to bed dreaming about a young girl who had a silly falling-out with her boyfriend and took thirty paracetamol but Didn't Mean It but her liver still inflamed and failed and her brain swelled and her body turned yellow, bloody and dead because some other poor fucker didn't get splattered in a car wreck. I don't want to kneel against a cold empty bed and beg that my faith be rewarded with understanding only to wake up once again with no answer to why these things are made to happen.

13: The Silence

In dull noon the hospital gates slip behind and reform in my rear-view mirror. I join the ring road swelling with Saturday-morning shopping traffic then travel south across the city. I take a filter lane and the road inclines as in meeting it silver towers dwindle to shops. I cross a roundabout at the top of the hill then like falling back towards the past I follow the long slope downwards in the direction of the university and the medical school.

I park on the road outside the block in which Rebecca and I once shared a flat but now it's hers alone. As I throw my car door shut something nips tender in my armpit.

I buzz. Receiving no answer I fish keys from my pocket then hesitate before buzzing again. 'Sorry!' she says in an electric hiss through the intercom and when the entry tone sounds and I push the door off its latch my heart is racing.

I ascend the single flight of stairs. Only halfway up I sense it's the last time. I want to halt at this step. I want to stop here and cry and not go on and turn back if it's not too late.

'Hi there.' Rebecca looks down from the open doorway. One glimpse reveals so much in her I've forgotten.

While I rummage through boxes, dropping items for junking into black plastic bags, she makes tea. I hear the chug of the kettle and the click of cupboards and the clash of mugs and in each note I'm transmitted a picture of the kitchen. She brings mine through and I thank her. She leans in the door frame sipping hers.

'Actually, that's *your* mug,' she says. 'You should take it with you.'

I think. Five seconds of my life evaporate in considering whether or not I need a fucking chunk of pottery. I say, 'No, I've already got a few.'

'One more won't hurt.'

'I can do without the clutter.'

She shakes her head in disbelief and says, 'Maybe you should be looking for a flat.'

I can't afford to move, not now my overdraft's shrinking at last. 'I am,' I lie and lift files out of the next box. 'Fuck. Notes from medical school. Like I'll ever need these.' I sling them into the rubbish bag.

She observes me from the doorway. She says, 'So how's work?'

'OK. Yours?'

'Hm, good.' Her gaze doesn't leave me. 'OK? You're sure?'

'Yeah. Why?'

'Nothing. I only wondered. Nothing.'

'No – what?'

I straighten up and face her.

'I only wondered . . . your hair, you haven't shaved . . .'

'We were on last night. The post-take round ran over. I didn't have time to shower and change. Sorry.'

'I've never seen your skin so bad.'

'I know,' I say in a flat tone without emphasis.

'And you're a bit, well, smelly.'

'I know,' I say the same way.

When I've filled two bags of rubbish I haul them out to the wheelie-bins at the back of the block. The lump in my armpit pulls as I stretch, throbs as I lower my arm. I slide my hand under my shirt. My fingertip encounters a tense hot bulge. I pinch it between thumb and forefinger and with a sudden hard crush I expel a teaspoonful of warm sticky fluid.

The stuff I'm going to keep packs into the boot of my car. I try to convince myself one day soon all those books, CDs, tennis rackets, football boots, bicycle pumps, lamps, luggage and photograph albums will be scattered round a stylish apartment but by tonight they'll be stowed in the darkness of my parents' attic.

When I'm finished I offer Rebecca my set of keys. She takes them and says nothing. Neither do I. Our flat is silent though it has us here together. Perhaps this is a moment when two people sense the same thing: that in a few minutes it will be silent again but with her left alone. I don't know because I don't ask.

On the stairs leaving I descend to the step where I paused on my way up, where I felt I should cry or turn back. I feel the same again, thinking of Rebecca in her silent empty place and myself in mine.

But I walk to my car and in it return to the ring road, this time heading north to the motorway, rehearsing the lies about my life I should tell my parents.

I get back late on Sunday. I redistribute the contents of my overnight bag around the room. Nothing's changed. From the basin I run water into a mug and decant a few teaspoonfuls on to the olive plant.

The next morning in the long main corridor I search for Donna among the bobbing heads and gliding trolleys. Some days when I've a minute or two to spare I venture as far down as the opening of the Surgical Unit in the hope that just then she's coming out on a break or escorting a patient to theatres. But she never is and I turn back acting as if for one moment I've lost my bearings and overshot my turning.

Every time my bleep chimes I snap my eyes down wishing for an unfamiliar number on the LED, an extension in a corridor somewhere quiet. There she hunches over the phone as a porter strolls past whistling and in a hesitant voice she asks if we can see each other again. But when my bleep goes off it's always a summons back to work.

It's always that, never Donna, never what I want. I feel it all building: like waste cramming a bin till the lid sits up like the top of a helmet and the bulge of rubbish is the eye slit of a demon perched in the corner of your kitchen taunting you about your dirtiness: like dishwater dribbling from a sink till the U-bend stenoses like a diseased artery and the stinking black swirl won't budge but stays there so every time you come to run water you smell it and have to look down in disgust: pressure that builds like silence.

14: The Cough

The pages slip between my fingers as I turn through article after article between pale blue covers. I pause to read a boxed bold-typed abstract that summarises a study of asthma in childhood. Then I flick on towards the back. This is where I get time to read the *BMJ*, when I'm sat on the toilet having a shit.

My bleep emits the trill of an arrest call. I snap off handfuls of toilet roll, wipe and look and hurl them into the bowl. There are still brown skids on the paper when the arrest call is repeated, giving me no choice but to pull up my trousers and run.

Rich turns to me as I plunge into Casualty and throws out his arms in a shrug then lets them fall to slap his thighs.

Behind him in the long vault of the department nurses cross between cubicles, patients with arms in slings idle by the plaster room and porters guide trolleys. The chatter jumps high and falls then rises again and in the lows come the crying of a baby and the wail of an ambulance siren.

'Does anyone know who called 222?' Rich asks out loud to the department.

Heads shake. Doctors and nurses go on about their duties.

A nurse I know glances up towards us. Her name's Carol. She's the severe-looking middle-aged one who helped me lavage Didn't Mean It. She holds her look long enough for me to examine its meaning. Her eyes flick towards resus then she recedes into a cubicle.

Out of the sounds around me I make a redefinition from a baby crying to a grown-up shrieking. 'Let's have a look in resus,' I say and lead Rich in the direction of the plastic doors of the ambulance entrance, then right.

A young black patient, maybe even as young as fourteen, is reclined on the treatment table. He's doing the screaming. The contours of his shoulder look wrong with the deltoid muscle lying too flat and the head of the humerus bulging forwards. A very short Asian Caz Officer applies traction to his upper arm while the A&E consultant, Mister M., bends the elbow and struggles to force the arm into rotation.

'Pull harder,' orders Mister M.

The Caz Officer rocks back on his heels, drawing his full weight on the arm. Mister M. angles the patient's elbow over his chest and forces the arm to roll out then in. The Shoulder Boy screams. His fingernails dig into the wipe-clean black plastic mattress of the treatment table and veins swell like vine ropes on his neck.

'Hi,' says Rich.

Mister M. and the Caz Officer swing round at us.

'Hello,' says Mister M.

Then he turns back to the Caz Officer and insists, 'You're not pulling! Pull very hard!'

'I *am* pulling,' says the Caz Officer.

'No, you're bloody not – now *pull.*'

The Shoulder Boy tenses. He grits his teeth. He grips the table.

The Caz Officer grasps and pulls and with his feet slipping and recovering like tug-of-war they make another effort to relocate the joint. Mister M. positions and forces and the patient shrieks.

'Anything we can do?' Rich says.

'Thank you, no,' says Mister M. 'This is nothing to do with you.'

Rich signals for us to leave. I don't want to go.

'Again,' says Mister M. and wipes sweat from his face.

The Caz Officer hesitates. 'Sir, perhaps we can try the Hippocrat method?'

'The *Hippocratic* method. No. We're doing Kocher's. Now — again.'

The Caz Officer applies traction and Mister M. attempts to wrench the shoulder back into place.

We all hear the crack when it comes. The shaft of the humerus buckles and the arm develops a new hinge halfway between elbow and shoulder. The boy's screaming crescendoes to the point where he loses his voice and open-mouthed with neck veins bulging he arches his back but no sound comes out for a second or two then it returns as a wail that trickles down to sobs.

'Shit,' says the Caz Officer.

Mister M. sighs and wipes the sweat from his face again. Then he turns towards us. With his eyes he throws Rich a challenge. Rich leaves. Mister M. transfers his look to me. I hold my position for only a moment before I feel Rich's arm on my elbow. I go, hearing Mister M. mutter to the Caz Officer, 'Now I'm going to have to take him to fucking theatre.'

In the main body of the department I ask, 'Where the hell's the registrar?'

Rich says, 'She resigned.'

'Maybe we should do something,' I say.

'*Do* something?' he says.

'*Say* something, I mean.'

'Like what?' he says. 'Who the fuck are we?'

I look for the nurse, Carol, the one I think wanted it stopped but couldn't make herself heard or was too frightened to speak out so she called a 222. I linger in the hall of the department and from here I can see through to the waiting area and the ambulance bay while from the other side of the hall I can still hear the shrieks of the Shoulder Boy.

This place where I stand divides the outside world from the hospital. It marks where the rules begin changing. Carol is nowhere to be seen and like her Rich and I recede into the interior and our own business.

I roll the notes trolley over the flat shining floor to the last bed in the last bay on the last ward. Doctor H. nods to the patient as he says his 'Hello, how are you today?' as Rich plucks the notes from my hands and as Anita stoops to inspect the obs chart.

The plate-glass windows overlook the far end of the hospital with its two car parks bordering Outpatients and the low red-brick buildings that house Geriatrics and Psychiatry. Darkness gathers. Rain spots the glass then runs down in drips. My eyes track a bead of rainwater as it trickles down the pane and swells and bursts on to the ledge.

Rich nudges me.

'This is Planet Earth calling,' says Doctor H.

'Sorry,' I say.

Later Rich turns to me and whispers, 'I could murder a curry tonight.'

'Don't you owe me one?'

'Yes, arsehole, I owe you one.'

After the ward round we're on the main corridor and I tell Rich, 'I think I left my notebook upstairs.' We make a time to meet later and he turns up the long slope.

I go back through the doors to the stairwell and stand on the landing watching the rain etch glistening lines on the window-pane. Black clouds squat on the horizon. Below, staff who came to work in fine weather sprint from the exit with newspapers on their heads like mortarboards. They duck into cars and steer out on to the roadway home as I once did.

My notebook sits in my pocket. I lied.

I descend to the main corridor and turn towards the Surgical Unit. I pause for a few seconds, revising my notes. A nurse tramps out of Orthopaedics alongside a middle-aged patient on crutches. She's not Donna but I approach her anyway and I ask her about the Shoulder Boy. She answers that he's not one of her patients but I should try checking on the ward.

I peer into the small lobby at the end of the Orthopaedic ward. I think about the Shoulder Boy but I also think about Donna.

I turn and head home.

'To paracetamol!' he says and we clink pints.

One of the waiters grins as he passes. He must assume our toast relates to anticipated hangovers instead of a bet on the outcome of a young girl's suicide.

'To paracetamol,' I say.

A waiter lays a pile of poppadoms between us. Rich and I spoon chopped onions and mango chutney on to small plates then break the poppadoms and scoop the onions and chutney.

'D'you ever think about doing something else?' I say.

'Like what?' he says.

'Anything,' I say.

'Sometimes.' Rich drinks and says, 'It's funny how, though they want you to be clever enough to train as a doctor, you've also got to be stupid enough to want to be one.'

'Who's "they"?'

'You know.' He munches through an outsize chunk of poppadom. 'The lot of 'em. The BMA, the GMC, the Royal Colleges.'

He downs his lager and signals to the waiter for another. I look over and show two fingers and he nods and goes to the bar to draw them from shiny brass pumps. When the drinks come, Rich drinks hard. 'I fucking hate the BMA,' he says. 'Don't you?'

'Are you a member?'

'I am, yeah. Only to get the *BMJ* – you know, for the job adverts at the back. That's about all they're good for.'

'I don't know. I thought they'd done some stuff to improve, er . . .'

'Improve what?'

'Improve . . . stuff.'

We both laugh.

'Nothing that's changed anything,' he says. '*Really changed anything.* The JDC's always run by some senior reg with a beard. How's someone like that supposed to be representative of us? Then, whenever there's some hospital scandal and they want a comment from the BMA, out comes some cunt in a bow tie. How's *that* supposed to be representative? A cunt in a bow tie? I'm cancelling my prescription.'

'Subscription.'

'What did I say?'

'Prescription.'

'And the GMC,' he says. 'And those fuckwits who said British beef was safe to eat when a third-year medical student could've told you BSE was already jumping the species barrier.'

'You're mixing everyone up. They're all different bodies.'

'They're all in it together. They all run medicine. And they're all cunts.'

Our starters arrive before the poppadoms are finished but we let the waiter take them away. I shift in my seat. My arse itches. It's itchy from this morning when I didn't have time to finish wiping.

130

Suddenly I have to say, 'D'you think he was OK in the end?'

Rich chews his sheekh kebab. I can tell he knows I mean the Shoulder Boy.

'I don't know,' he says.

'What if he wasn't?' I say.

'Then he wasn't,' he says.

We finish our starters and our drinks. We order another round and fiddle with the stainless-steel cutlery while we wait for our main courses. I fidget. I'm trying to rub my anus against the seat through my clothing.

'What's the matter with you?' Rich asks.

'Pruritus ani.'

A waiter guides a trolley to our table. He skims the plates with a cloth and lays them in front of us followed by a dish of pilau rice and two nan breads. A pair of sizzling Baltis jostle for space in the middle of the table and a sag aloo squeezes on at the side.

We begin eating and then I say, 'It's funny how all this stuff was there all along, for all of us to see. But when you're students you're blind. It's right in front of you and you're always looking somewhere else.'

He nods as he eats.

I eat too but I see the Shoulder Boy writhing in agony while two doctors break his fucking arm. Probably it's the drink. I'm weak against the wave of emotion. I feel moisture well in my eyes and blink it away. I say, 'Aren't we even supposed to care?'

'It was only a dislocation and a break,' says Rich. 'He'll be fine. If it's such a big deal, check in the morning. It won't be that hard to find out.'

'Don't you care?'

He drinks and says, 'I don't know. I don't know whether I care or not. I don't know if what I feel is me caring, or it's me

131

feeling something else, or if it's me not really feeling anything very much at all.'

I think about Mister M. 'The first time I saw him in action, I thought, I don't know, maybe he's having an off day. We all have those.'

'Everybody makes mistakes,' he says but down into his food.

'I know,' I say down into mine. I think of the Breathless Lady. She died three months ago. *I killed her* three months ago. Not feeling guilty all night, not hating myself, seems all of a sudden arrogant. I say, 'But then I thought it's not like he's just starting out. By now he should've dealt with his shortcomings. I don't know. Who am I to say?' I drink.

Then Rich says, 'Actually, there *is* a difference. There's making an honest mistake and learning from it, and there's being a fuckwit – and he's a fuckwit.'

'So how's he keep his job?'

'Two reasons. The first is no one wants to be seen to speak out. That'd make you a whistle-blower. Whistle-blowers get suspended. Whistle-blowers get . . . what's the word?'

'I don't know. What word?'

'Like being sent to Coventry.'

'Ostracised.'

'Thank you. Whistle-blowers get ostracised. Whistle-blowers don't get jobs.'

I ask, 'And the other reason?'

He shrugs. 'He's a consultant.'

We stumble into the pub in time for last orders. It's the one opposite the main entrance and some nights during the week it resembles an extension of the hospital social club. Doctors stand around us in clusters. The medics we know, the other specialties only by sight. Nurses crowd the bar. Most have come from finishing late shifts. They wear jackets over their uniforms and those with long hair have let it down.

'There's only two sure things in life,' Rich slurs. 'Death, and nurses.'

I push through to the bar and claim our last drinks of the night before the lights blink. Rich and I stand against a stone pillar towards the back of the pub with a couple of other SHOs. They talk about a stroke that turned out to be a brain tumour.

'Fucking patients,' says one of the SHOs, the Scot. 'They always want to throw up surprises.'

'Most just throw up,' I say.

In the middle of the pub people flow in convection currents. A large body shifts and I glimpse Donna with two friends, one in staff-nurse blue, the other like her in student-nurse white. Donna wears a denim jacket over her uniform but her hair remains scrunched back.

I stare taking my lager in sips. At last she glances up and when she sees me expression drains from her face. She looks back to her friends but she's not saying anything. I turn back into the conversation with Rich and the SHOs but I'm not saying anything either. I'm thinking. I'm thinking of Donna and I also think of finishing my drink and going to Casualty to scan the Shoulder Boy's notes.

When I look up Donna's crossing towards us with one of her friends, the staff nurse, who's older with a pleasant open face. The friend lays her hand on Rich's elbow and he turns and smiles and says, 'Hello, there.'

'D'you have a light?' she says.

He lights her cigarette and Donna's and then his own. He knows the staff nurse and they start talking in volleys. Uncomfortable Donna edges to the side.

'Hello, you,' I say.

'Hello, you,' she says back.

She looks down into her empty glass and across to the dark bar.

'Closing time,' I say.

She nods and I think she's going to go so I say, 'How's Orthopaedics going?'

'OK,' she says.

'It's pretty shite, actually, isn't it?'

'It is!' she says and laughs.

'Old dears with bones like eggshell and boy racers with not a brain cell between their ears. There's a good reason those idiots get smashed to pieces. It's so they won't live to pass on their genes.'

Her friend glances over her shoulder at us and then back to Rich.

Donna waves her cigarette at me and says, 'Sorry, d'you want one?'

'I don't smoke.'

'That's right, you don't,' she says.

I say to her, 'I was hoping I'd get to see you again.'

'Yeah,' she answers and I don't know what she means but I'm drunk so I say, 'You never bleeped me.'

She colours red. She looks to her friend but gets only the back of her head as she carries on talking to Rich and her hand reaches out to touch his arm again.

'I've been busy,' Donna says.

'Doing what?'

'Don't give me a hard time. If you're going to give me a hard time then I'm going to go.'

I say, 'I miss seeing you.'

She stays. She looks down at her empty glass for the second time. She says, 'I've been doing a lot of thinking.'

'What about?'

'Lots of things. It's pretty complicated.'

'About me, ever?'

'Yes.'

'And what did you think?'

'Maybe the same as you. That I missed seeing you.'

'Maybe?'

'More than maybe.' She laughs but still manages to look sad.

Her friend glances round and says, 'I'll see you, Donna,' and Rich says his 'Goodbye' to me and they walk out into the night together.

I edge forwards and say,

'Come back with me tonight.'

I'm expecting rejection. But somewhere in her thoughts and feelings since the last time we were together she must've found the thought or feeling that causes her to set her glass aside, nod her head and with a glance to the door say,

'Yes.'

Overhead clouds drift like grey continents. Rain drizzles on to our bare heads and forms a cold wet film on our faces and the backs of our hands. We stop to kiss and by the time we walk on again the rain has darkened the shoulders of our jackets.

I say, 'You were on Orthopaedics tonight?'

'Yeah,' she says.

'You didn't have a patient come to you, did you, a kid, maybe fourteen or fifteen, with a dislocated shoulder?'

'Why?'

'I was there in Caz when he came through. Just wondered.'

'It's really sad,' she says. 'He'd fractured his humerus too and there was a problem with the blood supply . . .'

I stop and turn her towards me and I kiss her again because I don't want to hear. I've heard enough of this talk and it comes out choking me like toxic fumes.

In my room our cold wet faces press against each other and

my fingers fumble open the buttons of her uniform. Her bra lifts her breasts up to me like offerings and I slide my hands under her clothes to her back and unclasp it so that I can accept them naked against my face and then gulp her nipples into my mouth.

Her fingers burrow under the long hair at the back of my head and pull me into her chest. I smell the dirty scent of her skin after its day in the hospital. I smell the damp of her hair and clothes. She hooks my jumper over my head and lets it fall, then my T-shirt, and now her hands glide over my bare chest and back.

I part her uniform from her shoulders and she helps slide it off her arms and it drops to her ankles. She steps out of it in only her knickers and our bodies fold together under the glow through a gap in the curtains of the quad lights outside.

On the floor, too impatient for bed, I feel the rub of carpet on my arms and knees and the warm life of her body under me. I smell again the damp in her hair and the grime of her skin. I curl to slip off my trousers and underpants and she helps me.

Kisses crush our lips. As our tongues entwine and spit bubbles on to our chins I taste the tobacco and drink on her breath and she the spices on mine. Her hand creeps into my groin and with a spasm my balls tighten and rise and I wish I'd had more sex in my life, wish I wasn't as nervous as a teenager.

She registers the tenseness of my body and pulls me close so her pelvis rubs against mine. In the softness of her lips and skin and breasts I relax. I feel my body joining hers and with this feeling springs an erection that she senses as it pushes into her crotch and it makes her smile.

I slide my hand over the hump of her pubic bones and down into the hair. My fingers find warmth and wetness and I begin to massage her clitoris with short gentle upward strokes. She squirms and spasms pass along her body in waves as she throws her arms back and I kiss the thin tight skin of her abdomen.

136

She hooks her thumbs over the side straps of her knickers and pushes them down. I slide them along her thighs and off over her feet then descend. She shifts beneath me in tiny spasms and lets out whimpers as her hairs bristle against my chin and her secretions dribble round my mouth and my tongue's arching tip slides over her.

Then she lays her hands flat over my shoulder blades and draws me up in centripetal waves. I climb to her lips and after kisses I pluck a condom from a packet in the drawer by the bed.

My thumb locates the opening of her vagina and with my other fingers I guide myself inside. I plunge into her and her body feels like wet leaves I'm falling into, falling into warm wet leaves after a lifetime indoors and rising again for sunlight to blast my eyes after a lifetime underground.

I grasp her buttocks and pull her pelvis hard into mine. She tenses and moans and the stink of sweat and of her secretions leaks all round us. I feel my semen rising, pressure building, pressure from trapped effluent, stinking detrital waters that were meant to be sewage, meant to be flushed away. The pressure chokes me, chokes me, till I cough my come like phlegm, like emptying into her my disease.

15: The Present

Her head lies on my chest. Her breath brushes my skin. I smell her hair and her body and my body and the bed stinks of sweat and sex. I hear the patter of rain on the path below my window. She goes before morning. I watch her dress in the grey light and then I turn under the blanket to sleep until my alarm wakes me at eight thirty. I gather my clothes from around the room and they all reek of curry and cigarette smoke.

On the ward I think of her. I press my stethoscope to the spent skin of an eighty-year-old and his breath rasps in my ears, each breath counting down to his last, and I think of her body naked beneath me and her hot gasps on my neck.

Her shift finishes at three and at three ten I get a bleep. She waits for me at the door to my block and I promise her I'll get my key copied and then we go up for sex. As she takes it off I see stains of patients' body fluids on her uniform and her body smells of sweat and dirt. Afterwards she holds me in an embrace while I answer bleeps on the phone in my room. When I have to go she tells me the Shoulder Boy has nerve damage and will be left with only partial use of his arm.

In the morning I detect long brown hairs on the pillow and my first thought is of her, not the Breathless Lady or the Shoulder Boy. I wash and shave and cream the red flashes of eczema on my forehead. They've stopped itching where my hair covers them and the ones on my cheeks have all but vanished. I try brushing it but my hair still falls down over my ears in tangles.

In the night I lie on top of the bedcovers with my hands behind my head and a CD playing. She taps the door and I let her in. While she smokes a cigarette I make her a cup of tea and serve it to her in the less chipped mug. I ask her how her day went. 'OK,' she says. She asks me about mine. 'OK,' I say.

We have sex and I lie beside her. My finger draws a line in the gutters between her ribs. I work up until the last gutter levels into her axillary tail, then I count down again to the hard ridge of her lowest rib, then back up again, each time making the same dimpling line in her skin. Later she rolls on to her side facing me. Her waist dips and rises again to the crest of her hip. She gazes into my eyes without expression and then we kiss. When she goes I fall to sleep in the narrow bed still warm from her body.

Over the next few weeks I look out for Carol, the casualty nurse who called 222 to try to save the Shoulder Boy's arm, but I don't see her around. The patient himself is being seen in Orthopaedic Outpatients. His arm will be strapped for eight weeks and they estimate he'll recover 50 per cent use.

Late at night Donna sits on the edge of my bed. I kneel behind her and reach round to cup her breasts in my hands. I lay my chin on her shoulder. My cheek nuzzles against hers and we peer out of the window of my room over the quad into the fogging city lights.

Winter first arrives in a wind that rushes between the hospital buildings as if through ravines. Trudging up towards the wards from the flats I grasp my white coat by the lapels and tighten it around me. Then the following week brings a snow fall that dusts the grass and shrubs and paints a white outline on the trees.

Maybe once he had a beer belly but it's gone the way of the house and the wife and the clean clothes. His skin is white, his arms and legs bone thin. His abdomen creases in rolls, rolls of skin, not fat. A beard tangles over the whole lower half of his face streaked grey and clumped with debris. He can't shave because of the tremors.

I'm asking questions. Vomit breath stinks out the cubicle.

'What colour was it? Was it food or liquid you'd taken down earlier? Was it dark green? Was it red with blood? Was it very dark brown like coffee grounds? Was it a lighter brown? Did it smell of shit?'

'Coffee grounds,' he says as if he's said it before.

He half rolls and his skinny white body contorts in spasm twice before red vomit erupts from his mouth and splatters on to the floor at our feet. The nurse and I hold him on his side till the antiperistaltic spasms pass. He spits clots on to the floor while I run a grey Venflon into a vein on the back of his hand and through it we flood a bottle of Haemaccel.

Then I bleep Rich and tell him about Coffee Grounds and he agrees that it could be varices so he needs a scope.

Rich and I together pass a central line while we wait for the endoscopist to come in from home. The blood on the floor near our feet congeals to purple jelly. We track Coffee Grounds' pulse and blood pressure. His heart ticks over at ninety beats a minute, ours nearer a hundred and twenty.

He doesn't puke blood again. We transfer him to the endoscopy suite where the endoscopist, an SPR, says, 'I'll take it from here,' and the doors swing shut and Rich and I plod back to Casualty with its chest pains and strokes and bronchitises and off legses.

On the floor of his cubicle I make out the faint pink blemish where the cleaner has tried to mop off Coffee Grounds' bloody vomit, has tried to erase the memory of him. I do the same. I give up on him as I must. I move on without inertia.

The next day the post-take round trundles through the hospital and we find Coffee Grounds lying on the ward with healing fluids funnelling through the central line we put into him the night before.

The day after I think he must've gone. Then I read the name over the bed and recognise the central line and realise it's him. He's shaved off his beard. The tremors are only mild now we're controlling his alcohol withdrawal with diazepam. He doesn't smile. That would be asking too much of the demons. Instead he shows me a thumbs up.

She reclines on the disordered covers of the bed. My hand flutters across her abdomen. The thin muscle twitches at my touch. Lying on her back her belly is a flat basin between the ridges of her lowest ribs and the crests of her hips and pubis. With my tongue I trace a line along her linea alba down to her navel where I lick round and in before descending to her vagina. Laying her palms on my shoulders she says, 'I have my period,' and draws me upwards.

My lips skim across the hard crest of her hip bone and follow upwards along her faint linea semilunaris to her ribs. I stroke each intercostal sulcus counting up to her breast. I'm learning every line of her body, every curve and ridge.

Her nipples stand hard. I bite her left one with a pressure just less than pain and she lets out a gasp and pulls me round on to her with her arms, bringing me up with her kisses and guiding my pelvis on to hers.

Instead I plant kisses down her neck, into her supraclavicular fossa, over the high margin of her clavicle and back to her breasts. She grasps my penis with her hand and rubs it against the warm wet opening of her vagina, arching her back as she does so, with her other hand on my buttock pressing me down on to her.

'You don't mind about my period?' she says.

'No,' I say.

'You don't have to use a condom this time.'

'You're sure?'

'Yes,' she says.

I enter and I'm gulped by the unattenuated warmth and wetness of her inside. My skin tingles. I grow harder than usual and she feels it because she moans and smiles. We know I'm going to come too soon but she drives me on anyway, surrendering her orgasm in favour of mine, and a few seconds later for the first time she feels me spurt inside her.

Now I fall in alongside her and we nap as perspiration cools on our bodies.

Then she wakes me and we touch and within seconds I'm hard again. Forgoing foreplay we fuck. I know my latent period will be longer having come once already. We arch in long slow strokes. Our bodies grow warm, exchanging heat. Her mouth tastes of sweat, her hair smells of it. I feel her draw herself tighter with each beat, each gasp longer and louder. I relax because she's coming and I am too.

Afterwards she uses my white coat as a dressing gown and takes a shower. Blood in red and black streaks of which some are moist and some crusted smears my dick. I soap it and wipe it at the sink.

When it's time for her to go she stubs out her cigarette and we dress without speaking and then I open the curtains to daylight. Her civvies drop into the bag that contained her uniform. In the mirror over the sink she cuffs back her hair with a scrunchy and plucks her glasses and cigarettes off the bedside cabinet and leaves to begin her shift.

I tip her tobacco ash into the bin then open the bed covers to the air and with a handful of tissues dab dry the red melange of blood and vaginal secretions. It's a Saturday afternoon. I'm not on call this weekend. I'm here for her.

Now I gather my things and drive north to visit friends. I return on Sunday night in time for the end of her next shift. My eyes flick at once to the scarlet patch on the bed sheet and I smile, remember her.

Weeks later I clerk in a homeless man after he's been found in a doorway barely conscious. He chokes and spits and black-brown mulch splatters the floor and I recognise its resemblance to coffee grounds. Him I don't recognise at first but then I study the beard returning in wisps and the swollen distorted face with the broken cheekbone and razor slash and it's Coffee Grounds.

With the nurses I strip off his clothes and try to straighten his legs but can't. In the end we have to cut him out of his trousers. After he got mugged he'd been squatting semi-conscious on his legs so long they're blue and his toes are black and people were just walking by while he'd been like this for days and I can't feel any pulses anywhere below the femorals.

The German SHO who was dealing with Coffee Grounds before me pinches the blue flesh. 'No feeling,' he says. 'Look.' He gathers a roll of wasted muscle and impales it with a white needle. Coffee Grounds feels nothing. '*Du alter Scheisskerl*,' the SHO says to him, '*wir werden dich in zwei Hälften schneiden.*' Laughing he leaves.

I picture Donna. I picture the minutest detail of her, the lines and curves and ridges I've explored and learned. Her body is here in my mind as I examine the rest of him knowing whatever I do he's going to the surgeons and they're going to cut off his legs.

At last I get my hair cut. The red flares of eczema have vanished

143

and now I can push my hair up off my forehead. My scalp feels bare. Cold whips my ears as I trudge down from the hospital towards the flats. I'm on call this weekend. Things have gone quiet and Rich's told me we have no patients expected for at least an hour.

She's waiting for me in my room wearing civvies. Her next shift isn't till Monday but she's managed to excuse herself from family, friends, fiancé or all fucking three, I don't know. As we undress she says, 'You've had a haircut.'

'Yeah,' I say.

'I've got something new to show you,' she says.

She takes me in her mouth and strokes the base of my penis with nodding fingers and I pulse to the pinch of her teeth and the wet heat of her mouth. I feel the cool sheet under my back and her long brown hair tickles as it falls over her face on to my skin. The scent of her body is clean and fresh, how she is before work changes her body. She drinks hot tea and when her mouth engulfs me again it's hot and shocking.

I say, 'I like your new thing.'

My pulses grow stronger and I sense my semen gathering. She must register me getting harder in her mouth because her fingers start working in short fast strokes. I feel my come rising and I put out a rising moan to let her know and then I do come.

I touch her hair. My fingers fall through it in long slow caresses.

She crosses to the sink and spits and runs the tap and scoops a handful of water into her mouth and spits again.

I gaze at her body as she stands with her back to me. My eyes trace the curves of her shoulders and waist and legs. I remember from minutes ago not the feeling of her mouth around my penis but of my hand caressing her hair and when doing so and looking at her I contemplate telling her she's beautiful though she isn't though she is. She turns and catches my look and glances away in embarrassment.

As I shift to make room for her on the narrow bed I wince. I twist round and examine my shoulder blade. She kneels on the bed straddling my backside and with her fingers squeezes the spot till I feel it rupture and leak.

She edges closer to me and her fingers glide along my arm and down to my hand over and over again while my thumb strokes her face from the cheekbone to the corner of her mouth and down on to the curve of her chin. We lie together, only her body and mine, no anxieties churning through our minds. I forget the patients and the diseases and even the sleeplessness and in forgetting fall asleep.

When my bleep goes off it's an emergency we didn't know about. I pull on my clothes and tie my shoelaces on the edge of the bed.

'I might be back soon,' I say. 'You know how these things can turn to sausage meat before you've even got going.'

'I don't know how long I can stay. Not long.'

'I'll call if I'm coming back.'

The case is a massive MI who's in VT. Not long after Rich and I get there we see the fast sawtooth lines on the monitor scatter into the jumble of VF. The anaesthetist tubes him and I apply the first shock of two-hundred Joules with the left-hand paddle to the side of his sternum and the right-hand to the side of his nipple. He tenses and rises like a body in ecstasy. Before anyone gets hands on again I charge, call, 'Clear,' and shock again. We're still staring at jumble on the monitor. I dial the charger to three hundred and sixty joules and shock a third time. Rich injects adrenaline and a nurse performs chest compressions and the anaesthetist bags him.

I glance at my watch and hope Rich'll call it off so I can get away from this dying body and back to a living one.

We cycle through the protocol into three more three-sixty shocks, adrenaline, another cycle this time adding atropine, a fourth cycle with added lignocaine, a fifth with bicarb. Energy drains from me knowing Donna will have gone before I can return to her.

But the nurse says, 'I think he's had enough,' and leaves. Rich calls after her but she waves a hand over her head and the doors close behind her. The anaesthetist shakes his head in disbelief. Rich's eyes flame with anger. 'Fucking bitch,' he says. 'Fucking cunt bitch nurses,' he says.

'Yeah,' I say and mean it.

We carry on, just the three of us, Rich, the anaesthetist and I. I shove down on the patient's chest counting out the compressions so the anaesthetist can time his ventilations. Beneath my crossed palms I feel the hard edgy give and rebound of the breastbone on the heel of my left hand. The body grows pale under me. The skin becomes cold and papery in the dry air of the resus room.

At twenty minutes into the resuscitation we've lost count of the number of shocks but we shock him again. As if to show frame by frame life's power to cling to life the random topography of the monitor screen blinks and jumps and twists and organises into peaks and troughs with a rate of about forty. All three of us reach for the carotid pulse at the same time but I get there first. I feel the slap of blood pressure. 'There's a pulse,' I say.

'Sinus brady,' says Rich.

My hand reaches again for the carotid artery. Smiling I nod to Rich.

We gaze at the body on the table in the middle of the big room. Perhaps it's only imagination but I think I witness pink re-entering his skin. I'm certain it's only my imagination when I feel warmth re-entering the room. Rich perches on a stool in the corner already writing up the notes. I take blood samples from the Venflon. I take gases from the radial artery and when I do his arm twitches so I have to hold it in place.

The anaesthetist twists the Ambu bag off the end of the endotracheal tube. Its spout is open to the air. The patient's chest rises and falls. We wait. It rises and falls again and this time we hear the suck of air and then the blow from the end of the tube.

'He's breathing for himself now,' says the anaesthetist.

I turn to Rich and say, 'What else've we got?'

'Nothing yet.' In a funny voice he adds, 'The natives, they are not so restless today.'

'Going to be a rough night then,' I say.

With a sudden spastic motion the patient's arm flicks up at the anaesthetist's face then the other arm too and the patient is awake and flinging weak slaps at the doctor looming over him. The anaesthetist snatches at the patient's arms trying to wrestle them down to his sides while Rich and I leap across the room to assist.

'It's OK, it's OK,' says the anaesthetist. 'You left us but you're back. You're back now.'

The arms fall away. The anaesthetist strokes the patient's brow. The patient peers up with wide confused eyes like child's eyes.

'You went away but you're back now,' says the anaesthetist.

I pad out and as I do I glance at the clock with some regret.

I see the nurse who walked out on us standing at the far end of the department, just standing around talking with another nurse. I march towards her past the mostly empty cubicles and a surgical houseman on the telephone struggling to find a bed for

147

her patient and when I reach the nurse she's laughing about something with her friend.

'I just wanted to let you know we recovered the patient to a sinus brady and right now he's breathing for himself. Not that you could give a shit.'

I turn and stride away from them.

The nurse calls after me, 'Hey! – who d'you think you are, talking to me like –?'

'Fuck you,' I say without looking back.

Outside in the ambulance bay I cross under the glowing Accident and Emergency sign. The sky's faded to grey and lamps have now spotlit the roadway round towards the hospital flats. I thrust my hands into the tight spaces left in my white coat pockets crammed with books and equipment and trudge home.

As the door to my room swings open I glimpse her asleep on my bed. I click the door behind me and hang my white coat on the hook. For a few seconds I stand and study her. She wears a jumper over her naked torso and knickers and her legs are bare. Her brown hair falls across her eye and cheek. As she breathes her chest rises in long movements. I don't know if she's beautiful or I just think she is because sometimes I see beauty in the jagging line of a heart monitor or in liquid that glistens through a drip or in the strong clean lines of a hospital corridor.

I wonder if when she's on the wards she acts like the caz nurse who stomped out of resus. I wonder what she'd think if I let her know that like most of my colleagues sometimes I find myself hating nurses.

But when I kiss her she opens herself to me. Soon our breath rushes and sweat leaks from our skin. As we touch and turn and touch, as we part and become one part and part again, our bodies conjoin in the biological imperative of life's struggle for life. Elsewhere bodies suffer, decay and die but we, we are immortal.

The rota condemns our firm to being on call for Christmas Eve and New Year's Day and one day-night-day in between. My sister and I agree to go home for Christmas Day. I start searching for a New Year's Eve party I can go to but still be able to get back for work the next morning.

Tonight is black. A layer of cold air clings to the window. I lean out of bed and turn the radiator tap till it hits the stop. Pipes gurgle and as we both slide under the blankets the room soon flushes with heat.

We have sex then a nap.

Before she goes she lays a small parcel and a card on my desk with a gesture of awkwardness. I offer her my gift in return. She takes it saying, 'You shouldn't have.'

It's so cold tonight I insist on walking with her to her car. Neither of us examines my logic. We walk out into the bitterness. Her car's parked under a light opposite the main entrance. Though we're shivering we don't hurry. I turn her towards me and we kiss. Our faces are numb. She eases away but I don't want to let her go.

'Get in,' she says.

She starts the engine and turns the dial to the thickest band of red so the heater blasts out a current of cold air that over time becomes lukewarm.

We kiss for half an hour until for the fourth or fifth time she says, 'I've got to go.'

With my work and her work, with my social arrangements and hers, we can't see each other again until after New Year. It's only natural she should be with her fiancé.

I watch her car turn out of the car park and its tail lights progress down the roadway till it turns again and vanishes behind buildings.

On Christmas Morning the post-take round finishes at eleven

o'clock. Doctor H. thanks us all and wishes us merry Christmas. Rich and I shake hands. We'll be back at work in a day and a half.

In my room I call my parents to say I'm on my way and start packing a bag. I pick her present from the desk and dig open the wrapping with my thumbnail. It's a CD. I slide it into the player and stack the box on top of the others. My present to her was a bottle of scent, the one I'd sometimes seen her dab on before leaving. I consider my row of CDs and her toiletries and realise our knowledge of each other derives solely from our contact within this room.

I open her Christmas card and it uses the word 'love' and I feel foolish for wondering if she means anything by it.

Carrying my bag and wearing a coat I cross the quad where the grass lies beneath a layer of frost and crunches under my boots. I duck into my car and accelerate out of the present towards our next moment together.

16: The Suspicion

Early in January her shifts switch to nights. Some time between seven and eight in the evening she unlocks the outer door with the key I've had copied for her and walks up the flight of stairs to my room. I put on a CD and put out the lights. The quad's amber glow filters through a gap in the curtain. In this light her body appears the colour of ivory. After we shed our clothes our skins feel cold against each other. Later we're hot and breathless and the bed beneath our bodies mops the damp of our sweat.

Often before she has to go we nap in each other's warmth. Other times we make tea and sit together on the bed cradling the mugs on our laps and usually she'll smoke a cigarette or two. When I put aside my mug or she stubs out her cigarette early it's a signal to the other and we kiss and fall back on to the mattress side by side or one on top of the other. Then at half past nine she leaves for work.

I watch some TV. I endure the negative creep of evening. At ten o'clock I put out the light.

From the darkness of her grave I'm visited by the Breathless Lady. Ice crystals encrust the headstone. In the ground below maggots writhe in her eye sockets. Worms crawl in and out of holes in her chest cavity. They eat the flesh off her bones but not the hard black fossil at her core. They curl round it. They creep over it. But they don't eat the blood clot I missed.

151

There's someone in my room. I hear her steps. I hear her breathing. I struggle to lift my head but I'm paralysed, my body mired in sleep while my mind's climbed out of it. I try to cry out, to make her go away, but my voice has been snatched from my throat.

'It's me,' she says taking off her uniform.

'What time is it?'

'Five thirty. I told the sister I wasn't feeling well and she let me go early.'

She stands over the bed and with my eyes graded to darkness I watch her strip to bra and knickers and the erection is immediate. She's shivering but I swing out of bed and pull down her knickers as she unclasps her bra and falling to my knees find her clitoris with my tongue. The smells of her crotch fill my nostrils, the smells of sweat and piss and tiredness.

When I pull her down to the carpet where we have sex cold stiffens our bodies, the only two hot spots in the room our confluent mouths and our confluent loins.

In the morning the tone of my alarm wakes us at eight thirty. We seek each other with kisses and the breath we share smells stale. She blinks at the time on the LED and then in panic she's scurrying around the room after her clothes.

'Shit,' she says. 'I'm going to have to use your shower.'

She's back in only a couple of minutes. She fastens the clasp of her bra on her front then turns it round into place and hooks her arms through the straps. She puts on her uniform and puts her coat over it while stepping into her shoes. In the mirror she brushes her wet hair.

'Shit,' she says again.

She kisses me without lingering and then I hear her running downstairs and the outer door slams behind her. Later when I get dressed I find on the bedside cabinet the half-full pack of cigarettes she's forgotten. I shut the lid and place them on the desk.

Then I see Carol for the last time. She's in smart civvies emerging from the doors outside the medical wards with someone in a dark blue Hospital Security puffa jacket and I run across the car park to intercept her. When I get close I notice she's crying.

She turns to me and I don't know what to say.

She says, 'You don't know the half of it.'

She slips into her car and starts the engine then speeds away crunching the gears.

The man from Hospital Security tracks her little car till it passes out of the hospital exit. He glances at me and says, 'Fuck it. Fuck it. Fuck it,' then trudges back indoors.

I shiver in the cold. On the staff work rota in Casualty her name's been obliterated by a black marker as if she never existed. I ask but no one will say anything.

Later I'm feeding coins into the vending machine in the patients' waiting area when the German SHO joins the queue behind me.

'Is Carol on today?' I decide to ask.

'That bitch?' He shrugs. 'They sacked her.'

'What for?'

'Why? Because she wrote some letter to the management. She said bad things about the Casualty department and the consultant also. So they suspended her.'

'Now she's gone for good?'

He grunts and waves me out of his way so he can punch the buttons on the machine.

On the ward round the next day Doctor H. spars with Rich and me and when we can we bounce back with banter. At one

153

point we encounter another ward round led by a consultant I'll call Doctor V.

Rich leans his shoulders in our direction and whispers, 'That's the one.'

'Which one?' I say.

Aware that Doctor H. is eavesdropping Rich bites his tongue. But without looking up from a chest X-ray he's studying Doctor H. says, 'The one who after a hospital party was seen by Hospital Security fucking his secretary over the bonnet of his Volvo estate in the gravel car park behind Biochemistry.'

I whisper, 'Does he know people know?'

Doctor H. says, 'I don't think he does,' and we all smirk.

The three of us with our trolley glide past Doctor V. who's conferring over a set of notes in a huddle with his houseman and SHO. Doctor V. glances up as Doctor H. passes. Doctor H. shows Doctor V. the chest X-ray he's carrying.

'Over-penetrated,' says Doctor H. and drops it back in its sleeve. Rich and I snigger behind our hands. Doctor V. blushes and fumbles with the notes he's holding.

Leaving the ward Doctor H. turns to Rich and me laughing and says, 'Now he knows.'

We finish bang on lunchtime, a moment determined by hunger rather than working practice. Doctor H. strides up the long main corridor and I follow not long after. At the click of footsteps he glances back and pauses for me to catch up.

'Can't resist the call of the canteen either?' he says.

As we walk he says, 'Have you thought much about what you want to do after house jobs?'

'I was thinking gen med.'

'That's great,' he says. 'Listen, I know some people think it's better to visit pastures new, but I happen to believe we've got a really solid SHO rotation here.' He shrugs. 'Better the devil you know.'

With a grin I say, 'Which way round d'you mean?' and he smiles back at me.

Then I say, 'But there's something I'd like to ask.'

'Fire away.'

We reach the entrance hall and break out into a cold bright day in January.

I say, 'If you saw another doctor harm a patient, what would you do?'

'Harm them how?'

'Trying to relocate a shoulder and instead fucking up some poor kid's arm.'

He halts. I turn to face him and I catch the spark of recognition in his eyes. The wind feels cold all of a sudden so I shelter my hands in my white coat pockets.

'Look,' he sighs, 'these things happen. We're only just beginning to recognise that being a hospital patient is a high-risk experience. We're estimating that anywhere between thirty-five and seventy thousand deaths in hospitals each year are caused by medical mistakes. We're estimating probably two hundred thousand patients per year are harmed in some way. That's one in ten. One in ten hospital patients suffers an adverse event due wholly or in part to clinical error. You're young and inexperienced. You're full of desire to "do the right thing". You should recognise that all doctors, even the best and most experienced ones, from time to time cock things up.'

He nods in conclusion and turns in the direction of the canteen.

'What if you were convinced of another doctor's negligence?' I persist. 'Not merely a mistake. *Negligence*. Would you let the hospital know so that if it was preventable it might be stopped from happening again?'

'That would make me a whistle-blower,' he says.

We approach the outer doors of the canteen.

'I think what I'm saying,' he says, 'is I would keep my mouth firmly shut.'

In the canteen we part. He sits on the table of suits, the consultants' table, the men and women whose patronage plots the course of their underlings' careers. I reside among the white coats, the juniors, and my mouth drains dry.

In my room I wait for her. At seven thirty, the usual time, I put on a CD and lie on the bed with my hands behind my head staring at the ceiling.

At eight thirty I get up and water the olive plant that remains leafless and fruitless after two months. I pick up the packet of cigarettes Donna left behind and toss them up in the air a few times before putting them back on the desk where they've lain unopened for two days.

At nine o'clock I hear the bang of the outer door and footsteps ascending the stairs. She shuts the door behind her and advances into the middle of the room.

She says, 'He's started asking questions.'

I don't know his name, the fiancé, and she never mentions it. I don't ever ask.

Now she says, 'It started after the morning when I overslept.' Her hand slides into her coat pocket and she produces a packet of cigarettes, plucks one out, lights it and with nervy fingers kisses it to her lips.

'What kind of questions?' I say.

'He slips them in. Sly. Mentions something he did a couple of weeks ago when I wasn't around and says, "I can't remember – what were *you* up to that night?" '

'You think he's trying to catch you out?'

She nods. She leans back on the edge of the desk and folds her arms under her breasts. Her right arm levers up to her mouth and she takes a drag of smoke then breathes it out.

'Has he?' I say.

'I don't know.'

I sit up.

'What d'you want to do?' I say.

'What do you want to do?' she says back.

We both glance at the clock. She stubs out her cigarette in favour of a greater addiction. I put out the light and strip. She wiggles off her knickers and hikes up her uniform and we fuck on the bed.

At nine twenty-five she soaps her hand at the sink and uses it to wash her vulva. Then her knickers go back up and her uniform back down.

'What now?' she says.

I gaze through the parting of the curtains out over the city. In a clear black sky I count stars and a crescent moon.

'Now you go to work,' I say.

At the end of the following day I sit alone in the doctors' mess and sip tea from a chipped mug. Rich comes in with two other SHOs and says, 'Wait till you see this.'

He puts a video in the player and fumbles with the remote control. Nothing happens and Rich starts mumbling in frustration. One of the other SHOs snatches the remote off him and switches to the video channel.

'Just wait till you fucking see this,' Rich says to me.

A picture forms from outsize pixels in black and white with time codes running in the corner of the frame. From a high angle it shows a car park at night deserted apart from a single vehicle. After a few seconds a woman carrying a full wine glass in her hand paces into shot. The car door swings open and out steps a man. The camera angle distorts them into tops of heads with stumpy figures below. They look around then start kissing. The woman, the secretary, lifts her dress and the man, Doctor V., bends her over the car bonnet.

'Where'd you get it from?' I ask.

'There's a bloke in Hospital Security who's running 'em off,' says Rich.

Doctor V. drops his trousers but steps out of them with only one leg so they fetter his other ankle. The paleness of his buttocks leaks over the picture as they begin to rock back and forth.

'How long does it go on for?' I ask.

'Nearly five minutes,' says one of the SHOs, the Scot.

'And it's like this?'

'Yeah,' says Rich. 'It's like this.'

I sigh.

'What?' he demands.

'It's an ugly middle-aged bloke shagging an ugly middle-aged woman, blurry, and in black and white.'

The three of them turn back to the video. The woman, the secretary, twists her neck in a strange fashion. They lean forward with eager squinting eyes but then they see she's trying to take a gulp of wine so they rock back. We return to watching the pale smudge that's Doctor V.'s arse, watch it nodding back and forth, back and forth.

Eventually Rich says, 'This cost me ten fucking quid.'

So Rich talks himself into returning the tape to Hospital Security. I stand outside as the fat man in a dark blue V-neck jumper and dark blue trousers opens the door, the man who escorted Carol the suspended nurse off the premises.

Rich says, 'This video you sold me . . .'

The security man surveys the corridor for eavesdroppers and counts only me, another white coat.

'. . . is crap.'

When the security man moves, a band on his jumper containing his belly's greatest girth stretches into a net pattern. Through the gap in the door I scan a bank of video monitors. In an empty corridor two figures in suits stand talking. They are Doctor H. and Mister M.

'I'm sorry, Doc,' the security man says. 'Would you like to have your money back then?'

'Yes, please.'

'Well, you can't. Now fuck off.'

The last image I glimpse is Doctor H. and Mister M. parting with a nod and smile before the security man closes the door laughing.

17: The Acid

In the night I'm called to one of the wards to see a blue bloater but a man who's not so old, perhaps sixty-five. His hands and mouth are blue, his nose purple. Inside rotten lungs can't exchange enough oxygen for carbon dioxide, making the blood acid; kidneys fight the acid by retaining fluid; fluid bursts out of his circulation into his tissues, swelling his body from abdomen to toes, pooling there under pressure his heart's too weak to relieve.

I give drugs that in a less severe case might relieve the swelling and breathlessness but I know in his they'll do nothing, nothing at all. His cold bloodless skin reeks of sweat from life's effort to cling on to life.

Then I emerge from the interior into cold night and plunge through dark made dusk by hospital lights. In my room I warm my hands on the radiator then a few minutes later her night shift ends and a few minutes after that she comes into my bed. She squats on top of me and I clinch her breasts as she angles forward to take me inside her and then eases herself up and down.

When we're finished and I've wilted I slide off the condom and wrap it in tissues and in the dark I register the thud of them dropping in the bin.

'I think he knows,' she says.

Rolling to face her I kiss the tip of her shoulder. My hand floats across her breast and down into the dip of her abdomen.

160

'I'm on nights for two more weeks,' she says. 'When I go back to days . . . He'll be at work. It'll be easier . . . '

My fingertip strokes line after line on her sternum. Then at last I tell her. I tell her, 'I'm finishing at the end of the month. The middle of next week.'

She remains motionless under my touch like a doll.

'D'you know where you're going?' she says.

'Back up north,' I say.

'For how long?'

'Six months.'

'Then?'

'Then . . . I don't know yet.'

She says nothing. I roll on to my back and soon sleep claims me.

I hear my bleep. The LED glows on top of the bedside cabinet signalling four digits I recognise at once.

'I have to go,' I say.

'Will you be long?'

'Not with this one. There's a big bloke with a black robe and a scythe standing over his bed.'

'I'll stay,' she decides.

I get there and the Blue Bloater's rasped his last breaths. I record no pulse under cold clammy skin, no sounds in his chest, nothing but a wide unchanging stare when I shine a light in his eyes. In his notes I pronounce him dead and in the sister's office on the thick pad of death certificates that looks like a giant chequebook I log the cause of death.

Then I clamber back into bed. It smells of the sex we've had. Under me the sheets bear the denser colder texture of sweat. Grey dawn filters through the curtains on to her body. She appears thin and grey like a corpse.

Her fingers crawl over my chest and down into my groin. She makes me hard at once and then takes me in her mouth.

With her fingers she strangles the base of my penis. Trapped blood turns acid. My muscles ache from oxygen lack. I remember the Blue Bloater with his dying rasps. They're all there in my mind to be revived, not only him but also the Breathless Lady and Didn't Mean It and the Vague Yellow Woman and even Grey Meat. I throb as cells swamped with carbon dioxide cry out for O_2. I remember the Young Headache Man's dick turning black and having to be cut off. I remember Coffee Grounds' body ending at his hips and the other half of him incinerated as hospital waste. In accelerating beats of pain she drives me to come. When I do I gasp at the surge of relief as she releases the acid blood and my tissues respire again.

She doesn't visit the sink. She curls across me and lays her face on my chest and our warm skins unite.

'He wants us to move in together soon,' she says. 'Before the summer. Before we get . . . before the wedding.'

I place one hand on the soft skin of her neck and with the other I caress long strands of her brown hair.

'I suppose it was silly,' she says.

'What was?'

'To think we could keep on like this for ever,' she says.

'Everything ends,' I say.

Her bare back chills and I draw blankets across us and we hold each other close.

My bleep goes off again and I unhook an arm to answer it. She lies across me as she's done for half an hour, not moving, me not moving under her, just holding her. As I answer the call I feel her skin shift against mine. She senses the weariness in my voice that means I'm going to be gone a while this time.

I hang up. I search for the words that say the things I want to say.

Without lifting her head from my chest she says, 'You're going.'

'Yeah,' I answer.

Moments pass before she says, 'I've got to go too.'

I release my hold on her. We rise from the bed. She washes at the sink while I discard my theatre blues and dress in my day clothes. She steps into her uniform and throws on a coat. For the first time we descend the stairs together and step out of the block into the cold air of the quad. We face each other. I reach out and lay a hand on her arm. She covers it for a moment with her other hand then lets go.

'Bye, then,' she says.

'Bye,' I say.

She follows the path towards the car park and home and I go into the hospital.

The patient is comatose and breathing fast. When I lean close to listen to her chest a sweet scent hangs in the air that I've never smelled before but I guess what it must be. I call in a nurse and ask her to do a BM.

A toddler clings in his arms and an older child hides behind his legs as the history comes from her husband. His hands are dirty and he wears a donkey jacket with council insignia.

She's been feeling weak for two weeks. She's been tired all the time like in bad flu. This morning the older kid couldn't wake her and he phoned his dad who called an ambulance over his mobile and rushed here from his shift.

When I pinch the skin on the back of her hand it stands in a ridge for a moment before levelling. I press the pulp of her thumb till it blanches then in letting go I observe the sluggish return of pink. She's dehydrated.

The nurse feeds the narrow plastic strip into the glucose

163

machine. She pricks the patient's fingertip and squeezes a drop of blood onto the part of the strip still showing.

'Has she been unusually thirsty?' I want to know.

'Yes,' he says.

'And passing a lot of water?'

'Yes,' he says.

'Got a reading yet?' I ask the nurse.

'Not yet,' she says. She's waiting for the display to count down from thirty seconds to zero.

'This will tell us if her blood sugar is high,' I explain to the husband. 'There's a strange sweet smell on her breath. You might be able to smell it. It's a substance called acetone. Sometimes it's a sign of a blood-sugar problem.'

'Fifty-five,' the nurse announces.

'Get me insulin, ten units IV, and we need a litre bag of normal saline, please.'

The nurse strides out to get the materials. I pass a Venflon and tell the husband, 'I think she has diabetes. Her blood sugar is very high and that's caused her to be extremely dehydrated. We're going to give her treatment to bring the sugar down and replace fluids with a drip.'

'Is she going to be alright?' he asks me.

'It's serious,' I say. 'We'll know exactly how serious when all her blood tests are in. I'm sorry I can't be more definite.'

He says nothing. The kids cling on. I get the Venflon in and draw off blood into tubes and flush it. In among the bones of her wrist that feel like paving stones under the skin I find her radial pulse again. This time I prick it with a needle and scarlet blood leaps into the syringe. I don't look at her face or her kids' faces. When I lean across her to give the insulin and then attach the infusion I smell her sweet breath again. 'Wide open,' I tell the nurse and she adjusts the drip to stream in at maximum flow. When I glance up at the husband his eyes are glistening.

164

'I've got to get these bloods to the lab,' I say, 'We'll do everything we can.'

Out in the department I bleep Rich then label the blood tubes 'URGENT'. I call the labs and call a porter. I write up insulin via a syringe driver and hand it to the nurse. When the first bag of saline's gone through I write up the next then start on the notes.

Rich strolls into Caz as I'm on the phone taking down results from the lab. He reads the numbers I transcribe into the notes.

'Bad DKA,' he says. 'How long's she been a betty?'

'Since I made this diagnosis,' I say.

'She needs to go to ITU,' he says.

We send Sweet Breath off with all her infusions running and the husband and kids trailing. From my seat at the station with the phone and the forms I peer as they recede, as the sounds of the department recede. I only hear them. The toddler insists on walking. He totters with a wide-legged high-stepping gait, holding his older brother's hand, who holds his dad's. The father pulls at them both to keep up with the trolley as it rattles over the floor but they're all held back to the toddler's pace so the porter slows for them to keep up. The train creeps forwards in this way for half a minute before their father's patience breaks and he scoops the toddler into his arms. The toddler kicks and screams but his father ignores him and the procession accelerates out of the department before being gulped into the interior. The toddler's protests echo back along the corridor till they fade.

Now I hear words. Someone is speaking in a shrill voice to a young woman in a cubicle nearby. Through the slit in the curtains I glimpse her dyed blonde hair and dark roots. She's overweight and she's laying a palm flat across the front of her chest then waving it back and forth saying she feels breathless. The shrill voice belongs to the short Asian SHO who abetted

Mister M. in wrecking the Shoulder Boy's arm. He's saying, 'Go home. This is not for A&E. See your GP if you don't get better tomorrow.'

'Have you done gases?' I'm at the slit in the curtain and the SHO steps out to join me. 'I couldn't help hearing. Did you do gases?'

'You,' he says, recognising me. 'What's it your business about gases?' he says.

'Her history. She could've had a PE. You could do gases and you'd know.'

'Who are you, actually?'

'I'm the medical houseman on call. Well, I was. We handed over at nine.'

'This patient isn't a medical patient.'

'I know. I'm making a suggestion, that's all.'

'I haven't referred her to you. I'm an SHO. You're a houseman.'

'Can I do gases?'

'I'm sending her home.'

'You've discharged her then. I can do gases.'

He says, 'I really don't care what you do.'

The SHO pads up the department away from me holding a look over his shoulder for three or four steps. He's very short and for the first time I notice his eyes have a yellow tinge.

I explain to the woman that I'd like to do a blood test. I turn her wrist palm-up and arch it down. I locate the radial pulse with my fingertip and then as with Sweet Breath only a few minutes ago I drive a needle into the tiny beating bulge under the skin. I hurry the sample round to the machine in Biochemistry and run it through. If only I'd done this for the Breathless Lady I'd've diagnosed her PE and she wouldn't have died or if she had it wouldn't've been my fault.

A minute later a print-out emerges from the machine like a

white tongue being stuck out. Her blood oxygen is low. Yes, she's had a PE.

I order Tinziparin at once. While the PE Woman reclines on the trolley in the cubicle with an oxygen mask covering her face a nurse pushes the first injection under the skin of her abdomen. Over the phone I transfer her to today's team. I grab a coffee from the machine in the patients' waiting room and return to write up the notes.

Today's RMO ambles in. He's the Scottish SHO, Rich's mate. I tell him, 'She's twenty-eight, no significant PMH, taking an OCP, smoker, no other regular meds. Presented with sudden-onset dyspnoea, nil else. On examination, tachycardic and tachypneoic. Chest clear. No calf tenderness. ABGs show hypoxia. I think she's had a PE.'

He considers the figures and says, 'I think she has too.' He takes the notes and with a grin steals my coffee.

'Thieving bugger,' I say and laugh.

I put on my white coat and smile that I got a second chance not to be lost to the profession by my mistake but to be improved by it. Medicine that betrays me in my training, my supervision and my workload owes me that much at least. My steps spring over the floor as I stride through the long corridor towards the medical wards and at last in her grave the Breathless Lady's blood clot is crumbling to powder.

18: The Rabbit Hutch

Sweet Breath's numbers fall over the course of her first day and night on ITU. Her glucose comes down, her pH normalises, her dehydration reverses. The effect is like the tide going out so the following morning we can see the stones on the beach. There's something wrong with what's revealed, with the part of her that can't be described by a thing as simple as a string of numbers.

When we examine her she groans. Doctor H. holds her eyes open one at a time with his thumb. Her arms flail and fall as if they're lumps of meat while her legs don't move at all. Drugs and fluids flow in via a central line. An arterial line pierces her wrist. Urine drains out through a catheter.

'Why isn't she waking up this morning?' the husband asks.

Doctor H. answers, 'The diabetes coming on so suddenly and without treatment means her blood sugar got a long way out of control. That's had all manner of effects on the chemistry of her blood. It's affected its acidity. It's affected the concentration of certain important substances. Although these derangements have been corrected, they've caused her brain to swell.'

He stares at us all, him on one side of the bed, Doctor H., Anita, Rich and me on the other.

Doctor H. doesn't say soon the swelling's going to crush her six-inch-wide brain through a hole in the base of her skull half an inch across and probably by now the damage is irreversible.

He says, 'We're going to do everything we can to bring the swelling down.'

The husband stares at us. After a few seconds he nods.

'Are there any questions you want to ask?' Doctor H. says.

He shakes his head.

The firm troops to the nurses' station while I pluck the notes out of the trolley. Hospital Records have located the old ones and I unpick the binders to add yesterday's crisp new pages.

There's only an Obs & Gynae file – her two pregnancies and nothing else but then tucked in the back I encounter two caz cards. The first is dated three days ago. There's no proper history or examination, no tests done, and the patient was advised to see her GP. The second is dated the day before yesterday. Again the history's vague and no action recommended. But in the line across the top written by the nurse it gives the pulse, the blood pressure, the temperature and circled *BM=18*. The signature is unreadable but the one below, countersigning and adding *TATT – Δ: ?depressed ?malingerer (?AOA!)*, is not: Mister M.

None of them picked up on the high blood-sugar measurement. I don't know whether the rest of the history was there and included the thirst and the passing water. I don't know any of that but I do know it would've saved her from all this if someone had only realised she might have diabetes.

Doctor H. talks into the phone to another consultant. Anita has located some results clipped behind the nurses' station and is busy circling the important ones with a red biro she carries especially for this purpose. And Rich makes his favourite joke again: 'This place used to be called the Intensive *Care* Unit, till they realised no one did.'

My first feeling is shame. I'm ashamed of medicine, the profession I once held above all others. But more I'm ashamed of myself. I'm ashamed of having approved of this secret society because it granted me a second chance after I killed the Breathless Lady. Now I see it acts without discrimination between error and negligence, between inexperience and incompetence, between remorse and arrogance. The code of silence is absolute. It shields us all alike.

And I sift through all the other things I feel. I feel sad. I feel angry. I feel powerless. I could show the caz cards to Doctor H. right now. I could find the caz officers and tell them what's happening to their patient. I could even confront Doctor H.'s chum himself, Mister M. I could do any of these things if I thought for one second someone might give a shit.

In my room I'm already preparing for the move though my job doesn't finish till next week. I'll travel north on Tuesday night and commence my new post at nine o'clock the following morning.

I've set out a cardboard box into which I'm stacking my belongings. In the corner of the room lies a black rubbish bag for the stuff I'm junking.

When I look at the bed I think of Donna and our bodies against each other, sweat chilling on our skins as we glide into sleep. I have her number. I could call her. I haven't. She has mine. She could bleep me. She hasn't.

My gaze rests on the olive plant. I consider its leafless fruitless form with grey twigs sprouting at angles off each other from a stem rising out of grey soil. My hands cradle it across the room and I hang it over the rubbish bag. Attachments to lost causes create inertia. I must be able to turn and to accelerate without the effort of overcoming my rest mass. But when I hold back I know I'm not ready to give up on it, not yet.

Next I go through the bedside cabinet and find old journals and on-call rotas that fly straight into the rubbish bag. At the bottom of the drawer I come across my copy of the New

Testament. It's been many weeks since I searched its pages for an explanation to the things I've seen. There's no answer because there's no God in this place. I know that now. And if God can't penetrate the interior then He can't be anywhere we need Him to be. I throw the book in the bin.

Following corridors inwards I trudge to the lifts by the opening of the Surgical Unit. I step in alone and of the buttons numbered to fifteen I punch the one marked '5'. The numbers light in sequence till the doors part and I'm spat out opposite the frosted double doors of ITU.

I hang my white coat on one of the hooks outside and go straight to the sink by the office. I wash my hands in a pink gob of Hibiscrub and dry them on paper towels and pad past the beds of motionless bodies. Monitors intone the rhythm of life. Ventilators breathe. Infusions circulate. But no one here is alive in the sense that I am.

Then I see Sweet Breath tubed to a ventilator with her husband and kids round her as if they're visiting a tomb. And I see the future. It's her in a wheelchair with drool streaming from the corner of her mouth and being turned every two hours in the night to stop her getting bedsores and her eyes welling up when she looks at her kids because she can't say words any more and now even the little one can.

The husband glances up at me with red eyes. The children are silent now. I don't know what they've been told but they can see. I ask him if the ITU specialists are keeping him informed and I express my sympathy.

'She won't lie down for long,' he says. 'She's a fighter.'

Some idiot up here's said this crap to him or he's seen it on TV so he's playing his role.

'That's good,' I say, playing mine. 'That's the best thing she could be.'

171

Over the bed he's stuck up a photo of her with one of the kids. I say I have to go now. I don't want to look. I don't want to see that she's a person.

I return from ITU to learn there's an admission waiting for me in Casualty. I plod back along the corridor and over the next hour clerk in a congestive heart failure. I make myself not think of Sweet Breath, not turn in my mind's eye to look at the photograph over the bed and see her in it as she was before.

By four thirty my whole body wilts from two nights on call and a weekend looming. Of the tasks listed in my notebook half are struck through, carried out. The other half stare back at me.

I'm not thinking about Sweet Breath, not peering into the photograph and picturing a wife and mother. I can't be poured into a mould shaped by other people's feelings so as to feel moment to moment what they feel and not be distorted by it. I can't go to ITU or wherever and go beyond bearing witness and risk becoming part of it and not finish up spent. I must always be the scalpel that glints and cuts and never becomes blunt. I must always be that blur in the back of the scene, present for an instant then appearing no more in the narrative of other people's lives.

So if this is the way it's got to be I ask myself whether I want it. I'm asking myself for the first time since I was a schoolkid who'd seen fuck all of the world, just a kid seduced by the myths of medicine. Now I'm someone who's done the job and seen what it's really like and felt what it does to you and become what it turns you into. I'm asking if I want to stay in medicine.

When I was a little boy I remember finding rabbits crammed in a hutch and out of mischief releasing the latch but none of them ran away. Instead their paws scratched at the straw under them in panic, backing into each other, cowering from the opening. They'd been caged since birth.

Now it's my turn. I can stay here, the only place I know, the only place I can be a doctor, or plunge into the big scary unknown. I'm staring out of the rabbit hutch.

Then a nurse asks me to prescribe an IV and just to do something, anything, I decide to draw it up myself. I step into the treatment room and take down a pack of drug ampoules from the shelf. I break open a syringe, bayonet it with a sheathed needle then I snap open one of the ampoules and it splinters in my fingers. Three or four pieces of glass embed themselves in my flesh. Though the blood's delayed the pain is instant.

Shuffling to the tap I run water over the tiny wounds and with my other hand extract shards of glass. Blood pinks the stream as it swirls down the plughole. The cold water numbs the pain and the bleeding eases off and I still want to be a doctor, I still want to do the job and that means staying in this world because it's the only one there is, but I'm crying, crying like I haven't since I was a kid, with tears flooding my face and snot drooling from my nose while on the ward normal business continues, it all continues, it all continues.

I'm twenty-three years old.

PART THREE

God's Locum

Life robs us of ourselves,
piece by small piece.
What is eventually left
is someone else.

John Updike

Six months later.

19: The SHO

My second First of August falls on a Wednesday. I finish my six-month surgical house job on Tuesday evening and travel down overnight to be ready for work the next day. I don't even have time to unpack. On my first morning as an SHO my consultant, Doctor O., bleeps me at nine a.m. exactly and suggests we meet on our home ward. We shake hands. 'Pleased to meet you,' she says. 'Let me tell you a few things about what I like and what I don't like and then there'll be no misunderstandings.'

'No problem,' I say.

Doctor O. is Doctor V.'s replacement. Doctor V. transferred to a post in another region after someone sent his wife the video of him shagging his secretary over the bonnet of his Volvo. When he demanded to know who'd have that kind of grudge against him, every junior doctor who'd ever worked for him raised their hand.

'There's no SPR routinely attached to this firm,' says Doctor O. 'One will be available to you on call. The rest of the time you answer directly to me. The house officer should be here any minute. Her name's Sally. I think she's bright. Give her support when she needs it. The hospital has adopted the house officers' curfew. That means no house officer works between midnight and eight the next morning when on call. The SHO covers. Good news for her, bad news for you. I like notes to be readable and whenever possible contemporaneous. I don't like pejorative remarks about patients or other doctors. I respond to candour. If results aren't back or a procedure I've ordered hasn't been carried out, don't confabulate – just come straight out and say. If something's wrong, tell me. I'll listen. In return, if I think something's wrong, I'll tell you and you'll listen. Don't use foul language to the nurses no matter how much you might believe they deserve it. Answer patients' questions. If you don't know the answer, tell them you don't know the answer. If patients or relatives want to speak to me, call my secretary to make an appointment for them. Unlike my predecessor, she and I aren't having an affair. Do up your top button. If your collars are too tight, buy new shirts. Shave every morning. I carry a bleep in the hospital. I always answer it. Out of hours, you can call me on my mobile. If in doubt, call me. I'd rather be bleeped at some horrendous hour of the night than be red-faced in front of the coroner in the morning. Any questions?'

'No.'

'I have Outpatients this morning. Take Sally through her duties. Take as long as it takes. Then come and help me out in clinic. OK, that's it.'

'That's it,' I say and she goes.

I fasten the top button of my shirt and hike up my tie.

Sally pads on to the ward. I recognise her by the look of fear in her eyes.

'Hi,' I say.

We shake hands.

'Hi,' she says.

'How about a nice cup of tea? We'll steal the nurses'.'

She smiles and nods. Her breath is fast, her eyes darting. We sit at the nurses' station and I show her all the forms and charts she needs to become familiar with. She asks questions, lots of questions, and I answer them all. When her bleep goes off for the first time she flusters but I show her the buttons to press to read and save the message.

'Everything they taught you in medical school,' I say, 'you may as well forget right now. Learn about chest pain and MI and COAD and strokes and off legs and diabetes. The other shit you'll never see and, if you do see it, you won't have a clue what to do, so call me, and if I don't know what to do we'll keep going up the line till we find someone who does. Take blood as much as you can. Get good at it. Pass Venflons. Get very good at it. If I'm around, I'll supervise you in any practical procedure you like, whether the patient needs it or not. Your need's more important than theirs. And if someone's breathless and you don't know why, do gases because it might be a PE.'

She's short and plump with a busy walk and a lopsided smile and over the next few weeks I watch her change. After the dry hospital air and its long hours have given her three bouts of conjunctivitis she gives up the struggle with contact lenses and trades them for spectacles. Another week and she's dispensed with make-up and tied her hair in a ponytail. Meals get skipped so she pinches chocolates out of the boxes the nurses leave out. By the end of the first month she's wearing theatre blues and trainers and like a puppy's her nose becomes an index of her well-being: in good times it's snub and kind of pretty but most days it's dry and inflamed. Meanwhile I buy new shirts and shave every morning.

Through sunlight I cross from the wards to Medical Records where the consultants have their offices and their secretaries type discharge summaries and letters to GPs.

Doctor O.'s secretary smiles and says, 'Hello.'

'Hello,' I say. By now I've stopped picturing her bent back over the bonnet of Doctor V.'s Volvo being given one.

Once a week I have to find an hour to come here and review

183

our patients' notes so I can compose discharge summaries into a dictaphone for her to type and send out and for the GPs to not read and throw straight in the bin.

'Her Ladyship wants to see you,' she says. She taps the door and pushes it open for me and I go into Doctor O.'s office.

Folders of notes stack chest high on a table in the corner of Doctor O.'s office, waiting to be piled into a shopping trolley and rolled down the corridor to the Depository. She opens a set to me and I recognise a page of my neat blue script. She shows me the name on the cover which is Sweet Breath's name.

Leaning on the edge of her desk she says, 'Do you remember this patient?'

'Yes,' I say.

'I noticed a particular line you wrote: *Pt s/b A&E x 2 in last 3/7 – BM 18 but no action taken.* It's not very prominent, but it's there nonetheless.'

'Yes. It's there.'

'My problem is there aren't any caz cards. There's no record she was ever seen by anyone in Casualty. They've been conveniently "lost" by Medical Records.'

I don't know what to say so I don't say anything.

She shuts the file and lays it on the desk beside her.

'Do you remember what the caz cards said?' she asks.

'I'd have to think about it.'

She sighs. 'You wouldn't recall who saw the patient in Casualty?'

'Can I ask why you're looking into this case?'

'No,' she says. She indicates the file. 'This patient presented in DKA, got cerebral oedema, brain damage and now she lives in a wheelchair without the power of speech. I'd like to know if beforehand she was seen in Casualty with signs of incipient diabetes and nothing was done about it.'

Again I stall. 'I'd have to think about it.'

Doctor O. jumps up from the edge of her desk and paces away and says, 'What do you "have" to think about?'

'My reference for a start.'

'Your reference?'

'Without a good reference, I'm unemployable.'

'I write your reference,' she says.

'Exactly,' I say.

'I want you to tell me what you know not because you want a shiny reference out of me but because you think it's the ethical course of action.'

In the face of her anger my mouth drains dry. I stutter, 'Look, I, I'm sorry.'

'Stop looking so frightened. There's nothing to be frightened about.' She smiles, wanting me to relax.

I say, 'Please understand. You're asking me to trust you and I don't know because I don't know why you're asking me this.'

'OK. Let me ask you something else. What do people think of the clinical standards in A&E at this hospital?'

'They think they're shit.'

'And I'm trying to do something to improve them. But first I need evidence there's a problem. Understand? Now please tell me what you can remember.'

I gulp. 'I still don't know if I should.'

'Why?'

'Because it'd make me a whistle-blower.'

She paces to the door and flings it open. 'Fine. You think about it.'

'I'm sorry,' I mumble.

'Whatever,' she says and watches me through the door and closes it behind me.

In Caz I glimpse Mister M. He wears a navy-blue suit and from time to time he swaps the jacket for a white coat. That means he's about to go up to theatre or into resus or to carry out a procedure of some kind. My eyes don't follow. I don't flash forward to bungles and heartlessness, to disability and death. He goes about his business. I go about mine. I have to consider my career. I'm an SHO now.

Then one day I see Sweet Breath again. Her husband is steering her wheelchair along the main corridor towards Physiotherapy. His eyes are fixed ahead, his face blank. If he recognises me it doesn't show. I look down at her. She's slumped to one side with her arms twisted in permanent in-turned rictus with hands half clawed and drool glistening at the corner of her mouth. As I pass by her eyes roll and she emits a sound. I slow, maybe to stop, maybe just to make sure it's her, but the wheelchair with its silent blank-faced driver rolls on towards their appointment. My stride barely breaks as I pick up and head for mine.

My new room overlooks the quad in the direction of the path that slopes down to the main road. At an angle to the left lies my old block and one floor up the window of my old room where Donna and I would peer out sometimes at night before turning back into the bed and into each other.

The miniature olive tree sits on the desk. Green leaves sprout from its thin grey branches and black fruits dangle below. The leaves are thinner and paler than the ones it bore when it lived with Rebecca and me and the olives smaller but it didn't die. It evolved to suit its environment.

20: The Sensitivity

A male nurse pastes a note on a drug chart and chucks it on the pile on top of the nurses' station and walks away. A few minutes later Sally picks it up and reads what it says. It says: *Temp 37.5 - ?UTI.*

'Yours or mine?' she says.

'Don't mind,' I say.

'I'll go,' she says.

'OK,' I say.

She strolls out of sight while I study a chest X-ray on the light box. Ten minutes later she returns with the male nurse, saying to him, 'If you send off a CSU, I'll write him up for an antibiotic.' She hoists thick notes out of the trolley. 'Catheterised yesterday,' she says in my direction. 'Now pyrexial, no obvious focus of infection. Probably a UTI.'

'Probably a UTI,' I say.

She fills in forms for the CSU and for FBC and U and E's in the morning while I travel to the neighbouring ward to chase up a blood result.

Ten minutes later the male nurse hurries me back. Sally stoops at the patient's bedside and with her stethoscope listens to his chest. His skin is red and his eyes, lips and tongue are swollen. His respiration accelerates and he emits a wheeze and his fight for breath begins.

At the bedside lie his notes. On their front I read: *ALLERGIC TO PENICILLIN.*

'You didn't give him pen by mistake, did you?' I want to know.

'No – *no* – of course not,' Sally snaps.

'I think you're having a reaction to the injection,' I tell the wheezing patient.

The male nurse runs the curtains round, grabs the sphyg off the wall and wraps the cuff round the Wheezer's upper arm.

'Forget about that,' I say. 'Get us a mask for sixty per cent oxygen, two hundred of hydrocortisone, ten of chlorpheniramine, five milligrams of salbutamol to be nebulised, adrenaline and Gelofusine on stand by.'

'Shall we lie him flat?' he asks.

'Leave that to me. Just get what I've asked for, please. Sally, help him.'

The male nurse shoots me a wounded look. Sally lingers twitching with anxiety so I push her out after the nurse.

I hook my left arm under the Wheezer's knees and my right round his shoulders and shuffle him down the bed then lift the catch at the head of the bed and slope the backrest to forty-five degrees. I've made a compromise between lying him flat to raise his blood pressure and sitting him up to strengthen his breathing.

Smiling at him I say, 'You're going to be fine. This kind of thing happens all the time. You're in the right place.'

He nods but his resps have hiked to thirty or forty a minute. I stride out of the curtains into the bay and steal an oxygen mask and line from another patient and wriggle it over the Wheezer's face and turn the flow out of the wall to maximum.

His resps keep going at forty. Short fast wheezes get shorter and faster. Sweat films his face and pastes the pyjamas to his back. Then I see in his eyes the look that he needs air to breathe and air to drive the effort of breathing and the less air he gets the harder he has to work, but the harder he works the more air he needs, and the look is that it's beaten him.

'Shit,' I say.

The Wheezer falls silent. He can't move enough air to make a noise. He stops breathing. I palpate his sweaty neck and the carotid artery answers with a pulse.

I jump out of the curtains and run to the opening of the bay and call out, 'Adrenaline, one milligram, right away, please.' The ward sister leaning over the station glances up and I say to her, 'Call a 222. Respiratory arrest.'

The rest of the patients read newspapers or stare down at their bed sheets. They pretend nothing's happening like it's a fart in a lift instead of a man dying. I scramble back to the Wheezer and pull his body flat with three or four hard jerks of his legs.

The sister and the male nurse bump the crash trolley through the gap in the curtains, nearly tipping it over. The ECG leads and the defibrillator leads entangle in Sally's hands and she starts clawing at them. From the trolley the male nurse plucks a Guedel airway, laryngoscope, endotracheal tube and brown Venflon and looks for someone to offload them to. He offers them to Sally then to me with his hands oscillating at two cycles per second like a tacky shop-window display.

I say, 'Give me the adrenaline, please.'

He clatters the Guedel airway, the laryngoscope, the endotracheal tube and the Venflon back on the trolley and flings me an adrenaline Minijet. I snap off the cap, twist on a needle and squirt it into the Venflon in the back of the Wheezer's hand.

'The hydrocortisone and chlorpheniramine now, please.' As I give them I say, 'Forget the neb for now but get the Gelo up and running straight away, please.' The sister connects the narrow pipe to the Wheezer's Venflon and hooks the bag on the stand. I say, 'Give me the Guedel airway now, please,' and the male nurse claws through the instruments he's just dropped on the trolley and finds it and passes it to me. Stooping I force it into the Wheezer's mouth upside down then roll it over to arch down over his tongue into the back of his throat.

Now the sister starts pumping the foot pedal to raise the bed to a working height.

'Ambu bag, please.'

I snap the oxygen mask off his face and replace it with the black plastic bag-and-mask, locking it over his nose and mouth with fingers clenched round the convexity of the mask and under his chin.

At last Sally connects the heart monitor. I catch her haunted look as the nurse pumps on the pedal, pumps and pumps to raise the bed, while the Wheezer's heart pumps, 160, 170, 180 beats per minute, pumps and pumps into flabby toneless blood vessels till that heart is spent and then the monitor draws a thick flat line and emits a long flat tone.

'Kill that alarm,' I say and the sister punches a button on the front of the machine.

In the silence we hear the gush of oxygen out of the wall into the Ambu bag, the plastic rustle of my hand squeezing the bag as I force the oxygen through the airway into the Wheezer's throat and the hiss of the bag refilling.

'What happened to him?' asks the sister.

I ignore her.

'Adrenaline, one milligram, please. Sally, start chest compressions, please.'

Sally stares at the monitor. Blushing with guilt the male nurse waves the Minijet and this time I squirt it through the Venflon in his arm.

'What happened to him?' the sister repeats.

'Shut up, please,' I tell her.

I lean over and punch Sally on the arm.

'Sally. He's dead at the moment. There's nothing you can do to make things any worse. So chest compressions, please.'

Tears break out of Sally's eyes and trickle down her cheeks. In a trance she feels for the inferior end of the sternum, measures two finger spaces up, places the heel of her left hand like a foundation stone, wraps the fingers of her right hand over and starts pumping the Wheezer's chest. From time to time she wipes the drips from her nose with the back of her hand.

'Shit, where are they?' I say. 'Put out the 222 again. All we need is the anaesthetist, no one else.'

The male nurse scurries out.

'Laryngoscope, please. And the narrowest ET tube you've got.'

The sister snatches the laryngoscope over to me and I snap the curved chrome blade out to a right angle and putting the Ambu bag and mask aside I plunge it into the Wheezer's mouth. Everything looks wrong, badly wrong, with blue walls where there ought to be pink, a tongue like the apple in a suckling pig's mouth and tissues so swollen they're folding over each other. As every chest compression judders the inflated masses of flesh I try to make myself believe a dip is the opening of the trachea.

'Sally, stop compressions and give another milligram of adrenaline.'

The picture settles to stillness. I drive the tip of the endotracheal tube into the dip, twisting and prodding and getting nowhere.

'Shit. Phone the paediatric ward. We need a much narrower tube.'

'What size?' the sister says.

'I don't know. They'll know.'

She runs out and for a few seconds Sally and I are alone with the Wheezer.

I whisper, 'If you didn't give him pen, what did you give him?'

'Cef,' she says.

'Cef-what?'

'Cefuroxime, 750 milligrams IV.'

'There's cross-sensitivity between cephalosporins and penicillins,' I tell her.

'I didn't know,' she says and sobs and wipes tears and snot from her face with the back of her hand before carrying on chest compressions.

The male nurse enters with the anaesthetist who's round as a beach ball and after running through corridors he's nearly as breathless as our patient. I register tufts of wiry black body hair curling out of his theatre vest as he takes the laryngoscope and looks down the Wheezer's throat.

'Shit,' he gasps.

Then the bulb blinks out on the laryngoscope.

'Shit,' he gasps again.

The nurse picks up the Resuscitation Officer's Report Sheet from the trolley and says, 'It should've been checked this morning.'

'Forget it,' gasps the anaesthetist. 'Fucking – get us – another one.'

He takes over bagging.

'What – happened?' he says.

'Anaphylactic shock,' I say.

'What caused – it?'

I don't glance at Sally or even hesitate. 'We don't know yet,' I say.

The nurse brings a working laryngoscope and the sister a slimline endotracheal tube and the anaesthetist struggles for ten

192

minutes before he succeeds in ramming it through the swollen tissues of the Wheezer's throat into his lungs, though by then at least he's got his breath back. We pump in 100 per cent oxygen hard via the Ambu bag. His heartbeat returns a few minutes later. By then his brain's been starved of oxygen for nearly half an hour.

When we stop squeezing the bag no reflex prompts him to gasp for air. The anaesthetist taps him on the forehead like knocking on a door. 'Anyone home?'

There's no answer. He's going to have to connect the Wheezer to a ventilator that'll do the work of breathing for him. So he's transferred into the only empty ITU bed in the hospital – as it happens the only empty ITU bed in the region.

21: The Charts

The nurses watch us as I walk Sally towards the sister's office and I hear her start to speak. 'Don't say a word to anybody,' I tell her. I reach for the phone on the nurses' station and bleep Doctor O. The sister busies herself with some emergency fussing. The guilty-looking male nurse goes on a break. The round hairy-bodied anaesthetist vanishes. But theirs have all been supporting roles. As we step into the office Sally's head turns to me dead and automatic like a doll's head and her gaze crosses with mine and her look of guilt proclaims herself and herself alone the author of the Wheezer's demise.

I close the door and say, 'This wasn't your fault. You didn't know that patients who're allergic to penicillin can have a reaction to cefuroxime. Someone should've told you.'

'It's no one else's fault,' she says. 'It's mine.'

'The patient's got a penicillin allergy, but the notes don't carry a warning to avoid cephalosporins as well. The nurse drew up the drug, and gave it, and never took a moment to check.'

She's not listening only staring at the floor. I know the process that's begun. In her head she's replaying the micro-events of the last hour. She's picturing the nurse drawing up the cefuroxime and then laying the syringe on the work surface of the treatment room. Now she stares into the moment, into the quantum uncertainty from which all futures branch. The instrument of destruction is tiny. If only it was the black bowling-ball burning-fused bomb of a *Tom and Jerry* cartoon then they might've known. If only Sally's pleading stare could alert the nurse to the error and stop him drawing up the drug. If only it could cause the BNF to fall open at the page and on it she reads, *Cautions: 1. Penicillin sensitivity...* But no: over and over again the permutations fold into the sole irrevocable reality wherein Sally prescribes the drug and it's injected into the Wheezer's body.

I say, 'Listen to me,' and she lifts her head. 'They say being in hospital is one of the most dangerous experiences anyone can have. One in ten patients comes to some kind of harm. A consultant killed a three-year-old girl because he turned the wrong tap and pumped her full of nitrous oxide instead of oxygen. A paediatrician killed a week-old baby because he flushed a tube with phenytoin that someone had left lying around. A houseman killed a patient because he was asked to give potassium and gave it as a bolus instead of as an infusion. Over the years *a dozen doctors* have killed chemotherapy patients because they've given them vincristine intrathecally rather than intravenously. In every case there were misunderstandings. In every case no one else said, "Wait – is this right?" In every case hospital policies created accidents that were just waiting to happen.'

Sally hunches small in her seat with cheeks red from tears and nose damp with snot. I say, 'Give me your bleep. Go home.'

She gathers herself to protest but nothing comes out but a mumble of, 'What about work?'

'I can cope. Especially now we've got one less patient to worry about.'

She tries to laugh but can't. With slow aching movements she unclips her bleep from the band of her skirt and presses it into my hand.

After she's gone I realise Doctor O. hasn't answered her bleep yet. I hail her twice more and when she still doesn't answer I try her mobile but after one ring I'm shunted into the network's voicemail service. I leave a message and wait. After an hour I call Switchboard.

'That bleep isn't active,' the operator tells me.

'Can I have her new bleep number, please?'

'There isn't one.'

'What's happened to the old one then?'

After a pause the operator says, 'Would you like to speak to my supervisor?'

'I'll speak to anyone if it'll help.'

She transfers me and a male voice says, 'That particular bleep is no longer active.'

'I need to contact her urgently about a patient. Do I have the right mobile number?' I start to quote it to him but he interrupts.

'I'm sorry, Doctor. I'm not at liberty to help you.' Then he hangs up.

I call Doctor O.'s secretary. I say, 'I don't seem to be able to contact her.'

There's another pause like the switchboard supervisor's. 'She's not available for the rest of the day,' she says.

'Will she be in tomorrow?'

'She's not available till further notice.'

'What's happened?'

She hesitates again. 'I don't know,' she says but it's clear she does.

Outside ITU my hand trembles as I hook up my white coat. I pad through the frosted double doors and the first distinction between this place and any other ward is in the landscape of noise. While I swing the lever over the sink and slide my hands into the stream of warm water I hear the breath sounds of machines: the clunk and hiss of ventilators, the beeps and tones of monitors. From the Hibiscrub dispenser I squirt a blob of pink fluid into my palm and rub it into a lather. I hear no voices behind me, no nurses chatting to each other, no ward rounds bustling, no patients calling out for attention. I rinse and swing shut the chrome lever and dry my hands on a paper towel and think. I think about the Wheezer and what I'm going to do about him.

His bed spans twice the size of one on the ward. He lies in a large area to himself – not that he's in any state to appreciate it – crowded by a ventilator, cardiac monitor, blood-pressure monitor, plethysmograph and automated infusers. Into him probe a ventilated endotracheal tube and a central line. Out of him run a urinary catheter, ECG leads, a blood-pressure cuff and an oxygen-saturation sensor.

I study his charts that are just numbers, lots of numbers. His notes feature an unreadable entry from the hair-ball anaesthetist who nearly gave himself an arrest running to answer the 222 call. Neither Sally nor I have written in his notes yet. I think about doing it now but I'm still unsure what story to tell. What am I going to do without a consultant? I peer at the Wheezer in his coma with his body being maintained by machines and the strongest impulse is to run away home.

A nurse approaches me. 'Is he yours?' she asks.

'Yes,' I say. 'He's mine.'

I watch the clock creep past five o'clock. Now we're into on-call time. I consult the rota and the consultant listed as on call for the night is Doctor H. That makes it a lot easier for me. His mobile's turned off too but I leave a message and wait and after half an hour of carrying out Sally's jobs on the ward one of the nurses tells me Doctor H. is on his way up to see me.

He begins, 'Being a new consultant – it isn't easy. Fitting in with colleagues who've worked in a certain way for years, some for decades. It isn't easy.'

Doctor H. shifts in his seat. He glances out of the window of the sister's office at the routines continuing on the ward outside then back to me and realises his arms are folded and in a deliberate adjustment of body language unfolds them and like a porn actor contorts his face into an unconvincing expression of languor.

'She came highly recommended. More than a few of us thought it was high time we appointed a woman consultant. Bring in the female perspective.'

'Get in touch with your feminine side? Whenever I do that it slaps my face and tells me to keep my hands to myself.'

He forces a smile. Then he shrugs. 'It's our fault, not hers. We got the wrong person.'

'Has she been sacked?'

'No. She's . . . left.'

'Left?'

'Yes,' he says. 'Left.'

'For good?'

'To all intents and purposes she has, given that she's no longer undertaking clinical duties.'

'I don't underst –'

'And that's why I'm talking to you now. Obviously we can't have you working without a consultant so on routine matters you'll be able to refer to me or when I'm on leave another designated consultant. Her clinics have been cancelled, as have her caths and echoes. We're working out a rota system to cover takes and ward rounds. In the meantime we're working very hard to find a suitable locum and I'm hopeful one will be appointed in the very near future.'

'I'm worried about my training. I'm supposed to learn from my seniors. I'm here to learn.'

'Yes,' he says, 'you're here to learn,' but adds no more.

'But –'

'This is a difficult time for all of us. Don't make it any harder.'

He moves to go but I persist with the question that's bothering me most.

'But who'll give me my reference?'

'What?'

'If I don't have a consultant, I can't have a reference.'

'We'll work something out.'

He's still trying to leave when I say, 'And we've got a patient who's gone to ITU today.'

'For fuck's sake.' He sighs. 'If he's that ill, he's probably going to die anyway.'

'I suppose.'

'Good. Look. This is a difficult time. We'll pull together and we'll get through it.'

Windows interrupt the long blank walls of the corridor and through them leak glowing squares of evening sun. I have to stop. I turn and peer through the glass towards a building that when I was a houseman was the construction site where I shattered the nail of my big toe on the night I killed the Breathless Lady. I don't know whether Doctor O. jumped or was pushed or whether she told them she was auditing A&E calamities or if she let on I might corroborate the failures in the case of Sweet Breath, and why would I know when I don't even know what the fuck this new building's for? This is a big hospital and I'm alone in it without top cover and I'm scared.

My bleep summons me from the window to a phone on the wall along the corridor.

'There are some relatives here who want to speak to someone,' says a nurse calling from the ward.

'What about?'

'About the patient who went to ITU.'

The sister who participated in the arrest finished at three and the late-shift sister is on. She gives me the first bit of good news regarding the Wheezer. There are no close relatives to kick up a stink, only an elderly neighbour and a niece. The sister ushers them into the office. She's middle-aged and very fat. Her corpulence has the benefit of filling most of the tiny room with navy-blue uniform. The uniform portrays the perfect balance of caring and officialdom, in itself representing the thousand souls and the hundred and fifty miles of corridor and the forty million tons of concrete of the hospital, and I want it here in this room like a talisman insisting to his neighbour and niece that the Wheezer has received and is receiving the full measure of the hospital's ministrations.

I follow and shut the door. The sister says very little because she only knows about the patient second-hand but she tells them she's very sorry about what happened, whatever that was. I wear my white coat and speak in metred tones that emphasise how serious his condition was and how heroic were our interventions.

'He developed a serious infection in his water. It was absolutely essential that we gave him the strongest antibiotic available. We knew he was allergic to penicillin, but it wasn't expected that he would have a reaction to a completely different kind of chemical. His infection was very, very serious. Untreated, it would've been life-threatening. Unfortunately, by a chance in a million, he did have a severe reaction. We did everything we could. At one point, he was actually dead, but we managed to bring him back. His condition at the moment is very serious, and I'm afraid you should prepare for the worst.

On behalf of all the doctors and nurses who're looking after him, please accept my deepest sympathy.'

The neighbour is a lady of the Wheezer's age with a moustache who's nodded throughout the speech and her momentum adds a couple of redundant nods after I've finished. The niece dresses like an office worker. She's in her late twenties with short straight peroxide-blonde hair and strong features. Inside a white blouse a black bra hammocks big breasts.

The niece says, 'Can we see him at all?'

Her low flat voice is rougher than expected but she has eyes like blue pebbles, high cheekbones and full red lips. The blouse opens at the neck and the bra is like a shadow on water.

The sister says, 'I'll phone them to find when would be a good time.'

'That's all right,' I say. 'I'll take you up there myself.'

The sister heaves herself up. 'I'm very sorry,' she repeats. 'If there's anything I can do . . .'

'You did everything you could,' says the neighbour.

The Wheezer's niece and neighbour stand at the foot of his bed flanked by an ITU nurse, hypnotised by the breaths of the ventilator and the beeps of the heart monitor, by the waveforms of the plethysmograph and the revolving wheels of the infusers. His eyes are taped shut. Bruises now mottle his skin where tubes have been inserted, infused their load till the vein ruptured and been replaced. A physiotherapist beats his chest and drains the debris he'd in life cough clear. The Wheezer is a mannequin without reason or sensation, inflated and deflated by a machine. The neighbour starts to sob.

I peer sideways at the niece. She isn't crying. She has a hardness to her.

'It'd be wrong of me to pretend he won't be here for some

time. There mightn't be any change for days, even weeks. The nurses will advise you of visiting times.' I look at the niece as I add, 'If you want to ask anything, ask them to bleep me and I'll come up.'

She looks back and in her hard flat voice says, 'Awright.'

I take his notes and drug chart into the office and lay them out on the desk in front of me. The drug chart that Sally filled in stares up at me with the words Cefuroxime 750 mg IV. I glance out through the slats of the blind and the staff are intent on their own business. I take a big breath and as I exhale I'm folding the drug chart in half then in quarters and then I slip it into the pocket of my white coat. On a blank sheet from the shelf on the wall I record that the Wheezer suffered anaphylactic shock while omitting the name of the drug he was given moments before. I enter an account of his resuscitation in detail, emphasising every piece of bad luck we encountered and how heroic were our reactions. Then I unclip the folder and insert these new pages before the anaesthetist's unreadable entry rather than after it. Inquests and investigations occur months even years after the event. By then memories have faded and documents assume primacy. Though I've told no lies there's no record of the patient ever having received cefuroxime.

I glance up as a nurse leads the niece and neighbour off the unit. Through the slats of the blind I watch the niece look back towards her uncle before leaving and her face is expressionless. As she turns her heavy breasts swing in the black bra under her white blouse.

I return the notes to the Wheezer's bedside and leave ITU. I descend five floors in the lift and stroll outwards through corridors whose air becomes cooler till I'm out of the hospital and in the freshness of night. From my pocket I shed the drug chart into a bin of hospital waste that's awaiting incineration. Then I head home.

Maybe being an SHO won't be so hard after all.

22: The Witch Finder

But Sally changes now the Wheezer's gone to ITU. The next morning I find her watching from just inside the frosted double doors. Her nose is red. The skin dries and when she scratches it it flutters off in flakes. The Wheezer is neither improving as she hopes nor dying as she fears, neither improving nor dying.

'The rels are fine,' I say in her ear. 'They're grateful for all we're doing for him. And the notes are buffed like the Crown jewels.'

She says nothing. She gazes at the consequence of her error. She peers at the rise and fall of the chest on a puppet whose strings are pulled by machines that beep and flash and doodle waveforms on monitor screens. At least the Breathless Lady's body died so her remains could be hidden in the ground.

Doctor H. joins us and glancing at his watch says, 'I haven't got long.' He scans the notes and charts and nods. 'I don't think there's anything we can be doing for him as physicians.' He wanders into the office and speaks to a man I don't recognise who wears a pink shirt with a purple tie tucked between the middle buttons. Five minutes later he ambles out again and says, 'All sorted.'

He looks at his watch. 'Good,' he says then goes.

The man in the pink shirt glances out through the slats of the blind covering the office window. He smiles. I furrow my brow. He strolls out and says, 'That's fine. He's ours now.'

I continue to look puzzled so he says, 'I'm the ITU consultant.' I'll call him Doctor T. Doctor T. bleeps his SHO, who is Rich. Doctor T. speaks to Rich about the Wheezer. By this time Sally and I have hit the wards. Later that morning Rich bleeps me.

'What happened to this bloke of yours on ITU?' he says.

'My houseman gave him cefuroxime when he was allergic to penicillin. He went into anaphylactic shock and got laryngeal oedema and it took too long to tube him so he's got cerebral anoxic damage.'

'Anybody notice?'

'No.'

He asks, 'What was the cefuroxime for?'

'UTI.'

'Shit. From a UTI to ITU.'

'A palindromic referral.'

He says, 'What was he in for in the first place?'

'Fuck all really,' I say. 'Tests mostly.'

'Don't you just love hospital? Come in to have your piss dipped or your shit sniffed and you wind up brain-dead on ITU.'

I laugh. 'That's *so* unfair,' I say. 'He's not officially brain-dead till two consultants test him for it.'

He laughs. 'The reason I wanted to know what really happened to him is because my boss wants me to give him Substance K and I need to check he meets the criteria.'

'Does he?'

'Yeah,' he says.

I can hear him scribbling.

'Why Substance K?' I say.

'The boss is running a trial of it in coma caused by cerebral anoxia.'

I pause. Then I say, 'What's Substance K?'

205

'Good question. You've heard of Substance P, the chemical transmitter involved in pain stimulation?'

'Yeah.'

'Well, it's nothing like that. Substance K is a chemical present in breast milk or fanny batter or something and no one knows what it does. Then last year there was an anecdotal report in an obscure journal of it improving outcome in cerebral anoxic damage. Quite why anyone would want to administer Substance K to such a patient baffles me, given that nobody knows – or for that matter cares – what if anything it does. But, inspired by this chance finding, they did a small trial in Holland and its results got reported in a slightly less obscure journal. The results cautiously supported a role for Substance K in improving blood supply to brain cells. Now the boss has set his heart on being the first in this country to prove the finding and report it non-obscurely.'

'And you're running it for him?'

'You know what it's like. This is a kingdom and he's the king. It'll be good for my reference and good for my CV. You could say there *is* a division of labour.'

'You do all the work and he takes all the credit.'

'Exactly.'

I tell Sally. *They're giving the Wheezer Substance K.* And I see it bring a glimmer to her eye.

We conduct a ward round with one of the consultant physicians. I keep it brief and he appreciates the narrow claim on his time. He asks for test results and from time to time examines a patient himself. He gives instructions and discusses articles from journals we've never heard of. It's no different from working for Doctor O. or Doctor H. or anyone.

I fill in forms and make calls as we go and Sally scribbles in the notes and pushes the trolley but I know her mind's elsewhere. *They're giving the Wheezer Substance K!* – a drug so new and powerful she's never heard of it. Of course it's going to work.

That evening I see the Wheezer's niece strutting along the corridor towards ITU. I see the blonde crop and the flare of her lipstick and I get a tachy.

'How's your uncle?' I say.

'He's, y'know, the same,' she says.

It's there again, the hardness, like she's counting every moment spent in this corridor talking to me against time she could be somewhere else. So I nod and continue up towards the wards.

'They've started some new thing,' she says.

I pause and turn and she adds, 'The doctor said it was the latest thing.'

'That sounds promising. I hope you start getting a bit of good news at long last.'

'Yeah, hope so,' she says. She smiles. She smiles the first smile.

The following week Sally and I are in Casualty and we see Rich busy in resus. A building worker lies on his side on the treatment table. A scaffold pole enters his flank and exits from the front of his abdomen. I wander through. He's alert and speaking to a fellow builder in a language I don't know that sounds Slavic.

'Hi,' I say.

'Oh, hi,' says Rich. 'Have I told you yet? My wife's expecting a baby.'

'Congratulations.' I nod toward the man with a pole through his middle. 'What happened to him?'

'Fell off a roof.'

'And?'

'Stable. Could well have missed all his vital organs.'

'Is he going to theatre?'

'We're just waiting.'

'What for?'

'The photographer of course.'

Mister M. strides past Sally and me and lines up his shot. The camera flashes. He moves round to another angle. The camera flashes again. 'Thank you,' he says and leaves.

'So who's giving the Substance K?' asks Sally.

We look at her and she looks anxious. Skin peels from the tip of her nose.

'Today's dose was due fifteen minutes ago,' she says.

'I'll give it later,' Rich says.

'I'll do it,' she says.

Rich shrugs.

Sally scurries to ITU. When I get there she's reading the data sheet that comes with the drug. She opens the box of supplies in the storeroom, breaks the neck of a glass ampoule, sucks the clear fluid into a five-millilitre syringe and expels the excess down to a precise volume commensurate with the Wheezer's weight. She cradles the syringe to his bedside and guides it into a port of his central line. Under pressure from her thumb the plunger glides down and millilitre by millilitre the elixir trickles into him.

Instead of turning away she gapes at the Wheezer's body. The pump of the ventilator rises and falls: the living object. The equal movement of the man's chest is only its shadow. Infusions bruise the Wheezer's arms and the central line humps his neck. With his mouth opened to gulp down the endotracheal tube his face is paralysed in a permanent silent scream.

The anaesthetist, the one from his resuscitation with the big fat stomach and the forest of body hair sprouting from his chest and back, works round the patients. When he reaches the

Wheezer he recognises him and taps his head like knocking on a door.

'Anyone home?' he says.

I turn Sally away from the bed and walk her back to the wards.

'Leave him to them now,' I say. 'There's nothing we can do. Try and put him out of your mind.'

She trudges alongside me through the bars of sunlight blazing from the windows of the long corridor and she scratches her nose till it spots blood. I sense the reel looping in her mind almost as if I can hear the projector whirring: the pictures of her hand etching the word CEFUROXIME into his drug chart like letters on a tombstone, the liquid swirling as it's carried to the Wheezer's bed, the plunger going down as it invades his blood. Without speaking we reach the end of the corridor and turn right and right again up the stairs towards our home ward.

'Back to the living,' I say but in return she's silent.

In the afternoon the secretary bleeps me.

'Could you do some discharge summaries later?' she asks.

'I wasn't planning to. Is there a rush on all of a sudden?'

'Yes,' she says. 'Five o'clock OK?'

'Five. OK.'

At five I go the back way out of the wards and along the path between privets to Medical Records. Having no outpatients' clinics now that Doctor O. isn't here I get more time to keep up to date. The secretary brews tea and I begin voicing discharge summaries into the dictaphone. I take notes from the pile on the shelf and review the entries then recount the patients' presenting complaints, their diagnoses, their courses of treatment, their outcomes and our plans for follow-up. When I started my letters extended to a page or two. Now they're no more than a couple of short paragraphs.

There are only six sets of notes. I stack them in the shopping trolley to be wheeled along to the depository at the end of the hall. I'm finished before the secretary's even finished making tea. As I plod through to question her the Hospital Security man looms in the corridor. Then Doctor O. appears behind him with her brow set hard and her eyes low and searching.

I glance at the secretary making tea and glint in recognition of her plan and she returns a wink.

The security man guards the doorway as Doctor O. loads personal effects into a case.

'How are you?' I ask her.

'Not great,' she says.

The security man interrupts, 'I don't think you're supposed to be consorting with other staff while you're here.'

'Give us a break, mate,' I say.

He puffs out his chest and fills the doorway. 'I've got me orders,' he says.

'Just piss off for a minute, will you?' says Doctor O.

He blinks. 'All right, love. Just pissing off for a minute then.' He turns his big back to us and slides into the hall. The secretary calls to him, 'Fancy a brew, love?' and he says, 'Ta, love, yeah, if there's one going.'

Doctor O. mutters, 'I suppose they've got a locum.'

'Not yet. They're looking.'

'How are you and Sally coping?'

'They've done a rota,' I say, 'so we get top cover when we need it. I try and teach Sally when I can, but they've cancelled your clinics and cardiology sessions so I'm not learning a whole lot myself.'

'I'm sorry,' she says.

'It's not your fault,' I say.

'It is,' she says. 'I thought I could get something done. I was wrong.'

With hesitation I say, 'I don't really know what happened.'

'I wrote a letter,' she says. 'I wrote a letter expressing concerns at negligent practice in the A&E department, and signed it. I requested a meeting to present evidence. At the meeting, no one wanted to hear what I had to say. They had the letter, and I'd signed it, and they suspended me.'

'What reason did they give?'

'They don't give reasons. They don't have to.'

'But they have to suspend you pending something,' I say.

'Pending an investigation,' she says. 'They won't say what it's an investigation into. But it's me. They haven't suspended anyone from A&E.'

She throws the last item, a framed photograph of her daughter, into the case and slams the lid.

'The witch finder is the one who gets burned as a witch,' she says.

She clicks the catch of her case and calls into the hall, 'I'm done here.'

The security man gulps his tea and lays the mug on the secretary's desk. 'Ta, love,' he says to her, then holds the door for Doctor O. as she says to me, 'Goodbye,' and we shake hands and she trudges out into the hall with her case and down the corridor and out between the hospital buildings towards the car park where the security guard watches her get into her car and he keeps on watching till she clears the hospital gates.

23: The Elixir

Blue Numbers is a dying man who's dying. I meet him at the point where night starts to feel like day again, when sunlight spreads back in through the windows and I become aware of weather again and footsteps and voices return to the long corridors of the hospital interior. The casualty nurse objects to him having morphine so I draw it up myself and when I press the clear fluid through his Venflon within a minute or two the knots in his cachectic body relax. I write him up for a bag of saline to keep him hydrated.

He has an end-stage lung cancer which is a bad-news cancer. In the outside world most illness is bad news and of course cancer is very bad news. But in the world of the hospital the scales work to a different setting. To me some types of cancer, the curable ones like Hodgkin's lymphoma or testicular seminoma, don't even count as bad news. Middle-ranking tumours like ones in your kidney or up your nose are a setback, but only the certain death of something like a late-stage lung carcinoma deserves to be called 'bad news'.

I say to the nurse, 'It's a cheerioma,' and we snigger.

There's nothing more to do. From here where the outside world meets this other one he's now conveyed deep into the interior.

At eight Sally joins me. 'How'd you sleep?' I say. She shrugs. Behind her glasses dark rings rim her eyes. She brings two coffees from the vending machine in the waiting room and offers me one. I sip it while dealing with the last patient of the take. 'Anything I can do?' she says. 'I'm done,' I say and we depart for the wards.

Doctor H. does the post-take round with us this time. Everyone's used to the arrangement by now. They've put Blue Numbers in a side room because it might distress the other patients to have him out in the open. When we see him he's stretching for a glass of water on the bedside cabinet. I hold the glass to his lips and he sips. He sips three times and runs out of strength. I return the glass to the cabinet and push it closer so he can reach.

'Are we actually allowed to write "*Not For 222*" any more?' asks Doctor H. with a grin.

'No,' I say. 'Not since a nice middle-class lady from the Home Counties found they'd put it on her notes. They've all seen on telly that no matter how fucked you are we can recover you from a cardiac arrest and they think it's true.'

Doctor H. laughs and says to Sally, 'In fact less than ten per cent of resuscitations are successful. In elderly patients with serious illness it's almost unheard of. If they're sick enough to arrest, they die. If they don't arrest and they recover and return to a decent quality of life, that means they weren't sick enough to bloody arrest in the first place.'

Sally sighs in boredom at the banter and dangles her pen over the notes.

'Don't write "Not For Twos",' I say. 'But, if he arrests, don't try bringing him back.'

She lifts her pen and shuts the notes.

After the round we rip into the jobs I've agreed with Doctor H. I finish on the ward and wander next door after Sally but she's nowhere to be seen so I bleep her.

'Where are you?' I say.

'ITU,' she says.

When I get there she's giving the Wheezer his Substance K. Her eyes are dark and emollient glazes her nose. I was ready to chew her out but instead I say, 'Why're you doing this?'

'Rich was busy.'

'How'd you know he was busy?'

'I check up on him,' she says without looking up.

The machines surrounding him beep like metronomes and as she trickles the magic fluid into his central line she wills him to wake.

'We've got to keep up the treatment,' she says. 'It takes time to work.'

I help her with the central line and say, 'It's only a matter of time.'

At the end of the afternoon I check on Blue Numbers. His dinner of fatty meat and limp vegetables and gravy long since congealed into brown jelly languishes untouched and out of reach over the foot of the bed. No one wondered if he was hungry and no one questioned if he was hungry how he'd manage to feed.

The original bag of saline hangs on the high hook over his bed, drained but not replaced. His arm extends for the glass of water on the bedside cabinet but he's twisted away somehow and can't roll back or shuffle back. His fingers twitch open and stretch, they stretch and miss, stretch and twitch closed, over and over again.

I give him the water and he takes sips. His pyjama sleeve has rolled up and I glimpse the blue numbers tattooed on his forearm like a sixty-year-old bar code. I cradle his head and hold the glass for him. I put it to his lips and he sips. The wasted muscles of his face twitch then sag. A few minutes later he is strong enough to try again. I sit on his bed with his head in my

214

arms and my bleep chiming every ten minutes and it takes him an hour to drink the glass of water.

When at last I come out I duck into the sluice room and splash water over my face and wash my hands. I hunch over the sink and peer into the draining plughole till I'm myself again. Then I stride out and to the first nurse I find I say, 'Why wasn't the next bag of saline put up?'

'We was getting round to it,' she says.

'Do you know what it's like to be thirsty, really thirsty, so thirsty you could die of it? He'll be dead before the day's out. Is it asking too much for you lot not to make it fucking torture?'

'Don't you swear at me,' she says.

'Just put the next fucking bag of saline up *now*.'

I start walking away and she turns to cry or stamp her feet or whatever this one does when someone's told her she's fucked up. Then afterwards she'll tell the others what a cunt I am.

In the main entrance I see the Wheezer's niece. I hesitate. I think about carrying on where I'm going (to CCU) or pretending to have business down the corridor and stroll with her to ITU. She lifts her eyes from the floor up to me so I step towards her.

'Hi,' I say.

'Hello,' she says.

'How is he?' I say.

'The same,' she says. 'Y'know.'

Conversation dries. I say, 'I was just heading off to the canteen for a cup of tea – why not join me?' She hesitates. 'Everyone needs a break some time,' I say.

'OK,' she says.

The canteen only bustles around lunchtime. With the clock nearing six the niece and I sit among empty tables. An Asian doctor eats alone while reading a journal. A trio of nurses from the same ward taking their break together pick at sandwiches.

'D'you think he'll ever get better?' she asks me.

I say, 'It's hard to tell, in these cases.'

'S'pose it must be.'

She kisses her red lips to the cup in front of her and they leave a print on the white porcelain.

'You're not that close, are you?' I say.

'No,' she says. 'I don't hardly see him. That's our family for you.'

I sense she's thinking about saying more but she doesn't. Her head goes down to her drink and my eyes run over her strong face and into the opening of her blouse.

'So where d'you work?' I say.

'I do part-time in a betting shop,' she says.

She reaches into her bag asking, 'Am I allowed to smoke in here?' I shake my head and she says, 'I s'pose I shouldn't, anyway, in front of, y'know, a doctor.'

'Doctors smoke too. And drink and do all the bad things everyone else does.'

I ask her where she lives and it's an estate on the south side of the city. She says it's near one of the stops on the Cross-City Line.

So I say, 'I've been to the pub by the railway station, just up from there. What's it called? The Railway Tavern or the Steam Inn or something.'

'I know the one. It's, y'know, all right.'

'D'you fancy meeting for a drink in there? I'm not on call tomorrow night.'

She's surprised. 'I thought there was some kind of rule against it,' she says.

'Rule against what?'

'You was asking me out, wasn't you?'

'There *is* an ethical consideration, yeah, but it only stops me going out with your uncle.'

She manages a small laugh. 'I dunno,' she says.

'Why?'

'It's funny,' she says. 'Y'know, you asking, with me uncle . . . y'know.'

'Yeah,' I say.

I change the subject and we talk for twenty minutes. She's lived in the city all her life. She left school at sixteen and not long after gave birth to a girl who's now nine years old. The father for reasons he tried to explain but couldn't left after three months and for a while returned once a year or so till he stopped coming at all, for reasons he tried to explain but couldn't. I make her laugh a couple of times. It's an uncertain laugh she has as if she doesn't know herself whether she gets the joke, like the head of a tortoise emerging from its shell unsure if it's safe to come out. But the hardness in her voice begins to break.

My bleep goes off. 'I've got to go,' I say.

Before I do I ask her out again and this time she says, 'OK.'

The next night I'm sitting in the pub by the suburban railway station, sitting there with the Wheezer's niece.

We drink. I think to myself she's only here with me because she has a wrong image of me as successful and respectable and even well off, but I also think to myself she has a beautiful face – a kind of beautiful, anyway – with those eyes and those cheekbones and that mouth, though I doubt anyone ever tells her.

Conversation passes between us in platitudes. We have nothing in common. She has an idea of what I am because I'm a doctor. And I collaborate with the deceit. Showered and shaved, my skin cleansed, my body scented, everything about me lies about my job. I'm showing her what she expects to see

217

so why not tell her what she expects to hear? – the stuff that tallies with her image of young doctors from television soap operas while the truth I swallow in drowning gulps of lager.

Growing up she will've been the sort of girl I had to watch go off with the lippy confident boys. She was impressed by their rebellion so she shared their cigarettes and gave herself to them in parks at sunset and later on the back seats of cars. To her boys like me never even existed. But soon she's thinking I'm different from the men she knows round here or the ones she meets in clubs, the ones who take her to bed then disappear when they find out about the daughter or go back to their wives and girlfriends when they've had what they were looking for. All the hardness with all its defence has left her voice.

'You're sure you won't get, y'know, struck off,' she says.

'You're not a patient. I'm not even your uncle's doctor any more. You're just someone I've met through work.'

This is the first time we've mentioned the Wheezer. She nods and says nothing more so I buy us more drinks. But later when pissed and disinhibited she asks me to tell her straight. 'Will he die?'

'Who doesn't?' I say.

Before last orders she suggests we go back to her place.

'It's only five minutes' walk,' she says. 'Me girl's at one of the neighbour's.'

She unlocks the front door and the place smells of chip fat. The lights come on but one bulb stays dark, burned out in the socket. On this warm summer night the air hangs stale and clammy but all the windows are shut, as they have to be, and most have locks. She bolts the door behind us then grabs me. She laughs when I appear startled, but I tell her it's fine, she just took me by surprise. She walks me into the bedroom, the one bedroom, and in it lies the one bed she shares with her kid.

There she undresses me faster than I undress her. A roll of

218

pale belly fat sags over the band of her knickers. Her bottom is round, her hips wide. On her upper arm sticks a nicotine replacement patch. I break open the upper hook on the clasp of her bra but her fingers take over. With calculation she throws back her shoulders and as the bra falls away her breasts burst loose and fall like seals leaping out of the water and flopping on to the ice. They're big with wide dark areolae and large nipples. My erection springs the way she expects and she tumbles me on to the bed and plunges her mouth round my dick.

I'm disturbed by the coylessness. My balls twitch and rise. I fight to relax. I should've had more sex in my life. I should've had more tawdry one-night stands so now I need them they'd be second nature. I stretch back and let it happen. I throw my arms above my head and stare at the ceiling while she works the base of my penis with nodding fingers and I pulse to the pinch of her teeth and the wet heat of her mouth.

The hot bed sticks to my back. Her cheap perfume fills my nostrils. A train rattles over the tracks nearby and the ceiling trembles and then the pulses of my penis become weaker. I'm losing my hard-on. She must register me dwindling in her mouth because her fingers start working in short fast strokes but still I'm falling away and those strokes roughen to tugs, harden like her voice can.

I slide myself out from under her. I glimpse her head turn but I show her my back, avoiding her eyes, and stand to draw the curtains – as if this is the problem – leaving a gap to let in the glow of the city lights. I stoop and gather her and lay her on top of the bed covers. As she falls on to her back her breasts droop into her armpits. I paw their doughy mass and with my tongue rub over the bumps of her Montgomery's tubercles. My fingers connect with a lump. They float round it and press and move and press again till I know it's about an inch across, rubbery and mobile with a well-defined edge.

She senses nothing.

My hand traces down to her belly where I cup handfuls of soft flesh. She turns her cheek into the pillows and flops her arms above her head, rounding her breasts, flattening her stomach. The fat lies in three shelves, one above the navel, one below, plus the mound of her vaginis mons. Where they meet they fold over each other in a soft wide crease.

She lifts her bum off the bed and slides down her knickers. 'I ain't a natural blonde,' she laughs. Her pubic hair is black and wiry. I register a scar dimpling its border and I imagine it being cut in the hospital by a doctor like me. 'That's me Caesarean,' she says.

Then she stretches for a condom like Blue Numbers for the glass of water. She tears the wrapping and pinches it out and together we roll it down my shaft. My hand begins to massage her clitoris. Her vagina leaks strong-smelling juices. The smell clogs the air of this hot room with locked windows. She opens her legs to me. She opens her arms. She's opening her whole body to me, eyes blank, blank with resignation. Her muscles offer no resistance. They are in surrender.

So we fuck. My belly lies on the softness of hers, my chest presses into big doughy breasts. I sink into the fleshy softness of this woman. I could lie here in her warmth, lie here on top of her soft gentle flesh and sleep till morning. I could forget Blue Numbers and sleep till morning.

I shrink inside her so I drive harder. It's no use. I go limp.

'Is it me?' she says.

'No,' I say.

'It's me, innit?' she says.

'No.'

We lie together, saying nothing, lying in the unreceding stink of sex. Another passing train quakes this little house. I sense she knows the timetable, knows my failure took place between

22.59 and 23.03, knows in precise minutes how unfulfilling it was.

A bladder full of beer bulges against my sphincter and I ask her, 'Where's your toilet?'

'Next door on the left,' she answers.

I pad into the room and the soles of my feet recognise linoleum. I peel off the condom and wrap it in toilet roll so it'll dampen and sink and drop it into the toilet bowl. My urethra's kinked after sex so urine sprays and splatters against the porcelain, some into the water, some on to the lino. I know she's lying on the bed listening to me piss and I feel embarrassed.

When I return I'm near to telling her I have to go. But she takes my hand and draws me down on to the bed. I lie on my back and she rolls on to her knees to straddle me. Her breasts dangle into my face and in them I notice deep-lying blue veins patterned like Medusa heads. I suck on her nipples as she wanks me to hardness again. Soon I'm reaching for another condom ready for the act she offers without ceremony. This time my plunges are fast and hard. My breath rushes and sweat pours from my skin. Her face turns into the pillow. Her eyes close. Her body drains of will.

I can only guess at what she feels. Maybe she thinks of a relative on a life-support machine in a building full of other men and women who edge closer to death than she's ever been. Maybe she thinks I live and work in that life–death world and she might think I *understand*. Death and sex, sex and death, are too confusing for her, a civilian – not like me for whom it's normal. But maybe she thinks nothing of these things, maybe only that.

Her big soft body gathers me but I picture Donna. I remember us fucking in that narrow bed and on the floor. I think of Donna's body bucking under me like a wasp impaled by a pin and it helps me come.

I lie on the bed beside her and when neither of us speaks it's suffocating, suffocating in this stinking airless room. Eventually I say, 'I need to get home.'

'You don't have to go,' she says.

I lie. I say, 'I'm on an early shift.'

'Oh. OK.'

I find my clothes and dress. I'm glad I'm here instead of at mine trying to get rid of her while sweeping the room for earrings and hairbands she might've left so she could call the next day asking after them or expect me to phone saying I've found them.

She stares into the ceiling holding her eyes up and away. I say, 'I think you may have a lump in your breast. Don't worry – it's not serious. I think it's something called a fibroadenoma. It's benign. It's not cancer. But you need to see your GP to make sure.'

For a time she says nothing so I carry on dressing. Then she says, 'Shouldn't I get seen at the hospital? I've been trying to give up smoking. It's the smoking, innit? Can you sort me an appointment?'

'No,' I say. 'You have to see your GP. He or she will make sure you're referred to the right doctor.'

'My doctor's a he,' she says.

'He,' I say. Then, 'It's not the smoking. If you're still worried, call me.'

She says nothing. She knows from the way I said it not to call me.

I button the last button on my shirt and tell her, 'I'll be able to catch the last train.'

'OK,' she says.

'Well . . . bye, then,' I say.

Her gaze grips the ceiling. I linger for a moment then recede. She says, 'You must really hate me.'

'I don't hate you. Don't be silly.' I return. I lean down and kiss her red lips. Then I go.

Long winding tracks steer the train back towards the city hub. For half a mile we parallel the slick effluent flow of a waterway before a bridge lifts us up and away. Housing estates and factory units fall behind. Office buildings glide towards us.

Après-jism dribbles on to my thigh and I find myself thinking back over the last eight months. Mostly I worked. I wasn't like one of the other housemen who on call one night was told by Switchboard, 'Congratulations, Doctor, you've now answered your bleep from every floor of the Nurses' Home.' But for me there was a staff nurse and before her an occupational therapist. Before them a student nurse. Before her an Australian physio. Before her another staff nurse. And before her – Donna. I remember the curves and dips of her body. I remember the feel of her skin against mine. I remember her long brown hair and my fingers falling through its strands.

I consider the past and for once in my life I also know the future. I know from now on every time I wander the hospital I'll peer along the corridors looking for the shock of blonde hair and the flare of red lipstick that belong to the Wheezer's niece, looking for them to make sure she's not there. She expected me to be different from the men who're hard as her who fuck her and dump her and use her and discard her but I'm not I suppose.

At midnight the train lobs me out on to the platform. Into the payphone I pump 20p and punch out the numbers I know by heart. Seconds drag by as my signal fumbles like a drunk through the network till it's answered by that long flat tone not dissimilar to the cardiac alarm that accompanies a flat line. I shouldn't be surprised that after eight months Donna's changed her mobile phone.

I slam the handset back on the hook and linger for a moment

223

on the platform where over its angled sheltering roof glimmer the lights of the hospital towers. Then I cross the empty main road and climb the path into the hospital grounds. On the ward the eyes of the night staff flick up from their whispers but they say nothing and turn back to gossip as I let myself into Blue Numbers' room and there alone in the dark give him water.

24: The History

We're on take today and Sally bleeps me from Casualty. She's admitting patients while I look after the wards but when they come in a glut I wander down there to help her out. A registrar from another firm is on call with us and while we wait for a locum consultant to be appointed the rota assigns us Doctor H. for the night. But so far there's been no need to involve either of them because the admissions have presented only run-of-the-mill problems: two heart attacks, two anginas, two strokes, three chronic bronchitises, two off legses, one stomach ulcer, one meningitis, one pulmonary TB, one lung cancer, one brain haemorrhage and one cardiac arrest.

For patients such as these the intervention of medicine is almost always predestined. The ones with treatable conditions get treated. The ones with untreatable conditions get worse or sometimes better for a while but in the end they go. When there's nothing you can do you do nothing. You're no more than the historian of life's closing chapter. In the notes you record symptoms, signs and results and go on till you come to the last line.

We don't get the first proper sickie, the first one whose illness concerns me, till seven that evening. He's in his sixties, this patient, and no one's come in with him. So when the moment intervenes in which the curtains of the cubicle exclude the synecdochic outside world of waiting area, atrium and ambulance bay he becomes alone with us in the interior space of the hospital.

Now this patient leans forward on the trolley and oxygen flows from a metal tank through into a mask on his face. A rhinophyma bobbles his nose like a ripe strawberry. Muscles on his arms and chest that bulged in youth now sag like bellies. His hair is flaxen and years of sun have tanned and toughened his skin to leather. Our bodies appear etiolated in comparison as Sally and I pass a Venflon and take blood and poke and prod and listen. We are the infirm with our pallid blemished skins and tired eyes and grease-blackened hair.

Sally says, 'The GP letter says it's bronchitis.'

'Who's the GP?' I say. She reads out his name and I don't react but I know from seeing his referrals in the past he doesn't know anything about medicine.

The patient's skin burns: the admitting nurse has recorded a high fever on the top line of the caz card. Pulse is fast, blood pressure normal, respiratory rate high. I lay my left hand flat on the patient's back and drum the end of the middle finger with the tip of my right one. The percussion note resonates across his lung fields. I unravel my tubes and listen over his back. Breath sounds are low but with few crackles. When he inhales I hear a harsh wheeze. I ask him to say, 'Ninety-nine', and it's transmitted as just a murmur.

Looking past the bulbous red strawberry nose I ask him, 'Have you had problems with bronchitis in the past?' He shakes his head. 'How's your throat?'

'Sore,' he says, but his voice isn't affected.

I shine my pen torch into his mouth and identify inflammation at the back of his throat. I listen to his chest again. I listen over his throat with the diaphragm of my stethoscope. The inspiratory wheeze sounds harsh, sounds sandpapery. 'This is beginning to sound like stridor,' I tell Sally. To him I say, 'How d'you feel? Rotten?'

'Yes,' he says.

'I want another doctor to see you,' I tell him.

At the phone on the desk in the middle of the department I bleep the registrar.

'What's worrying you?' Sally asks.

'We don't have a diagnosis so we won't know what to do if he carries on getting worse.' I scribble a couple of paragraphs on the end of Sally's clerking notes. His story has become ours to tell. Now I look at her and say, 'Learn this look. This is my worried look.'

The phone purrs and I scoop up the handset on the first ring. The registrar is Anita, who started as Doctor H.'s SPR last year when Rich and I worked for him.

'He needs an ENT opinion of course,' she concludes, 'but I'm in the middle of dealing with someone the fucking surgeons have been trying very hard to refer to Pathology Outpatients. I'll see your chap soon as I can. Am I right he's staying in Casualty, right?'

'Yeah.'

'Give me his name.'

I'm doing paperwork at the station in the middle of the department when I hear a scuffle in one of the cubicles at the far end. '*Fuck off,*' I hear. '*Fuckers.*' I lean round to view the entertainment. A uniformed policeman faces the curtains saying, 'You want to calm right down, mate.' One of the caz officers hangs back not fancying the idea of taking a history from whichever of tonight's alkies and indigents is pissed and first up for scrapping.

A figure lurches towards the copper. '*Cunt.*'

The copper straight-arm bounces the man back into the

cubicle. I hear equipment clatter and the man slump to the floor.

I only got a glimpse but it was Sweet Breath's husband.

Rising from my chair I pad down the department to where the copper stands over the slumped figure. The copper pulls the curtain. I open it as he kicks Sweet Breath's husband in the stomach making him spew vomit over the floor.

'Fuck off, Doc,' says the copper – 'he ain't ready for you yet.'

'I know him. Leave him alone.'

The copper raises open palms. 'You're welcome to him,' he says.

I bend close to the man on the floor and say, 'I'm one of the doctors who looked after your wife. I'm the one you saw here the day we brought her into hospital.'

He says, 'Not one of them other cunts?'

'No. Not one of them other cunts. I'm the one who recognised how ill she was.'

He lies in his puke and begins to weep. I look round. The caz officer is still lingering outside the cubicle not fancying it. The policeman loiters. 'If you want him, he's all yours,' he says.

'He's mine,' I say.

Shaking his head the policeman leaves. The caz officer posts the caz card in the box outside the cubicle and turns towards other cases.

With a paper towel I wipe Sweet Breath's husband's face and then I help him on to the trolley. He has a black eye, a cut lip and on his left hand I recognise the boggy bulge of a fractured fourth metacarpal.

'So you're a southpaw,' I say.

He looks down at his hand.

'Who'd you punch?' I ask.

'Not "who" – what. A wall.'

'Why?'

'So it wouldn't be a "who".'

I ask him, 'What happened tonight?'

He peers down into his puke. 'We go out in the street so she gets fresh air. People just turn their heads and look away.'

'I won't,' I say. 'Tell me what happened tonight.'

'I ain't been out in months,' he says. His hand slides over his face to wipe specks of puke from his mouth and dab the tears in his eyes. 'Not in months. I got laid off cos I couldn't keep up me shifts. Her mother's not well herself. Her sister don't wanna know. I ain't got me parents no more. It's been the neighbours and people from the council but I'm doing near all of it. Looking after her, night and day. The kids an' all. She screams in the night. Not "screams". It comes out different. But it's screaming. I gotta rub her arms and legs till it stops. Sometimes it's hours. The kids come through wanting to know why their mum's like she is.

'Some mates from work, my old work, they say, "Come out. Everyone needs a night out once in a while. Come out." A friend looks after her and the kids. I say, "One night. I can have one night." Soon as I'm walking down the street it starts.'

'What starts?'

'People. I know what they're thinking – "He oughta be home looking after his sick missus. What kind of bloke goes out on the piss with his mates when he's got his sick missus needs looking after?" I have a drink and I have another and another and another. Then I'm looking for a fight. I just wanna punch the world. She can't talk, she can't hardly move. She pisses herself. She shits herself. I have to hold her over the toilet and wipe her fucking arse for her.'

'Are you getting help at home?'

'Nothing like enough. It costs money. I ain't earning. Sometimes I think it'd be better if she'd've died. I think that. Our life, me and the kids, we'd be better off if she was dead. No cunt gives a fuck. She was sick and no one believed us. I've asked what happened. There's a solicitor asking what happened. I got legal aid. But the hospital still ain't said. This solicitor reckons it could take years to get to court. All I wanna know is what happened. I wanna know why she was seen and no one done nothing.' His head sinks. 'I just wanna know what happened.'

He raises his wounded hand. 'Now look at this. How'm I supposed to do anything for her with this?'

I give him another paper towel and he wipes the tears and snot and puke from his face. 'I'm going to do two things. I'm going to fix your hand right now. The other thing is I'm going to make sure you get help at home.'

'How?'

'I'm going to talk to someone.'

'Tonight?'

'Tonight. Give me your hand.' He holds it out to me. 'I can fuck around with anaesthetic but it'll hurt just as bad.'

'Just do it,' he says.

To put traction on the bones I draw on his fingers then with the heel of my hand I crunch the fracture back into place. He yelps. 'Now we'll strap it up. Normally the casualty doctors would call you back to fracture clinic but that's a lot of hassle you don't need. If the bone pops out again or you need to see someone about it, come to Casualty and tell them to bleep me direct.' I write out my name and bleep number on a piece of paper.

Then I spend an hour on the phone being passed from department to department till I find someone from social services who with a begrudging sigh agrees to make a home visit the day after tomorrow. I got angry when all the others said, 'It's not my problem.' I've got no right being angry. I've been saying it too.

Sally sips black tea in the doctors' mess. Lank hair hangs over her ears and with one finger she winds it in tangles round the arm of her glasses. She discards her cup. 'I can't drink this shit,' she says.

'Did you get something to eat tonight?' I say.

She shrugs and says, 'I'm fine.' Her skin is white. On automatic I scan her lips, palpebral conjunctivae and fingernails. She looks anaemic but then so do I. She looks weary, sick, beaten and cowed, but then so do I, so does everyone in this fucking place. 'I'm fine,' she says again.

We split and sweep the wards before she goes to bed at midnight.

I come across Strawberry on one of the medical wards. From the nurses' station I can hear his stridor and I search the gloom till I see him lit by a lamp over his bed, sat up, hands on knees, tossing back head and shoulders to pull in every breath and then on expiration hunching down to a ball. His eyes peer into mine with fear and confusion.

'What're we doing with him?' asks the night nurse.

I plug in my tubes and listen over his neck and chest to rasps of tightening obstruction. His pulse pounds along at a hundred and twenty. His fever soars. Sweat drenches his torso.

'Shit,' I say.

I crack open his notes and in the folder there's nothing, nothing but my admission clerking, nothing on the drug chart but the oxygen I wrote up.

'Shit.'

Plucking the handset off the phone I punch out four numbers to access the bleep system, four more to signal Anita, four more to relay this extension, slam it down and wait. 'Give him a neb and roids,' I tell the nurse even though I doubt they'll do anything but they'll make everyone here believe I'm treating him. 'Five of salbutamol over oxygen; two hundred of hydrocortisone IV.' My fingers tap out a rhythm on the wooden surface of the nurses' station. One ring of the phone and it's swinging up to my ear. The caller begins, 'I wonder if you can help me –' I snap, 'Clear this line,' and hang up. I write up the neb on the drug chart for the nurse as she passes. The phone rings again and I hoist it and hear Anita's voice. 'Did you see this chap or not?' I want to know.

'What?' she says.

'Didn't you see him?'

'I was tied up with the surgical patient and when I phoned Caz they said he'd been transferred out so I assumed ENT had taken him – why, didn't they?'

'No. I don't know why he was transferred. Caz must've got full. No one said anything to us.'

'So what was the ENT assessment?' she says.

'There isn't one. They haven't seen him.'

'I thought you were going to refer him to them.'

'What?' I say.

She says, 'I thought you were going to refer him – you know, when you called me about him, I said, "He needs an ENT opinion." '

'But I thought you meant you'd get one,' I say back – 'you'd get one after you'd seen him.'

'But that's not what I meant at all.'

'But that's the way it sounded.'

The night nurse crosses behind me towards Strawberry taking him the nebuliser. She waggles the syringe of hydrocortisone at me and I flick back a nod.

I say, 'I'm really worried about him, Anita. He's iller. His stridor's worse. I think he's got a critical airway.'

'Fuck,' Anita says. 'I'm at home – you see I forgot my overnight stuff and now I'm fifteen minutes away. I thought everything had gone quiet. Fuck.'

'I'm getting an ENT opinion right now.'

'Yes, yes – do it.'

'I'm doing it.'

I ditch the phone and run my finger down the handwritten list of bleep numbers pinned to a shelf of the nurses' station then put out a call to the ENT registrar on call then dash to Strawberry as the nurse plunges the hydrocortisone injection through his Venflon.

Now I'm waiting for ENT to return my bleep. His condition is treatable but only by them. So I write in the notes. People think doctors wield the power of life and death. We don't. Often we're no more than observers. So I record the event I'm witnessing but failing to avert as if I'm taking part from the remote high ground of the historian.

Then while I'm waiting I see her. She wears the pale blue uniform of a staff nurse. The diamond on her ring finger has been succeeded by a wedding band. She's changed her black-rimmed glasses for brown. She's returning with a colleague from break and they're stowing their bags in the sister's office when she happens to glance round and see me too. Seeing her I get a kick in the balls. Seeing her I tremble.

'Hello,' I say.

'Hello,' Donna says back.

'I didn't know you worked here.'

'Just started,' she says.

'Right,' I say.

'I didn't know you were coming back here either. To this hospital.'

'It's just something that happened,' I say. 'Not planned.'

'So you're an SHO now?' she says.

The phone rings and I snatch it up, saying to Donna, 'You haven't caught me at a good time,' even managing a wry grin.

'This is the RMO,' I tell the ENT reg. 'I've got a sixty-three-

233

year-old man severely dyspnoeic with worsening stridor after a short history of sore throat.'

'Has your registrar seen him?' he says in a plummy accent.

'What?'

He tuts. 'You know. As per hospital policy.'

'My registrar isn't available right now.'

'Sorry. Only take referrals from registrars and above. In the past, been a lot of abuse of the system.'

'This guy's got a critical airway.'

'Sorry. Need your registrar to see him.'

'Can't you get up here? Please.'

'Policy. Sorry.'

Click.

'Fuck,' I say.

Donna says, 'D'you need anything?'

'A crike set.'

'What?'

'Joking. I wouldn't even know where to start.'

I bleep Sally to be an extra pair of hands. I bleep the medical reg again. I go and take a look at Strawberry. The neb's gone through and he's still fighting for air through a narrowing throat. Saliva drools out of the corners of his mouth and down his chin. This is when I know, this is when I know I'm losing this one. His throat's closing off so he can't even swallow his own spit. First it's watertight. Then it becomes airtight.

The phone rings and I scramble back to the nurses' station to tell Anita about the ENT reg. Over her response run the sounds of travel and traffic. 'I'll call him,' she's saying. 'Give me his bleep number. Get an anaesthetist there.'

I bleep the on-call anaesthetist.

Minutes count down. My eyes keep flicking to the top of the ward in expectation of the ENT registrar's entrance or the anaesthetist's.

'What's he got?' Donna asks me throwing a glance at Strawberry.

'I think it might be acute epiglottitis. I daren't look down his throat because it can precipitate complete occlusion of the airway.'

Peering up at the clock I realise even Sally isn't going to show. It's ten past midnight. She's in bed with her bleep switched off. Anita's speeding along a hospital approach trying to persuade some ENT cunt (who probably wears a bow tie) to get off his arse and see a patient who's about to choke to death and the anaesthetist must be in theatre helping the surgeons create yet another future holder of a disabled parking badge.

No one's emerging out of the darkness at the top of the ward. When I turn back it's Donna's eyes I look into and I say what I have to say. I say, 'Ring around for a crike set.'

25: The Wound

I have a minute or two. I write in the notes the story so far. I'm writing the next paragraph in a man's life.

'No one's got a crike set,' Donna says coming off the phone.

'Who hasn't?'

'Any of the wards up this end.'

'Call ENT. We need either a cricothyroidotomy kit or a Mini-Trach set.'

She returns to the phone and starts dialling. I see her finger trembling and I reach out with my hand and see that it's trembling too. We touch and she lets out a smile like a breath of panic.

The nurse posted at Strawberry's bedside flaps her arm at me. I stride through into the bay. The curtains have been pulled round and the brilliance of the overhead lamp bounces off them hurting my gloom-adapted eyes. His nose is still big and bright and red but his lips are blue and a film of drool leaks over his chin. Every intake of breath scrapes out a high-pitched rasp.

The rasps get quieter. Less air squeezes through his throat. It's closing off now.

His eyes are animal eyes filled with the dumb dread of slaughter.

The last sound from his throat is a whimper and then he's drowning. His mouth gapes over and over again in silent futile gulps. His head tosses back and forth. Spit falls. His hands claw the bed and the rasps return but they are the scratching of his fingernails on the sheets.

His only chance is if I carry out a procedure I've never done, never been trained to do, never even seen being done. I touch his hand and say, 'I'm going to help you.'

I run out and Donna's still on the phone. Before I can ask she says, 'They think they've got one – someone's looking for it.'

'Put out a 222,' I shout grabbing a brown Venflon from the tray in the treatment room. 'Then bring oxygen tubes.'

Her voice rises to match the panic in mine as she says, 'I don't know what you mean.'

'The tubes, the tubes. The things that come out of the wall from the, the outlet into a mask. Just bring, just bring a load of stuff.'

I run back to Strawberry with the brown Venflon and as his fingernails claw the bed I say, 'This is going to hurt,' and push him back on the bed and tell the nurse, 'Hold his arms.' She clasps them but he's strong and he pushes her away and me away and claws the sheets so hard he rips them. 'Fucking *hold him!*' I say and already sniffing back tears of panic she locks her hands to his wrists. Donna runs in with handfuls of tubes and I tell her, 'Hold him down.'

I wipe his throat with a Steret and then with my left hand push back his chin. He struggles to come upright and he's a strong old bugger but I jerk it back hard. I run my right index finger down to the notch of his Adam's apple and into the dip between it and the cricoid cartilage. I unsheathe the Venflon and unscrew the cap and twist on a two-mil syringe. Strawberry sees the long thick needle and tries to writhe free but we hold him still and then bringing my elbow up and over I drive the cannula down into the dip in his Adam's apple. Blood trickles down his neck as I push through. Blood flashes into the neck of the syringe. I drive deeper to where there's no more blood and draw back on the syringe but the plunger's stuck fast. I nudge a little deeper and pull back again and this time the syringe fills with air. I'm in the windpipe but he's still clawing at us, drowning in front of our eyes.

I snap off the syringe and remove the needle leaving the plastic tube of the Venflon sticking through his throat. A minute tide of air hisses in and out. I tell Donna, 'I need a three-way tap.' She snatches one and I fit it to the Venflon then I attach a line and Donna runs it to the oxygen outlet on the wall.

'Turn it up to fifteen litres,' I say. Oxygen hisses down the line making it writhe off the end of the three-way tap. I grab the line again and tell Donna, 'Shut off the oxygen.' I snap it back over the port of the three-way tap with my fingertips though Strawberry twists and squirms in our grasp. 'Turn it back up slowly,' I say. The hiss builds and the oxygen flows down the line into the tap and into tube and into his windpipe.

We're allowing him to breathe in. We also have to let him breathe out. I turn the three-way tap for a few seconds so his lungs can push out CO_2. Blood bubbles out of the Venflon tube. When I realign the three-way tap the join hisses with gas escaping from the seal. None is flowing down into his windpipe.

Between clenched teeth I murmur, 'The fucking tube's come out of position.'

Pinching it between thumb and forefinger I try to wiggle it back into the windpipe but the resistance I get is telling me it's kinked and buried somewhere else.

My composure fractures. 'Fuck, I don't know what I'm doing, I don't even know what I'm doing.' Donna and the night nurse peer at me in horror. 'Fuck, fuck,' I say. 'Give me another Venflon.'

Donna scoops one out of the pile of tubes and lines she dropped at the foot of the bed, peels off the plastic cover and offers it to me. All the time Strawberry shreds the sheets with his fingernails. I withdraw the Venflon tube from his throat and the hole fills with blood. It gurgles and bubbles as he struggles to draw air through it. I watch the tiny wound invaginate with his inward gasp then blow out beads of blood with expiration. The bleeding leaks into his windpipe and he tries to cough it clear but there's nowhere for it to go, no passage up through a closed throat.

I force a new syringe back on to the new Venflon and slide the needle tip back through the hole in the front of his neck. It's around this time the clawing stops. With him motionless I advance the needle while drawing back on the syringe, looking for that pipe of air that runs down to his lungs. Instead I draw back blood, blood and more blood.

When Anita arrives the night nurse is weeping behind her hands and Donna and I are fumbling with bloodied hands to pass yet another tube through the congealing gravy of blood and saliva coating the dead man's throat. Anita hangs her head. When I try to take an oxygen line direct from the wall outlet and poke it into the hole in the dead man's neck she slaps my hands and says, 'Just fucking stop, for fuck's sake, just fucking stop.' My bleep goes off and I fingerprint it with his blood as I press the button to read the LED before going to the nurses' station to accept my next patient. Then I write an entry in Strawberry's notes that goes all the way to the last line.

Doctor H. pads through the door of the sister's office. I'm slumped in the chair facing the wall. I've washed my hands but I couldn't get the blood out from under my fingernails so there it remains in purple crescents.

He says, 'Why don't you tell me what happened?'

'Lots of things happened.'

'Tell me,' he says. 'I'm listening,' he says.

Footsteps gallop on to the ward outside and I turn to glimpse a breathless streak of theatre blues: the anaesthetist arriving from theatre fifteen minutes after we put out the 222. It's him again, gasping, the one with the gut and the body hair like an Italian beach vendor. He peers in and sees us so Doctor H. kicks shut the door to keep him out.

I struggle for the first words but when I find them the rest follow. 'The GP refers the patient to us. So he's in the system as a general medical patient. But after I assess him and speak to the reg about him, we suspect he needs to be seen by ENT instead. This is where the hospital policy fucks him. ENT won't accept the referral unless it's made at registrar-to-registrar level. But Anita never sees the patient because one of the caz nurses moves him out to the ward without telling any of the doctors, so when she hears the patient's not in Caz she assumes he's been turfed to ENT. On the ward none of the nurses call us to say he's getting worse. They're waiting till we come round before midnight. Now we need an ENT surgeon urgently. He insists on the policy being followed, insists on Anita seeing the patient first. Only Anita has picked that very moment to nip out of the hospital. No one's got a Mini-Trach. We put out a 222 call but the anaesthetist is busy in theatre. He's only just arrived now – quarter of an hour late.'

He furrows his brow and says, 'So . . .'

But I continue, 'So let's identify every single thing that went wrong and change policy to stop it happening again. If a patient's in Casualty and he's under the wrong doctors, the referral can be made by the juniors involved. If a patient's moved out of Caz, the nurses have to clear it with his doctors first. If a doctor needs to leave the hospital, someone of at least equal grade should be on standby. Mini-Trachs should be put

240

on the crash trolley on all hospital wards. There's probably more. I can't think.'

He nods. 'You should put your thoughts on paper. Write a letter.' He acts like he's going to say something more but he doesn't. Then he mutters, 'I know you've just had a bloody awful experience, but d'you always look this scruffy on call?'

I glance down at my stained shirt and loose tie. 'Sometimes,' I say.

'I'm being unfair,' he says. 'This isn't a good time. Yes, I'm being unfair.'

'I can't help the stain,' I say. 'Is it my tie?'

'No, I'm being unfair.'

'It's my tie?'

'The tie. Yes, it's the tie.'

'Right,' I say and stare back at him in my stained shirt and loose tie.

He says, 'Let's talk in the morning. I hope things go better during the rest of the night.' Then he gets up to go.

'Who should I send it to?' I say.

Looking back at me he says, 'Send what to?'

'The letter.'

'The letter.' He thinks. 'Send it to me,' he says, then he goes.

My bleep goes off twice before it induces me to get up out of the chair. Stepping out I notice the anaesthetist, the one from the Wheezer's intubation, slip through Strawberry's closed curtains. I catch up with him and over the body he says, 'God, I'm sorry. Really couldn't leave theatre.'

He looks down at Strawberry's throat and says, 'This is a right old mess.' Then he steps to the top of the bed and raps the dead man on the forehead. 'Anyone home?' he says.

I walk towards him and as he looks up with his usual stupid smirk I strike him hard on the bridge of the nose and he stumbles back against the wall.

In my room I don't sleep. When I close my eyes I hear a choking man's fingernails scratching his bed sheets. When I open them I stare at a crescent moon framed by the gap in the curtains.

I flick on the bedside lamp and hunched over a pad on my lap I begin writing the letter about the chain of errors that led to Strawberry's death, a chain of events I've recorded but failed to influence as if they were no nearer me than history.

Footsteps creep up to my door and then I hear a hand tapping. It's six a.m. and still dark outside.

I open the door and it's her.

She slips into the room. She turns towards me as if to say something but her gaze falls down and away towards the floor. My arm stretches towards her and her hand comes up to meet mine. We linger at arm's length and one of us, I can't even feel which one it is, draws on the other's hand. Our arms hinge down into a V as we step close and she lays her cheek against my chest. I lay my free hand on the back of her head and release her hair from its bunch. Then in slow downward strokes my fingers glide through its long brown strands.

When later we're in bed I draw myself up on my knees and lift her calves on to my shoulders and with my first stroke plunge deep into her. She gasps and cries out and as she claws my back I feel stinging tracks of pain. Her fingernails slice through my layer of numbness, my chitin, and I'm grateful to feel something, anything, electrified not to be feeling nothing.

In return I pin down her shoulders and ram hard to her cervix. She squeals and I ask her if she's OK and she says only,

'Harder.'

26: The Face

When I wake I'm alone. Light filters through the curtains on to the clock that reads seven thirty and I remember the night. I remember the dead man with a throat like it was savaged by a dog. I remember every line and curve of Donna's body, not that I've ever forgotten them. My sheets stink of our sweat, her vagina, our condom and my come. My mouth remembers the warm wet taste of hers, my tongue the juice and piss of her vulva. I remember or maybe I dreamed a crescent moon over the bed.

I stagger to the sink and pain streaks my back like a branding iron. After I throw water over my face my head sinks into the basin and I wish she wasn't gone. I should never have let it end when my first house job ended. I should've told her what I felt about her, only I didn't have a name for it, not then, not now.

The outer door creaks before I hear footsteps come to mine, a tap, and then she's slipping back into the room. She's in her pale blue staff nurse's uniform with a denim jacket over it and her hair down. 'I didn't want to wake you when I got dressed,' she says. 'I wanted to let you sleep.'

From her pocket she takes a bottle of ointment she must've stolen from the ward. She pools some in her palms and as she does so I notice purple crescents under her fingernails like the ones under mine, coloured in by the cakes of my blood and Strawberry's.

Then she rubs the ointment into the scratches on my back. Tears cloud my eyes and they might be because it stings, only might be.

'I thought you were gone,' I say.

'I'm not gone,' she says.

The post-take round surveys all yesterday's admissions plus the ones who came in during the night. Midway through the morning Sally peels off to make a call.

'Has he had his dose this morning?' she wants to know. She listens and says, 'I'll do it.'

At the end Doctor H. excuses himself to a clinic, saying nothing to me about Strawberry. His eyes flick up into mine as I peer at him. 'I'm sorry,' he says. 'I really do have to go.'

Sally and I share the list of assignments. She heads downstairs towards CCU but I know at the bottom of the steps she'll turn left instead of right and at the far end of the long corridor ascend to ITU. I know she's hurrying away to give the Wheezer his daily injection of Substance K.

After work I take the scribbles I made in the night to the secretary's office and on the computer type them up as a letter. In it I state all the errors that led to the death of the patient and the measures that in my opinion should be instituted to prevent a repeat of the tragedy.

This is where Doctor O. probably sat when she composed the document they suspended her for. I examine every line I've written. I blame no individuals. I'm clear my criticisms describe a systemic failure and the only faults I list are ones it's possible to correct.

Then I ask myself a simple question I haven't raised before. Why am I doing this? The helplessness I felt last night will pass. The memory of Strawberry will pass. Soon I'll realise the guilt I feel is baseless. I killed the Breathless Lady. I didn't kill

Strawberry. I didn't have either the specialist training or the right equipment. The hospital let me down.

I look back over my letter and censor any phrases that imply the hospital let me down. No, it's a wonderful place. I address the letter to Doctor H. I sign it and post it with the internal mail.

Half an hour later I break out in a sweat and I can feel the pounding of my heart. I run back and with trembling hands fumble through the stack of mail till I recover the letter.

The moon is real. Through my window that night I locate the crescent hung in the sky above the city lights. I wonder if there's a method that could tell me whether it's waxing or waning but if there is I don't know it. If I were giving its history then at this moment I'd be unable to say whether I was contemplating a phenomenon in bloom or one in decay.

Before sleep I read my letter over again. I can't project how Doctor H. will respond. I can't make myself objective as if I'm a stranger to my own thoughts. I wedge the envelope on my desk between the stack of CDs and the pot of the olive plant. There I find it the next evening when I finish work, and the next evening after that.

One day I show it to Rich. He reads it and says nothing till he's finished it and folded it and offered it back to me. He says, 'Don't send it.'

'Why?'

'You send this and none of the consultants'll give you a reference. Without a reference you're unemployable.'

I say, 'Maybe I'm thinking, "Fuck the reference. Just do it." '

He says, 'What will it change?'

I say back, 'What will your baby change when it arrives? Will it stop you fucking around?'

He bends towards me, bigger than me, bends his pale eyes

and light brown face towards mine. I expect a retort or even a slap but he leans away again, shakes his head and walks off. He wasn't there. He didn't see what happened to Strawberry, didn't see me butchering his throat, didn't hear the scratching of his fingernails on the bed. So, no, he won't know what it'll change.

Donna's arms loop round my back and our bare chests press against each other. She says, 'Do it like you did it before.'

'I don't feel the same,' I say.

'Please,' she says.

I rise to my knees. My hands skim over the bulges of her breasts and into the dip of her waist and under her buttocks. She twists as I lift her and her twisting ripples the thin sheets of muscle that cover her abdomen. Her skin is almost translucent. In that moment I know it's an image I'll never lose and it'll always give me a hard-on no matter how long I live or who else I get to fuck.

She shifts down the bed and lifts her legs and I enter her as they touch my shoulders. I angle forward, curling her spine, and the flesh of her belly gathers in thin folds. Then I ease deeper inside her, in and out with slow rocking motions. She gazes up at me and I down her at her. I accelerate, plunge farther. She moans. Then with a jerk of my hips I thrust so deep and hard she yelps.

'Deeper,' she says. 'Harder,' she says.

Afterwards we lie against each other like spoons. Her face nuzzles the back of my head, her small soft breasts my back, her knees inside my knees, one body moulding into another.

'Was there anyone,' she says, 'when you were away?'

'Some,' I say.

'Many?'

'No.'

'Who were they?' she says.

'Nurses,' I say. 'A physio. An OT.'

With a fingernail she inspects the scabs on my back. The edge of one has dried and she flakes off the crust and brushes it on to the sheet beneath us.

Then she says, 'What were they like?'

'They were different,' I say.

On the skin at the back of my neck I sense her mocking smile as she says, 'A blonde one, a posh one, a black one – like Spice Girls – is that how they were?'

'I didn't mean different from each other,' I say. 'Different from you.'

My eyes search the windowed rectangle of sky till from cloud they unmask the fattening moon.

'What about you?' I say.

'Me?'

'Have there been any others for you?'

'No,' she says, and then after a pause she adds, 'only him.'

'Your husband.'

She says nothing. I feel her breath quicken on my neck.

'Your husband,' I repeat.

'My husband,' she surrenders.

It's nine twenty-five. Her night shift begins in five minutes. She swings out of bed and in the phosphor glow of the clock's LED she hikes up her uniform and cuffs back her hair. In silence without moving I watch her from the bed as she pulls on her coat and lifts her bag from the chair by the desk and turns for the door.

As it swings shut behind her the door blows a current of air across my desk and in it the envelope containing my letter wags. It wags like it's waving at me, waving to remind me I've not sent it because I'm a coward, I'm a fucking coward.

The following morning I run into Doctor H. I see him try to

avoid me but when he realises I've already made eye contact he aborts the evasion. 'Good news,' he chirps. 'We're very close to making an appointment to the locum consultant position.'

'That's good,' I say. 'I was worried I was going to get into bad habits.'

'Good,' he says. Then swallowed by awkwardness he adds in a less hearty voice, 'Good, good.'

'I never wrote that letter,' I say. 'About the mismanagement of that ENT case.'

'No?'

'No. I decided it's best left in your hands.'

He cheers up so much I think he's going to pat me on the back or give me a friendly punch on the arm. He doesn't but he says, 'That's absolutely the right way to go. Yes. I'm glad. I'm very glad you've . . . In fact, we're giving it detailed considera-tion. But these things take time.'

'When d'you expect I'll hear?'

'Hear?'

'About any policy changes.'

'Oh,' he says and sinks back into a sulk. 'You'll, er, you'll hear soon.'

In the side room Blue Numbers surprises us all by continuing to live. He murmurs fragments of words and his breath is a wet rasp. When he coughs what he coughs up is sometimes red (fresh blood), sometimes black (old blood), sometimes green (infection). The lung cancer's metastasised to his skeleton. Secondary tumours seed his bones so now they ache all the time. He flits in and out of consciousness. For the pain we're giving him ever bigger doses of diamorphine.

The physiotherapist bleeps me because she was beating his chest to relieve congestion when she heard a sound like the snap of celery. I come to the ward and we talk at the nurses' station.

She's a big woman who wears the uniform of white tunic and dark blue trousers.

'I think we should stop physio,' I say.

'He's very prone to pneumonias,' she says. 'If he gets one, he's very weak.'

'I know,' I say.

'According to the notes he's still for 222.'

'That's the notes. Next to this bloke you'd stand more chance of reviving a Christmas turkey.'

She writes an entry in the notes absolving herself of responsibility and I countersign it.

In the side room I slide my hand over Blue Numbers' ribs. When I locate the fracture he shifts in discomfort and lets out a barely audible moan. Uncushioned by flesh the bones of his wasted body stick out like rails. I wish for pneumonia and the end it'll bring.

Through the gloom I come to her ward at midnight. This is my first shift on call since Strawberry died four nights ago. At the nurses' station I work through the drug charts left out by the staff, all the time looking out for her in the shadows. I hear the squeak of the drug trolley's axles but it's pushed by the night sister. I hear footsteps emerging from the sluice room but they belong to an auxiliary who's singing hymns to herself.

I resite a Venflon. I examine a woman who's complaining of chest pain. The night sister chaperones. Chocolate-brown moles mottle the woman's skin over her shoulders and her one breast. The other side is a brawny pad scarred by a mastectomy that I don't react to.

Back at the nurses' station I write in the notes. The door of the side room opens and she steps out wearing gloves and a disposable polythene apron over her uniform that she discards into a bin reserved for clinical waste. When she sees me she hesitates but then she shuffles into a bay to carry out an unnecessary task.

I loom in the opening of the bay. She looks up at me. I sit back down at the nurses' station and pretend to work. She takes the seat beside me and opens the Kardex to make notes.

'You hurt me,' she says.

'I'm sorry,' I say. 'I'm sorry I hurt you.'

'Things are a certain way. They're a certain way but not because I planned them.'

'I know.' I lay my hand on hers and after a second feel her grip.

She says, 'I didn't know my life would be like this.'

With a hard-on I wait in the corridor between the pools of brightness spreading from the strip lights spaced overhead. She appears wearing a jacket over her uniform as if she's taking one of her breaks. We lock ourselves in the disabled bathroom where I lay my bleeps side by side on the ceramic shelf of the toilet. She hikes up her uniform and slides off her knickers and I part my white coat and drop my trousers. She wiggles down my underpants and gripping the handrail we fuck.

Strawberry's post-mortem reveals he died of acute epiglottitis. The tissues of his throat grew so swollen they blocked his windpipe. The only treatment that could've saved him was a full tracheostomy performed by an ENT surgeon. Even a successful crike would've only provided enough oxygen to keep him alive for half an hour.

In the morgue they cut out all his organs and weigh them and some they'll probably stash in jars. Now bloodless the wound on his neck appears as a flap of lacerated skin over his Adam's apple as if he might only have cut himself shaving. Blue lips are grey, flaxen hair is grey, scratching fingernails are now still and grey. His struggle for life was expressed in vivid colours but now death has drained away those colours and with them stolen his body's power to tell the tale. Even the bright red of his nose is gone for good.

But in this moment with Donna I sense her warmth and wetness gulping me in. Her hands burrow under my shirt and then her fingers rip into my back. Her wetness oozes into my pubic hair. I smell the rising scent of her juice and with every stroke hear the slurp of my dick swaying in and out of her. She spreads open my shirt and bites my shoulder till skin capillaries burst into a purple wound. These are the things I feel: her cunt, her fingers and her mouth, my dick so hard it aches, and nothing else. There's nothing else to feel.

Blue Numbers' cancer spreads to his liver. I picture tumour pellets growing like pimples of mould. His skin and eyes become dirty yellow-brown. The bile salts make his skin itch so he scratches it.

I prescribe him chlorpheniramine but it never helps the itching very much as far as I can tell. I ask but he mumbles. If I thought it'd make any difference I'd scan his head for cerebral mets.

When one day he scratches into the tissue of his leg I get a sense of what that word 'tissue' really means. Soon he'll be digging down to bone.

For days Doctor H. reverts to avoiding me till the afternoon I find an official envelope in my pigeonhole outside the doctors' mess. There's one in every doctor's slot. It's from the hospital manager. It reads:

It is hospital policy to keep standards of clinical care under constant review. I remind all junior medical staff that clean, smart dress is expected at all times. Thank you for your co-operation in this matter.

251

I remember Doctor H. saying I looked scruffy when he saw me on call after Strawberry's death. And this is all they care about: whether or not I straighten my fucking tie. This is all they care about.

Later Sally calls me down to Caz to see a patient. 'He's twenty-eight,' she says, 'unemployed. He's had a severe headache and now he's got no feeling in his left arm or leg.'

'Any recent head injury?'

'No,' she says.

'Nausea or vomiting? Flashing lights? Loss of consciousness?'

'No.'

'Seizures, photophobia, visual field defects, neck stiffness, hypertension, cardiac arrhythmias, weight loss?'

'No.'

I affect the look of a man being sold a car that's two welded together.

'Sorry,' she says.

After picking up the Caz card she's begun to fill out I visit the patient in the cubicle. Sometimes you see a face you just want to hit with a shovel. His black hair shines with grease and his fat cheeks and chins droop towards a stained black heavy metal T-shirt and he wears tan-tinted glasses through which he blinks like a lizard.

'What appears to be the bother?' I say.

'I can't feel anything down one side of my body,' says the Lizard.

I manipulate his arm and leg. He has a pale pear-shaped body that leaks BO. 'You had a headache and then this happened?'

'Yes, Doctor.'

'Was it a very bad headache?'

'Yes.'

'Do you still have it?'

'A bit.'

'Where?'

'All over.'

I tut and test reflexes by swinging a patella hammer on to his knees and elbows.

'And you can move your arm and leg OK?' I say.

'A bit.'

I endure the ritual of testing sensation. I find a cotton-wool bud and make him close his eyes then stroke various pieces of skin and afterwards prick them with a pin. I bend joints to odd angles and ask him if he knows where they're pointing. I say, 'You're sure you can't feel anything?'

'Yes,' he says.

Sally fills the gap in the curtains. 'What d'you reckon?' she says.

I peer into the Lizard's eyes. He peers back and blinks: blink, blink, blink. Through a slit in the curtain behind him I glimpse the waiting area and beyond it the windows fronting the hospital. I pull the curtain slam-shut on the outside world.

'Give me a Venflon,' I say to Sally.

'What colour?'

'Green.'

She hands me the packet and I break it open. I unsheathe the cover then slide off the cannula. The bare three-inch-long needle glints under the strip lights. I clench the Lizard's fingers in my fist and ram the needle under his middle fingernail till he screams. He bucks and gasps and wrenches his hand free. He peers up at me motionless except for his lizard blink through tinted glasses. It goes blink, blink, blink. A bead of blood trickles out from his nail on to his fingertip. Open-mouthed Sally doesn't say a word.

'You're a malingerer,' I tell him. 'Now get the fuck out of my hospital.'

If the bosses don't care then why should I? And when you stop caring that's when you realise something. You realise no one from outside is watching. No one is watching me examine patients and talk to relatives and write up notes and fill in charts. They're not watching because they don't want to see what I see. They let the interior be my world.

That night I wait for Donna in my little hospital room with the olive plant and the narrow single bed and the on-call rota pinned to the wall. The full moon glows above the hospital towers and I glimpse its face. I know that now it will begin to dwindle back to a crescent. But I know this only because I'm familiar with its cycle. When I first saw Blue Numbers' crumbling body there was nothing to tell me he'd take this long to go. When I gazed into Strawberry's face with its red bulb of a nose there was nothing to tell me he'd die. There were no things to tell me except the knowledge that everything dies and in dying everything suffers.

Doctors have no more power over life and death than any other living organism. All we do is bear closer witness. Everything we feel and everyone we know will one day be extinct. And when I gaze into my own face in the mirror I see nothing that promises me any different. I see a face and I don't know if it's one in bloom or one in decay.

27: The Locum

The hospital appoints a locum consultant, Doctor E. His first round with us is on a Tuesday morning and the three of us, he, Sally and I, plod round the wards. By now it's the middle of November. Doctor O. was suspended a month ago; the hospital has still to give the grounds.

Beyond the frosted double entry doors machines intone the mechanical rhythms of ITU. Sally and I lead Doctor E. to one of our patients who twenty-four hours ago was having sex with his boyfriend and his blood pressure climbed and ruptured the wall of an artery in his head. He had a brain haemorrhage and already the physical signs of life have vanished so we define the patient by a string of numbers. Our locum consultant nods as Sally recites pulse, blood pressure, respiratory rate, oxygen saturation, blood pH, the list goes on and on. After she's finished I ask him, 'When he dies, d'you want us to get a PM?'

'Yes,' he says.

Sally gazes across a row of comatose bodies to the man in the end bed, the Wheezer. The ventilator inflates his chest with metronomic regularity. Ripples on monitor screens describe the contractions of heart muscle. She shuffles to the foot of the Wheezer's bed and on the charts confirms his daily dose of Substance K. I glance around for the blonde hair and red lips of his niece but she probably stopped visiting him weeks ago – after all, what's new to see? Instead I recognise Rich's broad frame cross–cut by the slatted blind of the office window. In the doorway I say, 'Hello.'

'Hello, mush,' he says.

'I shouldn't have left it this long before I apologised. I apologise.'

'Fuhgeddaboudid,' he says like a Mafioso.

'Fuhgeddaboudid,' I repeat and laugh.

He reaches past me to close the door and asks, 'You didn't send it, did you? The letter?'

''Course not,' I say.

He smiles. 'Good,' he says. 'They might *not've* suspended you. Seems like they only suspend consultants. If they started suspending juniors there'd be no one to do the real work. You know, there's consultants who've been suspended on full pay for *years* without charges ever being brought. There's one bloke in Cornwall got suspended fifteen years ago and they still haven't told him why. Of course he works in some nothing specialty like haematology or microbiology where he won't be missed.'

I peer out between the slats at Sally studying the Wheezer's charts. 'How's he doing on his Substance K?' I ask.

'No change,' he says.

'So how many patients have you tried it on?' I ask.

He looks around to ensure no one's about to step through the office door. 'Eleven,' he says.

'And how many got better?'

'None.'

'None out of eleven?'

'No,' he says.

'Sounds to me like Substance K doesn't work.'

'No,' he says. 'Substance K doesn't work.'

'You won't get a paper out of the trial if it's negative,' I say. 'I know.'

'No one wants to know about drugs that don't work.'

'I know.'

'"Man Bites Dog" – now that's a story.'

'I know.'

'Are you going to fake the results?'

He shrugs. 'I haven't decided,' he says.

At the end of the ward round the firm lunches together in the canteen. We've visited thirty-one patients in four hours. Doctor E. sits with us, not on the consultants' table. 'Tell me something,' he says: 'is it always this busy?'

'No,' I say. 'Today was a good day.'

He laughs. He's Nigerian. He went to medical school in Moscow and after coming here he got his MRCP. He's never held a permanent consultant appointment. No one will appoint him to one because he's African and trained in Russia. So he does locums.

'I heard about someone like that,' I say. 'He was called Slocum but his name kept getting misprinted on the rota.'

In return he asks me about myself. I give him the unremarkable details of medical school and house jobs and starting an SHO rotation in general medicine. I don't tell him I killed the Breathless Lady and then I mutilated Strawberry's throat.

He turns to Sally. She picks at her food. She redistributes it round her plate with her knife and fork but I don't see her swallow any of it. 'I'm just the house officer,' she says. 'No one special.'

Then the usual volley of bleeps truncates lunch so she and I trudge up the main corridor back towards the medical wards. Her skin is white, pink flakes peel from her nose, dark crescents underhang her eyes.

'How is he?' I say, meaning the Wheezer.

'They thought he'd got a PVS,' she says. 'But they don't think that any more.'

'He's still ventilated. Wouldn't PVS mean he could get by without?'

'That's why they think he hasn't got it,' she says.

I say, 'It's been a long while now. Maybe the time's come for them to consider switching him off?'

Incredulity shakes her head. 'But they're giving him Substance K,' she says.

A pair of tests twenty-four hours apart confirms Fucking His Boyfriend is brain-dead. The next day the family comes for the death certificate but it hasn't been filled in because we want a PM. This is the first they know about it.

The Hospital Registry bleeps Sally to come and speak with them. Though our knowledge of autopsies is small the job of requesting them is best left to clinicians. Pathologists can be such weirdos families feel like they're receiving a visit from Nosferatu. So they sit in a chintzy waiting room till someone who's been qualified a few months and knows nothing about autopsies explains why they should agree to their son/brother/ boyfriend being hacked up and fails to mention that most pathologists will stash their organs in pickle jars.

A few minutes later Sally bleeps me. 'Why d'we want a PM?' she asks me.

I call Doctor E. 'Why d'we want a PM?' I ask him.

He says, 'PM rates are low at the moment. I want us to have the highest PM rate of all the medical firms.'

'Why?'

'It's always good to be number one.' Then he sighs as he adds, 'But if you can't get one, you can't get one.'

I say, 'I can get one.'

When I arrive in the waiting room I usher the family into the office. An air of embarrassment mingles with their grief. He died during anal intercourse. It's only surpassed by victims of autoerotic asphyxiation who technically have wanked themselves to death.

'Firstly let me express my deep sympathy for your loss.'

'Thank you,' they mumble.

'What I'm asking is the hardest thing I can ask you in your time of grief. I want you to consider allowing us to find out exactly what caused someone you love to die.'

'No,' says the mother.

'No,' says the father.

'No,' says the brother/boyfriend.

Sally glances at me with a look of told-you-so but I don't even look back at her. I say, 'He might've died of something hereditary. One of you could be next.' I click my fingers – 'Just like that.'

I shove the form across the table and with only a second's hesitation the father whips out a pen.

On call tonight we admit patients as a team till midnight then Sally retires to bed. The hospital's undeviating twenty-one Celsius makes me sweat inside my white coat as if it's a blanket. I hook it over the back of a chair and strip my tie. I drop a pen into the breast pocket of my pale blue shirt and loop my stethoscope round the back of my neck.

At three thirty I'm in Caz clerking in an AE of COAD. My bleep chimes. I glance down at the LED and a pulse thrills through my dick as I glimpse the unexpected double-hash prefix Donna's begun using followed by an extension number. On the phone at the station in the middle of the department I speak to her in a whisper.

'I've got some time,' she says. 'But if you're busy . . .'

Cutting short taking the history I listen to a couple of the patient's breaths and his lungs are humming the same tune as every other pair of knackered old bellows I've ever heard. It takes me another three minutes to snatch blood gases, scribble up oxygen, nebs, steroids and antibiotics, and toss him on to the queue for a chest X-ray. I say nothing to the nurses before wrapping on my white coat and slipping out the exit.

Wind breathes through the ambulance bay. In confluent pools of light I jog along the tarmac track that leads down to the flats. Beyond the lamps leaves rustle in the dark and with the air tasting cold and clean they make me feel part of the living planet again.

In my room she's stripped and lying face down on the bed. Without speaking I swing off my white coat and then the rest of my clothes before lifting her by the hips. Just the touch, just the touch of her body and I'm hard, just the scent of her bare skin. As she kneels on the edge of the bed I stand behind and she guides me in. I cling on to her breasts as I rock in and out on my heels.

Her body tenses as she rises towards orgasm. My hands slide down her sides and grasp her hips and then my pelvis bashes her buttocks sending ripples through their soft flesh till in quick strong beats I make her come.

Tired I carry on. Her cunt dries and she moans with every grating stroke but I keep on till I'm released inside her. My dick aches from being engorged, its foreskin grazed.

I say, 'No one makes me hard like you do.'

'No one?' she says.

'No one,' I say.

She smiles and opens her arms to me. On the bed we lie in an embrace and together watch the glowing digits of the clock count down to four a.m., the end of her break.

Then she says, 'I've put in to carry on on nights.'

My lips brush her neck and my hand glides over her ribs into the dip of her waist and back up again to her breast.

'They're always short of people and the pay's better,' she says.

'That's not the reason,' I say.

'No,' she says, 'that's not the reason.'

She rolls towards me and we kiss. Her fingers renew my erection. I wince as the flesh stretches and when she begins to masturbate me the scarring skin cracks.

'Do you want me to stop?' she says.

'No,' I say.

'Come on me,' she says. 'Come on my body.'

She shifts under me and I straddle her. As she pumps me blood spots her hand.

'Do you want me to stop?' she says again.

'No,' I say.

After minutes her hand cramps so she swaps to the other. When I moan she arches her back, deepening the dip of her belly and the lines of her ribs and I become even harder, hard to bursting, pained to bursting, and then I do burst. She gasps as she feels the warm sticky come on her belly. She rubs it into her skin and I fall on her and I feel it between us like glue.

At four at the sink she rinses between her legs and over her abdomen then puts on her uniform, scrunches back her hair and from the bedside cabinet picks up her glasses and cigarettes. But in leaving she hesitates.

I hold out my hand.

Taking it she says the thing she's said before. She says, 'I didn't know my life would be like this.'

'Who does?' I say.

I draw her hand towards me and she comes back to bed. Her face lies on my chest and her hair falls down on to my skin in soft tickling strands. 'I have to go,' she says. 'I know,' I say. But she doesn't go. We nap for the few short minutes till my bleep wakes us. The first thing I feel is how much my dick hurts.

The bleep isn't about the COAD I abandoned in Caz. It's one of the nurses calling me to see Blue Numbers.

He's screaming in pain but he's too weak to make the noise. As his back arches his mouth gapes and his limbs twist and instead of a shriek the sound that escapes from his throat is a moan. Then his body falls limp.

'Where's the pain?' I say. 'In your stomach? In your chest? In your bones?' I look down into his blank yellow eyes and they're wide and glassy and he says nothing.

After a few seconds his back rises again and his head pitches back and with writhing limbs he lets out another long low moan before flopping back. I boost the rate of diamorph he's getting from his driver.

The effect only lasts a few minutes. Then it gets worse. His fingernails dig into the cotton sheet beneath him. His knuckles blanch. The tendons on the back of his hands stick out like rods. He begins to claw the mattress with both hands with such force it breaks nails from their beds and arches his wasted body. I look down into his eyes again and though they're blank and glassy like animal eyes I know behind them somewhere there remains what's left of a human mind.

I divert the nurse by asking her to phone Blue Numbers' relatives though I know he hasn't got any. As soon as she goes I remove the syringe from the driver. I hold it up to the light and count in it twenty millilitres of diamorphine. I clasp the scratching arm that bears a Venflon and I inject five mils then ten then fifteen. I look down at him as I give the overdose and I say nothing.

Blue Numbers stops scratching within a minute. When he's dead in front of me I palm the syringe into my white coat pocket and later write in the notes nothing apart from *Respiratory arrest – pronounced dead 04.55.*

Casualty – the front of house – still bustles but night has emptied the hospital interior. The clicking of my heels echoes along blank walls. In this city within a city the rare glimmers of outside life don't begin for more than a mile that's a mile through concrete, glass and steel.

I know the interior at night. I know every one of its long empty corridors and its tall empty stairwells. When I gaze down them I see no eyes looking back. I'm a tiny ant in a world of concrete and glass where the laws are different and no one from outside is peering in. No one is looking in because they don't want to, because they don't want to know what it's like.

But I can gaze out. In a stairwell I stand in front of windows that divide air of constant twenty-one Celsius from that of outside that fluctuates with weather and seasons. In this interior of twenty-four-hour illumination there's no light and shade bar life and death. Out there on the outside people slumber in their beds. Those people dream and love and watch television and believe it's real and read newspaper headlines and think they can judge. But they don't know anything. Even if it mashes my hands to pulp I want to beat on these windows till they burst and for the blast of sound to radiate into their beds and for the bursting of these windows to burst their eardrums. I want them to wake to glass shattering into a thousand crystal splinters, *I want them to wake up*, the blind unconscious oblivious cunts.

In my room I examine thin pink scabs mottling my foreskin. With hand-cups of water drawn from the sink I quench the stinging.

Then I take the syringe from my pocket. I attach it to a butterfly and pop the butterfly into a vein on my left forearm and being careful not to dislodge it I draw back to see a stem of bright blood snake back to the syringe. Then I push. I feel cold enter my arm and over a few seconds a tingle as 2.5 mils of diamorph pass into my bloodstream.

I pull out the butterfly and press a Steret over the puncture in my arm. The antiseptic stings. The square of material blots red. Then the first wave hits me like drunkenness. I feel like I've downed four pints in an instant. Convinced I'm going to vomit I totter to the sink.

There's no God. There's no God here. If there's no God then I must act in His place.

My vision blurs and I crawl back to the bed without being sick. I lie down and fall to sleep. They have to bleep me four times before I stir.

I strip to the waist and rinse my skin with cold water. My muscles tense and relax, tense and relax. My fists clench and open, clench and open. In a burst of rage I snatch the olive plant off the desk and smash it into the bin in the corner of the room. I stamp it in with my foot, crush it, crush it, stupid weak thing that may have survived but it'll never prevail, the pitiful piss-green puke-yellow excuse for a living thing.

Donna comes again at seven, after her shift. At once we fuck and I feel the scabs ripping open on my wounded dick.

'What's wrong?' she says.

'Nothing,' I say.

28: The Critical Hour

On CCU I see Anita for the first time since Strawberry died. She's presenting a patient to four medical students. Though they wear white coats I know they're students by their green name badges. Anita's hand jabs at the monitor and at an ECG in her other hand and at the patient. The students ring the end of the bed and as Anita gabbles through lists of causes and lists of symptoms and lists of everything their eyes glaze over.

The group troops out to the nurses' station where I'm organising a transfer to the University Hospital so one of my patients can have an angioplasty. Anita slaps up a chest X-ray. 'What can you see here?' she asks the students. I glance round: the patient has a pacemaker and a tiny bit of pulmonary oedema.

None of the students says anything at first. One is a big rugby-playing type who looks like he's got caught in too many scrums that've collapsed. The other boy is fat with glasses. The first girl is tall with a flat-footed walk. But the second girl is beautiful. To my jaded eyes everyone and everything looks grey but not her.

'Anyone?' says Anita.

'He's got a pacemaker,' she says, the beautiful one.

'Anything else?'

'Pleural effusions?' she guesses.

'No, that's not right,' says Anita. 'Pleural effusions appear as solid white zones at the bottom of the lungs with a fluid level and sometimes a meniscus but the hazing you see here is quite different –'

'Pul–' she interrupts trying to correct herself but Anita cuts her off by raising her voice to finish with, '– it's pulmonary oedema.'

The beautiful student purses her lips feeling slighted.

Anita jabs a finger at the square outline squatting in front of the heart and says, 'And of course you see this patient also has a permanent cardiac pacemaker inserted.'

I say, 'The thing about pacemakers is to look at the position of the wire.' The students rotate towards me. 'You're all looking at the box, aren't you? Big metal box in the chest. You haven't even noticed the wire coming out of it. I had a mate who, when he was a houseman on a cardiology firm, was given the job of looking at chest X-rays to make sure pacemakers had been fitted correctly. Except no one had told him he was supposed to be checking the position of the wire that comes out of the box, making sure it goes into the right place in the heart. So every one he looked at, he went, "Yeah, brilliant, the metal box is still in the patient," and approved them all. Three of them were readmitted with arrhythmias before anyone twigged what'd been happening.'

The students laugh the kind of forced nervous laughter that gets common as the start of house jobs approaches, all except the tall girl. Instead she asks, 'Where should the wire go?'

Anita thumps the X-ray on the light box with her finger. 'There,' she says glaring at me. She tells them all, 'Listen, I think we're going to have to leave it now because I really do have a lot of work to do and I'm afraid I've got to go so goodbye.'

After Anita goes the students linger by the nurses' station. They have nothing to do, no one to teach them. They glance towards me. I'm busy arranging the transfer of my patient. Sighing they file off the ward and disperse till lectures after lunch back at the medical school, their practical training for today finished by mid-morning.

Later Anita reappears. I say to her, 'Didn't know we were getting students.'

She pulls a face. 'They get sent to us and the first thing the consultants say is we're too busy to teach so you do it and I'm busy enough myself. What do I care about teaching? I should be learning.'

That night Donna is late. In my room I turn the syringe of clear liquid through my hands and in it as it turns the mineral glows of the bedside clock refract into a green rainbow. With this I took a life. With this I took the place of God when He wasn't there.

For half an hour I worry she's not coming, she's stopped coming. I miss her like missing my drug. When Donna raps on the door at half past eight I stow it back in the drawer and I use her to answer my craving.

Afterwards we lie on the narrow bed where drawing on a cigarette she examines the wounds on my foreskin. She blows smoke on them then laughing she kisses them. 'There, there,' she says. The sweat on our skin cools as she finishes her cigarette and before our bodies chill we wrap blankets round us.

I say, 'If I asked you, would you leave him?'

At first she says nothing. She twists under the blankets and curls her legs over mine. Her hand brushes my chest. She says, 'You've never asked.'

'No,' I say. 'But if I did.'

'You haven't,' she says.

Her hand on my chest quivers and then I feel her breath weigh on my skin. I bundle the blankets in my arms and hug them round her.

'What's wrong?' I say.

'Nothing,' she says.

267

The following morning I see the quartet of medical students loitering on a ward. Anita was supposed to be teaching them again but this time she claims she's been called to endoscopy. That would be that, another day's clinical training lost.

'I've got half an hour,' I say. 'I suppose I could teach you.'

'Thanks,' they say with shock.

'Any of you put in a Venflon yet?' I get shaking heads. 'Taken blood?' More shakes. So I supervise them as with trembling fingers they take blood from a patient who doesn't need his blood taking and put in Venflons on patients who don't need theirs changing.

I save the patient with the easiest veins for her, the beautiful one, whose name is Victoria. The skin over her cheekbones, her perfect cheekbones, glows red as she struggles to advance the clumsy plastic cannula.

'Too deep,' I say. 'Make the angle shallower. Aim to skim the vein and let the needle bite on the wall.'

She holds her breath. The Venflon pierces the vein and blood flashes into the chamber.

'In it goes now. Slide it in.'

She runs in the tube and pulls out the needle. Her lips part showing even white teeth. Her blonde hair shimmers. Her skin without a single flaw gleams. Her face is the face of an angel.

'Now,' I say, 'to some *really* important stuff.' I point to the fat one with glasses. 'Matthew, unbutton your white coat. Never wear the white coat buttoned. It makes you look like a paedophile.' The others laugh. Matthew unbuttons.

'Next. Stethoscopes. Wear them round your neck – like this.' I loop mine behind my head and set the earpieces on the front of one shoulder and the bell on the front of the other. They copy.

Then I pluck a sleeve of X-rays out of the notes trolley and lead the students to a light box. I give them one each and show them how in one movement you slap the film on to the box and flip its edge under the clip. 'It's all in the wrist,' I say. Laughing, they take it in turns. The rugger bugger, Angus, is the first to get it right and we give him a round of applause.

In her hand I notice Victoria is holding a CT scan of someone's head. 'OK, now we're into registrar territory. This'll look very impressive in your exam. Victoria, put the CT on the box in the correct orientation.'

She squints at the crowded gallery of images, turning them through ninety degrees, then flipping them over, then turning them back again, never making up her mind.

'OK,' I interrupt. 'I'll close my eyes. You turn it any way you want then give it back to me.'

I lay a palm on my face and a few seconds later Victoria says, 'Ready.' I open my eyes, give one glance to the CT and sling it on to the light box the right way up and facing the right way.

Pulling the film off the box I point out a small indentation in its edge. 'Here's the secret. This little dent always goes in the top right corner.' Victoria and the others smirk. 'Just look for the dent. Forget about all these fiddly little pictures. Put one of these babies up the way I've shown you and in the exam you'll walk a grade A. Shit, they'll probably make you a professor.'

Esther, the tall flat-footed girl, interrupts, 'We're supposed to be doing the heart today.'

'OK,' I sigh. I take them to one of my patients who has cardiac failure. I explain his condition as if the heart were a blocked sink.

Matthew says, 'What about atrial myxoma?'

'Never seen a case,' I tell him, 'because rare conditions are *rare*. In medical school, they make you think, if you hear the sound of precipitation hitting the roof, it must be raining frogs. It never rains frogs in this hospital. It just rains rain.'

'But we've got to know it for the exam,' he says.

'Apart from straight after an MI, if someone has heart failure it's almost always because they've got long-standing cardio-vascular or respiratory disease. If it was something more exotic you'd have to send them for an echocardiogram. That's where the myxoma would be diagnosed, not at the bedside. All that kind of stuff is Victorian medicine. Doctors couldn't intervene so they sat at the bedside recording all these weird and wonderful signs and when the patients died they made the diagnoses at post-mortem. It's different now. Learn the basics of *managing* disease. Learn the things you'll have to do as doctors.'

Esther says, 'Sorry, I know you're only trying to help, but it's one of the conditions we're supposed to know about.'

'It's true,' says Victoria. 'That's what they'll ask us about in the exam.'

I mumble. 'I'm sorry. I can't remember the signs of atrial myxoma.'

For the rest of the morning I think about Victoria as if she were a single vision of loveliness from a lost summer, a girl standing on a platform in a pretty dress as my train pulls out of the station or a face in the crowd on the quay as my boat puts to sea, never to be seen again. I like to think she's untouched. She's as yet uncorrupted by this world.

From the window of my room I study the wind gathering dead brown leaves in cyclones. Then night joins Donna and me. Fucking and then lying together, my dick aches from how hard she makes me. I touch her body and at once I feel myself stiffening again. She turns into me and soon we're fucking again with no foreplay.

Afterwards she says, 'Sometimes I wish we could go out. For a drink or a meal, or to the pictures.'

I say, 'We can.'

270

'We can't,' she says.

And I find I'm thinking of Victoria. I'm thinking she's a virgin with odourless skin and soft white pubic hair.

'What's wrong?' she says.

'Nothing,' I say.

The following week outpatients' clinics resume. While Sally looks after the wards Doctor E. and I split the medical students into two pairs and sit them in the corners of our consulting rooms. I get the rugby-playing bloke (Angus) and Esther, the tall flat-footed girl. Whenever a halfway interesting case comes in I duck my head through the connecting doors to Doctor E.'s suite and suggest the other two students might like to see it too. Victoria glides in beside Matthew, the fat one with glasses. I think she's the most beautiful girl I've ever seen. When she returns to Doctor E.'s clinic animation drains from my voice.

The nurse is busy so I step into the waiting area to summon the next patient. As I call his name I glance round the room to track who's going to respond. Among a bank of seats outside a different clinic sits Sweet Breath's husband and facing him in a wheelchair Sweet Breath herself. He looks up as I call my patient's name and as I scan the room our eyes meet.

'I'm sorry,' I tell the man who shuffles towards me, 'go through – I'll be a couple of minutes.'

I cross the room and sit for a minute with Sweet Breath and her husband. She makes a noise when she sees me that's a noise of recognition. I smile at her and I say, 'Hello.' She makes a different noise now that's the sound that'd be words if her tongue and palate could move as she wants them to. She tries again and becomes frustrated. Her husband lays his hand on her twitching waving arm and she tries to push it away but she has no control of her limb. So she falls silent and tear ducts empty into her rolling eyes.

271

Her husband's unshaven so a dark paste of stubble straps the bottom half of his face. Darkness rings his eyes. Even if I couldn't smell it on his breath I'd know from the hand tremor he's drinking too much.

'Are you getting more help?' I say.

'Some,' he says.

'What about your compensation claim?'

'The solicitor says there ain't a case. There's no proper records or nothing she was seen, that's what he says. We've told him to keep on to 'em. He says it'll be years before we hear anything.'

I say, 'I'm sorry.'

'Fuck it,' he says.

He looks down. Sweet Breath shakes her head and lets out a shrill moan. I turn to go but he stops me. He says, 'It ain't just the money.'

'What is it?'

'I wanna know what they done to her. We trust you people – we come in here and . . . I wanna know what they done to her. And I want 'em to look us in the eye, not hide behind lawyers, look us in the eye and say, "Sorry." '

Now I'm standing here in front of him knowing what I know but not able to tell him because without any evidence it'll be no help to his case unless I agree to testify against the hospital and if I do that I'll be a whistle-blower and I'm more concerned about being suspended and ostracised than I am about helping him and his wife. I look away. I've become yet another of the ones who can't look him in the eye.

Mid-clinic we're entitled to a ten-minute tea break. The two students and I drink from clean white cups. The cups come with saucers and there are even biscuits. I've forgotten that apart from the outpatients themselves I like Outpatients.

'Got house jobs sorted yet?' I ask them.

272

'Yeah,' says Angus.

'Yeah,' says Esther.

'Any thoughts on what you want to do?'

'Surgery,' says Angus, the rugger bugger.

'Because it's intellectually undemanding?'

He laughs.

'No,' I say, 'I'm asking. Why d'you want to do surgery?'

He hesitates. 'I don't know. Just fancy it, I suppose.'

I glance at Esther. 'Paeds,' she says.

'Why?' I say.

'The same. Just fancy it.'

'Let me ask you something. Why'd you guys want to be doctors in the first place? Can you even remember?'

'*Yes*,' Esther says.

'So what was it?'

'I wanted to help people. Present tense: I *want* to help people.'

'I did too,' I confess. 'When I was a kid I wanted to help people and I wanted to save lives. And what if in your job you find you can't?'

'I don't think like that,' she says. 'I don't believe that's what'll happen.'

I turn to Angus. 'And you? Why'd you want to be a doctor?'

'The same,' he says.

'You wanted to help people and save lives?'

'Yes,' he says.

'And?' I say.

'And what?'

'And what else tipped you into deciding to apply to medical school? The apocryphal stories about medics taking morgue corpses on pub crawls?'

He laughs and says, 'Might have.'

'And what else?' I say.

'The real reason?'

'The real reason.'

'Well,' he says, 'the real reason – apart from all the helping people stuff – was that doctors seemed to do loads of cool things and sometimes they got to shag really fit women.'

Esther purses her lips in disgust.

I ask him, 'Which doctors?'

'On TV.'

'You're right,' I say. 'That's exactly like it is on TV. I think I thought the same as you when I was seventeen.'

He grins and shrugs.

Swivelling in my chair I peer at them both and say, 'You want to know something? If you can, just get out. I'm not saying you're not up to it. You are. But, if you can, trust me, just get the fuck out.'

They exchange a look. They don't know whether I'm serious.

'I mean it. Just get out. Before it's too late and there's nowhere left to go.'

They peer into their cups of tea. We get cups and saucers with biscuits: *This can't be a bad life, can it?* they must think. They look at each other and in their look I see mockery, disbelief, dismissal. Our break ends and the clinic continues. They don't say another word to me till it's over. Even then they just mumble, 'Goodbye.'

As I lie in a bed that smells of our sex my hands trace the dips and crests of Donna's body. I feel the warmth of her skin, warmth tinged by the wetness of spit and perspiration. Soon we're napping in each other's arms but my bleep goes off. I'm still inside her. I roll for the phone and my shrunk dick slips out of her. A caz nurse says, 'There's a patient for you.'

'Haven't you called Sally?' I say back.

274

'This is for you,' she says. 'You'd better come straight away.'

Dressing I gaze at Donna where she sleeps. Her knees curl up to her chest and vertebrae line the middle of her back with a chain of humps and dimples. I set the alarm for nine twenty, in time to wake her for her shift, then brush her cheek with my lips. 'Bye,' she murmurs.

Dead leaves squelch underfoot as I cross the wet grass of the quad. Wind rushes between hospital buildings and clouds blanket the sky. Nothing about the world has changed. I read no portent.

In resus two patients slump on trolleys being cut out of their clothes. Smoke has blackened their bodies. They cough and moan. As the nurses scissor their clothes I see their bodies aren't black but more of a grey colour. A few parts are bright red.

Mister M. and a caz officer struggle to get an intravenous line into one of the patients. She looks to have 40 per cent full-thickness burns. Mister M. is searching for a vein in the arm, hunting from the elbow down. The arm ends early, its fingers melted into a clump. The burns are painless because they're deep enough to have destroyed nerve endings but the swelling's too severe for Mister M. to cannulate a vein.

'I'm going to do a cut–down,' he says.

I ask, 'D'you want me to try a central line?'

Mister M. ignores me and begins to slice into the skin of the patient's ankle.

'I can't see!' the patient keeps shrieking in an accent I think sounds Middle Eastern and calling out to the other patient, 'Where are you? I can't see! I can't see!' Fire has vaporised the patient's eyelids and scorched her unprotected eyes. The rest of her face has swollen and blistered. I can smell the vaporised flesh. It smells like roast pork.

The other patient's burns are worse, probably 60 per cent. Though the deepest ones are painless, the patient is crying out.

In her eyes and nose and mouth I recognise Down's syndrome. The tissues covering her trunk are so swollen they're impeding chest expansion. One hundred per cent oxygen isn't enough.

'Escharotomy,' says Mister M.

She screams though not from pain as the registrar carves three long straight scalpel incisions in vertical lines from the collarbones to the bottom of the ribcage. The swollen tissue parts like the flesh of a peach being thumbed open and the chest expands to take in breaths through shrieks and calls to the other patient.

A nurse who's cutting clothes grabs my arm and says, 'This one's yours.' As she shoves me away I glance back at the patients: a twenty-five-year-old mother with melted eyes, face and hands, and her six-year-old daughter, screaming for her mother to stop the doctors hurting her.

'This one's yours,' the nurse repeats and there on the side not even on a trolley is a six-month-old baby. She shakes her head and says, 'Do what you can,' before scurrying back to the other two who are the ones who stand a chance.

'Where are paeds?' I say. 'Where are the paediatricians?'

No one answers. It's just me in the corner of the resus room with the dead baby. I wipe the soot from its face but the skin is cold. With my index finger I sweep round its mouth and throat for foreign bodies. It doesn't even gag. Turning the outlet up to fifteen litres per minute I hose oxygen into the baby's mouth. When nothing happens I roll the baby over, chest on to my palm, and slap its back five times to dislodge any airway obstructions. Its arms and legs dangle towards the floor. Its body is heavy and cold, its skin livid. Then I feel for a pulse on its cold neck then bag in a couple of breaths before beginning chest compression with the tips of my index and middle fingers.

Behind me I hear voices. Mister M. is shouting at the others, 'I'm doing a bloody cut-down and that's final.' The little girl is shrieking for her mother not understanding why these strangers

276

are hurting her so much. The mother who's blinded is calling back that she can't see her little girl. Then she calls out to know about the baby. I don't turn. I don't say anything. I finish the cycle of chest compressions and give oxygen again.

'I need help here,' I say. 'I need help to intubate.'

No one answers.

'I need help here,' I repeat. 'Where's the anaesthetist?'

No one's listening. They're fighting for the two live ones.

I decide to intubate anyway. From the shelf I grab a slim endotracheal tube and lighting the baby's throat with a laryngoscope I try to wiggle it into the windpipe. It takes two or three goes, maybe a minute, but I get it in. I pump twice on the bag and see the baby's chest rise twice. I feel for a pulse. There's no pulse. I swing a defibrillator into position and read a rhythm through the paddles. The screen draws the flat line of asystole. I pluck an adrenaline Minijet off the crash trolley but I can't see any veins so I attach a green needle and spear between the ribs into the heart. I squirt in one-tenth of an adult dose which is a guess. As I withdraw the needle there's no blood just a clean puncture mark. Then I resume the cycle of oxygen and chest compressions.

Using the defib paddles I read the rhythm again and it's still asystole. I shock anyway. There's no reason left not to.

'I'm calling this one off,' I say but no one's listening. I haven't even looked to see if it's a boy or a girl. When I glance down at the dead baby I see my own hands blackened by soot.

By now the nurses are loading the six-year-old with Down's on to a trolley. Covered in dressings and a space blanket she's got blood and fluids running and she's going to ITU. She's calling out for her mother and her mother is calling back.

Mister M. continues to struggle with the cut-down. He's sliced open the flesh of the mother's ankle in search of the long saphenous vein but he can't locate it.

'Bloody thing . . . ' he's muttering. 'If I can only . . . Bloody thing.'

One of the nurses has prepped the central line but she's forced to idle at the head end and throw imploring looks at the other doctors. She looks at me. I'm about to react.

Another nurse scurries in from outside. 'There's another smoke inhalation,' she says.

'One for the RMO, I think,' says Mister M.

'OK,' I say. The nurse with the central line peers at me as I leave. I look away.

I follow the other nurse out of resus into the hall and along to a cubicle at the other end of the department. There's a policeman outside and another inside, the one who kicked Sweet Breath's husband when he was on the floor.

Handcuffs lock the Smoke Inhalation to the trolley. Soot cakes the face and hands of this fat unshaven man of about forty with long bushy hair swept across a balding scalp.

'Why handcuffs?' I want to know.

'He's the one started the fire,' the copper answers.

'I'd like to examine him alone, if that's OK.'

'No fucking way,' he says.

The other policeman calls him out with a flick of his head.

'Have it your own fucking way,' says the copper, the one who assaulted Sweet Breath's husband. 'We'll be right outside.'

I draw the curtains and turn up the Smoke Inhalation's oxygen to 100 per cent. When I put the mask to his face he pushes it away. I say, 'I need to listen to your chest, please.'

'What the fuck for?' says the Smoke Inhalation then coughs for about twenty seconds.

'I think that kind of answers the question for you.'

But when I reach towards him with my stethoscope the Smoke Inhalation pushes me away. 'Fuck off,' he says.

'I need to listen to your chest. There could be lung damage

278

that if we don't treat now will give you chest problems for the rest of your life.'

This time the Smoke Inhalation complies. Though soot smudges his face and hands I see no burns. My stethoscope prowls his chest in small leaps, transmitting two breaths from every spot I press it. Wheezes and crackles pop in my ears.

I offer him the oxygen mask again. I ask him, 'Why'd you start the fire?'

The Smoke Inhalation pushes the mask away. He coughs again and this time spits black phlegm on to the floor next to the trolley. I pluck a styrofoam bowl off the shelf and sit it in his lap. 'Use this.' He spits again, on to the floor again. 'Please don't do that. Why did you do it?'

'Fuck off.'

'Did you know there was a family in that house?'

'Fuck 'em,' he says.

'The baby's dead. The little girl's got less than a fifty per cent chance of survival.'

The Smoke Inhalation spits again, leaving a black bubbling coin to blister the floor. 'Fuck 'em.'

I say, 'You've got a reaction in your lungs to the smoke you breathed in. I'm going to give you an injection and some fluids.'

He shrugs. I sweep open the curtains and the policemen step in. The younger one, the violent one, tinkles the handcuffs.

'You're fucking cuffing me again?' he says. 'I'm ill. I'm fucking ill and you're cuffing me. Fucking tell 'em, Doc.'

I say, 'He's got inflammation of his lungs from inhaling smoke. I'm going to give him some steroids.'

'See?' says the Smoke Inhalation.

'Do we cuff him or don't we?' says the copper.

'It's up to you,' I say and with a smile he locks the handcuffs round the chrome trolley rail.

In the storeroom I swing open the drug cupboard door. My

finger taps each packet as I read the names till I find one containing hydrocortisone ampoules. My hand lingers on it but doesn't bring it down from the shelf. Instead I choose potassium. As I draw it up I remember the dead weight of a baby in my hands with its arms and legs dangling towards the ground. I remember cold skin covering a body that's heavy in all the wrong places, pale or livid in all the wrong places.

The Venflon pierces a vein in the back of the Smoke Inhalation's forearm. He winces and clenches a fist at me but the policemen restrain him. Trembling I screw the syringe into the injection port. I study the clear fluid that with pressure from my thumb will drain into his blood and stop his heart.

Out in the department a porter wheels the six-year-old girl flanked by a nurse and an anaesthetist. The girl cries out for her mother. I watch them mount the slope of the corridor and beginning the journey to ITU then either to death or a lifetime of operations they turn out of sight into the interior of the hospital.

My thumb presses the plunger. The pressure builds till it punches open the valve of the injection port and the first dribble of liquid creeps towards the Smoke Inhalation's bloodstream.

At the curtains appears the nurse from resus who was holding the central line that no one dared put in.

'You've got to do something,' she says. She sniffs and flicks a tear from her eye. 'Please,' she says. 'He wouldn't call in the paediatricians because they won't be pushed around by him. He won't call the anaesthetist because he thinks it shows A&E can't handle a crash on its own.'

I stare down at the syringe of potassium hoping she'll just go away. I want her to go so why doesn't she? She stands by the curtains on the hospital side of the cubicle beckoning me back in.

'Fuck it,' I say and pluck out the syringe and throw it in the sharps box.

'Hey, what the fuck's going on now?' the Smoke Inhalation asks.

I ignore him and with the nurse I go back to resus and as soon as I'm through the doors she prepares the central line and I start feeling for landmarks under the patient's clavicle.

'What the bloody hell do you think you're playing at?' says Mister M.

'I'm putting in a central line.'

'Not without my say-so you're not.'

'I think it's time for you just to shut up.'

All the others look away removing themselves from the confrontation.

Mister M.'s eyes catch fire and he says, '*How dare you even contemplate talking to me like –?*'

I snarl, 'Fuck off.'

My hands are trembling now, trembling I'm not going to get this line in. With the central-line needle I dig under the collarbone, pushing under the skin towards the opposite shoulder aiming for the subclavian. Mister M.'s huffs carry up from the patient's feet. She twists on the trolley. 'Hold still,' I say to her. 'Please hold still.'

'My baby?' she cries.

'Please hold still,' I say.

'My baby?' she cries again.

'We're treating your baby now,' I say. 'We're doing everything we can.'

I push deeper and I see blood from the subclavian gush into the syringe. I twist off the syringe and against the spurt of blood I feed a guide wire through the needle. Next I withdraw the needle. To ream a big hole in the skin I ram a dilator over the guide wire and wiggle it and discard it then thread the central line over the guide wire. All the while blood seeps from the wound and the woman cries out for me to stop hurting her and I feel her blood hot and sticky between my fingers. I slide out the guide wire and at last begin stitching the central line in place as the nurse begins connecting the bags of fluid that've been languishing on the side for fifteen minutes. 'Well done,' she whispers.

Mister M. claps his hands. 'Come on, everyone, let's get moving. The critical hour. Chop-chop!'

His eyes patrol the room and rest on mine. I stiffen as he opens his mouth but a nurse interrupts to say to me, 'The father's in the relatives' room – d'you think you might talk to him?'

'Yes, now, go,' says Mister M. and drops his look back to his patient.

I push out of resus into the department. I wash my hands then tread round the bottom cubicles towards the small room behind a varnished wooden door. My eyes fix on the door handle and every step carries me to the threshold. Inside waits a man who doesn't yet know his baby's dead and his little girl will probably die and his wife is blind and disfigured for life. This is the long walk when you wonder how they'll react, when you wonder how much of their pain they'll try to make you feel.

When I reach the door I don't pause. To pause is fatal. I rap on it with my knuckles and swing it open and step in and shut it behind me. Then my eyes swing up and I introduce myself. He wears an anorak over a waiter's uniform and he's middle-aged, perhaps as much as twenty years older than his wife. Now I wonder if I misunderstood the nurse when she said 'the father'. Perhaps he's the woman's father and the children's grandfather. I can't allow it to faze me so in the same clear measured metre as my introduction I say, 'We're doing everything we can but your family all have serious injuries. Your wife has bad burns and I'm afraid her eyes are affected. She may become blind.

Your little girl's burns are worse. They may be so bad that she won't survive. We did our very best but, I'm sorry, your baby has passed away.'

In the same Middle Eastern accent as his wife he just says, 'Yes.' She must be his wife. They must be his children. Surely he would've corrected me otherwise. His head sags and I stare into thinning curls of wiry black hair. On automatic I continue,

'I know this is terrible news. This is hard to take in. But your wife and little girl are in good hands. We're going to transfer them to our Intensive Treatment Unit. They'll receive the best care we can give.'

'They throw stones at my home,' he says. 'They know when I am at work. Then they throw stones. My wife, in the street, they spit on her.'

Now he begins to sob.

'I'm sorry,' I say. 'I should go back.'

He manages to nod and I walk out. In the hall I can hear the screams still coming from resus and the shouts of the Smoke Inhalation. He's shouting, 'I'm fucking ill. Where's my fucking treatment?' As I pass the cubicle he sees me and says, 'There he is, the fucker. Oi, where's my fucking treatment?'

'Fuck you,' I say.

Trembling and hyperventilating I break out into the cold air of the ambulance bay. I choke back tears and almost fall against the outer wall of the building. Against my cheek I feel the bricks' punctate roughness. Fighting not to cry out I push my face against the masonry and scrape my cheek till the graze hurts so much I have to stop.

The lithium wind breathes on my face, chilling my skin, and I fill and empty my lungs with it but I can't stop shaking. I wish I'd been able without compunction to inject the bastard with potassium. That is what in that moment I wanted to be. In order

283

to introduce justice into the world around me I nearly became not a saver of life but a taker.

Light spreads from the atrium through the windows into the forecourt. An ambulance pulls up and its beacon flashes so that my white coat and white skin blink to blue. The bay slopes up to the roadway where lamps make dots of light like a necklace round the perimeter track. Beyond the hospital the city lights are winking out for the night. Darkness only begins outside the hospital but tonight and every night it cloaks half the Earth.

29: The Horse

But tonight my bleep won't stop singing. In this place only the dead sleep. No one dies in the ambulance before they get here. No one gets better all of a sudden and decides they'd rather go home. From midnight till nine I work snatching ten or fifteen minutes of rest at a time, rest being solitude in substitute for sleep. When at last sunlight leaks like oil from the windows my body is spent.

By now Donna's gone home. I try the mobile and a man's voice answers it so I hang up. The graze on my cheek is clean and as stubble grows through it's becoming less conspicuous. But even a wound that heals doesn't do so without leaving some kind of scar.

In the doctors' mess I make myself a cup of tea. There I see Victoria by herself waiting for the other medical students. I surprise her by making her a cup. I ask her, 'Would you like to come out for a drink sometime?'

'Oh,' she says. 'When?' she says.

I say, 'Tonight.'

She hesitates and then she says, 'It's great that you've shown an interest in teaching us when loads of people don't, but I really only want to be friends.'

I know she isn't interested in me but I pretend, I cling on, I say, 'Just friends. Tonight, then.'

The other three students appear in the doorway. I whisper

the name of a pub near the medical school, one I know she'll know. She nods in surrender then she gets to her feet and scurries to the others.

Before I'm ready to confront the rest of the day, the day after I nearly murdered someone, I'm bleeped to the morgue. One of my dead patients is dead of something interesting that's interesting at least to the pathologist and she wants to share it with me and by now I'm more engaged by reasons people die than by reasons we live.

I stride into the morgue and the pathologist greets me with a smile of welcome. She points me towards her workbench. On it I see a chopping board, the kind you find in a kitchen. Splayed out across it with its tiny arms and tiny legs is the baby from last night. Its tiny limp arms and tiny limp legs dangle over the edges on to the bench. Its body's slit open navel to neck. Maybe even it's strung out and pegged like the frog in a school biology lesson but I don't know because I turn away so fast, so fast for the rest of my life I'll never know if there are strings or pegs or I've just imagined them.

That evening I take the remaining two and a half mils of diamorph. When the rush comes I'm ready for it, I'm steady for it. When the nausea passes I'm still sat on the bed propped up against the wall.

I swing the butterfly in my hand. I swing it like a shoelace. I pinch the plastic wings between my thumb and forefinger and with the needle scratch an inch-long cut in my forearm. I feel pain. It comes in answer to my craving to feel something, anything that normal people get to feel. I etch deeper till it bleeds, till blood bursts out like come, till I feel its release. Then I turn the needle at an angle and make a second lac across the first. I make a cross on my arm and watch the blood dribble

286

over my skin. I gasp in ecstasy at the tickling creep of warm wet living liquid.

A bus carries me across the city till the giant pale grey obelisk of the University Hospital calls out my stop. In the pub I wait for her and as the yawing hands of the clock above the bar insist she's not coming I swallow drowning gulps of lager. I used to come here when I was a student. This place hasn't changed since then. It remains dead every night of the week except Friday, with the same pictures on the wall and the same rings printed on table tops like fractals of the Olympic emblem and the same mix of locals and medical students negotiating a border truce. This place may not have changed but I have.

Then I see her scanning the room.

I buy her first drink, my fourth. She's nervous. She's nervous because of how I'm acting. When she buys cigarettes from the machine and lights one it makes me think I'm wrong about her being a virgin. Tobacco soots her lungs so maybe there's grime and corruption throughout her body. When she puts the cigarette to her lips and draws in a mouthful of smoke I remember the apocryphal story of the student who like everyone else in her histology class scraped a few cells off the inside of her cheek to study under the microscope but then she saw a type of cell that wasn't in the textbook so she asked the tutor to take a look and he identified it as a sperm. She offers me a cigarette and I giggle. I giggle about the girl at the microscope with a mouthful of blow-job debris and I giggle at the incongruity of saying, 'No, thanks,' to a cigarette when I'm pissed and opiated.

She asks me, 'What's so funny?' and I answer, 'Nothing,' and she frowns.

But I look at her and I still don't want to believe she's not pure. Soon after drinking the next round I say, 'If someone's breathless, you should always think of a pulmonary embolism.

287

All you have to do is take gases.' I throw my hand on hers. 'Tell me you won't forget. Tell me you'll never forget that.'

Victoria pulls her hand away. 'You're weirding me out. Maybe it wasn't such a great idea for me to come here.'

'I just want to protect you.'

She sneers in disbelief. '*What?*'

'Listen to me. *Listen*. You're still untouched by it all. You're uncorrupted. It's not like you ever imagine it's going to be.'

'I've heard that before,' she says. 'I've heard it, like, a zillion times. I'm sick of listening to cynical housemen and SHOs.'

'They're telling the *truth*.'

'It's *not* true. Just because it is *to you* doesn't mean it will be to anyone else.'

'But I want you to know the truth. I want to spare you what it's done to me.'

She steps back and makes gestures with her hands that in their flurries seem experimental and mean nothing. I fear she's going to leave so I start gabbling. 'I know you don't see it. It's like, it's like when they used to paint horses. You know how they used to show horses in paintings when they were galloping across meadows and over fences and shit? They used to have them with all four of their legs sticking out in every direction. You've seen those old pictures, right, you've seen them?'

'Mmm,' she says because she doesn't want to encourage me but under my imploring stare she adds, 'yeah, I think so.'

'Well, that's how they used to think horses ran because it was before films and photographs and shit. It was the artists' freeze-frame view. And everyone believed it. Then years later, ages later, when they'd invented photography, someone took a series of photographs of a horse galloping. And when they looked at them everyone saw that horses don't run with all their legs sticking out, they run like, well, like we know horses run.'

She says, 'I don't get what this has got to do with anything.'

'Wait. *Wait*. I'm getting to it. So immediately after they've proved how horses run, artists start painting 'em that way, the *right way*. And guess what happens? People looked at these paintings, and, because they've been used to seeing 'em the old way for so long, they say, "These paintings are stupid. Horses don't run like this. They run with all their legs sticking out." D'you see? D'you see what I'm trying to say? Everyone's so used to thinking about medicine the way it's talked about by people who know fuck-all about it or the way you imagine it as an ideal that they don't believe you when you tell them the truth.'

'I don't know what this is all about,' she says and she's raising her voice so people turn and look. 'I don't think this is even anything to do with me.'

'It is, it is to do with you. Because you're innocent. That's what they use to betray you. Your innocence. They take all your expectations, all your idealism – There's no God. If there *was* there'd be no suffering and there'd be justice. It's medicine. It's not what you think it is.'

'I think I'd better go,' she says lurching away.

'Don't you see, don't you see? – that's what *I* thought when they said it to me. But it's not true. The job isn't what you think it's going to be and it changes you and I don't want it to do to you what it's done to me, don't want it to turn you into what it's turned me into –'

'I'm going.'

She strides out. I want to follow her but more I want to sit here, I just want to sit here for a while surrounded by chatter and jukebox music and people who don't know what I've done. That'll make me feel better. Just sitting here for a while. Then I'll be fine again. Then I'll be myself again.

In my bed I sleep for a few hours. I sleep off the lager and heroin and then I wake but nothing has changed. Things aren't returning to what they were and I stare through the window of my room into the fading glimmers of the outside world knowing they never will return to what they were no matter how much longer I sleep.

Donna taps on the door at 7 a.m., at the end of her shift. 'I came before but you weren't here,' she says. She sits on the edge of the bed. 'What's wrong?' she says.

I don't even get the word out. I try to say, 'Nothing,' but I don't even get the word out before my shoulders heave and tears flood my face.

She cradles me in her arms and at last I let myself fall. I fight to wipe the tears and snot from my face, to recover, but I can't. I can't even lift my head from her lap.

'What's wrong?' she says. 'What is it?' she says.

I find my voice but what comes out is just a croak. I croak, 'I want to be me again.'

She cuddles me and all I can do is cling on and let her body hood my head with soft comforting darkness.

PART FOUR

Blowing The Whistle

But cursed are dullards whom no cannon stuns,
That they should be as stones;
Wretched are they, and mean
With paucity that never was simplicity.
By choice they made themselves immune
To pity and whatever moans in man
Before the last sea and hapless stars;
Whatever mourns when many leave these shores,
Whatever shares
The eternal reciprocity of tears.

From 'Insensibility', Wilfred Owen

30: The Butterfly

Machines beep and on monitor screens they stencil waves. When an alarm shrieks the nurse makes soft plimsoll steps to the bedside and there he or she pushes the RESET button so the same tuneless song can resume. I study the machines and the body before me and the others around me. Some lie in coma. Others are doctors like me and they're standing and speaking but nothing of what they say is registering.

As a child I wanted to be a doctor when I grew up but now I am a doctor I've also grown up. Yet nothing outside of me has altered. No process in the physical world has altered to reflect the thing I've become. My spirit resembles the bodies of the old as through disease bits have grown on and bits have been cut away. But nothing is expanding to occupy the vacuum of what I've lost in the last one and a half of my twenty-four years; no pressure is shifting to balance what's been grafted on, and when I move through these hospital vaults I displace the same volumes of air.

When I begin listening again the ITU consultant, Doctor T., is saying, 'Given the persisting absence of neurological response, I consider it now appropriate to test for brain death.'

'I think so, yes,' agrees Doctor E.

As they drift away from the Wheezer's bedside to begin the paperwork Sally asks me, 'Why can't we give him a bit longer?'

I say, 'Because he's deader than Elvis.'

Rich frowns at the deadness in my voice and whispers to Sally, 'They'll do one set of brainstem tests today and repeat them tomorrow. You could say that's giving him another twenty-four hours.'

She says, 'But he's not even that old.'

I say, 'He's dead: you can't get much older than that.' Then I begin to wander away from the bed where the Wheezer's lain for the past four months under a bank of monitors whose beeps and wavy lines have fabricated his only signs of life. Yet Sally remains as if standing vigil and for a moment I manage to gather enough energy to deal with someone else's feelings but mine, someone else's torment but mine, and I say to her, 'This'll all be over. This'll all be over tomorrow.'

She nods and says, 'Yes.'

'We ought to get back to the wards now. There's too much to do to be standing round here.'

She says nothing back but turns with Rich and me for the frosted double doors where we pick our white coats out of the ones on hooks and proceed to the lifts where Rich pushes the button displaying a down arrow.

'How does this affect your study?' I ask him.

'It doesn't,' he says.

I say nothing back. Now I don't give a shit about Rich's study or anything else for that matter. I think he mistakes my silence for tact. He says, 'Because, even though we're switching him off, he did better on Substance K than he'd've done without.'

Sally glances round at him but even when he infers this is a cue to elaborate she's already folding back into her own thoughts. He shakes his head at us. 'No. Not really. Only according to my "results".'

A motorised whirr delivers the lift to this floor and after the ping that goes with the flashing light the doors part and the three of us step in to join someone in theatre blues. I glance at Sally as the doors close and her eyes are fixed on the jumping lights with her face white and blank. On the next floor down the person in blues, either a theatre nurse or an ODA, marches out and as it's just us three white coats again I say something if only to kick through the deadness surrounding me.

'You've faked them?' I say.

'Who doesn't?' Rich says.

We descend another floor and the doors open but no one's waiting. I lean forward to punch the close-doors button and in doing so I glance at Sally's profile and observe in her face the same fixed blank look.

'Who doesn't?' Rich repeats but I know his voice so well that I recognise the inflection's wrong, that he's masking his feelings beneath indiscreet jollity. 'Everyone does it, because there's this pressure to reproduce positive results, and those original positive results were probably people faking them in the first place. It's the system: you can't change it, and, this way, everyone's happy. My boss is happy because he's going to be the first in this country to prove that Substance K benefits patients with cerebral anoxic damage. The relatives of patients are happy because they think something positive's being done. The drug company's happy. Their shareholders are happy. And I'm happy. I don't piss off my boss, I get a great couple of lines on my CV, I get a leg-up towards an SPR post. This is my fucking career. You can't change the system so you do what you need to do to prosper within it. Everyone does it. It's hardly such a big deal. Patients with cerebral anoxic damage are fucked to begin with. Giving 'em Substance K's hardly going to make things any worse. Who gives a shit?'

The doors open on to the ground floor and we wander out into the corridor. Rich opens his mouth like he's got even more crap to come out with but he hasn't. He hasn't got any more to say. So he turns in the opposite direction and Sally and I trudge towards the medical wards. 'Are you all right?' I ask her.

'It'll be over tomorrow,' she says.

'Listen, I can't come to the ward just yet. I've got a meeting. I might be some time. I don't know.'

'OK,' she says.

Sally recedes through doors and by the third set I lose sight of her. I tread a busy corridor and all along it I concentrate on my feet in an attempt to render my normal walk instead of a guilty nearly-murderer's walk. Grey clouds mat the squares of sky framed by high windows and though daylight is weak I miss it as with the next corridor I plunge deeper into the interior where the light is harsh and electric. Among the people ahead of me I detect a dark uniform. A policewoman is walking towards me. I begin to sweat and hyperventilate and then she passes. She might even have glanced at me and smiled and I might even have thought she was attractive. I don't know. I half expect more of them to be waiting when I knock on Doctor H.'s door but of a different type: sour men in suits exuding halitosis.

I stumble, 'You wanted, wanted to see me –'

'Come through, please,' he says.

Doctor H. widens the door so I can see a figure standing by the bookcase who turns to reveal he's Mister M. Now I'm shaking. They can both see I'm shaking. Even if I hide my hands and plant my feet it's still here in my voice like a tremolo. Mister M. sits and seating himself Doctor H. indicates a third chair that I tread to and lower myself into and before I'm all the way down he starts, 'I've called you here to discuss a very serious allegation. Normally there'd be a disciplinary protocol for this kind of thing but I believe that we can reach some kind of resolution that might obviate that. That's why I've agreed to mediate.'

'This kind of conduct just isn't acceptable,' says Mister M.

and though Doctor H. sighs and raises a palm to halt him he continues, 'The very foundations of hospital practice are teamwork and professional respect. As soon as one person starts thinking the rules don't apply to him, then the whole system falls apart.'

I stop trembling. I should feel like dancing round the office as I realise they're 'only' talking about my insubordination but I'm dead inside. I say nothing. I don't even lift my eyes to theirs. I act like I'm not part of the scene but instead of being the blurred figure flashing through I'm static and Doctor H. and Mister M. and everything else appear in motion around me as if I'm furniture.

'What would be a start,' says Mister M., 'would be if he even *acknowledged* it. If he even –'

This time when Doctor H. raises his hand he knows to follow fast with speech. He says, 'Let's just be absolutely clear about the issue in question. Last Thursday night – Thursday November nineteenth – the Accident and Emergency department dealt with three patients recovered from a house fire.' He counts them as three. He doesn't mention the fourth who was the Smoke Inhalation and the man I came close to murdering.

Mister M.'s impatience conquers him and he interrupts, 'There's no "question" about it. I gave you a clear instruction and you disobeyed it –'

'You inserted a central line –' Doctor H. counter-interrupts.

'– and compounded it with the rudest, most offensive conduct I've ever –'

'– and, when the instruction was repeated, you responded with foul and abusive language.'

They finish and I look from one to the other. My hands and feet have stopped their trembling and in a steady voice I say, 'Yes, I know.'

'So what, may I ask, do you have to say for yourself?' says Mister M.

'Nothing,' I say.

Doctor H. blows a big sigh and says, 'Shit.' He leans across his desk and says, 'We're trying to help you here. None of us want this to become a disciplinary matter. If there's been a misunderstanding or there's been a personality clash, now's the time to reach some form of accord so, as I say, we can avoid it becoming . . . I'm repeating myself . . . becoming a disciplinary matter.'

I say nothing.

Mister M. says, 'An apology would be the least – the very least – I'd accept.'

'I'm sorry,' I say then negate it with a shrug.

Mister M. gasps and throws his hands up in the air. I don't even look up. 'What?' he snaps. 'You think a consultant's in the wrong, who's leading his department in the treatment of three simultaneous cases of major trauma, doing all that only to be abused by some silly prick of an SHO?'

Doctor H. flags Mister M. to calm down and says to me, 'This is out of character. Maybe it was banter that got out of hand. I don't know. I wasn't there. But great offence has been taken and I don't believe it's asking too much for you to provide some kind of statement of regret. You're far from being a bad doctor. You're normally a team player. You can be a smartarse at times, a bit of a smug bastard, but normally a team player. From what I've heard perhaps this was a distressing case and perhaps you allowed it to cloud your judgement. I won't say you shouldn't ever get emotionally involved because that's bullshit. But I'm certainly here because I want to help you out of this hole you've dug yourself into. Cultivating the ability to get on with your seniors is an essential prerequisite for success as a junior hospital doctor.'

'I know,' I say.

'Good,' he says.

'As soon as someone's labelled a troublemaker,' says Mister M., 'that's it. That's it for him.'

'I know,' I say.

Doctor H. sighs again and leans farther over his desk and says, 'Are you going to say *anything* in your own defence?'

'You don't want me to defend myself. You want me to say I was wrong and to apologise and to promise it'll never happen again.'

Doctor H. grins his wry grin and says, 'That'd be nice.'

'This is pointless,' says Mister M. 'This turd hasn't shown one iota of regret.'

Doctor H. waves at Mister M. again but this time his flicking wrist betrays annoyance.

I say, 'I'm prepared to express regret. I regret that it wasn't possible in the situation described for the patient to receive the appropriate standard of medical care and at the same time for the chain of command to be preserved.'

Doctor H. sighs yet again. '*Shit*,' he says.

Mister M. says, 'What *exactly* is the accusation you're making?'

'I'm saying, for reasons best known to yourself, you refused to call in the appropriate medical specialists to deal with a paediatric emergency and an anaesthetic emergency. In regard to the management of the adult patient, you might've said, "Go ahead, try the central line, I'll keep trying to get this cut-down." But, no, you had to make it about your ego and your authority.'

Mister M. leaps to his feet and shouts, '*How dare you? How dare you?*'

'OK,' says Doctor H. coming round the desk to intervene between us, 'I can see there's no point carrying on with this meeting. This matter will be dealt with at a formal hearing to be notified next week. Unless the complaint is withdrawn.'

'No,' says Mister M., 'the complaint is most certainly *not* withdrawn.'

'Next week, then,' concludes Doctor H.

I hoist myself to my feet and slouch towards the door without even looking round. In the hall outside I experience a moment when I believe I can still go back in and say how sorry I am, how I might be acting disturbed and I need sick leave and it could still be swept under the carpet with the sort of sympathetic noises the seniors like making from time to time to appear more humane if only to their wives. But I don't.

Now I'm plunging through corridors towards A&E. I look through the cubicles and in resus till I find the nurse who persuaded me to put in the central line. 'I need a witness,' I tell her. 'You know he should've called in paeds and an anaesthetist.'

'Yes,' she says.

'You saw him fumbling with the cut-down. You realised the patient should've had a central line.'

'Yes,' she says.

'So you'll testify on my behalf?'

She hesitates. After a few seconds she asks, 'And say what?'

'What d'you think? That the patient needed a central line and you asked me to put one in her because the consultant wasn't managing the case properly.'

'I can't say that,' she says.

'Why can't you say that?'

She says, 'Because that'd make me a whistle-blower, wouldn't it?'

One of my patients on the ward is an Oriental man who speaks little English and the nurses bleep me to report that although we're treating him for a stomach ulcer he's complaining of some sort of problem with his back. When I lift the tail of his hospital gown I find between his spine and right shoulder blade a carbuncle that's bulging as tense and purple as a plum. I brandish a needle and scalpel and he nods and this constitutes informed consent. Many of our patients don't speak much English and because the hospital translators never seem to be in the hospital we end up practising this form of veterinary medicine.

I plunge local anaesthetic into the skin, slice out an incision and peer in. Membranes honeycomb off each other, sectioning the abscess into chambers. I compress the walls with my thumbs and a river of bloodstained pus erupts down the Chinese Carbuncle Man's back. I slice through more membranes and squeeze out more pus but every time I think I've eradicated the infection I find another chamber that's deeper, better hidden, better protected.

In my room I lie on the narrow bed staring at the ceiling till daylight fades and I'm peering through grey at the outline of the bulb and the tops of the cupboards. A slit of window is open to suck out the scent of Donna's cigarette ash. I tip out the secret drawer and from it strip syringes and butterflies still in their packets and drop them in the bin. I've suffered no cravings for diamorph and I don't want it any more.

When Donna taps and enters I go to her and kiss her mouth. 'How are you?' she says.

I make us tea and she smokes a cigarette. Then we lie on the bed and though we undress we don't have sex.

'Is it all right if we just talk a while?' I say.

'OK,' she says.

We cling together in an embrace while I tell her about my meeting with Doctor H. and Mister M. Afterwards she kisses my chest. I feel the brush of her breath on my skin.

'How d'you feel?' she asks.

'What d'you mean?'

'D'you ever wonder if you should be doing this job? I do.'

'And what d'you think?' I say.

'I think I can take it,' she says. 'I think this is the right job for me. And you?'

'The same,' I say.

I loop my arm across the bare skin of her back. I feel the ridges of her shoulder blades on my forearm and as I kiss her hair I take in its scent. She's clean and fresh before her shift, still clean and fresh because I've not leaked sweat and spit and spunk on her.

'Let's go out one day,' I say.

Her breath presses against me. I feel her weight change.

'Why not?' I say.

'You know why.'

'I'd like to. Just once. One weekend. Go somewhere far away from here.'

'I can't,' she says. 'Don't ask me.'

'I'm asking,' I say.

'Don't,' she says.

She lifts her head and kisses my chin.

'What are you going to do?' she says.

I've been thinking about it all evening and not reached a decision. I'm on my own now. I know no one will back me and maybe I'll even be without Donna. But when she asks me I'm naked beside her and an answer forms on my lips and it feels good to hear me say it, feels like me again, so I say it. But I only say part of it. I don't say the part about my own self-destruction. I only say the part that's, 'I'm going to get the bastards.'

31: The Exit

The Wheezer's niece glances at me through her eyelashes and I see her cheeks flush red like her lips. I cast my gaze to the floor. Doctor T. says, 'We're ready now.' A middle-aged man who Rich says is the Wheezer's bumpkin brother from Somerset nods and Doctor T. presses the button and turns off the machine. The whooshes of mechanical inspiration and expiration halt. The beeps of the cardiac monitor persist for the few heartbeats expected before the myocardium runs out of oxygen.

But when the beeps don't stop I look up from the floor and peer into the monitor then at Rich. He frowns and Sally's face opens and the brother and the niece turn to Doctor T. He stares at the line on the screen continuing to sketch peaks and troughs with the speaker continuing to intone the rhythm of life holding on to life. The Wheezer's going to take a breath. Sally's eyes dart from the screen to the body and back again. Her face is bright and its brightness wills the man to live.

Then of course it ends. The beeps fade and the monitor shows no more upstrokes and downstrokes but just a flat white line stringing from left to right across the bare black screen.

Satisfied, the niece and the brother go into the office for a few kind words courtesy of Doctor T. When they come out again the niece glances in my direction and for a moment I worry she's going to approach me. I wonder about her breast lump. I wonder if she got it checked out or if she was too scared to. But instead the brother huffs at her with impatience so they turn and leave ITU and then leave the hospital altogether.

'Must've parked his tractor on a yellow line,' I mutter to Rich.

Sally is watching the nurses remove the tubes and lines from the Wheezer's body. The endotracheal tube slides out of his throat trailing streaks of phlegm and blood. The central line has melted into the tissues under his collarbone so when they pull it out a few clumps of flesh come attached. They pluck a Venflon from his arm and tug out of his urethra the catheter whose tip has been floating in his bladder so it's coated with congealed urine. They wheel the ventilator into the corner and soon the porters will come to zip him into a body bag for transfer to the morgue. On the phone outside the office I hear the ITU sister passing the message that they've got a vacant bed and they're ready to accept another patient.

'It's over,' I say to Sally. 'You can put it all behind you now.'

'It's over,' she says.

In Outpatients' reception I ask the secretary to give me the occasion of Sweet Breath's next appointment. I have lies prepared but I don't need them. Without even glancing at my name badge she punches into the computer then scribbles out the information on a slip of paper and hands it to me across the counter. 'Thank you,' I say. I consider the date and it's next week so I'm going to have to move fast.

I present a list of names to Doctor E.'s secretary. She's the same woman who was Doctor O.'s secretary, the former Doctor V.'s secretary who shagged him over the bonnet of his Volvo.

'Can you obtain these patients' notes?' I ask her.

'No problem,' she says.

Later that day she bleeps me. 'There's a problem,' she says. 'One of the notes has been sequestered by the legal department.'

I bleep Rich and ask him, 'What's the official code for the Substance K trial?' He gives me the details and I stalk off in search of the legal department. I locate it in the new building that's sprung up within the hospital grounds that when I was a houseman was the construction site where I shattered the nail of my big toe on the night I killed the Breathless Lady.

The assistant is very helpful. I quote the official description of the Substance K trial and tell her I need use of the notes for a couple of hours as part of the research project. When she brings them out they're sealed in a transparent plastic envelope inside which they're bound by criss-crossed elastic bands. She breaks the seal and hands them over. I sign a document to state they're in my care. 'I'll have them back by the end of the day,' I promise.

She smiles and says, 'No problem,' and I stroll out with Sweet Breath's notes tucked under my arm.

I rendezvous with Doctor E.'s secretary and she hands over a folder containing among others Strawberry's notes and the Shoulder Boy's notes and I hide them all in my room.

At the end of the afternoon the legal department assistant bleeps me to say, 'According to our records, Doctor, you're holding a patient's notes which have to be returned.'

I say, 'I finished with them ages ago. I gave them to a porter to bring back.'

'Oh,' she says.

'These things happen. Big hospital.'

'Big hospital,' she says.

Optics glint in the mirror behind the bar and in it I glimpse my own reflection. I gaze down and I'm there with a spoon face in the lustre of the pumps. The picture doesn't lie. I might like to pretend I'm Serpico but I'm still the doctor who killed the Breathless Lady.

When I glance up again the barmaid asks me my order and I come back with the name of a bottled beer I notice cooling in the fridge behind her. I take my first sip while I wait for change. The glass neck is cold in my hand and the liquid chills my lips and palate.

I take my change and turn at an angle to lean on the bar as while reading a newspaper I throw looks to the door that's fogged by condensation. She arrives ten minutes later and we shake hands.

'It wasn't too far for you to come?' Doctor O. asks unbuttoning her coat.

'No problem. I relish every opportunity to experience this city's public transport system. What would you like to drink?'

'No, no, I'll get it,' she says.

'I'll get it. I'm the one in work.'

Doctor O. grins but I see she doesn't enjoy the joke. 'Sorry,' I say and buy her a drink. She folds her coat over a neighbouring chair while I drop my jacket on to the back of mine and here we sit at a table in the corner where a stubby candle dribbles wax onto a saucer and I rock my beer bottle on its edge in arcs across the dark hardwood table.

'How's it going?' I ask her.

'It's a piece of shit,' she says. 'I'm taking legal advice. But lawyers just love to move slowly. If tomorrow in work you see one in cardiac arrest, spend six months exchanging documents before you start treating him. See how they like it.'

'D'you hear the one about the lawyer who went potholing? Before he could leap out of the way, a stalagmite grew through his foot.'

She unzips her bag and without lifting out the packet she produces a cigarette. 'Want one?' she says. Dipping the beer bottle from my mouth I shake my head. 'Filthy habit,' she says and lights it and then waves away the smoke.

308

'Have the hospital given grounds yet?' I say.

'Grounds for the suspension? No. Look, I don't mean to be rude but I'm not in the mood for discussing my fall from grace. Sorry.' She stares into her glass of wine before draining a sip.

'I'm going to blow the whistle,' I say and she looks up. 'I'm going to come clean about the diabetic misdiagnosis, and about some other things too. There are four cases I've got intimate knowledge of. The one you already know about is the diabetic who's now in a wheelchair, as I've just mentioned. There's a boy who had his arm wrecked. There's a man who died of acute epiglottitis. And there's one other.'

'D'you want a piece of advice?' she says.

'I know what you're going to say.'

'What am I going to say?'

'You're going to say, "Don't do it."'

'No. That's not what I'm going to say.'

'Then what are you going to say?'

She says, 'I'm going to say, "*Really, really* don't do it." I thought like you. I thought I could fight the system. I waited till I was a consultant before I spoke out, because I thought by then I'd have the power to put things right. And they still managed to screw me. What makes you think you'll fare any better?'

I take a sip of my beer. 'Nothing,' I say.

'Then why're you doing it?'

'Because I'm a doctor. Because we're supposed to help people.'

She finishes her wine and stubs out her cigarette and I watch its last emission climb in a spiral rarefying into the air above. She shifts with a sharp movement like I've upset her somehow. 'I'm going home,' she says. 'Good luck.' Then she clinks her wine glass on the table, picks up her bag and coat and crosses the bar to the door.

Through the windows I watch her blurred figure reach the

street and throw up her arm to hail a taxi but it doesn't stop. She fumbles in her bag and with some juggling lights another cigarette. Then she glances back towards the bar and sees me peering out at her. She's crying. I stand to go to her but with her next hail a taxi pulls up and she clambers in. As she glides out of sight I slump back down and try to finish my beer but I can't because I feel sick now with fear.

The clock on the wall above the waiting area in Outpatients edges towards the time of Sweet Breath's appointment and I begin to worry she's going to DNA. A sister approaches me and asks, 'Are you doing a clinic, Doctor?'

'No, Sister,' I say.

'May I ask what you're doing here?'

'I'm waiting for someone.'

She glares at me in disapproval. I think she imagines I'm loitering so as to sexually harass one of the nurses. Then I hear the tyres of a wheelchair squeaking across the floor and I turn away from the sister to glimpse Sweet Breath's husband parking her adjacent to a crowded bank of seats. He doesn't look up as I pad towards them. She sees me first. She makes a low noise. I never know whether it's a greeting or whether it's an accusation since maybe in her mind I'm among those she blames for her condition.

'Hello,' I say.

He looks up and when he recognises me he lowers his eyes to the back axle of the wheelchair where with his foot he's kicking on the brakes. 'What d'you want?' he says.

'I can help you,' I say.

'I don't need no help. Believe it or not, I'm used to this by now.'

'I mean I can help you with your lawsuit against the hospital.'

Now he looks up. He says, 'I want 'em to admit they made

310

mistakes. I want 'em to say they're the ones done this to her. And when all's said and done I want 'em to look me in the eye and say they're sorry.'

'They will,' I promise.

The long, long corridor slips behind me and I pass through the swing doors at its end. There are no windows and my eyes are mole's eyes under the crackling strip lights. Arrows point into a set of steps and I follow them down to a pair of oak doors. When I push through them the floor under my feet becomes carpeted and around me I don't see any more uniforms, only suits, and the smells aren't hospital smells but those of offices. I'm treading deeper into the interior than ever before.

At an L-shaped reception desk I give my name and the receptionist advises me to take a seat. After removing my white coat and folding it over my arm I sink into a soft leather chair where in front of me on a square glass coffee table lie magazines arranged in a spiral-staircase pattern. In my hands I hold a beige A4 envelope that I place on my lap and from it I slide a set of documents atop which rests the letter instructing me to attend a formal disciplinary hearing today.

I wait ten minutes. Then a man my age wearing a boxy suit emerges from a door to my left and throws a glance to the receptionist who stabs a finger in my direction. 'Would you come in now, Doctor?' he says to me. I stand and straighten my tie and then I follow him through that door to the left.

In the room a long narrow wooden table reflects light showering from the ceiling. Four men in suits horseshoe the far end: from left to right they're Doctor H., someone I don't know at the head of the table, Mister M. and another person I don't know. The man at the head of the table indicates a chair facing them all. 'Please sit down,' he says. The young guy who walked me in pushes a glass of water in front of me and then takes a seat by the wall where with a pad balanced on his knees he begins to make notes. The man at the head of the table tells me his name and says, 'I'm the Medical Director.' That leaves only one man I don't know and he's the man on the far right who's middle-aged and has retaliated against male-pattern baldness with an all-over number-two cut.

'First off,' says the Medical Director, 'let me say how much we all regret that efforts to deal with this matter informally proved unsuccessful.'

I say, 'And first off I'd like to ask a question.'

'You'll get your chance,' mutters Mister M.

'No,' I say, 'I think I'll ask my question now: By what authority am I being charged? Because it seems to me that, if there was a case against me, it should be referred to the General Medical Council.'

'No one wants to go that far,' says the Medical Director, 'unless we have to.'

'As far as I understand it, I'm being accused of insubordination. I know of no guidelines that prohibit clinical disagreement between doctors.'

'I'm sure you're well aware,' says the Medical Director, 'of the greater authority of a consultant's clinical judgement and your failure —'

'I know all that shit. I think I was right to do what I did. You people insist I was wrong. But it only amounts to a departure from medical etiquette. For this to be a disciplinary matter, surely you have to prove my action was negligent. And negligence should be referred to the GMC. Do you think I was negligent?'

The Medical Director stumbles, 'No one wants to label —'

'*Do you think I was negligent? Yes or no?*'

'No one's accusing you of negligence,' says the Medical Director.

Doctor H. who's clever enough to anticipate my comeback winces just before I say, 'If there's no negligence involved, then I don't have a case to answer. I've got nothing against marsupials, but this is a kangaroo court.'

'This isn't a kangaroo court,' says Mister M. 'This is a legitimate disciplinary committee and you'll be bound by its verdict whether you like it or lump it.'

No one else says anything. Mysterious Number-Two Cut scribbles a line on a notebook. Doctor H. gazes into space appearing embarrassed about the whole set-up.

I say, 'Then I'd like to put forward an argument in my defence.'

'Of course,' says the Medical Director.

'This is sounding less like a defence and more like an attack,' mutters Doctor H. and then I'm shocked when he chucks me a wink.

I stumble before I say, 'I observed a failure to provide prompt, appropriate treatment and concluded that a patient's life was in jeopardy.'

'Do we really have to listen to this shit?' says Mister M.

'Yes, you do,' I say back but Mister M. is rising and strolling to the trolley by the back wall where he pours himself a cup of coffee from a cafetière. 'Anyone else for tea or coffee?' he says.

Trying to ignore him I say, 'I judged that it was necessary to depart from the consultant's course of treatment in order to act in the patient's best interests. This was a clinical difference of opinion. Given that you ask me to accept that a consultant's opinion is, a priori, superior to an SHO's, I'd agree that this is almost invariably true. However, through first-hand experience, I've come to doubt this particular consultant's clinical competence.'

Without even turning round Mister M. spits, 'Oh, please!' but before he can continue I pluck the documents out of my

313

envelope that relate to Sweet Breath and the Shoulder Boy and throw them across the table. 'These are photocopies.'

Mister M. spins round from his coffee distribution. Doctor H. and the Medical Director exchange glances and even the boxy-suited stenographer looks up from his note-taking.

I carry on, 'They demonstrate two previous cases, one in which failure to diagnose diabetes led to a patient's severe disability and another in which failure to carry out a safe shoulder relocation caused a functional limb deficit.'

Next I shove the other half of the documents across the table. They're Strawberry's notes and the Breathless Lady's. 'In addition, I've assembled documents relating to two other cases. In the death of a patient from acute epiglottitis, I provide evidence of a catalogue of errors, all of which relate to hospital policy. When these comments were presented at the time, no action was taken. The fourth case is of a failure to diagnose a pulmonary embolism in a patient who subsequently died. The family is unaware of medical error contributing to the death and this information would allow them to make a claim for compensation.'

Mister M. huffs but produces nothing resembling speech. Doctor H. stays calm as he flicks through the documents on the table and doesn't even look up at mention of his unwillingness to act after Strawberry's death. None of them have looked yet at the notes on the Breathless Lady that prove the fatal error was mine.

Eventually Mister M. says, 'I'm sure there's a breach of patient confidentiality involved here. Not to mention slander against me.' No one pays him any attention.

The Medical Director says, 'What's the purpose of all this?'

'I'd like you to consider policy changes to stop these tragedies occurring again. I'd like you to institute an inquiry into the running of the Accident and Emergency department. Rather than entangling them in litigation that takes so long they're likely to die before it's concluded, I'd like you to settle out of court to compensate these patients and their families. I'd like you to establish a reporting system so members of staff can notify errors or near errors, and the information be used to make policy changes to prevent them happening again. The system should be confidential and anonymous, and anyone reporting an error should be able to do so with impunity. Finally, I'd like these patients or their relatives to be told the truth about what happened to them, not lied to and fobbed off. I'd like them to be told by the doctors involved, not by lawyers, and for the doctors to say they're sorry. I think that's all.'

The Medical Director shakes his head in disbelief. 'I think you might have to accept that the balance of power in this room is somewhat in our favour.'

'In this room, maybe. But all this happened in the hospital, and I think you might have to accept that, out there, compared to me, you don't know shit.'

Doctor H. looks across to me and says, 'And if we don't do what you say – what then?'

'In the case of the diabetic patient, the solicitor acting for her husband had always been informed her notes were "lost". Ironically, last week they *were* removed from this hospital's legal department and no one's even got round to tracing their whereabouts. It's highly likely they've fallen into the hands of this solicitor. A similar case at a different hospital led to a damages award of 8.3 million pounds.'

The Medical Director clears his throat and starts to say something more than once before he settles on, 'I think we'll adjourn things here. Perhaps you could wait outside whilst we deliberate on, these, er, matters.'

As I turn to go Doctor H. says, 'Why're you doing this?' but I don't answer.

Out in the reception area I retake my seat and as I do so I see the door of the meeting room swing shut. I glimpse a narrowing frame that contains Mister M. flinging his arms in rage and Doctor H. shrugging before the edge of the door and the door frame fold together like a shutter. On my side of the door I'm surprised that there stands the man I don't know, Number-Two Cut, and then to my greater surprise he wanders towards me.

'Sorry about that,' he says.

'Why're you sorry?'

'I don't think it went very well for you.'

'Who are you?' I ask him.

'I've been appointed by the BMA,' he says. 'I'm your representative. Sorry, I've got to be somewhere else.' He offers his hand. 'Bad luck,' he says. He shakes my hand then strolls out of the exit.

32: The Spectre

I slump back in the soft leather chair and my white coat blankets my lap. My stethoscope's rubber earplugs poke out from a pocket so I flick them with my fingertip over and over again to watch them oscillate on their metal prongs.

Maybe right now in the boardroom they're studying the documents. They're coming across the Breathless Lady's file and reading that a year and a half ago a houseman told her that her PE was an anxiety attack then a couple of hours later she was dead. They'll look into the case and everything will come out at last – the chain of errors, the cover-up, and my guilt. Things will go back to the way they were. Medicine will be the noble profession again. I will be the person I was before.

My bleep goes off and I ignore it but when it goes again with the same message I decide I may as well respond to it. The receptionist lets me use her phone and at the other end a nurse says, 'Would you come to the ward and write up some TTOs?'

'Sounds uncannily like a houseman's chore to me.'

'But Sally's off.'

'She shouldn't be.'

'Well, we've been bleeping her all morning and there's been no answer.'

I fob off the nurse and try bleeping Sally myself. I prefix my message with my own bleep number so she'll know it's me contacting her. When she doesn't answer I worry.

317

Ditching the phone I scurry across the carpet to the exit and as I mount the bare stairs I throw on my white coat and by the time I'm back in the corridors I'm running. Soon there are windows and as these vaults tunnel out and spiral out then cold grey daylight begins to appear in them. The air grows cooler and fresher in my throat and on my skin.

I begin on CCU. I dial Sally's bleep number and then I listen out. Through the beeps of monitors and the chatter of staff and patients I try to pick out the chime of my signal being received. I move to the next ward and the next and the next. Eventually I hear a remote sound. I'm on one of the medical wards and I don't locate the noise before it stops so I bleep her again. This time I can associate its origin with the aisle leading off the ward but I'm not sure if I'm just mistaking it for another sound. I bleep once more and while the signal travels through the air I sprint into the aisle and when the bleep responds I know it's out here somewhere. I run down towards the nurses' locker room and find it empty but the staff toilet in the alley next to it displays the red swathe of occupation. When I knock on the door I do so feeling foolish but there's no reply so I rap harder. When still there's no reply I say, 'Anyone in there?' and then I say it again louder but still there's no sound from inside. 'Shit,' I say out loud to myself and then run back to the ward from where I phone Maintenance to send someone up with a tool kit. When the man arrives he's short with a big moustache and sounds Spanish or Greek. He begins to unscrew the hinges and I ask him to hurry and he says, 'Patience, my friend, patience.' When the hinges are released I lean on the door to force a gap and through the gap I glimpse the hem of a white coat and the legs of someone slumped on the floor. 'There's a doctor in here,' I say to the man from Maintenance, 'and I think she might be seriously ill.' He turns into a ball of fury kicking at the door and shouting so loud that people dribble off the wards to investigate the commotion. Together we knock the door off the frame and slide Sally out into the alley. She's pale and comatose with a thready pulse and sweat has chilled on her skin. A narrow trickle of blood has dried by her elbow where she punctured a vein. In the bathroom I register a used syringe and butterfly on the floor but no drugs. I search the bins but can't find any empty vials. A sheet of paper balances on the ceramic shelf of the toilet and I know at once it's a suicide note and I know she meant to kill herself because of the note and because of the steps she's taken to avoid detection and conceal her choice of overdose drug. Asking one of the nurses to bleep Rich because he's someone I can trust we turn Sally into the recovery position and I start examining her while a ward sister cuffs her arm with a sphyg.

'Pupils are reactive,' I say. 'Dilated. Not opiates.'

While we measure pulse, blood pressure and temperature I pass a Venflon and from it drain off a syringe of blood for tests. Rich arrives and together we go through a checklist in *The Oxford Handbook* but we still can't figure out what she might've taken. A nurse passes us Sally's suicide note and I read, '*I became a doctor to save lives. No one told me it had to be at the expense of my own.*' Rich and I pause for a moment and he says, 'Fuck.' That's all either of us says.

'The rest of it is just fucking scribble,' I say squinting at some lines she must've tried to add as she was losing consciousness.

'But nothing about what she took?' he says.

'If there was, I'd've kind of mentioned it.'

By now we've connected her to a cardiac monitor and though her pulse is weak and racing her heart's in sinus and a Guedel airway arches over her tongue to protect her windpipe. 'OK,' I sigh. 'You're on the wards and you want to top yourself. You inject something IV. What?'

'Potassium,' says Rich — 'no, she'd be dead already.'

I say, 'Atenolol or digoxin or something – no, she's in sinus.'
'Insulin,' he says.

'Too much chance that instead of dying you'd end up brain-fucked on ITU – ' At exactly the same moment we both say, 'Shit!' and while I'm calling for a BM he's calling for fifty mils of 50 per cent dex.

I hold Sally's wrist and with my fingertip I feel the weak splash of her pulse. Her pale skin is corpse white apart from the permanent rawness round the tip of her nose. Sweat has evaporated from her skin and now it's sticky.

The dex arrives first. Rich and I exchange looks about whether we should wait for the BM. 'Fuck it,' he says. 'Fuck it,' I say. I hold up her arm and uncap the Venflon port and he rams in the neck of the syringe and starts plunging in the sugar solution. I say to the nearest nurse, 'Get a bag of saline to flush this with, please,' and he darts back towards the ward.

The dex works fast. Sally's blood sugar climbs at once and her eyelids flicker. Then her eyes open and she moans and then she's sick on my trousers. 'Let's get her into a bed,' I say and Rich gives the nurses a wink.

In looking down at Sally I feel a sense of incongruity. People I know are real people. They don't get ill and die. The ones who come into the hospital from the outside to suffer and die are spectres who've dwelt in a virtual world without past or future or connection to me. The image in front of me is bizarre, as bizarre as gazing down on my own corpse.

I'm rinsing the puke stains off my trousers in the toilets on the landing outside the ward when my bleep goes off with an unfamiliar number. At the sink I wring them out then standing in my socks and underpants I dry them in the dragon breath of the hand blower. I put them back on and wander on to the ward where Sally is being monitored and infused and though she's going to recover her head hides under a blanket.

We've both chosen self-destruction, she by her method, I by mine.

I wander round to the office where I pick up the phone to answer my bleep. At the other end of the line the caller's gasping for breath and takes a few seconds to get any words out. 'This is Hospital Security. Doc . . . where the bleeding hell are you?'

'M20.'

'I've been all over the bloody hospital hunting high and low for you. Just wait there, will you?'

Five minutes later the corpulent security man stumbles on to the ward.

'I've been instructed to escort you off the premises,' he gasps. 'Sorry, mate. You've been suspended.'

33: The Lone Gunman

The security man guides me to his office where he asks me to hand over my badge and my bleep and my security pass. I unclip my bleep from my belt, slide the switch to OFF and lay it on his desk. I unpin my badge from the lapel of my white coat and the plastic rectangle of black lettering on a white background arcs down in my hand to the desk. But the day it was issued I stuffed my security pass into a pocket of my white coat and I've not seen it since. He sighs. 'They all bloody lose 'em,' he says. Behind him a gallery of CCTV monitors displays hospital scenes as he flips my bleep on its side and transcribes its serial number on to a worksheet before dropping it in a shoebox with three others of which one must be Doctor O.'s.

Then he escorts me out through corridors. Staff spot us together, walking but not speaking, and they hold their looks till I'm about to return them and then they snap their eyes into the floor. We burrow out from the interior and when the air becomes fresh and cold I know we've reached the borderland with the outside world and my ordeal's almost over. My head sinks and when he holds the door open for me I can't even say, 'Thank you.'

'It's worse with the nurses,' he says. 'They usually cry.'

In the car park he watches over me clambering into my car. 'You won't let on, will you, Doc?' he says. 'You know, about me having to phone you to find out where you was. They like me to ... swoop.' He imitates a flying action with his hands: 'Swoop,' he says.

'If anyone asks, that's what I'll tell 'em. You "swooped".'

'Cheers, Doc. No hard feelings, eh?'

We shake hands then he watches me drive out of the gates. He must be indoors again by the time I drive back in and park up by my room. There I slump in my car not moving for an hour. I feel so tired. That's the primary sensation. I feel so *weary*.

I peer at the hospital buildings and at the staff coming and going. I'm sad for Sally but I'm sadder for me and for that I hate myself. This cycle of self-destruction is spinning me down and now it's too late, it's too late to stop it. I try to believe that because I'm not crying I'm handling it well, oh so very well.

Eventually I shamble up to my room and in there I hook my white coat on the back of the door and when I turn I survey this little place with my TV and CDs and the on-call rota on the wall and not even the little olive tree any more. Now I recognise I've come here because I've got nowhere else to go and with my badgeless white coat hanging off the door like a ghost this is when I cry.

I compose myself before I phone Donna. She promises to come round as soon as she can.

'How is she now?' she asks when she arrives.

'Normoglycaemic. Her lytes are returning to normal and there doesn't appear to be any residual damage.'

'Why'd she do it?' she says.

'The job, I suppose,' I say.

After we fuck we lie against each other and I'm comforted by the warmth of her skin on my front and the hot currents of the radiator on my back.

I say, 'I had my hearing today. They suspended me.'

She says nothing for perhaps a minute. I can hear her breath and smell her body but I can't sense her thoughts. I say, 'When I handed over my bleep and badge, it was like in an American cop show, when they make the guy turn in his badge and gun. I'm Dr Dirty Harry Callaghan. They're takin' me off the bronchitis case. Goddammit – I been workin' the Bronx for five years. This is a forty-four Littmann, the most powerful stethoscope in the world . . .'

'It's not a joke,' she says. 'You got suspended.'

'I know,' I say.

'You got suspended and you didn't tell me.'

'I know.'

'So . . .?' she says.

'So . . . what?'

She snaps, 'You know what! Talk to me!'

'Here's talking to you,' I say. 'When did you last fuck your husband? Today? Yesterday? The day before? Did you come? Did you make the same noises as when you come with me? Did you suck his dick like you suck mine?'

She slaps my face so hard my head flips.

As she hurries into her uniform I slump at the edge of the bed with the sting of her hand radiating from my cheek. She twists her buttons together hand over hand almost as fast as fastening a zip. My fingers trace the bruising side of my face and I say,

'Don't go.'

She stops dressing. She starts crying. I hold her in my arms.

'Please don't go,' I say.

She keeps on crying but she doesn't go.

Though suspended I'm not sacked so I remain on the payroll. My salary will continue to take its monthly nibble out of my student overdraft. Also I'm still entitled to my hospital room. But the next morning when I go up to the ward to visit Sally I'm turned away. The sister says, 'If anyone found out you were

324

on hospital premises, they'd want to know who knew you were here. Sorry. Nothing personal.' I suppose I ought to be content with just not being homeless or destitute.

When I return to the flats I close the door and as I do so my white coat swings on the hook so the stethoscope poking out of a pocket scrapes on the wood. The room smells of cigarettes and sex. From the tap I draw a mug of water. There's nothing on TV. I shuffle through my CDs but I'm not in the mood for music. I have no books besides textbooks and nowhere to go. Then I hear a beep and reach down for my bleep but the sound's coming from another room and my bleep languishes in a fucking shoebox somewhere. I draw the curtains and bury myself under the covers.

For the first week mostly I sleep. I force myself to eat regular meals. I conduct minor errands that expose me to fresh air. I feel like I'm discovering the outside world all over again. My body recharges. I feel energy re-entering my muscles. I reattune to a circadian rhythm. And after Donna and I fuck I don't nap because I want to do it again. She asks me how I'm feeling and I tell her, 'OK. Surprisingly OK.'

Yet after the first week the holiday is over. I lie in in the mornings not because I'm still sleepy but because I've got nowhere to go. The energy that's returned starts to slacken away as my muscles wilt and my belly fattens because I'm no longer trawling the wards each day performing the equivalent of a ten-mile hike.

I contact the BMA every day. The person who's dealing with my case turns out to be Number-Two Cut. 'I'm afraid your case is at the bottom of a very tall pile,' he says. 'In your region alone there are currently twenty-seven doctors on suspension.'

'But I haven't *done* anything,' I say.

'Neither have most of them,' he says.

The hospital depresses me so for a few days I hole up at my parents' but tell them I'm on study leave. There I spend hours in my room pretending to pore over textbooks but I'm more likely to be watching TV or masturbating or both.

I watch a newscast about a hospital in the West Country where for years there've been whispers the surgeons aren't much good at operating on baby hearts – which is no handicap to most doctors, except for these blokes it's their chosen specialty. Some anaesthetist's blown the whistle so hard that the poor bugger's having to emigrate to Australia.

I flick to a hospital soap in which the staff all have time to hold patients' hands and the nurses are matriarchial and the doctors patriarchal and none of them ever fucks up. Then I zap back to the news to glimpse a consultant gynaecologist ducking into the GMC to face charges of slicing through women's insides like a golfer trying to hack his ball out of the rough. On another channel the TV cops are solving yet another crime rather than bungling their investigation of a racist murder or framing a man with a low IQ for a rape he didn't commit. Our public services are failing while television plays hour after hour of incorruptible policemen catching criminals, of crusading lawyers keeping the innocent out of prison, of streetwise social workers rescuing children from abuse, of heroic doctors sticking needles in tension pneumos . . . I'm flicking between the real world and the drama of reassurance and I feel like I'm the only person watching who recognises the mendacity, sees it clear enough to want to kick in the TV screen.

I drink. I endeavour to see my school friends as often as possible but unlike them I don't have work in the morning or a teething baby to soothe so I'm the one who wants to ensure we get another round in before last orders and maybe go to a club or float a Balti on a stomach full of lager.

I can't tolerate returning to the hospital but the days are

passing and soon two weeks have elapsed and my parents become suspicious.

I return to my hospital room and on the way back I try not to think of anything but sex. Donna meets me that night and the first thing of her I sense is the smell of her cunt already wet inside her jeans and it seems so long since we had sex that I fear I'm going to spurt before we even get naked.

'I've been thinking about what you said,' she says.

She's sat on the bed with her back against the wall smoking a cigarette. In profile the outline of her breast curves in a crescent from beneath her nipple to her axillary tail. When she exhales she flicks the smoke away and it makes them wobble. She draws her knees up to her chest and her belly concertinas into skinny folds.

'About us going away.'

I'm lying on my back with my hands behind my head. My dick flops across my groin leaking a buttery smudge into my pubic hair.

'Where?' I say.

'Somewhere,' she says. 'I can say I'm doing an IV course next weekend.'

'Next weekend?'

'You still want to?' she says.

'Yes,' I say.

Her cigarette is only half smoked but she quenches it in the ashtray balanced on the bed sheets then lays it aside. At this signal I make more room beside me. Twisting on to all fours she stalks over the bed and with her hair falling into my face she lowers her mouth to mine. Her hand skims my midriff and like examining an old person and encountering an added-on body bit she squeezes its newly formed flab. 'Too soft,' she says. Then she descends to feel what's happening with my penis and smiles. 'That's better,' she says.

In my mail I receive a letter from the hospital requiring me to attend another hearing. I put on a jacket and tie and though I'm wearing neither uniform nor ID I pass unchallenged into the hospital interior. In the management unit I spit my name at the receptionist and at the appointed time she says, 'Go through.' When I shuffle into the boardroom I find it empty apart from Doctor H.

'Are we early?'

'No,' he says. 'Sit down,' he says.

I take a seat at the table while he pours himself a coffee. Without asking he pours me a cup too and then he sits opposite.

'So . . . ' he says. 'Here we are, then.'

'Here we are.'

He says, 'I believe there's something you don't understand. It's that this hospital, or any other for that matter, is never going to admit its policies could harm patients. It's never going to openly agree to its practices being remodelled or staff being retrained like they were some puppy dog that shits on your carpet. It's never going to openly agree to making its internal quality-control system more effective because that would be tantamount to admitting things have been a bloody shambles all along.'

'I know,' I say.

'So why did you do this to yourself?'

'I wanted to change things,' I say.

'You can't,' he says. 'No one can.'

'I know,' I say.

'The system harms one in every ten patients who come into hospital because it's too big and too old. Medical-school training is totally fucked up and you people come on to the wards

328

knowing bugger all. You're expected to get trained in little nibbles of an apprenticeship, in between treating seriously sick patients. No wonder mistakes are made. And it carries right on through. Consultants get appointed who haven't seen enough clinical medicine or done enough operations. Doctors at every level make mistakes. And what are we going to do about it? Come clean and say the whole system's a mess and seventy thousand patients a year get killed because of it and another two hundred thousand patients a year get seriously harmed because of it? It'd be like the airlines saying, "Our planes crash because we don't build them very well and some of our pilots don't fly them very well." No one wants to hear that. The politicians don't. The general public don't. So what happens when something goes wrong? We cover it up, of course. Invariably, we succeed, unless someone decides to go and blow the whistle.

'The problem when you blow the whistle is this. This is the problem: as doctors, we're all equally at the mercy of this culture of blame. We're all in the same boat because whether as doctors we make an honest mistake or we commit a huge clanging act of incompetence, the system treats us the same. We're all eligible to become the scapegoat. The managers have a word for it. They call it "blame-storming". Any of the people implicated in your evidence could be that scapegoat. In the case of the diabetic woman who's now severely handicapped, it could be the GP who saw her first, either of the caz officers who saw her, the nurse who detected the high BM but didn't impress it on the medical staff, or the consultant in charge of the department. In the case of the woman who died of a PE, it could be the registrar who insisted she was a Munchausen or the houseman who didn't get the spiral CT or the nurses who didn't call anyone even though she continued to be breathless.'

'It was my fault,' I say. 'It was my fault she died.'

'She was a Munchausen,' he says.

'She wasn't a Munchausen. It was my fault she died.'

He shrugs. 'Maybe. Maybe not. Anyway, it's not important. What is important is that you failed to perform a successful cricothyroidotomy in the case of acute epiglottitis.'

My body slumps in my chair. I stare over Doctor H.'s shoulder into the wall. They're not even acknowledging my culpability in the death of the Breathless Lady. Instead it's Strawberry they're blaming me for. When I raise my coffee cup it rattles against the saucer.

He continues, 'So when someone blows the whistle, the hospital has to start looking for a scapegoat. The hospital looks for the lone gunman – the individual, acting alone, acting counter to his training, who, through a gross act of incompetence, unrelated to the day-to-day running of the institution, the individual who's caused a patient to die or be harmed. And once he or she's been blamed, everyone's happy. Joe Public says, "One rotten apple. They oughta be struck off." The politicians can say, "The safety of patients remains our highest priority," but without actually having to do anything or spend any money. And the hospital's clean off the hook. And the absolute best person to portray as the lone gunman is the whistle-blower himself – so much so that it's become a patellar reflex to suspend first and work out charges later.'

Gulping I say, 'Will I be charged with serious professional misconduct?'

'Yes,' he says. 'Or even manslaughter. We'll refer it to the GMC. It doesn't matter whether they find you guilty or not. Who knows with them? But by the time the case comes up a good few years will have gone by and, after being suspended that long, you'll be unemployable.'

'All this to make an example of me?'

'Yes,' he says. 'All this to make an example of you.'

'You've won,' I say.

'No,' he sighs. 'Chances are the compensation claims will be successful. You know now we've had to house a whole legal department here. Nationwide, litigation costs amount to enough to build sixteen new hospitals. I don't think any of us can consider ourselves winners.'

He takes a sip from his coffee. He says, 'It's not all bad news. The hospital will do anything it can to make this embarrassing situation go away. So, if you agree to leave the SHO rotation at the end of the year, they'll drop the charges and we'll provide you with a first-rate reference. Come the First of August, you'll be some other hospital's problem.'

Pushing his coffee away from him he stands and gathers his things. 'You know what?' he says. 'I think you'll take the deal. You'll take the deal, because deep down you're one of us.'

He strides out of the door behind me and I'm left alone in the room facing his coffee cup with his dregs inking the bottom while my own reflection floats in the varnish of the table.

34: The Addiction

Through the little car's windscreen we see a road that snakes with humps and bends being swallowed by the bonnet in front and hear it squealing under the tyres below. Now darkness gathers round. It begins in the grey hills to the east and over meadows and hedges it creeps towards us. Behind us a haze sinks into the basin that we're climbing out of and ahead a turning rises into view.

Like glowing antennae the headlight beams probe ahead and they're stark against the dying light and when they strike the signpost I see we should take the turning. A few minutes later we glide into the village and soon our tyres crunch on the gravel drive of the B&B.

In the lobby the manageress notices Donna's wedding ring and checks us in as 'Mr and Mrs'. Donna blushes but neither of us corrects her. We're late so we don't unpack. We go straight to a pub where men with beards lean against the bar and big furry dogs sleep on their owners' feet.

We set our drinks on a table by an open fire.

'This is nice,' she says.

'Yes,' I say.

Warm now, we shed our coats and lay them on a third chair. Being together in a public place discomforts me. The physical language of our relationship has been formed in a hospital room ten foot by twelve with no one present to witness. If in reaching for the ashtray her palm were now to brush over the back of my hand I might take her hand and draw her into me and we'd lower ourselves to the floor and start fucking. But here we can't. Here we have to act like two different people. We have to become whole people.

We have a couple of drinks but instead of finding somewhere to eat we decide to trek back to the B&B. Stars glitter in the black sky. The night and its silence unsettle us both because in the city traffic rumbles like a constant remote earthquake and the lights of homes and industry fog the heavens. Through freezing air I fumble for her hand. Coats double our size so in embracing we feel like strangers to each other. By the roadside we kiss and with the heat of our breath tickling our faces we dribble warm spit into each other's mouths but still she feels like a different person to me. When we reach the B&B our faces and hands are numb but we rush upstairs to our room and as we strip off the bulking layers of clothing we're reverting from strangers back to our true naked selves.

Still cold, her nipples are rigid. 'Keep those away from me,' I say. 'They could have my eye out.'

'You don't suit the cold, do you?' she replies with a nod towards my dick. 'A button mushroom, that's what I'd call it,' she says and giggles.

'It's a wiggly worm that's coming to get you. It's an evil weevil!' Laughing we tumble into bed and as we start to kiss each other's naked bodies I feel the stretching pain of a cold erection.

Tonight is our first night in a double bed. When we roll to change position we still fling out our arms to stop ourselves falling off the edge, only to feel another yard of mattress between us and gravity. We wheel round in a rotating arc until our heads are at the foot of the bed and still no part of our bodies has been lost over the side. At last we stretch out to sleep revelling in the space for our limbs.

But in the night, in sleep, our bodies interlock. An arm burrows under a back, a leg hinges over a hip. We reform into the compact two-headed twin-bodied chimera that lives in the narrow bed in that little hospital room because that's who we are.

At dawn I find her still here with me for the first time in weeks maybe in months. In my hospital room I might stir in the middle of the night and then I'll always find her side of the bed empty and the sheets damp and chill and realise she's at work on a distant ward. By morning I've claimed the narrow bed all for myself. Yet this morning even while still in sleep I recognise the body beside me. I smell the stale scent of cigarettes and alcohol on her breath. I smell the vinegar odour of her armpit. I smell the last of her perfume.

We make love again and then open the curtains on a glistening frost-covered landscape. Like children running into a garden we leap into the new day, the second day. Mud made ice crunches under our boots as we hike into the hills. I feel like a mole that's burrowed above ground for the first time in eighteen months. My skin tingles with cold. Wind stings my eyes. The bulk of so many layers of clothing restricts my movement and though they're insulating they're not as insulating as layers of concrete.

Together we peer down towards one of the lakes. Mist is lifting and the sun is beginning to filter through. Off the shore waterfowl dip and skim and lay white trails through the black waters. Donna's hand reaches out in exploration and then it finds mine. I hook my arm round the bulked-out cushion of her waist.

Then I ask something. I ask, 'Why did you change your mind?'

'About coming here?' she says.

'Yes.'

'I didn't change my mind. I made it up.'

The first hard rays of sunlight burst through the mist and strike our eyes. Bare trees flicker from grey to brown, mud from grey to black, grass from grey to green. I gaze into the strands of Donna's hair counting half a dozen different shades of dark brown I've never seen before. Splinters of colour fleck her irises, colours unexpressed in that gloomy little hospital room, colours whose names I don't even know. This is the first time I've seen her in unfiltered sunlight and she's beautiful.

'And the first time?' I say. 'Why did you change your mind then?'

'The first time?'

'Last year. After we'd gone out for a drink and we snogged by the flats. Then you said you couldn't see me. But later I met you in the pub and you changed your mind.'

'It was just something,' she says.

'What?'

'It's not important.'

I say, 'Tell me.'

She gazes down towards the lake over which sunlight creeps like oil and it's making the ducks' foamy trails glisten like jewels. She says, 'There was this woman who gave birth and the baby was fine but at the delivery they noticed a problem with this woman. They noticed a mass on her cervix so they had to do a biopsy. It was CA cervix. They went back and looked at her smear from before she got pregnant and it'd been missed. That day they got a routine FBC back that showed low red cells, low white cells and low platelets.'

'It had already invaded the marrow.'

'They kept topping her up with transfusions but it only took a couple of days. She was dead before her baby was a week old.'

'How old was she?'

'Twenty-seven,' she says.

'How old are you?'

'Twenty-two,' she says.

We tread a trail down to the lake. It takes us half an hour of zigzagging down the hillside before we reach the shore. There our boots scrape over pebbles while sunlight dapples the water with glowing white leaves.

She plucks up a stone and flings it across the surface but instead of skipping off its first impact it sinks with a plop. 'Watch and learn, my girl,' I say. 'Watch and learn.' I select a flat stone and project it low and fast over the water. In flight it tips on its side and the edge collides with a surface ripple and my stone disappears in a spurt of foam. Donna erupts with giggles and as I make protestations for a second chance they begin to sound ridiculous in my ears and I too begin to laugh. Here, if only for the moment, we can be two different people.

Not long later we trek back up the hillside to the lay-by where the car is parked. We follow a road south to a picturesque village in which for lunch we visit a pub. In the afternoon we mooch in and out of shops looking at lots but buying little. In one window she points out a toy koala bear and calls it, 'Cute', but I insist it's horrible.

Just as day turns grey we drive back to the hotel and by the time we're up in our room again it's dark outside. I open the radiators to full while Donna slips across the landing for a hot bath and when she returns the room is warm. We lie on the bed and I throw open her dressing gown just to see her body. I kiss her breasts and my hand skims over the hard edge of her ribcage down over her belly into her pubic hair.

'Tell me a secret,' she says. 'Tell me something you've never told anyone else.'

I kiss the soft thin meat of her belly. My finger caresses her nipple then the caresses contract to circles that rub it erect. I say, 'Once, in Casualty, I treated a patient who'd torched a house and burned a mother and burned to death her baby and, later, it turned out, her other child, and I started to kill him with a shot of potassium, but I didn't have the guts to carry it out.'

Her hand locates my balls and she cups them like little eggs. Her other hand spiders through my hair to the back of my neck and with it she draws my cheek to hers. 'Now you tell me something,' I say. 'Something you'd never tell anyone else.'

'I have done,' she says.

'The woman who died a few days after her baby was born?'

'Yes,' she says.

'You didn't tell your husband?'

'How'd he ever understand?' she says.

She rolls towards me and as her body begins to heave with sorrow I hold her close. I hush her and hug her. But she grasps my dick and begins to rub it against her vulva. I get hard and she wet and when she says, 'Just fuck me, just fucking rape me,' I pin back her shoulders and drive into her. I'm feeling her cunt round my dick and her tongue in my mouth and I'm not feeling the crushing suffocating guilt of the doctor who didn't kill the arsonist though the bastard deserved it but did kill the Breathless Lady who didn't. My tongue fills her throat like I'm plugging a dyke and I'm doing the same to her. I'm filling her empty spaces with other things to feel.

In the morning while Donna dozes I steal her car and sneak to the shop with the koala bear in the window. I race back and lay it on the bed for her to find. When she sees it she detonates with laughter and throws arms round me kissing me.

Without warning I say, 'Leave him.'

She holds on to me but says nothing, perhaps pretending I didn't say what I said.

'Leave him, for me,' I say.

'I wish you wouldn't ask,' she says.

'Why?' I say.

'Because it means I have to answer,' she says.

'You don't have to answer.'

'Yes, I do,' she says.

Today, the third day, the last day, we venture west. Rain spatters the windscreen as we steer the winding route between bulbous green hills. By the time we reach our destination the rain's swelled to drops the size of grapes that smack our faces and thump our hoods. We duck back in the car and wait for the storm to pass. It drums on the roof and double-glazes the windscreen and the heat of our bodies mists the windows.

'What are you going to do?' she asks me. 'Take the deal?'

'I don't know. If I do, it'll feel like this has all been for nothing.'

'You've given the diabetic woman the chance to claim compensation. That'll change their lives. You've made the hospital acknowledge the damage they did to that boy's shoulder. I wouldn't call that nothing.'

'They'll discredit me. No one'll get compensation, or an apology, or even an explanation. No one.'

'Yes, they will,' she says. 'The hospital think they can make you carry the blame for that man's crike, by intimidating everyone else involved, by making everyone say you acted alone, you were a loose cannon, you were the lone gunman. But they're wrong. *I* was there. They may think I'll be like the others, but they're wrong, because they don't know what you are to me.'

She kisses my cheek. I turn and my lips join hers. Then I feel her hand clasp mine.

'Yes,' she says. 'The answer's yes. I'll leave him.'

338

The rain peters out to drizzle and we venture out on to the ridge. Below us the road snakes down and away into the distance and disappears into a smudged horizon that hides the lakes. We tread a gravel path through evergreens and it lifts us up to a summit. From this position our eyes scan hundreds of square miles of open terrain. Across a valley another summit nuzzles the cloud base. In this moment we're surveying a world that even to its edges is without pain or suffering.

Donna says, 'But maybe it's better on the inside.'

At first I mistake her meaning and I experience a sudden hunger for the interior. I miss the concrete and brick and glass. I miss the constant weatherless climate. I miss the bodies of the old with their bits added on and bits taken away. I miss the rhythm of machines and the smell of antiseptic and the secret vaults that taste of healing. My body aches for it all in the way it's never craved cigarettes, never even craved heroin, but in the way it's been addicted to one other thing only and that thing is here with me now.

'What's that expression?' she says. 'Better to be on the inside pissing out than on the outside pissing in? Maybe, even if you take the deal, one day you'll be able to get your message across some other way, some other way that doesn't even occur to you now.'

I nod as now I understand her. I smile.

'It's not how I planned it,' I say.

'It never is,' she says. 'So take the deal.'

She hugs me. I kiss her. Then I say, 'D'you think I'm like them? That's what they said: "You're one of us".'

'No, you're not like them.'

'But I will be if I go back. I will be one day.'

35: The End

I return to work and under the terms of my pact I begin applying to other hospitals for the next First of August.

On the wards sets of forms appear. They're called clinical incident forms. They come in giant chequebooks the same way death certificates do. At a meeting in the Postgraduate Centre banks of medical staff listen while Doctor H. explains what they're for.

He says, 'Their purpose is to create an official route for hospital staff to report clinical episodes that may have given them cause for concern.'

From the row behind Rich leans forward to tap my shoulder. He says, 'What's he talking about? Fuck-ups?'

'I think so.'

'Then they'd better have printed hundreds.'

Someone asks, 'Can we fill them in anonymously?'

Mister M. interrupts to say, 'If you've got an observation to make, you should be prepared to stand by it, shouldn't you?'

Doctor H. thinks before saying, 'Let's see, shall we? I hope it doesn't come to that.'

Someone else asks, 'After they've been filled in, who reads them?'

'We're forming a Clinical Risk Management Committee.'

'Who's on it?'

'Well, so far . . . me . . .'

Doctor H. grins and thus permits laughter and it ripples round the room from stiff faces. Then he continues his presentation. He explains that the time has come when hospitals must formulate a new governance committed to detecting and modifying practices that put patients at risk. Not once does he look my way.

After the meeting the consultants huddle and Mister M. appears no less an architect of this new governance than any of them. Only now do I notice the absence of anaesthetists and paediatricians. Doctor O. isn't in the huddle either. She isn't here at all. Because of her refusal to recant her concerns about the A&E department she's still suspended without charge. The hospital management have tossed her out into the cold and they are the same regime that for reasons I don't know and I'll never be allowed to know can't resolve the feud between A&E, Paeds and Gas that's risking patients' lives.

I think of Doctor O. as I trudge out of the building. I clutch my arms across my chest, pulling my white coat tight against the freezing air, and wonder how many patients have been crippled or killed, how many incompetents have been left at liberty to prosper, how many whistle-blowers have seen their careers ruined, till enough of those bastards inside in the warm thought maybe, just maybe, it was time to change things.

A second-division medical journal accepts Rich's Substance K research paper for publication. A few days later his wife gives birth to a baby boy weighing 7lb11oz who they name Jack.

'From now on, I'm going to do better,' he says to me one day. 'I'm a family man. I'm going to be turning over a new leaf.'

'I believe you,' I say and like him I'm not telling the truth. After a silence he says, 'You know, this job – either you can handle it, or you can't. When I first met you, I thought, "There's

341

someone who's not going to make it. There's someone who's soft in the centre."'

I say nothing.

With a glimmer of regret he adds, 'I haven't changed. The job didn't do this to me. I must always have been like this.'

The following week I'm notified I've been short-listed by a number of other hospitals. Doctor H. has been true to his word and given me a first-class set of references. It's something they've done before, except that those other doctors they wanted rid of were incompetent.

I have my first interview and the same day I'm offered a new job. I accept. I'll take up my post on the First Wednesday of August.

Doctor H. chairs the inaugural meeting of the Clinical Risk Management Committee. They examine an incident in which someone was given the wrong drugs because he had the same name as another patient. No one suffered any harm so the SHO had no qualms about filling in a clinical incident form. 'Obviously,' she says, 'if anyone'd died, I'd've thought twice.' From now on doctors and nurses must ensure a patient's name corresponds to his or her registration number before administering any treatment. This procedure results in delay and frustration and within a week some doctors go back to taking short-cuts. They soon learn which nurses will report them and which won't so they only do it when they know their actions won't be found out. They have no fear of getting caught and why would they when deep in the interior they're so used to no one watching them?

In the last week of January I get a bleep from a nurse in Outpatients. 'There's someone here who's asking to see you.'

I finish writing the notes I'm making and then I wander

down the long corridors of the interior to the Outpatients' Department. In the waiting area stands Sweet Breath's husband and in her wheelchair sits Sweet Breath herself. For a moment I stiffen but he smiles at me and holds out his hand. As I approach I see he's clean shaven with clear hopeful eyes. We shake hands.

'They've agreed to make a settlement,' he says. 'Out of court, it is.'

'Not as good as winning the Lottery, though, is it?'

'It ain't bloody far off,' he says. Then he sighs. He says, 'But . . .'

'But what?' I ask.

He says, 'No one's held his hand up and said he's the one's left her the way she is. They fuck up people's lives, but they can just walk away. They just walk away.'

Sally doesn't come back to work till this final week. People ask her how she is and in a quiet voice she says, 'Okay.'

On the last day of the job, the last day of January, I take her for a drink. She says little at first. I look past her through the fogged windows of the pub into the gloom outside where streetlights glow in yellow smudges.

Sally says, 'I'm not taking up my next job. I need time to think. I need time to decide whether medicine's really for me.'

'If you're lucky,' I say, 'you'll decide it's not.'

'I'm not lucky,' she says.

Glancing at my empty glass she makes a sound that might be the start of her saying something but nothing comes out. Her face is pale. Her hands are thin. A medical accident can also cripple the ones who walk away.

She rises and goes to the bar. A couple of minutes later she returns with two more drinks.

For a few moments she swirls her glass and watches the liquid

343

ripple then flatten. 'I've seen the new clinical incident forms,' she says. 'So, d'you think they'll work?'

'In some places. Not all hospitals are like this one. But the culture won't go away overnight. Every few months a new case is going to come to light. Surgeons hacking up people's insides, pathologists pickling babies' brains, GPs fiddling with their patients' fannies. All while their colleagues think, "Ho-hum, there goes old whatsisname, at it again with the hacking stroke pickling stroke fiddling." Every time one of those stories comes out, it makes it harder for people in the outside world to understand that medical accidents are a different thing – harder still for them not to want blood.'

Peering into her drink she says, 'Doctors protected by the system who don't deserve to be. Colleagues who turn a blind eye.'

'Yes.'

'Us, then.'

I think of the Wheezer. I say, 'I didn't know how his family would've reacted. The hospital, either. They don't want to know that no one's bothered to establish a fail-safe system for handling patients with penicillin allergy – that's too scary, and too hard to believe. It's much easier to imagine it's one doctor acting with appalling negligence, and demand she's punished for it. The system won't protect you if you're honest – but it will do, as long as you and your colleagues lie. You made an honest mistake. It wasn't appalling negligence. It was different. So I chose to protect you.'

'Answer me one thing,' she says. 'How do you know that the one mistake I made, the one you covered up – how d'you know it's not the first in a long line, and, every time I do it, my colleagues won't say, "It's fine – it's just an honest mistake – accidents happen"? Like you, they'll say it time after time, till I'm a consultant or a GP somewhere, and by then it *is* appalling negligence. How d'you know that won't be me? How d'you know that's not the way it always happens?'

In answer to her question I look down. In answer I say, 'I don't.'

The last time I see Mister M. is in Casualty. To me he's always been like those men I sometimes see on the news as they duck through a baying crowd into the GMC. They're figures of hate bred by a system few outsiders can understand. Now I wonder if he started like me with a mistake like the one that killed the Breathless Lady. I wonder if he was protected like Rich protected me and then like I protected Sally. I wonder if he felt the guilt and then thought he could make it right just by learning from his mistake. I wonder if he didn't confess because all he had that he'd worked for seemed too much to give up. Guilt and self-criticism ended up being a couple more emotions you don't want to lug around with you.

These questions crowd into my mind and he looks at me as I stare at him. Then he turns and slips through the plastic doors into resus. Up until the end this is all I'll ever know of him. All I'll ever know is that when I stare at him he stares right back at me. He can hold his gaze to mine without shame and with his eyes gleaming like mirrors because I made a mistake and I covered it up and now I think I can walk away believing everything's all right but it'll never be all right, never, till I stop walking away and I'll never be different, never, as long as like him I keep hiding in the interior.

Snow dusts walls and rooftops but it isn't sticking on the roads or pavements. We sit in Donna's car that's parked in mid-afternoon in an ordinary urban street. My heart drums my chest. My mouth runs dry. My hands on my lap are shaking.

I say, 'He knows you're here?'

'Yes,' she says.

'With me?'

She gulps. 'Yes,' she says. 'He knows everything.'

'So what happens now?'

She thinks. 'I don't know. Does anyone?'

'No,' I say. But I lean across and kiss her.

She turns off the engine but I don't move yet. We begin to shiver. In shivering I think we're not impervious to nature. One day our bodies too will wither and perish.

'What d'you want?' she says.

'I want . . .' I stumble. She grips my hand. I think I want a chance to get it right next time. I think I want a day when nothing bad happens, when it's warm again, and after this day in the hospital when nothing bad happens I lie with her on a bed in a room that's a proper person's room, in a house even, with a breeze breathing through the window brushing over our naked skins with sounds of the outside world coming in and they're happy sounds. I say, 'I want another First of August.'

That's as far ahead as anyone can look and maybe even that's too far but at least this person beside me knows that too. She and I know what the rest of the fucking ignorant world acts like it doesn't.

'Go in,' she says. She kisses my cheek. 'I'll be here waiting when you come out.'

'I might be a long time.'

'I'll still be here,' she says.

I kiss her again because I know she will.

I open the car door into this February flurry. I cross the street and though by now I know the address off by heart I check it yet again on the notepaper in my hand before I edge towards the front door of the house. This is the hardest journey I've ever made. This is worse than any walk to the relatives' room to tell them who's alive and who's dead. It's worse because I'm out

346

here on the outside instead of deep within my world that's protected by layers of concrete. I'm out here where I have no power. I have no power at all.

My leg muscles wilt and for a moment I think I'm about to stumble and fall. I recover my balance and peer across the street to Donna who looks out from the car in concern. I'm ready to run and she's about to get out but I manage to wave at her and she halts. I turn back towards the house and this time I ring the bell.

While I wait snowflakes flutter down from the sky. My eyelashes trap them but fragile as living things they melt before I can even blink. They melt like the dead.

Footsteps shuffle to the door and I hear voices collect inside the house. When the door opens I look up from my feet and I hold out an arm that's trembling all the way down from the shoulder. The Breathless Lady's stepson shakes my hand and I begin to get myself under control.

'I told everyone you'd phoned,' he says. 'We're all here.'

In the little house I sit in their living room and to the Breathless Lady's family I tell the truth about what happened that night when I was called to see her and I made a mistake and because of my mistake she died. They listen in silence and the first time I sob one of the women offers me a tissue but I say, 'It's OK,' because I made sure I brought a handkerchief. Though often I'm staring into the floor and I'm wiping tears from my face I carry on until after an hour I've told them everything. I say, 'I'm sorry.' At last I've finished and they've heard every part of everything I've done.

Now I look up. Now I look up to be judged.

Acknowledgement

The author thanks Doctor Fiona McDonald MRCP, for her advice on the text's medical content.

Glossary

222 A telephone number dialled to put out a cardiac arrest or crash call.

3/7 Three days.

AE of COAD Acute exacerbation of chronic obstructive airways disease.

Alky Alcoholic (traditionally defined as a person who drinks more than their doctor).

Ambu bag Black plastic bag squeezed by hand to provide artificial ventilation, either through a mask (hence 'to bag and mask') or an endotracheal tube.

AOA Adult-onset anencephaly, a non-existent condition, used as an insult. Anencephaly means being born without a brain and is incompatible with life.

Arterial line An indwelling cannula that permits repeated sampling of arterial blood.

Asystole Cardiac standstill, a flat line.

Betty: Diabetic (rare slang).

Bleeding oesophageal varices Varicose veins round the

gullet, usually caused by liver disease, which can burst and bleed in the stomach.

Blue bloater A person with severe lung disease and heart failure who turns blue because of low oxygen in the blood and bloats with fluid because of the heart failure.

BM A bedside measure of capillary blood glucose, sampled by a finger prick.

BMA British Medical Association, (in)effectively the doctors' trade union.

BMJ *British Medical Journal*.

BNF British National Formulary, an encyclopaedia of prescribing information.

Bolus A single, rapid injection.

Buff the notes Make Clintonesque records – exhaustive enough to gleam with medical competence, selective enough not to be flat-out lies.

Butterfly A small needle attached to plastic butterfly wings that sits in a vein for a short while.

CA Cancer.

Cachectic Severely emaciated by disease.

Cannula The plastic tube surrounding the introducer needle which is then left in the vein.

Caz card An A5-size record of A&E visits.

CCU Coronary Care Unit.

Central line A wide-calibre drip inserted into the subclavian vein, a large blood vessel running under the collarbone.

Cerebral anoxic damage Brain damage due to being starved of oxygen.

Cerebral mets Cerebral metastases, pieces of cancer that have spread to the brain.

Cheerioma A tumour that will cause the patient to wave goodbye to the living world ('Cheerio!').

COAD Chronic obstructive airways disease, a degenerative combination of bronchitis and emphysema.

CPR Cardiopulmonary resuscitation – any combination of chest compressions, artificial ventilation, drugs and defibrillation.

Crash An extreme emergency such as a cardiac arrest (in which the heart stops), or worse.

Crash bleep A bleep carried by the on-call medical houseman and SHO and the on-call anaesthetist that transmits 'crash' calls only.

Cricoid cartilage The shelf of cartilage beneath the Adam's apple (the thyroid cartilage).

Crike Cricothyroidotomy, a mini-tracheostomy, cutting a hole through the front of the neck to bypass a blocked airway. Tracheostomy: operation to create a (semi-)permanent opening through the neck into the windpipe.

Critical hour The first hour of treating a seriously injured patient, when therapeutic measures exert their most significant effect (aka 'the golden hour').

CSF Cerebrospinal fluid.

CSU Catheter sample of urine, sent to laboratory for analysis.

CT scan A detailed X-ray examination that portrays the anatomical planes of the body.

Cut down Surgical exposure of a vein to allow cannulation under direct vision.

CVA Cerebrovascular accident, a stroke.

Δ Symbol for diagnosis.

Defib Defibrillator, a machine that reads the heart rhythm and delivers electric shocks.

Defib pads Conductive pads placed strategically to focus the electric shock on the heart.

Diamorph Diamorphine, pharmaceutical heroin – a strong opiate painkiller.

DIC Disseminated intravascular coagulation, a life-threatening combination of clotting and bleeding.

DKA Diabetic ketoacidosis, wherein blood sugar and chemistry get so out of control the patient progresses to coma and death.

DNA Not attend an appointment (verb derived from 'Did Not Attend' stamped on patients' notes).

Dopamine A drug that raises blood pressure and improves the work of the heart, but in high doses has the side-effect of closing off blood flow to the extremities.

(24-hour syringe)driver A device used in palliative care to administer a slow infusion of painkiller.

ECG Electrocardiogram, a tracing of the electrical activity of the heart.

Endotracheal tube A pipe that passes down into the lungs to allow breathing.

ERCP Endoscopic retrograde cholangio-pancreatography, an investigative technique in liver and gall-bladder disease.

Escharotomy Cutting tightening skin to allow chest expansion.

Femorals The femoral arteries, the pulse of which are palpable in the groin.

FFP Fresh frozen plasma, an infusion containing blood-clotting factors.

Four bottles of the house red Four units of O negative blood – a transfusion that can be safely given in an emergency before the patient's blood group is known.

Fubar(bundy) Fucked up beyond all recognition (but unfortunately not dead yet).

Gas The Department of Anaesthetics (Gasman – anaesthetist).

Gases (arterial blood gases) A measure of oxygen, carbon dioxide and pH levels in blood extracted from an artery, a method of distinguishing between hyperventilation and genuine respiratory problems; also useful in cardiac arrest to gauge blood acidity.

Gastric lavage Siphoning off of stomach contents, colloquially 'pumping the stomach'.

Glasgow Coma Scale An index of conscious level based on a series of simple neurological observations, devised in a Glasgow hospital (not a scale of consciousness compared to the average Glaswegian).

GMC General Medical Council, the professional standards agency.

GU Gastric ulcer(ation).

Guedel airway A hard plastic tube with a mouthpiece and curved shaft that keeps the tongue from occluding the back of the throat.

Histology The study of body tissues on the microscopic level.

Hydrocortisone A steroid drug used to treat inflammatory conditions.

In sinus In sinus rhythm – normal rhythm.

Intrathecally Injected into the spinal fluid.

Ischial tuberosity Outcrop of pelvic bone normally deeply covered by the buttock.

ITU/ICU Intensive Treatment Unit/Intensive Care Unit.

JDC Junior Doctors' Committee of the British Medical Association.

Kardex A file containing the nurses' care notes (trade name).

Lac Laceration – cut.

Lipoma A benign growth made of fat.

Littmann A leading brand of stethoscope.

LP Lumbar puncture, a procedure to pierce the lining of the spinal cord and sample spinal fluid.

Lytes Electrolytes – indicators of blood chemistry.

Mane Latin for next morning.

Metastasised Cancer cells have migrated in the blood or

lymphatics or through the tissues from the primary tumour and started to multiply into secondary tumours in other sites.

MI Myocardial infarction, a heart attack.

Microemboli Microscopic blood clots, usually lodging in the lungs where they can cause breathing problems.

Minijet A pre-packet plastic syringe containing the standard dose of emergency drugs (trade name).

Mini-Trach (II) A kit containing a blade, introducer, tube, etc., for performing a tracheostomy (trade name).

MRCP Member(ship) of the Royal College of Physicians.

Munchausen Person suffering from the Munchausen syndrome – a psychiatric condition characterised by the simulation of disease in order to gain medical attention.

Myocardium The heart muscle.

NAD No abnormality detected (this abbreviation sometimes suggests such a cursory examination that it's facetiously taken to mean 'not actually done').

Non-steroidal (anti-inflammatory drug) An aspirin-like painkiller, a class of drugs known to exacerbate stomach disease.

Normoglycaemic Having a normal blood-sugar level.

Nosocomial illness An infection acquired in hospital either from other patients or staff (not uncommon by any means).

Not for 222 A do-not-resuscitate order.

Obs chart Record of nursing obs(ervations) – usually temperature, pulse, blood pressure and respiratory rate – clipped at the end of a patient's bed.

ODA Operating department assistant.

Oedema Swelling of a body part due to engorgement with tissue fluid.

Off legs A description of an elderly person whose condition has deteriorated to the point where they can't get up anymore.

On take Receiving emergency admissions. Hence 'the take': the period of time a firm is assigned to receive emergency admissions; also, collectively, those patients admitted.

OT Occupational therapist.

Oxford Handbook of Clinical Medicine, The (OHCM) A pocket reference used by virtually all hospital doctors.

P waves Little blips on the ECG and heart monitor that refer to the origin of the heartbeat.

Palpebral conjunctivae The membrane lining the eyelids.

Parotid gland A salivary gland in front of the ear (the thing that swells in mumps).

Patella hammer An instrument with a rubber end and plastic shaft for testing tendon reflexes (so named because of its use in the knee jerk, not because it was invented by Dr Patel).

Pathology Outpatients A euphemism for the morgue.

PDE Pissed, denies everything.

PE Pulmonary embolism, a blood clot in the lungs – fatal, if big enough.

Penetration A quality of an X-ray image analogous to exposure of photographic film.

PFO Pissed, fell over.

PGT Pissed, got thumped.

Phenytoin An anti-epileptic drug that can cause severe side-effects.

Potassium Normally an additive to slow infusions – when given as an intravenous bolus, this drug will cause cardiac arrest.

prn (of drug) to be given only if required, not at set times, e.g. a painkiller.

Pruritus ani Itching of the anus.

Psoriasis A chronic skin disease, sometimes confused with cirrhosis by malaprop patients – e.g. 'psoriasis of the liver'.

Pt Patient.

PVS Persistent vegetative state, where the body can survive but the mind is dead.

Redivac A surgical drain – a plastic tube temporarily stitched into a body cavity allowing post-operative blood, fluid, etc, to discharge to the outside world (trade name).

Rhinophyma Red lobular overgrowth of the tissues around the tip of the nose seen in some old men.

RMO Resident medical officer, a traditional term for the SHO or registrar on call for general medicine.

Royal Colleges Royal College of Physicians, Royal College of Surgeons, etc – the academic governing bodies of medical training.

S/B Seen by.

Scope Endoscope, an instrument for viewing the insides of the gullet, stomach and intestines.

Sharps box A yellow plastic container reserved for the disposal of needles etc.

SHO Senior house officer, the training grade between houseman and registrar.

Sinus brady Sinus bradycardia, a slow heart rhythm, but a lot better than having none at all.

Sphyg Sphygmomanometer, an instrument for measuring blood pressure.

Spiral CT (scan of chest) A detailed X-ray that can reveal blood clots in the lungs.

SPR Specialist registrar – the most senior 'junior' doctor, one grade below consultant.

Steret A small antiseptic wipe (trade name).

Subclavian The subclavian vein, a large blood vessel draining into the superior vena cava and on into the heart.

Subcut diamorph driver A subcutaneous infusion of diamorphine, a strong opiate painkiller (the active ingredient in heroin).

SVT Supraventricular tachycardia – a type of abnormally fast heart rhythm.

Tachy/Tachycardia A fast heartbeat.

Tachypnoeic Breathing fast.

TATT Tired all the time (the commonest presenting complaint heard by doctors).

Tension pneumo(thorax) Air in the chest cavity that can squeeze the heart and stop it beating – a rare presentation, but seen week in, week out at TV Hospital.

TTOs The medication a patient takes home (To Take Out).

Tubes Stethoscope.

Turf refer, transfer.

Upper GI bleed Haemorrhage from the gullet, stomach or duodenum (the upper gastrointestinal system).

UTI Urinary tract infection.

Venflon A needle-and-tube assembly that sits in a vein to provide repeated access to the bloodstream (trade name).

VF Ventricular fibrillation, spasms of the heart muscle not supporting circulation – an arrest.

VT Ventricular tachycardia: A potentially fatal abnormal heart rhythm.

penguin.co.uk/vintage